LORDS
of the
TWO LANDS
A Trilogy

Book One
RE ASCENDING

SECOND EDITION

This is a work of fiction.
The majority of the principal characters are actual persons
in the historical record, although their personalities and particular behaviors
are the creation of the Author's imagination.

ISBN 1-4392-1725-4
A Uraeus Book

Visit
www.booksurge.com
to order addiitional copies

Printed in the United States of America

Cover photograph and design by the Author

LORDS
of the
TWO
LANDS

A Trilogy of 18th Dynasty Egypt

Book One
RE ASCENDING

CHAZ DESOWL

URAEUS

AUTHOR'S FOREWORD

Re Ascending, Book One of a planned trilogy titled *Lords of the Two Lands*, is a fictionalized account of the first several generations of the House of Djehutymes, the family which ruled during the time labeled by historians as ancient Egypt's Eighteenth Dynasty. This overall period of some 250 years was arguably the high point of that 3,000-year civilization and the lifetime of several luminaries of antiquity, most notably (in *Re Ascending*) the woman who, against convention, ruled for two decades as a king and her nephew-stepson coregent who established the furthest boundaries of the Egyptian Empire, today called the New Kingdom.

The reader of *Re Ascending* will quickly discover that I have not followed the conventional approach to fictionalizing ancient Egypt. Many of the names of places, persons and deities, etc., commonly used today are anglicized (if in English) versions of what the ancient Hellenes (Greeks, or, more correctly, Macedonians) chose to rename things Egyptian when they ruled that country during its last 300-plus years before Egypt was absorbed by the Roman Empire. Thus, Egypt was actually known to the dynastic Egyptians as Kemet, which translates from hieroglyphs as the "Black Land" (alluding to the soil deposited by the annual inundation of the Nile (from Neilos, its Hellenic name). Even today Egyptologists stubbornly refer to the southern capital of the New Kingdom (modern-day Luxor) as Thebes, whereas the ancient Egyptians themselves called it Waset. Likewise, the northern capital was Mennufer before being renamed Memphis by the Macedonian Ptolemies. Karnak, on the other hand is Arabic; in antiquity the cult center of the god Amen-Re (at Waset) was Ipet Isut ("The Most Select of Places," in translation).

The personal name of four rulers of the Eighteenth Dynasty is today rendered as Thutmose (or Thutmoses, Tuthmosis and other variations) and numbered I, II, III and IV. This is because the Hellenes renamed the Egyptian god of the moon and of writing, Djehuty, as Thoth. Thus the Egyptians of the early Eighteenth Dynasty knew these rulers as Djehutymes ("Born of Djehuty"), and I have chosen to call them such, without the benefit of Roman numerals, which is a European way of keeping successive rulers of the same name differentiated, a contrivance unknown to the ancient Egyptians. A ruler's throne name (prenomen) served this purpose. In the same vein, the god of the Afterlife and ruler of the Underworld we today call Osiris (again his Hellenized name) was Asar to the Egyptians; and his sister-wife was Aset (some Egyptologists render it as Iset), not Isis, her Greek name.

Further on the matter of names, ancient Egyptians frequently — especially in the cases of rulers and nobility — employed short phrases to refer to an individual, effectively their "name." Thus "Amenhotep" when vocalized was heard by the ancients as "Amen is Pleased." I have followed that usage in *Re Ascending*, although employ Amenhotep when the name is not being spoken aloud by my characters. Hatshepsut is translated by Egyptologists as "First Among Noble Women," which I've taken the literary license of simplifying to "Noblest Woman," the same meaning but less of a mouthful. Likewise "Lasting is the Manifestation of Re" (Menkheperre) is conveniently shortened to Lasting Manifestation of Re; "Truth is the Soul of Re" (Maatkare) becomes True Soul of Re; et cetera.

I have used a good many terms throughout *Re Ascending* which might be unfamiliar to the general reader, so a Glossary has been iappended to the end of this volume for handy reference. Likewise find there an alphabetical listing of all of the novel's many characters, with a brief identification of each.

Most of the major characters are actual historical figures — albeit, in many cases little more is known about them than their names and perhaps titles (if they had any) — although a few, like Minmes, Prince-Count Amenemhat and Prince Tao (Taotios), are wholly my invention. The personalities, behaviors and interpersonal relationships of all *Re Ascending*'s historical personages are likewise created purely from imagination. Hatshepsut is no longer regarded by most present-day historians as a conniving wicked aunt-stepmother, and I've chosen to portray her as the savior of her somewhat-juvenile coregent's throne rather than as its usurper. Making Princess Neferure a nymphomaniac is without historical basis, as is the reason for her sudden disappearance from the historical stage. There is no evidence of Senenmut's sexual orientation, except that he appears never to have married or fathered children; his exile and recall are purely speculation, as well. Was youthful Horus-in-the-Nest Amenhotep (II) something of a hotheaded Prince Hal? From the historical record, as king he appears to have been more physical than cerebral is all that is really known. And so forth.

Many of the events depicted in *Re Ascending* are factually historical (the expedition to Punt, the march on and capture of Megiddo, the elephant hunt at Niye, etc.), while others are wholly made up (the attempted assassinations of Hatshepsut and her coregent and, later, of Menkheperre again; the sinking of the obelisks; Hatshepsut's retirement; the poisoning deaths of the three foreign wives; the tragic event at Menkheperre's funeral; and the list goes on).

The description of the political exhumation of Hatshepsut from her kingly sepulcher and her reinterment in the modest Tomb of Nurse In — and the latter's subsequent accidental discovery a few hundred years later — is theoretical, but as good an explanation as any. The recent (2006) so-called "100-percent certain" identification of Hatshepsut's mummy is 100-percent wrong in my view, as evidenced by my description of the physical appearances of the petite Mistress of the Two Lands and her tall, quite obese lifelong companion, In Sitre ("Fish, Daughter of Re").

Inasmuch as the story line of *Re Ascending* covers a rather long period,

I've chosen to not follow a conventional linear narrative (which would of necessity leave out large hunks of time, in any case), but rather to move the story of the early House of Djehutymes (the Eighteenth Dynasty) along by jumping back and forth between the now, the past and (to a lesser degree) the future. Hopefully this will not be overly confusing to the general reader.

Chaz Desowl

Chronologies

1

Royal Nurse In Sitre bent her considerable bulk and poured wine from a Great Green octopus-decorated jug into a faience goblet imitating a water lily. She replaced the fanciful ceramic on a low ebony table and slowly stood upright, her huge pendent breasts resuming their usual position at her rotund waist. Eyes closed, In sniffed the goblet rim.

"Is she ready?," croaked the barefooted tallish elderly woman in a loose linen sheath. An elaborately braided black wig belied her years, conspiring with the heavily cosmetic faux-youthfulness she affected. Her bead collar and inlaid bracelet were of the finest quality. The nails of both her fingers and toes were hennaed, as were the palms of her hands. In's great vanity was legendary — within the Dowager Great Royal Wife's residence, at least.

"No, Most Favored. There's still this."

A youthful bare-breasted maid-servant held aloft the massive tripartite wig she had been vigorously shaking — to free it of whatever vermin might have taken up residency since its last wearing, some long while before. She began to fuss with several of the out-of-place braids.

"Bring it and follow with me." The old nurse sipped twice from the lily-form vessel, then put it on the table. She measuredly moved her bulk across the sparsely furnished columned antechamber to a closed door in the wall opposite the portal through which she had entered only moments earlier. Knocking lightly with a gnarled knuckle on one of the polished cedar-wood paired panels, she announced and asked, "My Lady, it is Nurse Fish, Daughter of Re. May I enter?"

There was no audible reply from the adjoining room. In Sitre pressed her bewigged ear against the door panel

"Perhaps she's napping again, Most Favored," suggested the younger woman, who had followed as commanded by the nurse, still adjusting the wig's braids. "She dozes off frequently of late, as you well know."

A second knuckling was more forceful.

Who is it?" came a faint voice from within the private sitting chamber.

"Fish, Daughter of Re, Most Honorable Lady. It is now time. Son of Re Born of Djehuty, has arrived and awaits his scheduled audience."

"Enter then." The voice now was firmer.

The crone pulled wide the twin panels and waddled into a somewhat larger space, its higher ceiling also supported by half a dozen brightly painted wooden columns with papyri-form capitals. Furnishings there were also sparse, although richly appointed with ivory inlays and gold or gilded fittings. Seated on a low dais in the room's center, on a cushioned, fully gilded chair, with a small cedar-wood table in front of her, was another somewhat less-elderly woman, petitely frail in appearance.

Her wide cheeks and small pointed chin gave her face, with its tracery of faint feathery wrinkles, a triangular shape. The dome of forehead above her modestly beakish nose was very high, and wavy long dark-gray hair hung to her narrow bare shoulders. She was wearing an unadorned strapped linen sheath and had been applying eye makeup and still gripped a silver mirror in the bony narrow hand resting on her lap. She returned the applicator to a calcite kohl jar, the only object on the low table, placing the mirror alongside it. All the while Royal Nurse In, fleshy arms extended, bowed from the waist, insofar as her girth and agility allowed. The handmaiden followed suit, holding out the wig as if presenting an offering to the seated woman.

And she was Hatshepsut, formerly Mistress of the Two Lands Maatkare, but now in her long retirement, and once again but the widow — Dowager Great Royal Wife — of long-deceased Lord of the Two Lands Akheperenre. She was preparing to receive her former coregent, Lord of the Two Lands Menkheperre, Son of Re Djehutymes, alongside whom she had jointly ruled Kemet for a generation — not all that many years before. Hatshepsut could not remember exactly when he had last paid her a visit. She could, however, quite vividly remember the first time she had laid eyes on a tiny brown infant, third Djehutymes of that family name — the out-of-wedlock son of her late half-brother/husband by a commoner harim concubine, Lady Iset.

THIRTY FLOODINGS EARLIER
THE RESIDENCE, WASET

The late-afternoon breezes from the lush garden pleasantly cooled Hatshepsut as she sat on a cushioned armchair in the shaded loggia, re-reading for the third time the day's official documentation — provided earlier as always, according to established protocol, by the High Chamberlain. It was mostly bureaucratic boorish matter, certainly nothing that Lord of the Two Lands Akheperenre could be bothered with, such as whiney petitions, tedious law-court rulings, dull royal-estate accounts, demanding correspondences from the Khefti and other foreign wretches: that sort of ho-hum routine thing. It was stuff certain to drop His Majesty's double chin to his clavicles and exactly why he was only too happy to let his sister/wife be so focused on the minutiae of governing Kemet.

Hatshepsut bent forward to retrieve a faience goblet of wine from amid the helter skelter of papyrus rolls on the low table before her. She lifted the vessel, savoring the tangy-sweet Delta vintage. At that moment the loggia's paired cedar doors opened with a bang, and a wiry naked amber girl of six burst onto the porticoed space. She was King's Daughter Neferure, wearing her Sidelock of Horus, if nothing else. She dashed to her mother's chair. Taftet, the large striped pet feline bolted from under her mistress's seat, where she'd been napping. Her tail would not be pulled again by the hairless human monkey.

"They're here!" the small girl exclaimed, jumping up and down and clapping hands.

"*They*, Precious?"

"Papa and the new *baby!*" responded the child, gleefully. Followed by a conspiratorial whisper into Hatshepsut's ear, "And its *mother*." She giggled.

From the wide-open doors, where he was standing, Royal Tutor Senenmut also strode onto the loggia, coming in front of Hatshepsut, then bowing at the waist, arms extended.

"Your pardon, Your Highness." His voice as always was raspish.

"Stand," was the command from the seated woman attired in a strapped white sheath, but wearing neither jewelry nor wig, her own raven tresses cascading to her shoulders. "Speak."

Senenmut, taller than most men, resumed an upright position, so that his well-fed waist was all too evident. He was wearing a short curled wig, to hide his high forehead, and a linen tunic with a wraparound long kilt reaching to his ankles. For the umpteenth time, Hatshepsut mentally noted his too-pointed nose and rather weak chin, which promised the addition of wattles one day. She also thought again that he always seemed to list to one side slightly, when standing or walking.

Senenmut extended his arm to rest a gentle hand, protectively, on Neferure's shaved head, to quiet her squirming excitement. He had been her tutor since she was a mere toddler.

After bowing only his head, he looked directly at his royal benefactress. "What the First Born is announcing, my Lady of the Two Lands, is that Lord Great Form of Re is approaching. He is bearing, in his very own arms, the new infant, Born of Djehuty. And he is accompanied by that fresh seedling's mother, the, ah, *harim* woman, Iset."

Hatshepsut let the papyrus roll in her lap snap closed and she placed the wine goblet back onto the table with some force. "Our poor brother has the audacity to bring his bastard *and* wretched, simpering whore into my presence?" she hissed.

"Indeed, My Lady!"

"Well, I'm not *receiving*! Head them off."

Neferure already had lost interest and dashed into the garden, in pursuit of Taftet the cat.

"But *how*, My Lady? He is Lord of the Two Lands and I am but a lowly tutor."

"Simply close the doors, Brother of Mut, and wait as a barricade on the other side. Fold your arms. You are very good at that. Inform him, *them*, in no uncertain terms, that I am, yes, very much *indisposed*."

Hatshepsut tossed the papyrus roll onto the table with the other documents and rose. Barefooted, she quickly crossed the narrow expanse of cool painted-plaster floor and stepped down onto the very warm limestone paving of the garden path.

"Beauty!" she called after the small girl chasing a fleet feline some ways off. "She will *bite* again! Don't come crying to *me*, if she does!" At least Taftet's front claws had been yanked as a kitten. Hatshepsut stepped quickly away, following the curving path into the manicured garden and the too-familiar childish game of Catch the Cat.

Senenmut turned and retreated towards the wide-open door panels. Before he could reach them, however, the dark rectangle framed an excessively stout woman, arms akimbo. Royal Nurse In Sitre.

Senenmut continued advancing. "Step aside, Nurse Fish," he commanded, matter of factly.

"Where *is* she?" the bewigged crone demanded, standing her ground, arms now folded over her massive bosom.

"In the garden, with *my* princess. Now, a*side*, I said."

"*You* do not order *me*, tutor. I'm very much most *senior* here and I've come to alert Our Lady."

"She is *alerted* already. By *me*. And I've been commanded, by *her*, to stand guard at these doors. Would *you*, Nurse, compromise Noblest Woman's direct orders?" Senenmut's arms had also folded across his own far-less-fleshy bosom.

Before the dueling nannies' standoff could resolve, a faint commotion was heard coming down the adjoining long hallway. They both looked in that direction.

Advancing towards them were two ebony barefooted Medjay palace guards bearing gilded lances and attired in just white wraparound short loincloths with white-linen skullcaps. Immediately behind them lurched a fully naked bowlegged male dwarf, the always annoying King's First Companion, Khawi.

The trio preceded at a few paces Lord of the Two Lands Akheperenre, who slowly advanced out of the cool dimness into view, his reed sandals flip-flapping the hall's plaster floor. He wore a sheer white-linen tunic that covered his thick torso, over which, belted at his substantial waist, was a pleated royal kilt with triangular starched apron; no wig or other head-covering hid his well-advanced baldness, however; and he was without even a single item of jewelry. Akheperenre was carrying high on his barreled chest a small bundle swathed in blue linen: his recently delivered son, whose birth name was his own, and that of his father before him: Djehutymes; that is, as heard when vocalized, "Born of Djehuty," the Lord of the Moon and scribe to the gods.

Close on the heels of Lord of the Two Lands followed a barefooted short, thin youngish woman in a red-linen sheath, her head weighted forward by an immense braid-layered wig of the sort then popular at court. A three-stand beaded collar was her only jewelry. Her weak-chinned pale oval face was dominated by a prominent aquiline nose and close-set small eyes enhanced with considerable kohl. (A great beauty of the royal harim, she certainly was not. Mother of the new apparent heir, she indisputably was, confirmed by several eyewitnesses to the actual coming forth — if not to the act of conception.) She raised her receding chin and smiled weakly as the group came up to Nurse In and Tutor Senenmut, side-by-side, effectively filling the still-open portal to the private apartment of the Great Royal Wife and God's Wife of Amen Hatshepsut.

The two guards stepped to flank each side of the chambers' wide entrance and simultaneously turned to face towards the hall, lances resting across their black torsos. Little Khawi abruptly squatted on his stunted haunches, long flaccid penis nearly touching the floor; he tilted back his large shaved head and grinned wickedly up at the self-important servants of Hatshepsut.

Before either of them could react, Lord of the Two Lands halted and instructed, "An...nounce to m...my sis...ter that her hus...band a...awaits ad...admission to th...the presence of h...his First B...Born's mo...ther."

Both servants bowed from the waist. As would be expected, Senenmut was the first upright again, however, and quickly responded, "Your Majesty, Great Royal Wife Noblest Woman has told us, with absolutely no uncertainty, that she is presently *'indisposed'*."

"N...n...never so to *us*, daughter's t...t...t..tutor. Go fetch our 'indis...posed' s...s...sister and in...inform our f...f...father's daughter that *we* are here, *awaiting* her a...attendance. *Now!*" Akheperenre smiled sourly and bowed his bald-pated head to nuzzle and coo at the swaddled infant cradled in his arms; then, looking up, he once more advanced towards the human barrier, sandals again noisy on the floor. Khawi immediately jumped to his pigeon-toed feet to follow in his master's wake.

"As you command, Mighty Bull," replied Senenmut, just barely nodding his own bewigged head and stepping widely aside to admit Lord of the Two Lands to his spouse's personal space. He began to move backwards, to retreat into the garden, seeking her.

But the naked little Neferure suddenly emerged out of the bright sun and hopped back onto the shadowed loggia.

"Papa!" she screeched in her piping voice, running up to fiercely hug the stout man around his kilted thighs, effectively crushing the starched apron. She also stuck out her tongue at the dwarf, who, grinning, then returned the gesture in kind — his tongue much pinker and far longer.

Senenmut continued moving in reverse towards the edge of the porticoed platform. Nurse In Sitre also stepped widely aside, hesitant as whether or not to continue bowing to these uninvited persons, one the highest royalty of all.

"Let me *see* it, *hold* it!" demanded the small girl, bouncing excitedly.

"Sit t...t...there in the seat, P...Precious. He is n...not an 'it', a *toy*," replied her father. "He is y...your flesh-and-blood *bro...ther* and his name is B...B...Born of Dje...huty."

"Like *you*, Papa!"

"And like my own p...papa, too, be...loved Beauty of Re,"

The child wiggled herself onto the chair abandoned earlier by her mother, and held her arms wide to receive the linen-wrapped living doll her father gingerly held forth.

Once settled into the young girl's awkwardly encompassing arms, the bundle burst forth with a sudden loud squalling and attempted to squirm within the swaddlings. Lady Iset maternally stepped forward, arm extended. Then, looking towards an unmoved Akheperenre, she halted her impulse.

At that exact moment, the domestic tableau was joined by another principal. Coming out of the bright sun, briskly stepping back up the steps into the cool of the loggia, Hatshepsut strode to the chair where her daughter was perched and abruptly took the protesting infant from the girl. Motioning for Neferure to abandon the chair, she sat in her place, cradling her husband's bastard. Almost immediately, the bawling stopped. Neferure crossed to her father and, smiling up at him, embraced his heavy thigh, recrushing the wrinkled apron. Khawi was standing again beside Akheperenre, who patted the First Companion's large cranium without looking at him.

Hatshepsut bent her head, jet tresses falling off her shoulders, and lifted the edge of wrap draped across the newly born's brown face. Her first thought was: He has the *nose*! *Ours* and, doubly so, his wretched mother's, too. Poor little Falcon Beak! She did not, at the moment, realize that she'd just given the hapless babe the nickname she always would have for him. When she extended her index finger to the puckered mouth, the infant reached up with his tiny brown hand and gripped the appendage, tightly — remarkably tightly. He has something more of his grandfather than his personal name; he has his iron will, was her private thought. Then little Falcon Beak attempted to pull Hatshepsut's finger between his lips, to suck it.

Great Royal Wife abruptly withdrew her hand and looked at her brother/husband for the first time, but without making direct eye-contact. Then she turned her head towards the mound of Nurse In, who had assumed a squatting position, permitted by Hatshepsut in her presence.

"Daughter of Re, it seems the nestling here is hungry. Perhaps you should earn your keep." She held out the small bundle, as if to pass it to Nurse In. The protest erupted again.

"But Your Highness," the other woman protested, as she struggled to rise upright. "I'm not..."

"Of course not," replied Hatshepsut, matter of factly. "I was but jesting, dear Ancient One. Nestling here has his own wet nurse, has he not, Harim Lady Iset?" The question was directed at the anxious small woman still cowering in the shadow of Lord of the Two Lands. "Or are you with milk yourself?"

"Oh, *yes*, Highness!" the infant's mother squeaked, nodding. "And, no, I am *not*, Highness," shaking her head vigorously. The large wig slipped slightly askew.

"Well, step forward then and relieve Great Royal Wife of your squawking chick, before he wets himself. I won't be peed on by my husband's marital indiscretion!" She smiled bitterly at her pathetic rival — "Harim Mouse," she'd once dubbed her — holding out the baby bundle a second time.

Akheperenre mutely moved aside and gestured for his concubine to advance. The uncertain mother slowly walked to the seated Great Royal Wife, holding out her thin arms to receive her trophy son — which Hatshepsut quickly passed off, wiping her hands together in a dismissive gesture.

Looking again to Nurse In, now standing, the Great Royal Wife directed, "Daughter of Re, escort Harim Lady Iset back to her and the chick's quarters. And make certain he is fed to his contentment. By *his* wet nurse, of course."

The older woman moved to the mother and child, her own pendulous arms and breasts receptive as down-filled cushions. Lady Iset meekly shifted the bundle of her son to the assertive nurse, who moved to the doorway. Iset looked first towards the nodding Lord of the Two lands, then turned to follow.

At that moment Royal Daughter Neferure released the grasping hug of her father's thigh and streaked once again into the garden.

"Daughter!" Hatshepsut barked, then abandoned any further effort of restraining the unbridled First Born.

"S...Sister." Lord of the Two Lands nodded towards his Great Royal Wife and abruptly turned to catch up with the figures moving off down the dim hallway. The King's First Companion scrambled to follow. The squalling had stopped.

"*Brother*! Our business is not *finished*," pronounced Hatshepsut.

The thickset ruler of Kemet stopped in his tracks and turned back to his Great Royal Wife seated rigidly in her gilded chair. Khawi reversed himself as well, folding his short arms over his narrow chest.

"Yes, Nob...lest Wo...Woman."

"How dare you, *dare* you bring that squawking mistake into my presence, let alone drag along Harim Mouse? And your disgusting *pet*, too!"

"For you...you to finally meet Hor...us in the Nest, next L...L...Lord of the Two Lands, Sis...ter. And, officially, his mo...ther, too. A simple c...c...courtesy is all."

"He's a whore's *bastard*, plain and simple, name little Falcon Beak whatever you will, to our and your justified father's disgust. The *First Born*, my husband, is Beauty of Re, *our* daughter.

"B...Born first, granted. *Daugh...ter*, yes, but *n...not* Horus in the N...Nest, my sister. The two s...sons you successively gave us w...were lifeless f...f...from your bit...ter w...womb, as you re...member only too...too well. The new B...Born of Djehuty was sent by L...Lord Amen,

9

by...by way of dear, sweet I...set, to suc...suceed us on the...the Horus Throne, one d...day far off, of c...c...course. The be...be...loved daughter of our b...bodies then will be *his* G...G...Great Royal Wife, is...is all."

"Never! Not even if he should *survive* so long. Lord Amen-Re and our father meant for *us* to be Lord of the Two Lands, not you! We were named "Prince" before the court, as Beauty of Re *will* be, as well."

"*Not* be...before *we've* f...f...flown to the heavens! And wh...en that far-off time c...c...comes, in their wi...wisdom, the priests of L... Lord A...Amen, as be...before, will see no...no good reason to flaunt an...cient tra...dition in fa...fa...favor of a fe...female Horus-in-the-...the Nest, certainly n...not when a vig...vigorous male heir is in...in hand. A *third* B...Born of Dejhuty will be L...Lord of the Two Lands. *Accept* it, Si...Sister. It is the d...d...destiny of our family."

He turned on his heels and strode from the chamber, immediately followed by the lurching nude dwarf and then the Medjay escorts. The flapping of Akheperenre's sandals on the passageway's floor receded to silence.

Hatshepsut sat staring at the several scrolls jumbled on the table. After a long pause, she sighed, raised her head and looked towards Senenmut, who stood across the loggia, arms as always still folded on his chest, silent observer of the testy family scene just concluded. A hint of smile was apparent on his thin lips.

"Well?" Lady of the Two Lands asked wearily.

"Great Form of Re was in rare good form today, was he not, Your Highness? He didn't cower from you as is his usual manner. Perhaps his new fatherhood has stiffened his backbone."

"Thank you as always, Tutor, for your oh-so-astute observations. Now perhaps you should make certain that your one sole reason for being at the Residence has not gone and drowned herself in the garden pool. Or else the cat, for that matter."

Enough of this bastard business. Hatshepsut waved her hand as if brushing away a noisome fly, leaned forward and picked up a papyrus roll, perhaps the same one she had been reading before this interruption. It didn't really matter.

Senenmut had been dismissed for that day.

INUNDATION 29, AGAIN
WER-MER

The maid-servant finished adjusting the braided strands of the heavy wig, and Hatshepsut looked without much interest at her faint reflection in the silvered surface of the mirror. She supposed this was the best that could be done, considering what there was to begin with. She had long ago abandoned any pretense of vanity. The rouge helped plump her lips and the kohl did restore some her best feature; she had always been pleased to have been favored with her mother's sea-green eyes. The former Mistress of the Two Lands handed the mirror to the much younger woman, who, backing away, bowed low, holding the object forth in her outstretched hands as if it were a sacred instrument and she an acolyte.

"Inform Nurse Fish that Noblest Woman is ready." She touched the bead collar with which the girl had draped her narrow breast before settling the wig in place. She then adjusted the inlaid bracelet on one thin wrist. "And remind dear Ancient One that the audience with Lord Lasting Manifestation of Re is to be totally *private*, with no ears pressed to the door. Mind you *both*, no ears."

Stepping backwards off the dais and moving in reverse until her rump touched the cedar-wood double door, the maid turned, opened one and slipped quickly from the room, closing the panel behind her.

Hatshepsut bent forward to retrieve her Great Royal Wife's golden whisk-scepter from the ebony table at her knees, then decided against regalia and sat upright again. Waiting. After what seemed like a rather long time, there was a brief, firm knock at the door. She counted to five.

"Enter." Her command voice was still strong.

Another five-count and both panels fanned widely outward. Standing in the gap was the nephew/stepson with whom she had shared the Horus Throne of Kemet for some twenty floodings, and on whom she had not laid eyes for several seasons, at least two floodings, as best she remembered. Falcon Beak was a bit stockier now, his bull neck thicker, it seemed; but there was no fat on his frame. He clearly still kept active with his annual campaigning in Retenu and even further northeast. Today Lord of the Two Lands had eschewed the emblems of his kingship, save for the small inlaid-gold serpent at his brow, as if it were emerging from his short curled wig. His garments were a simple linen tunic and a kilt tied at the waist, but without girdle or an apron. He sported no jewelry and, as his custom, was barefooted. Menkheperre Djehutymes stepped through the doorway and the panels were quickly closed behind him, no doubt by Nurse In.

"Please have a chair, Born of Djehuty." She never addressed him by his throne name. The ebony armchair opposite the table from her was indicated.

"Dowager Great Royal Wife," he replied, quickly nodding his head and striding to her. He stepped onto the low dais and took the pillow-cushioned seat. "You are looking fit as ever, Noblest Woman. Time does not know you." Elbows on the chair arms, he tented his fingers before his broad chest, a habitual gesture which had secretly annoyed her all these long floodings.

"Flattery fails on an old woman's deaf ears." She smiled. "What do we owe the honor of a visit by Mighty Bull? We were thinking that you had *forgotten* about us here in our resort confinement."

"Not a day passes, Aunt, that we do not give you *some* thought. We are constantly reminded that 'True Soul of Re did this, True Soul of Re did that'. You are very well remembered, to be sure. And you are not *confined*. You can come visit at Mennufer whenever you choose, and Waset, too, as you well know. Your apartments in the Residences of both capitals are always kept ready in anticipation of your visit, announced or otherwise."

Hatshepsut ignored the latter remarks. "So, Born of Djehuty, why have you come all the way out here at this time? Surely not for our wise counsel."

"It is a courtesy call, Noblest Woman. We and our counselors have reached a decision that we felt you should learn directly from Our Person."

Hatshepsut held up a palm, as if to halt her former coregent's discourse.

"How rude of me, My Lord. We have not offered Mighty Bull a refreshment." Before he could respond, she clapped her hands twice, and the doors fanned open. Nurse In had undoubtedly been listening on the other side. "Daughter of Re, bring us wine and some fruit. Grapes. And be *quick* about it." She clapped again, and the doors were pulled closed. "As quick as Ancient One is capable of." Dowager Great Royal Wife smiled to herself and looked back to her guest. "Now, Born of Djehuty, you were about to make a pronouncement?"

Menkheperre gripped the arms of his chair. "Yes, Aunt." He paused. "My Majesty has determined that the Hidden One, Lord Amen-Re, requires a new Holy of Holies at his ever-expanding great mansion in Waset. So the present one there, which we raised together so many floodings ago, is even now being dismantled. Lord Hidden One's priests are very pleased. First Prophet Hapu is Well has declared he finally will go into his own retirement, once the new barque shrine is finished and inaugurated."

"We shouldn't think that you would need our permission to please our divine father, Lord Amen-Re. You never sought our permission to finally finish the great shrine we built together, but without a single reference to True Soul of Re in the scenes of the topmost registers, or so our flies on the wall reported." Hatshepsut was tempted to pick up the whisk-scepter and swat her former coregent. Good naturedly, of course.

"In that instance you had retired from the Throne, so the fact that Our Person is *sole* Living Horus was depicted. Obviously, Aunt, no permission is being asked this time either, since, as we said, demolition is already well underway, in fact nearly finished. My Majesty simply felt you deserved the courtesy of being *informed* by Our Person."

Hatshepsut chuckled. "As if our network of *spies* would inform us otherwise!"

Menkheperre abruptly stood, signaling the audience was over. "When the grand new Holy of Holies is completed, Aunt, it is our very personal desire that you come to Waset for the dedication. You might wish to see your old ally in his final role as First Prophet." The third Djehutymes nodded formally, said "Noblest Woman," turned, stepped off the dais and crossed to the closed door panels.

Before he could push these open, they fanned outward and there stood the old crone, In, and a pretty melon-breasted servant girl, the latter with a tray supporting two faience lily goblets and a large ceramic bowl of grapes. The women bowed their heads and stepped aside, so that Lord of the Two Lands could pass. When the doors to the outer chamber closed with a bang, they both looked up and into their mistress's sitting room.

"Bring the wine," demanded the seated woman within, who had pulled off her wig and tossed it onto the low table. "Falcon Beak has made us thirsty. *Very* thirsty."

INUNDATION 29, TWO SEASONS LATER
ON BOARD THE ROYAL YACHT, *ARROW OF RE*, APPROACHING WASET

D owager Great Royal Wife Hatshepsut dreams: The drumming which determined the cadence of the processional suddenly stops, and the slight swaying of the palanquin ceases a few moments later. Mistress of the Two Lands opens her eyes, sits bolt upright and leans forward from the deep, feather-filled cushions against which she has been lounging, yes, dozing; and she now attempts to peer through the yellow-linen gauze of the curtains of her carrying vehicle elevated on the shoulders of a dozen black men of wretched Wawat. It is a bright blur beyond. She sinks again into the comfort of the bolsters, closing her eyes again, thinking: *We will be told.*

Many moments later, she hears orders barked at her bearers, and senses that her conveyance is being quickly, smoothly lowered in two stages, from shoulders to arms' length, then to the ground itself. A few long moments more pass and there is the approaching sound of sandals crunching coarse sand, stopping close by one side of the palanquin.

"Your Majesty, we are arrived."

It is Nebet, the handsome young captain of her Medjay guard. The approaches of others are heard.

"Are you ready to exit, Your Majesty?" The captain again.

Maatkare Hatshesput reaches up and adjusts her tall crown, the uncomfortably heavy bulbous blue-leather *Khepresh*, studded all over with many gold bosses, her long hair wound and bound underneath it. It is a highly ceremonial occasion calling for this particular regalia. She would have preferred a wig. She clears her throat. Waits a moment.

"We are, Captain. You may pull aside the curtains."

Immediately the gauzy fabric is pushed wide, exposing the palanquin's diminutive occupant. The exterior glare is blinding. Many immobile figures are just visible in the immediate vicinity, all bowing from the waist in her direction. Maatkare swings her legs over the side of the inlaid-ebony conveyance, so that her gilded-leather sandals dangle a few inches above the sand. Immediately a small, low stool decorated with the Nine Bows representing Kemet's enemies is thrust under her soles. The large jet hand of the guards' captain is offered. Grasping it, ducking her head and tall crown to clear the roof cornice, the Mistress of the Two Lands is slowly, gracefully pulled into an upright position. The late-morning sun is ferocious, and with her free hand she shields her eyes. Instantly two Residence serving-maidens are adjusting her garments — especially the askew starched, pleated triangular apron worn over the king's short kilt — and are rearranging her elaborate beaded collar and the sheer white tunic which covers an otherwise bare torso.

Dropping the captain's hand and arching her back so that she is standing at her full short height, she looks directly into the black eyes of the young officer. He is perhaps the most handsome man in all of Kemet, she is thinking once again.

"We thank you as ever, Captain Nebet." Unsupported, she steps down off the stool onto the sand. "Now, where is God's Wife?" She looks hard to her left, at the row of some dozen palanquins, carrying chairs and chariots in file behind the one she has just exited. Several persons of the court are disembarking from these transports. The large yellow-curtained conveyance immediately behind her own shows no signs of activity, however.

Nebet responds in little more than a hoarse whisper. "God's Wife is very much ill this morning, Your Majesty. She begs your forbearance that she is unable to go further."

"Nonsense. This is a divine event and her presence is absolutely required, even if she must be carried to it, puking all the way! Fetch her, now, Captain." She forces a smile at him, but her eyes are flashing.

The dark-skinned officer bows stiffly, turns and strides to alongside the God's Wife's palanquin. He bends down to speak to the unseen person behind the curtains, then actually squats as an animated conversation ensues. Just as Maatkare's patience has frayed almost to its limit, Captain Nebet is pushing aside the curtain. In moments linen-sheathed legs swing out of the carrying vehicle and sandals reach the sand. The young officer rises to his full height and offers his brown hand, which is taken by a slender amber one. Then he is pulling to a standing position a post-teenage woman — who is enormously pregnant! Her very extended belly pushes against the somewhat-altered white sheath she is wearing. This is Neferure, God's Wife of Amen-Re, and the only child of Mistress of the Two Lands, Maatkare, Daughter of Re Hatshepsut. She hands Nebet the gilded scepter of her office and adjusts a short golden cylinder atop the curled wig she is wearing, a God's Wife's headgear. She then takes back the scepter with the spatula-shaped finial, raises it against one shoulder and rests her slender bare forearm along the officer's own offered arm. Together they slowly move to the awaiting short woman in the warrior's helmet-crown, stopping two paces from her. God's Wife Neferure quickly nods her head and speaks before her impatient mother can.

"I am really quite ill this morning, Your Majesty. I should be on my bed, not here in Re's glare and unbearable heat. I have no lines to speak today, that I am aware of."

"Protocol, however, specifically requires the God's Wife's *presence*, daughter. You know that very well. The Hidden One would be most displeased if you fail your holy duty to him because of a purely personal inconvenience, like the sickness of mornings. As father of the sacred life in your belly, Lord Amen-Re will let no harm come to you — or *it* — while you are performing your service, even if that is only your mute presence. So enough malingering, Beauty of Re. We are awaited."

With that Maatkare Hatshepsut takes the inlaid-gold-and-faience ruler's Crook and Flail from the open wooden case being held forth by the Keeper of Scepters, crosses these regal implements on her narrow chest. She then turns and begins striding up the incline of the wide long ramp, at the foot of which the royal procession had stopped. The drummers resume their cadence, but remain where they had halted earlier. God's Wife Neferure, having no choice, reluctantly slowly follows her mother in tandem. She is still supported by the muscular arm of Captain Nebet, who brightly smiles his encouragement towards her.

The dream continues: Mistress of the Two Lands Maatkare, Daughter of Re Hatshepsut halts after stepping a few paces onto the flat paved surface of the second terrace of Djeser Djeseru, "Holiest of Holy Places." This is her Mansion of Millions of Millions of Years, some long while under construction. In front of her is a small contingent of official welcomers. At its center and one step in front of the others is Overseer of All of Her Majesty's Works, Great Steward of Amen-Re Senenmut. Two each on either side of him stand the four shaved-bald prophets of Lord Amen-Re, First Prophet Hapusenub at the steward's immediate right. They and the many others in rank and file behind them are bowing from the waist, until Maatkare commands in full voice, simply, "Thank you." A score or more priests and courtiers rise upright again. The Daughter of Re looks above and beyond this ordered crowd, her attention on the soaring curtain of tan high ragged cliffs which rise sharply up to meet, in an even more jagged line, the cloudless light-blue sky.

Senenmut advances one pace closer to Maatkare Hatshepsut, without making eye contact — focusing perhaps on the rearing golden serpent on the brow of her crown — and he nods again.

"Welcome Majesty, Mistress of the Two Lands, to this day's dedication at your Holiest of Holy Places. All present trust you will find the newly finished avenue of your regal lion-effigies equal to your fullest expectations, and to those of the Great Lord Amen-Re, of course."

All the greeters bow at the waist again, but immediately rise to full height, in near unison, without any command to do so.

"Show us" is Mistress of the Two Lands expected response and command.

There is a lengthy inspection stroll along the paved avenue of the Second Terrace — all of the stone lion-effigies of differing sizes being individually and collectively impressive (if only vaguely suggesting her actual facial features). When Count Senenmut's droning narration is finally over, Maatkare Hatshepsut stands alone and rigid, again the center of all attention. After long moments, the Keeper of Scepters advances with his open wooden box and Mistress of the Two Lands surrenders her regalia. A bowing bald young *wab* priest then hands her an obsidian-bladed knife with a sheet-gold haft, which she holds with one hand to her breast.

The crowd of officiants parts and a large, fattened all-white bull is led forth by several young acolytes. It wears a massive garland of blooming flora in a long yoke draped over its humped shoulders, with another small beribboned wreath of blue cornflowers between its gold-capped horn stumps. The beast snorts repeatedly as it slowly lumbers along.

A lector priest now intones his tedious abracadabra. The Fourth Prophet finally steps in front of Maatkare Hatshepsut, bows from the waist, rises and takes the ritual knife which she thrusts towards him. He retreats in a formal half bow, shuffling backwards, to stand alongside the huge bovine with the round apprehensive brown eyes. Without further ceremony, the priest suddenly thrusts the serrated shiny blade deep into the wattles of the sacrifice, slicing the razor sharpness wide, away from himself. The white bull bellows as bright red sprays widely from its opened neck. It slumps to kneel on its forelegs, before crashing sideways into a massive heap. Blood has been flung so far as to have splattered several large bright drops on the triangular white apron of Her Majesty's ceremonial attire.

No sooner is the bull in its sudden-death throes, legs twitching, blood pooling, than an agonizing human scream echoes off the distant cliffs backdropping Djeser Djeseru. Turning to look behind her at the disturbance, Maatkare Hatshepsut sees the God's Wife writhing on the paving stones several paces away. Captain Nebet is kneeling beside the thrashing form of King's Daughter, King's Sister Neferure — attempting to subdue the thrashing slender bare limbs. But before the Daughter Re can take but two steps towards this terrible tableau, the God's Wife's belly-stretched plain sheath rips open. In moments her exposed greatly swollen abdomen splits wide, as well. In a geyser of wet red, a reptilian creature thrusts out. It twists its blood-slimed scaly double head this way and that. Then it springs forth, two mouths of pointed teeth clattering. Trailing scarlet slime, it skitters like a colossal scorpion across the limestone paving — directly towards where Mistress of the Two Lands Maatkare stands frozen, defenseless, unable to move out of its way.

A sharp knocking on her cabin's doorjamb mercifully yanked the Dowager Great Royal Wife back to reality. She sat bolt upright on the narrow bed against one long wall of the cabin amidship the river yacht, which for several days had been bearing her south to Waset, the Southern Iunu, Residence of Lord Hidden One, Amen-Re. The light in the narrow space was so weak that Hatshepsut remained disoriented for several moments, half trying to remember what she had been dreaming. Then there was a second urgent knock.

"Highness, it is Fish, Daughter of Re. Awake! We have arrived and will be docking momentarily. You must make ready. There would seem to be a considerable welcoming delegation on the quay."

"Thank you, Nurse. You may enter and assist, please." The former ruler of the Two Lands swung her small bare feet to the cabin's cool floor, as the door panel was unceremoniously slid aside and the wide silhouette of her life-long companion all but filled the bright rectangle. In Sitre shuffled into the dim cabin without further formalities. At her heels was Hatshepsut's pretty young body-servant, ready to repair her mistress's appearance. The nurse slid open two narrow window panels, admitting shafts of pale light into the interior gloom.

The crone extended her still-firm grip and pulled the shorter thin woman to a standing position. Immediately the maiden began smoothing Dowager Great Royal Wife's unadorned linen sheath, adjusting the wide shoulder straps, assisting her in slipping on the gilt-enhanced leather sandals discarded earlier by the bed. Next she fastened a many-stranded broad collar of gold-and-faience beadwork from behind — Hatshepsut herself pushing her longish grayed hair high on the back of her neck to enable this. A pair of bracelets next, and then a scarlet narrow sash was affixed around her hips, the long strands flowing down the front of her thighs to the knees. The girl reached for the massive braided-and-curled black wig on its stand atop the narrow table opposite the bed, but was halted by Hatshepsut's hand.

"First our headband with the cobra."

"But, Highness," the old nurse hoarsely objected.

"Shush, Ancient One! Falcon Beak can't deny us that tiny bit of former regalia, now can he? Will they shackle us and drag the Dowager Great Royal Wife off to Born of Djehuty's rumored dungeons?"

In shrugged her hunched shoulders. From a small gilded casket on the table, the handmaiden removed a narrow gold band with rearing golden serpent and placed it on Hatshepsut's head, centering the royal emblem on the high brow. She next lowered the heavy tripartite wig into place, adjusting stray strands of gray hair out of view, arranging the drape of the braids on her mistress's narrow shoulders. She adjusted these so that the inlaid little cobra seemed to be emerging directly, menacingly, from the dark wig. She then handed a Hathor mirror to the somewhat-older woman. Makeup had been applied before Her Highness' midday nap, and required no touching up. The overcast daylight from the narrow doorway and window slots was less than bright and Dowager Great Royal Wife's reflection minimal, but — after a brief glance — Hatshepsut nodded her approval.

"So, then, we are ready now for Falcon Beak and his legion of toadies!"

Hatshepsut emerged from the ship's cabin, closely followed on deck by her nurse and handmaiden. They crossed together to the handrail of the sleek vessel maneuvering alongside the harbor quay of Ipet Isut.

From where he sat enthroned on the low dais erected for this one-time event, Living Horus Menkheperre Djehutymes observed the tiny figures of three women standing at the railing of the royal yacht, *Arrow of Re,* then in the final stages of docking at the quay of the Mansion of Lord Hidden One in the Southern Iunu. He was wearing the tall felt White Crown of Upper Kemet and a simple unpleated kilt with narrow apron of hinged enamel-inlaid gold plates. His stocky bare brown torso was otherwise unadorned by jewelry and his feet on the low Nine Bows stool were, as usual, without sandals. The Crook and Flail scepters resting side by side on his lap, his elbows were positioned atop the side panels of the gold-detailed ebony chair serving as his portable throne. Hands tented above his chest, his extended fingers touched his smooth-shaven chin (no False Beard required that day). Menkheperre slightly cocked his head to listen to what was being whispered into one ear.

"Your Majesty will give the signal when the percussion is to commence and the carrying chairs are to be advanced, yes?" The speaker, bending forward from behind Living Horus's right shoulder, was wearisome Vizier of the South Rekhmire.

Lord of Upper and Lower Kemet Menkheperre, Son of Re Djehutymes merely nodded an affirmative. The bewigged rail-thin noble in the identifying white ankle-length full sheath of his lofty office rose up to his not very great height and withdrew one step backwards. Rekhmire stepped off the throne dais and resumed his place in the sizeable assembly of standing courtiers and priests murmuring among themselves in casual ranks behind Lord of the Two Lands. Standing, that is, but for one shaved-bald ancient elder in a long white kilt, who was hunkered on a stool alongside Vizier Rekhmire. This was First Prophet of Amen-Re Hapusenub, then well into his eighty-third flooding. His great age and high rank — and, in particular, his declining health — allowed him to be seated in the public presence of Lord of the Two Lands Menkheperre. This was, in fact, the much anticipated day of his retirement as highest officiant of the principal god of Kemet.

Also among the welcoming delegation, but no longer standing in the front rank as in times past, was a tall, round-shouldered, portly individual who leaned slightly to one side and was himself of considerably advanced years. Wearing his hallmark cap-wig of short black curls, his long nose more pointed and cheeks more deeply furled than ever by age, his receded chin made even weaker by its long drape of wattles, he was Count Senenmut. Once high-and-mighty of this-and-that-everything, he was now unspecified "personal advisor" to Lord of the Two Lands — whose wise counsel, truth be known, was rarely sought any longer by His Person. The elderly count had not laid eyes on Dowager Great Royal Wife Hatshepsut in very many floodings. In fact, he had never been able to learn if she even knew that he still lived, having been recalled from his lengthy "banishment" by Lord Menkheperre, hard upon Mistress of the Two Lands Maatkare's retirement. That day he was perhaps wondering if she would recognize him and, in doing so, acknowledge her old confidante.

As two of the women seated themselves in the carrying chairs taken on board *Arrow of Re* — the maid-servant, of course, would appropriately walk behind her mistress and the nurse — Menkheperre gestured for Count Intef to approach alongside the Horus Throne. Whispering into the bent ear of his Chamberlain, Lord of the Two Lands instructed that the princes Amenemhat and Menkheperre should advance and stand to the right of the dais, to be ready for their formal introduction to the "honored visitor" from the North. Intef nodded and stepped back to where the two youths in short kilts — one prepubescent with a Horus Sidelock, the other an older teenager sporting a shoulder-length braided wig — were standing in the front rank. He whispered to each in turn and they stepped forward in near unison, arm to shoulder, exactly as had been directed by their father.

Drumming commenced at Lord Menkheperre's gestured signal, and the gold-inlaid ebony carrying chair supporting the distant figure of his former coregent was hefted in two stages to the shoulders of eight men of Wawat oiled and gleaming in white short kilts. The plain conveyance fully occupied by her omnipresent noisome old woman-companion was also lifted just moments later — but at stiff arms' length by only four glossy jet-hued bearers. To the measured drum beat from the quay, this mini-procession advanced down the gangplank of *Arrow of Re*, crossed the quay and halted — with the percussion ceasing simultaneously — in front of the dais solely occupied by the youngish man wearing the White Crown of Upper Kemet (on whose broad bare chest the Crook and Flail scepters were now formally crossed).

Dowager Great Royal Wife Hatshepsut's chair was lowered in reverse of how it had been lifted. Nurse In Sitre was grounded less ceremoniously. After an appropriate few long moment's pause, the diminutive figure of once-upon-a-time Maatkare stood and accepted the offered hand of a captain of the Medjay guard who had stepped forward. She then exited her carrying chair with more grace than might be expected of a woman of her fairly advanced years. Stiffening her spine, clutching her fly-whisk scepter, she moved rigidly upright to exactly in front of the dais and occupied throne-chair. Stepping forward to within three paces of Lord of the Two Lands Menkheperre, she nodded just her head, then looked her nephew/stepson directly in his narrowed eyes, her small pointy chin jutting. He could not help but smile at this display of regal arrogance he'd known so well for the some twenty floodings she'd half-shared his Horus Throne. Son of Re Djehutymes simply nodded ever so slightly in return.

Staff of office in hand, Vizier Rehkmire now stepped forward to alongside His Majesty's dais. He cleared his throat.

"Greetings, Dowager Great Royal Wife Noblest Woman, and welcome to the Southern Iunu, for this great occasion of the dedication of Lord Hidden One's splendid new barque shrine, His gift from Mighty Bull, Living Horus, Lord of the Two Lands Lasting Manifestation of Re, Son of Re Born of Djehuty."

Before the officious scrawny man in the long full sheath billowing from under his armpits could drone on, the seated ruler spoke in a raised voice.

"Yes, greetings, Aunt. We trust your voyage was comfortable and without incident. We trust, as well, *Arrow of Re*'s crew attended to all of your needs."

"The food was richer than we have become accustomed to these last several floodings, but never mind, Nephew, it was a trip comfortable enough and mercifully without incident." Hashepsut's voice was that of a woman half her years. "And we are pleased to be present, at your kindest invitation. But may we dispense with the ho-hum formalities of welcome and get on with the serious business at hand of dedication? We tire easily at these events, Your Majesty perhaps recalls. And a seat of some sort would be appreciated, if we're to be at this one spot for long." Hatshepsut shifted her Fly-Whisk scepter from the crook of one arm to that of the other.

Still wanting to be in charge, was Menkheperre's thought. Perhaps this public easing of his former coregent's long retirement would prove to be not such a good idea, after all.

Later that Evening
Banquet Hall, the Residence

With Great Royal Wife Sitiah chattering away beside him, Lord of the Two Lands Menkheperre surveyed the array of dining guests at the farewell formal banquet he was hosting for First Prophet of Amen-Re Hapusenub, Retired. The very old priest, seated in the place of honor directly at his right side, was clearly struggling to stay awake, his sagging chin snapping up whenever he began to nod off. Perhaps, thought His Majesty, he should soon whisper a suggestion that the bewigged ancient priest might "retire" from the present festivities, if he so wished. Clearly Hapusenub's final sacerdotal duties at that afternoon's drawn-out barque-shrine dedication ceremonies had taken their toll, evidenced at the time by the First Prophet's frequent need to sit even when a particular ritual act called for him to be standing. His Majesty should have excused the priest from a subsequent inspection tour of the grand Renewal Festivities Hall under construction nearby the new Holy of Holies, but hadn't thought to do so at the time, being focused rather on impressing his former coregent with the unique building, which would reach its completion by the next flooding.

Looking past the several nubile fully naked dancing girls and the loin-clothed, shaved-and-oiled youths gyrating in graceful unison to percussion, pipe and string accompaniment in the open central space of the columned, brazier-lighted large hall, His Majesty was mostly intent on the grouping seated directly across from the royal dais. This included at its center that same former coregent, Dowager Great Royal Wife Hatshepsut, flanked on one side by Horus-in-the-Nest Menkheperre, and on the other by the youth's teenaged older half-brother, Amenemhat. Mighty Bull Menkheperre's namesake heir, as usual, sat hunched forward, his full concentration riveted on the plentiful female nudity of the entertainment. The stick-straight elder Royal Son, however, was clearly captivated by whatever stories of fanciful times past the old woman was relating. The Living Horus was decidedly curious if Hatshepsut had figured out yet exactly who the youth was.

Once the interlude of music and dancing performance concluded, to brief polite applause from the noble assembly, and the dozen young men and maidens had dashed away, the din of conversation rose again. Hatshepsut sipped from her golden wine goblet and listened attentively to the stammering young man on her right, as he belaboredly answered a question she had posed. Royal Son Amenemhat reminded her of someone, but she couldn't quite place who it was. Unlike his younger half-brother the Heir — son of Djehutymes's tedious Great Royal Wife — the youth didn't really look at all like his father, lacking Falcon Beak's, well, *beak*, was Hatshepsut's thought. Perhaps that was because he — so she had been told by Nurse In Sitre some years before — was the bastard of a harim whore (like father, like son!) and so probably favored that anonymous female. Still, there was something — the way he squinted and blinked, the pronounced bowed curve of his mouth when he smiled, the jug ears (visible now that he was not wearing a wig), especially his annoying speech — that recalled — yes, she had it! — her own despised half-brother and late husband, the second Djehutymes, at the same awkward young age.

When Prince Amenemhat concluded his drawn-out reply and reached for the refreshment waiting in his own golden goblet, the Dowager Great Royal Wife took the opportunity to ask, "Just how old are you, my boy?"

After sipping and swallowing, the lean brown youth replied, "Eigh..teen f...lood...ings, I've b...been told, Great La...dy."

Hatshepsut did a quick mental calculation and a cold chill ran down her spine. No, it absolutely couldn't be, but surely, well, was. Here beside her sat the grandson she'd never known existed, having been told that Neferure's bastard, like the God's Wife herself, had died in childbirth those years go! She glared across at her nephew/stepson and former coregent, the third Djehutymes — whose own attention for now was directed at the departure, with servants' assistance, of her loyal old colleague, the former First Prophet.

At that same moment there was a commotion among the banquet guests seated behind Hatshepsut. People were murmuring loudly, standing, chairs and stools being pushed back. Someone called out for the royal physician. Dowager Great Royal Wife also stood, along with the two princes. Lord of the Two Lands himself came off his dais and strode across the banquet hall's central open space, entering the parting crowd now on its feet several paces beyond her. She turned totally around to view only the backs of her neighbors.

"Just what is happening, Prince?" she directed at her earlier conversation companion. Young Amenemhat shrugged his narrow bare shoulders, as four of the Residence guardsmen followed in the wake of His Majesty.

"Is he dead?" someone unseen asked aloud from amid the courtiers' buzzing murmurs.

"High time, we can all but hope" was a low-voiced anonymous response nearby Hatshepsut and the royal youths. She could not tell who had spoken

Very soon a thickset mature man entered the banquet hall and passed into the standing crowd. Amenemhat told Hatshepsut in a whisper that he was Amenenope, His Majesty's personal physician. Several long moments later, the tall Medjay guards came back through the again-parting assembly, carrying aloft on their shoulders the prone figure of a stout elderly man, whose head was violently thrown back, mouth gaping open.

As the departing group crossed in front of Hatshepsut, she was absolutely stunned to recognize in profile the contorted features, pointed nose, furrowed cheeks, the askew out-of-style close-curled cap-wig: Brother of Mut, presumed deceased in exile long ago!

Two abrupt shocking revelations, one hard upon the other, that things were absolutely not at all as she had been led to believe these past floodings caused the former Mistress of the Two Lands to sink down onto her cushioned armchair, clutching and looking into her empty goblet. The third Djehutymes, Falcon Beak, certainly had some profound explaining to do!

*   *   *

2

From the vantage of her hiding place between the array of grounded carrying chairs and horseless chariots, six-floodings-old Heir's Elder Daughter Hatshepsut watched the distant small figure of her blindfolded younger sister, Neferubity, still counting slowly to 100. The two girls attired in just their sidelocks were playing hide-and-seek, to amuse themselves at the family outing underway in the large man-made clearing near Riverside. The "seeker," her shaved head bent towards her knees, was seated on the edge of a low platform supporting an airy, brightly painted small pavilion occupied by the mother of the two girls, Heir's Wife Ahmes. She lounged on large colorful bolsters, chatting with aged Dowager Great Royal Wife Ahmes Nefertari (upright on her portable chair) and several other reclined noblewomen. Their half-brother, Heir's Younger Son Djehutymes, hunkered cross-legged at one side of the group, gnawing on a leg of roasted duck. Immediately next to him, playing knucklebones, squatted his older cousin, Prince Tao, only son of Count Siamen, the Lord of the Two Lands' lame elder brother. Four women-servants were pouring wine, attending to the several low tables of eatables arranged among the picnickers. Two kilted male servants cooled the group with tall ostrich-feather fans.

Hatshepsut's and Neferubity's father, King's Heir Djehutymes, their other half-brother, Heir's Eldest Son Amenmes, Count Siamen and husbands of the noblewomen present were all off fowling from reed skiffs in the dense papyrus marshes that extended well beyond the clearing and screened The River from view.

Little Neferubity, finally finished her slow counting, sat upright and pulled away the cloth blindfold. With the women gossiping at her back, she stood and gazed about, looking for the likely place her big sister would be found hiding this time. Perhaps down the gradually sloping embankment and a few cubits into the tall papyrus stand. More probably somewhere in the midst of the carrying chairs. Or crouching on the other side of their bearers, who themselves were squatting in a group and joking with the tall Medjay guard. Or, even further away, behind the chariots. Or perhaps beyond those, where the horses were grazing, indifferently attended by their drivers, also hunkered or lounging. Possibly lurking in the shrubbery there, shielded by the trunk of a dom-palm.

Having decided against the thick curtain of papyrus, the small amber girl began moving across the clearing, directly towards Hatshepsut, now crouching as low as possible within the cluster of carrying chairs.

When her sister did not materialize after several long moments, Heir's Eldest Daughter risked a peek around the corner of the seat which was shielding her from Neferubity's view. Her mouth fell open at what she saw.

Not ten paces away stood the other child, rigid, stopped in her tracks, arms stiffly at her sides, fists tightly clenched. She was staring wide-eyed at the ground just in front of her. There, on the green grass, was what appeared, from Hatshepsut's viewpoint, to be a very thick long length of brown rope. Just as Heir's Eldest Daughter realized the truth, however, perhaps a third of the "rope" suddenly rose upwards into a swaying post, the towering end flared the size of a small plate. Cobra! the older girl exclaimed mentally.

As Hatshepsut was about to call out and implore that Neferubity keep standing totally still, the naked small girl abruptly turned completely around, to flee. But before she could even begin to dash away, the upright column of serpent lunged forward, sinking fangs into the narrow bare calf. It instantly pulled back and lowered itself onto the ground again, to begin slithering away. Neferubity and her sister screamed simultaneously, the victim dropping in her tracks to her knees, the single witness bolting from her hiding place.

Chattering in the pavilion immediately ceased, all attention there focused towards the small form sprawled face down on the verdant lawn, and also on Heir's Eldest Daughter, who was moving across the clipped grass in a wide semi-circle, attempting to brave an approach to her fallen younger sibling.

"Cobra! Cobra!" the panicked girl called out, now jumping up and down and jabbing her finger towards the serpent slowly gliding away in the direction of the papyrus stand.

Except for King's Mother Ahmes Nefertari, who remained regally rigid on her chair, the several women and two prepubescent boys scrambled to their feet and began stepping off the low pavilion platform, advancing into the sloped clearing. Simultaneously the chair porters and charioteers came running up to see what had happened. The group's single Medjay guard, short sword unsheathed from the scabbard belted at his waist, strode quickly towards where hysterical young Hatshepsut was pointing. Going behind the retreating cobra, he quickly lopped off its head. The thick long body writhed in loops several times before its movement completely ceased.

B y the time King's Heir Djehutymes, his teenage eldest surviving son, Amenmes, Count Siamen (dragging one leg) and the noblemen with whom they'd been hunting burst through the tall papyrus and into the clearing — alerted to the emergency there by a shrill whistle-call from captain of the charioteers — Heir's Younger Daughter Neferubity lay dead across her mother's lap. Heir's Wife Ahmes and the other women (except for the King's Mother, still seated in the pavilion, head bowed) had pulled off their wigs and were tearing at their natural hair, keening and rocking where they knelt. Heir's Eldest Daughter Hatshepsut squatted a short distance off, sucking on the coiled end of her sidelock. Heir's Younger Son, the boy Djehutymes, stood mute by the pavilion, his narrow back to the scene of tragedy and loud mourning. Prince Tao had wandered off to piss in the shrubs.

King's Heir Djehutymes dashed across the clearing and dropped to one knee beside sobbing wife Ahmes and unmoving Neferubity.

"What has happened, Moon Born?" One splayed hand gripped and gently shook his grieving spouse's bare shoulder, the other rested on the shaved small head of the girl, her mouth open as if in a frozen scream, vomit drying on her cheek and chin. Heir's Wife Ahmes seemed oblivious to her husband's arrival and question, continuing her rocking and wailing.

"Cobra," was the single-word answer offered by Hatshepsut from her squatting position apart from the distressed women. Her slender arm pointed towards the perimeter of the clearing and papyrus grove.

Young Amenmes crossed to where his little half-sister indicated, bent down and lifted high the five-foot length of headless snake. "This would seem to be the villain, My Lord," he said expressionlessly to his father, who had raised the lifeless child off her mother's lap and now stood upright, holding the small form clutched to his broad chest.

The nobles were all kneeling by their wives, embracing, consoling, attempting to quiet the wailings.

"Who saw what happened?" demanded the King's Heir.

"I did, Papa," Hatshepsut replied, standing and walking towards the stocky brown man dressed in a plain white kilt, without other adornment, his shaved head glistening with perspiration. She stood in front of him and took the dangling hand of her little sister.

"We were playing hide-and-seek. It was her turn to count. I was over there." She pointed to the carrying chairs. "When she finished she looked about, then started right for where I was, so I ducked low as possible." She sucked a deep breath and continued. "When she didn't come up, I peeked and saw her stopped and staring at the cobra, who was rearing up to strike. Before I could call out for Beautiful Bee to not move at all, she turned to run and she was bitten on the leg." The girl kissed the lifeless fingers. She looked up at her father's always stern falcon face and a tear flowed down her plump cheek. "I shouldn't have...." The sobs began.

"Now, now," King's Heir Djehutymes began, "It's not your —"

Suddenly there was a commotion among the porters and charioteers watching in a group at a respectful distance, having been joined by the serving women and fanners. These spectators had turned away to watch the approach of a single chariot racing very rapidly up the dusty narrow lane leading to the clearing. In moments the driver reined in his galloping horses and jumped from the halted vehicle, tossing the long reins to one of his stable fellows. The man dashed into the clearing and, oblivious to the dramatic scenario in progress there, strode directly to where the King's Heir stood with his two little daughters, one lifeless in his arms. The charioteer knelt on one knee, head bowed, awaiting acknowledgment.

"Speak," Djehutymes ordered.

"Great Lord, I bring an urgent message from the Residence."

"So, deliver it."

"It is very bad news, Great Lord. Mighty Bull Holy Soul of Re has fallen ill again, most gravely so, this time." His head still bowed, the messenger's voice quavered. "He may already have flown, by now, to the heavens, Great Lord."

This was the moment that the King's Heir had been both awaiting and dreading. "Born of Amen," he directed at his eldest son, "Come here and relieve me of your sister." The fifteen-year-old, a slimmer copy of his father, stepped forward and received the small body into his cradling arms. "Noblest Woman," Djehutymes spoke now to Hatshepsut, again clasping the cooling hand of her sister, "Be a brave big girl and go offer comfort your mother. Tell her that we must all go back to the Residence, immediately. *Immediately!*"

With that he turned and made his way through the still-keening women and their attendant husbands, past his self-absorbed wife without looking down at her, and up to his youngest son still standing, struck speechless, at the edge of the pavilion, where young Prince Tao now sat, jaw cupped by hands. He placed a heavy dry palm on the eight-floodings-old boy's damp shoulder.

"Go, Namesake. Assist your little sister and step-mother." He stepped up onto the low platform and crossed directly to the old woman seated there, hands clasped in her lap, bewigged head bowed, perhaps sleeping through all the mayhem. He dropped to one knee in front of her.

"Oh Greatest One," he began in a hoarse whisper.

Ahmes Nefertari's head jerked up. She *had* been dozing.

"Your Beautiful Bee is gone," the Dowager Great Royal Wife announced matter of factly in her rusty voice. The pinched face, grim as ever, was all but lost in the shadowy depths of the heavy black wig. But the squinting dark eyes flashed authority still.

"Yes, yes, Your Highness, Beautiful Bee is flown off; but we may have been cursed with two tragedies this day."

"How so, did the serpent get the other imp, as well?"

"Little Noblest Woman is heartbroken but wasn't harmed. No, Oh Greatest One, word has just come from the Residence that Son of Re has fallen ill again. Most seriously so. We must all return there in haste."

"Amen is Pleased? Is Ill? Again?" The old woman rose upright out of her chair with such sudden force that it toppled over behind her. "We must go to him. Immediately. Now!"

Djehutymes also stood. At her full height, Ahmes Nefertari came only to his chin. He offered her his arm. She hesitated, then accepted it. The King's Heir and the King's Mother began slowly moving across the wide pavilion.

"I suppose his whore-boy is with him," she stated flatly.

Djehutymes supposed that he was.

EIGHT FLOODINGS EARLIER, INUNDATION 11
REIGN OF DJESERKARE AMENHOTEP
THE RESIDENCE, MENNUFER

Dowager Great Royal Wife, King's Mother, God's Wife, God's Hand Ahmes Nefertari rounded the corner of the hallway leading to her son's private quarters in the Residence. There, his back to the apartment's closed doorway stood a very tall Medjay guard, chin resting on hands overlapped atop a bronze-tipped lance, its point-end on the floor: catnapping on watch, was the first thought of Her Highness, who was trailed at a few paces by her own spear-bearing guardsman, a man of Kemet, as she always insisted. At the sound of the approaching sandals squeaking on the gypsum-plastered surface, the muscular young Wawat mercenary came to rigid attention, chin high, gaze directed upward, towards the dim hallway's high ceiling.

When the advancing woman in a linen sheath-gown came up to within just feet of him, the guard moved his spear from a vertical position to a diagonal one, signaling barred passage. He continued looking somewhere over the short woman's massive wig.

After several long moments, an impatient Ahmes Nefertari spoke. "Stand aside, low one, so that we may enter."

"Lord Majesty say he not be disturbed," replied the ebony guard.

"Do you know who we are, wretch?" King's Mother asked, her head tilted so she was staring at the young man's wide raven face rather than his broad, well-cleaved chest. "Look at me, young fool."

The guardsman kept his chin up, but rolled his eyes low enough to see this haughty old female who was addressing him. As he did so, he caught the toothy smile of the bronze-faced guardsman close behind her.

"Well, now do you now know who we are?"

"Pardon, no, lady. Never seen."

"Our guard," King's Mother spoke over her shoulder to her armed attendant, "announce Her Highness's presence to this raw recruit."

The Kemetman came to attention himself. "Yes, Your Highness." Then to the Wawatman: "Stand aside, foreigner, to admit the King's Mother and God's Wife."

"Got orders right from Lord Majesty herself. No one in," was the slow reply.

"Do you want to be perched on a stake before nightfall?" Ahmes Nefertari was becoming angry. She stepped to one side. "Guard, if he won't move aside immediately, run him through," she ordered her escort.

Just then the double door-panels behind the stubborn Medjay fanned wide to reveal a quite stout tall individual in an ankle-length kilt but without a wig: Son of Re Amenhotep's youngish butler and personal body-servant, Suitnub — who peered around the triangular broad back of the young Medjay.

"Oh Great One, it is *you!*" he blurted, moving the ebony barrier physically aside with a forceful shove.

"Yes, butler, *me* Herself. I am here to address His Person on an urgent matter of State, and this dumb tree post refuses *Our* Person entrance."

"He has his orders directly from Mighty Bull, Oh Great One. His Majesty is, well, indisposed, and receiving no visitors this afternoon, Your Highness. Not even *you*, I am afraid, Oh Great One." Suitnub was wringing his fleshy hands — as eunuchs seemed always to do when distressed, was the Kemetman guard's private thought.

"Nonsense! No one refuses the God's Wife *anything*, not even Living Horus himself! Step *aside*, butler."

Ahmes Nefertari advanced and Suitnub did move aside, as ordered by the fearsome King's Mother. "Wait here," she instructed her escort, walking into the low-lit chamber, its high ceiling supported by several painted-wood columns. "Close the doors and stay outside, butler. Amuse the guards with your...whatever."

The doors closed behind her. The large room — illuminated only by narrow clerestory windows near the high ceiling — was scantly furnished with a few chairs, a couple of low tables, a chest on tall legs. This was actually the antechamber to the true inner sanctum of Lord of the Two Lands Djeserkare, Son of Re Amenhotep, which lay beyond another pair of doors in the wall opposite where the royal lady had entered. She crossed to these and, without any hesitation, pulled the tall panels fully open, passing through the wide portal into her son's bed chamber. Then she halted in her sandals.

In the center of the smaller, even darker columned space was a low dais supporting a wider-than-usual bed. And on this were two nude persons copulating, with accompanying grunts and groans.

Ahmes Nefertari was immediately certain that the thrusting bare buttocks she was staring at were not her son's, but those of someone far more slender than the stocky Mighty Bull. From her vantage point, all she could see of the penetrated person were bare legs wrapped around the narrow waist of the active participant, ankles hooked above the humping, naked derriere; and those calves were too muscular to be feminine. It was instantly apparent to God's Wife, God's Hand that Horus in the Flesh was playing woman for another male! Not that this difficult revelation surprised her overly — actually, not in the least — but she had never expected to actually witness the crass act itself, in person. His Majesty was "indisposed," to be sure!

Her entrance and presence went unnoticed, of course, and so the King's Mother quietly closed the wooden panels and lowered herself onto a stool conveniently positioned next to one door jamb, to continue watching this vulgar little Set-and-Horus reenactment to its foregone conclusion. Which occurred sooner than she was expecting, with several final hard thrusts by the penetrator and his loud moan of pure release. But it was not fully over. This person now raised upright, Living Horus's legs slipping away; and then something else seemed to be transpiring between the two males on the bed — that Dowager Great Royal Wife could not make out, except for some sort of rapid movement of the dominant person's left elbow. Finally, there was an audible groaning, which ceased momentarily. This topmost individual now lowered himself onto the other and the two embraced tightly, murmuring together. Then the top person sat upright again, stretched his thin arms over his head of close-cropped bright-copper hair, and abruptly dismounted the bed.

He proved to be a tallish, leanly muscled young male of not more than fifteen or sixteen inundations — who was a "mighty bull" in his own right, judging from her personal experience with the considerable appendage of her late brother/husband! In the dim light, however, he appeared rather, well, less-than-attractive facially, was her thought, with a longish pointed nose and a weakish chin under rather fleshy lips.

Bending to retrieve his abandoned kilt on the floor, and standing upright to rewind this around his waist, the semi-erect naked youth suddenly spotted the voyeur seated in the shadows by the door. He turned back to the person still supine on the bed, arm hooked across his eyes.

"Amen is Pleased, there's a *woman* here!"

"What the...?!" Lord of the Two Lands Djeserkare raised himself on his elbows, squinting into the dimness and exclaiming, "Amen's blue balls! Not *you*, Mother!"

T he clearly nervous man-boy had been dismissed through a side doorway of the bed chamber, which the King's Mother had not noticed previously; and Lord of the Two Lands was soon reattired sufficiently to conduct a private audience with the only fully important female in his life. They sat in gilded armchairs facing one another. There was a long silence before the blunt-featured Son of Re Amenhotep spoke, clearing his throat, first.

"So, our State Secret is now finally known — by *you*, Your Highness."

"I've long suspected as much; but I'm mostly disappointed in your *taste*, Son of Re. He is rather, well, just a bit *ugly*, at least in the face. And the orange hair of Set! I could have selected some serving boy that bests all the few beauties of the harim, if you'd but asked your mother's assistance."

"We have all the several choices we could want. He pleases us mostly because of his wit and wisdom beyond his years. He makes us laugh — sometimes so hard that we even weep — Our Mother."

"Is he a slave?"

"Oh, no, no! From an honest professional family at Iunu of the South. A scribal acolyte, actually, there in the Mansion of the Hidden One. He aspires to be a lector priest, although My Majesty has other plans for him now." Lord of the Two Lands coughed, covering his mouth with the square of linen he always carried.

"Just how *old* is he, Amen is Pleased? Surely just shorn of his sidelock."

"Eighteen floodings, he says, though we suspect one or two less. But, well, Your Highness, he seems far more experienced than whatever tender age." The familiar cough again. "He does know a great deal about *everything*."

"And his name?"

"Brother of Mut."

"How interesting. I shall have to ask the great Mother Goddess her opinion of this seductive sibling of hers from Iunu of the South — when next I speak with her." Ahmes Nefertiti smiled wickedly.

Young Senenmut, ear pressed to the door behind which he stood, only frowned.

A Few Passages of Re's Barque Later
The Residence, Mennufer

The breeze wafting through the columned loggia off of the Dowager Great Royal Wife's private sitting room was warmish, though welcomed. A fanner was not necessary that early afternoon. Three ebony armchairs were arranged facing towards the garden in an arc around a low cedar-wood table loaded with two ceramic platters, one piled with a varied assortment of fresh fruit, the other with a squat pyramidal arrangement of small sweet cakes. Three faience goblets brimming with the finest Delta vintage rested on the table as well. Two serving girls waited in the background.

Occupying the middle of the three chairs was God's Wife Ahmes Nefertari. She was attired for this midday gathering in a strapped plain red-linen sheath-dress, but without broad collar or other jewelry, and wearing no wig. Her grayed longish braided locks were pulled behind her ears, held in place by a thin plain-gold band fronted by a small inlaid Lady of Buto golden cobra. She was barefoot, long toenails marooned with henna.

To her right slouched Lord of the Two Lands Djeserkare, Son of Re Amenhotep. He, too, was dressed simply in just a pleated linen kilt without an apron, his soft belly protruding a little over the waistband. He wore no collar or head covering, or even a diadem, so was for now without the protection of the Lady of Buto. Amenhotep's closely cropped hair was receding and, though he was only twenty-six floodings old, graying a bit at the temples. Unadorned by jewelry, nevertheless his butler Suitnub had carefully applied kohl eyeliner and Ahmes Nefertari thought (to herself) that she could detect a bit of rouge on her son's thin lips. He wore simple woven-reed sandals and clutched, as always, his large linen handkerchief.

The third chair was empty, the invited luncheon guest not having yet arrived, but expected momentarily. While the Dowager Great Royal Wife and Lord of the Two Lands waited, she was relating — droning on — in great detail her new plans for another generous endowment of Delta vineyard acreage to the estates there of Lord Hidden One Amen-Re. His Majesty half listened, half daydreamed, totally disinterested. He lifted and sipped from his wine goblet, which he returned to the table, plucking up the sweet cake that topped the pastry pyramid, sniffing at it, then popping it in his mouth. When his mother asked a question, Son of Re Amenhotep was trying to decide if more honey should have been used in the confection.

"What, Mother? We were distracted by this sweet."

"I said —"

Just then the third party came onto the loggia, crossing to behind the awaiting empty chair and bowing his bewigged head towards his Lord and cousin, and then the God's Wife, his late father's sister. This was Generalissimo Djehutymes, only son of King's Son Asar Ahmes Sipari and the Lady Senisonbe, and recently widower of the Lady Asar Mutnefret. He was the father of four sons: Wadjmes (deceased), Amenmes, Remes and the infant Djehutymes (during whose birth Mutnefret breathed her last). Besides the childless Son of Re Amenhotep, Djehutymes was one of but two surviving adult males of the House of Tao, which was precisely the reason for that day's command lunch.

"My Lord, Oh Great One," Djehutymes came around the empty chair and sat down, arrow straight, without invitation to do so. Like his somewhat younger cousin, the Living Horus, he was stocky but clearly far more muscular, his abdomen still quite flat. Facially he favored his mother, his narrow nose being rather beaky, so he would not have been thought related to Amenhotep, the latter having the flared-nostrils and coarser features of Taosid men. In addition to his currently stylish tightly curled capwig, Djehutymes sported a simple bead collar, gold wrist bands and a plain linen kilt of the latest cut. Leather sandals shod his feet.

"It seems I over dressed for this occasion," he chuckled, leaning forward and lifting the goblet at his place, gesturing a silent toast to each of his dining companions and sipping the wine. "Delicious!" He returned the vessel to the table.

"You always cut a fine figure, General Born of Djehuty," said the God's Wife, reaching for and sipping from her own goblet. "Yes, it is good, isn't it? From the Hidden One's estates in the Eastern Delta. And a particularly good vintage, three floodings old, I am told."

Son of Re Amenhotep had come out of his slouch, perhaps in response to his somewhat older relative's military demeanor. "And how are the boys, Nephew?"

"Born of Amen is still missing his mother very much, has become irritable, even surly. Born of Re, however, being still a young boy, is more interested in toy soldiers than tears. My infant namesake sleeps a great deal, his wet-nurse tells me." He plucked a grape from the bunch on the fruit tray. "When awake he bawls a lot, but not for his mother, certainly."

"And you, Born of Djehuty, how are you holding up without your beloved Asar Beauty of Mut?" inquired Ahmes Nefertari. "Are you ready to marry again?" she asked unexpectedly, before he could respond to the God's Wife's first question.

"*Remarry*? I think not, Oh Great One."

"But we think *so*, do we not Amen is Pleased?"

"It is *your* thought, Your Highness," replied the Living Horus with a sigh, slouching again. He also reached for the fruit tray, taking a very ripe date and biting into it, so that juice ran down his chin, which he wiped away with his handkerchief.

"It is most appropriate that the Heir be married, even if the Living Horus himself is not, we think." Ahmes Nefertari smiled bitterly at her son, who was looking away into the garden, off to where two pet gazelle were grazing.

"I am afraid you have lost me, Oh Great One," inserted General Djehutymes. "What 'heir'?"

"Precisely the point, Nephew," began the God's Wife. "Inasmuch as Sacred Soul of Re, Amen is Pleased failed to impregnate his late sister-wife, Asar Beloved One of Amen, before she flew to heaven, and for some time now refuses to venture even into his harim — in favor of, ah, *other* recreation — the Two Lands are, as you well know, without a Horus-in-the-Nest. With Son of Re's health in question, I have decided that an Heir of the Blood must be determined sooner than later."

"It was not our fault for not *trying* that Great Royal Wife Asar Beloved One of Amen did not conceive, Mother!" replied Amenhotep, throwing the date pit into the garden, but missing his target, the gazelles there, by cubits. "She was already dying from her first day out of your womb. Wonder that she survived into her teens. Our other deceased sister, the most unlovely Asar Daughter of Amen, would have been a better breed sow, if a grandson was what you wanted! Although successfully bedding that loathsome bitch well might have been quite beyond even Our

Person's best pretense. And there is nothing 'in question' about our health!"

With all that Horus-in-the-Flesh began a fit of violent coughing and covered his mouth with the handkerchief. When this subsided, he emptied his goblet and held it aloft, signaling for a refill. One of the serving maidens rushed up with a jug and complied.

"If we may get back to the topic at hand," began the God's Wife, who had been impatiently waiting for the return to calm. "Since there are no prospects of a Son of His Body from the Living Horus, I have decided that he must adopt the Heir from among his cousins. Because you are the oldest of the grandsons of our own father, Asar Tao Perpetuated Like Re, and also the father yourself of three healthy — I presume — sons, it has been decided by me that you, General Born of Djehuty, shall immediately become Heir of the Blood and the Two Lands' Horus-in-the-Nest."

"But, Great One, what of King's Son Prince-Count Siamen? My uncle is —"

Ahmes Nefertari raised her small henna-stained palm, cutting her nephew short. "And when the time does come for *you* to ascend the Horus Throne and don the Double Crown, protocol and tradition require that there will be a Great Royal Wife at your side, to be God's Wife of Amen and Divine Hand. Thus, oh yes, you *shall* remarry, soon."

Before the thunderstruck generalissimo could object again, she continued. "And so I have decided that you take as wife our niece, your cousin, Princess Moon Born, only daughter of our long-gone sister, Asar Beloved One of Amen, with whom you shall have yet more sons undoubtedly, since she is both attractive, youthful and healthy. A Lord of the Two Lands can never have too many sons!"

"I don't know what to say, Oh Great One." Djehutymes turned to his younger cousin still intent on the gazelles. "Are you comfortable with this, My Lord?"

"It seems we have no input to the matter. It has all been decided for us," replied the Living Horus, who reached for the entire bunch of grapes, abruptly pushed back his chair and stood. "Is this tedious family business of yours finished, Mother? We have another important matter demanding our attention."

Ahmes Nefertari merely nodded her grayed head, reaching again for the wine. And the Lord of the Two Lands, coughing again, quickly departed the shaded loggia, disappearing into the Residence.

"That 'important matter' being his whore-boy, no doubt," God's Wife stated matter of factly, then sipped from her goblet.

The new Heir-appointed was almost certain he knew who she

meant.

Inundation 19 Again, Eight Floodings Later
Final Day of the Reign of Djeserkare Amenhotep
The Residence, Mennufer

When the Heir Djehutymes slipped into his cousin's dimly lighted bed chamber without announcing himself, he came upon a strange tableau. Lying amid several supportive bolsters on the wide bed on a central low dais, sweating profusely, breathing loudly and seemingly unconscious, was a wasted Djeserkare Amenhotep. His bare upper body was exposed, waist and legs covered by a rumpled white sheet. Hunched in a chair to one side was King's Mother Ahmes Nefertari, seeming smaller, even more shrunken than usual. Without a wig her patchy baldness was exposed. Bony hands folded in her lap, she seemed to be typically dozing — less likely praying. Perched on edge of the bed itself, at the Son of Re's side, was a wide-shouldered slender young man, who wiped the damp royal brow with a folded cloth. He looked up as the Heir approached the bed dais. This was King's Scribe Senenmut, Lord of the Two Lands' secretary and confidante — and secret "consort."

"Greetings, Heir of Horus," the youth smiled. "He is close, I think. Amen is Pleased has not fully awakened for a very long time. His breathing is increasingly more labored. The King's Physician has said there is nothing to do now but wait for the end. Her Highness dismissed him, Born of Ptah, the physician, awhile ago."

At the sound of speaking, God's Wife Ahmes Nefertari lifted her chin and blinked in the dim illumination provided by two tall braziers. "Oh, it is you, Heir Born of Djehuty. My thanks for coming. You will be Horus-in-the-Flesh by the time Re's barque disappears behind the horizon, I think."

"I have just been at the House of Beautification, Your Highness, where the preparations for our little daughter have begun. My wife would, should, be here but is taking today's terrible tragedy at The River very badly. She sends her greetings, Your Highness, nonetheless, and wishes Son of Re a swift flight to his place on the Barque of Re."

"Rushing us off, are you, Cousin and "Son *Not* of Our Body?" whispered the expiring Horus-in-the-Flesh, hoarsely but loudly, eyes still closed.

"You're back!" Senenmut enthused, gently placing his cool palm on the supine man's feverish wet brow.

"If we understood correctly, our royal condolence for loss of your daughter this day, Cousin Born of Djehuty. Perhaps we shall see Beautiful

Bee again. Soon." Son of Re's eyes opened, blinked, attempted to focus on his visitor.

"Greetings, Your Majesty," was the Heir's simple response.

"Are you ready for the great burden?"

"Yes. Fully, I hope, My Lord."

"Mother, are you still here?" Son of Re Amenhotep turned his head on the bolster, blinking. He listlessly raised his arm, hand drooping.

The God's Wife pushed herself upright with some difficulty and took the single step to the bedside, covering the damp royal hand of Horus-in-the-Flesh within the dry weak grip of both her own gnarled ones. "Still," was her terse reply.

"Excuse us our failures to realize your expectations of Our Person, Mother. Your Heir of choice will prove the strong ruler the Two Lands truly deserve." Turning back to his cousin, "Born of Djehuty, provide for our beloved Brother of Mut." With that, Djeserkare Amenhotep sighed deeply, opened his mouth for his *ba* to fly, and was on his way to the stars.

There was a long silence, three heads bowed.

"We shall announce his passing first thing on the morrow," stated Lord of the Two Lands Great Soul of Re, Son of Re Born of Djehuty, in his very first royal pronouncement. "Come with us, Brother of Mut, so that Her Highness may be alone with her grief and regrets."

The new Living Horus and his predecessor's secretary exited the death-chamber together. Following his new lord, wiping at his tears, young Senenmut could not have guessed at what the gods who determine the future had in store for him.

* * *

3

Chief King's Scribe Senenmut continued his reading aloud: *"His Majesty is Horus, whose kingdom is uncounted years. Subject to him are all islands of the Great Green, and the entire of Creation is under his heel, bodily Son of Re Born of Djehuty, living for ever and ever. The Hidden One, ruler above all gods, is creator of His Majesty's beauty; beloved is he of all gods of Waset, who give him Life, Stability, Prosperity, filling his heart with joy upon the Throne of Horus, where he leads all living beings like Re."*

The young man finished, paused, then looked up from the papyrus sheet spread wide before him on the low table where he sat cross-legged on the mat-covered sand in the spacious campaign quarters of Lord of the Two Lands Akheperkare. After a few long moments, he said, "That is all, Your Majesty."

The broad-backed man who stood looking through the tent-hatch spoke without turning around. Outside a pair of Medjay royal guards flanked the entrance, their spears at ease.

"Your way with words never stumbles, Brother of Mut, always so nicely smoothing our own wordy ramblings. Yes, that will be most satisfactory. Worthy for stone."

Silhouetted by the bright fat slice of noon-hour sunlight admitted through the open flap, Son of Re Djehutymes now turned to face his scribe across the tent. He was without head covering or adornment and wore only a simple kilt and leather sandals.

"Take your text to the engravers, so they shall begin cutting our declaration into the prepared great boulder over on Tombos. The sooner their task is finished, the sooner the conquering forces of the Black Land may set sail for the Belly of Stones. The Navy will have refloated the ships by the time we have struck camp and are marched to below the Third Cataract."

"Yes, Your Majesty." Senenmut stood tall and rolled up the several papyrus sheets, bowing just his head towards Akheperkare and moving around the low table.

"If you should spot either of our sons on your way to the river, send them to us. And the King's Daughter, if you happen across her path."

"Should I not encounter their highnesses then, do you wish that I go seeking each of them when I return from delivering the text, Your Majesty?"

"Yes, that is our desire, Brother of Mut. The Namesake will probably be moping alone in his tent, as always. Little Noblest Woman will be somewhere dashing about with her fat nurse huffing and puffing in tow, as always. Heir Born of Amen no doubt will be laughing over ribald jokes with rank-and-file troops in their camp, as always. Round the lot of them up and send or bring each here. No great hurry, actually." The Son of Re crossed to a provisions-filled folding side table positioned against the rear wall of the command tent. He picked up a Great Green jug sitting there and poured himself a tall tumbler of warm beer. "So, be gone!"

"Your Majesty." Senenmut bowed his skullcap-covered head, pushed aside the door flap, ducked a little and exited the tent into the blinding midday desert sun.

Lord of the Two Lands Akheperkare then seated himself in his camp chair, gulped some beer and arched his shaved head back, eyes closed, to muse on highlights of the present campaign, to first suppress and then impress the rebellious chieftains of wretched Wawat, as the barbarian natives called that Re-blasted barren land. It had proven a rather easy undertaking — except perhaps for the tedious long travel upstream by river and ashore (especially at the Belly of Stones) — and the Dirteaters had been subdued without much force; the barbarian cowards mostly just turned and ran when confronted with Kemet's sheer military might. Djehutymes had now led the army of Kemet further up Father of Inundations Hapu ("The River") than any of his predecessors, extending the previous control of the Black Land over the wretches there, as his stela here on Tombos Island would declare for eternity. He was thinking again about the new fortress he would order built near this point, when there was a commotion at his tent flap that returned him to the present, his head coming back up and his vision focusing on the silhouetted figures at the opening.

"Mighty Bull, order these damn Medjay thugs to allow me to pass! It's most urgent that I speak to you immediately!"

It was the old veteran marine admiral, Ahmes son of Ebana.

"Let him through," was the Son of Re's reflexive command, as he sat bolt upright on his chair.

The spears uncrossed and the grizzled familiar figure of Ebana's son came striding into the tent, stopping at rigid attention in front of his lord. Without formality he burst out: "There's been an accident in The River, Your Majesty! Horus-in-the-Nest was swimming with the men, then suddenly was struggling and then disappeared beneath the surface."

Lord of the Two Lands Akheperkare was already pulling on his tall blue *Khepresh* and dashing through the tent hatch into the blistering light of Re in Wawat. Son of Ebana was at his heels, continuing his dire narrative, as the ruler and admiral moved rapidly through the temporary village of tents. They were headed towards The River bank.

"Many men are in the water now, but have not found him! Sons of Sobek were reported this morning sunning on the opposite side of Father Hapu miles upstream, so some fools have jumped to the conclusion that one of those monsters grabbed the Heir, unseen below the water. Others think he merely cramped and went under, the Crown-Prince not being a particularly strong swimmer."

Shouts at riverside could now be heard and scores of others — soldiers, mercenaries and servants alike — were also streaming there. When Djehutymes and the veteran came close, the already assembled crowd parted and the two warriors hurried down the steeply sloping embankment to water's edge.

A dozen or more naked soldiers were in The River, some knee or waist deep, others further out actually diving beneath the brown surface, breaking water, gulping air and diving again. The Lord of the Two Lands could only stand helpless and watch with everyone else. Heavy grief descended on him, as he came to realize that beloved Heir Born of Amen was certainly drowned. Three sons taken from him now, with only the "spare," difficult namesake Prince Born of Djehuty, just ten floodings old, left to succeed to the Horus Throne, if his own days were numbered — as they ultimately would be. Swamped by these dark thoughts, the Son of Re didn't notice the small kilted form that had come alongside him — fearless tomboy only Daughter of the King, little Noblest Woman.

"What has happened, Papa?" she asked, taking his large hand.

Just then the girl spotted the skiff bearing her tutor, Senenmut, being maneuvered by its rower through the diving soldiers. He was returning from his mission to the far off big island in The River, just as he'd assured her he would soon, when she ran up to him on his way there.

Hatshepsut began waving to the distant tall figure with her free arm. He didn't wave back, however. A bit hurt, the girl looked up at her father, just as a tear coursed down his broad brown cheek.

L ord of the Two Lands Akheperkare, Son of Re Djehutymes sat enthroned on a low dais in his spacious campaign tent, his two surviving offspring standing rigidly arm to shoulder before him, Prince Djehutymes and Princess Hatshepsut. Several of his field commanders and a few non-combatant courtiers were arrayed to both sides of the ruler; the children's tutors, Minmaat and Senenmut, and Hatshepsut's nurse, In Sitre, were also present. He had just formally announced to them all that a half-eaten male body, presumed to be what survived of Crown-Prince Amenmes — but uncertainly so, as little was left but a limbless, headless mauled torso — had been recovered late that afternoon from a sandbar some distance downstream from the encampment of the Army of Kemet in Wawat. Son of Re was now mercilessly lecturing his visibly quaking new Heir.

"The worst part of this tragedy, young Born of Djehuty, is that you are now Horus-in-the-Nest, by default, which distresses us. You are still young, so hopefully may yet mature in some more positive way. But now we find you gluttonous, lazy and without apparent ambition, boy, and perhaps not as quick of wit as we would hope for in an Heir — all in sharp contrast to your sister, here, who has boundless energy and seeming unlimited curiosity. Plus keen intelligence. Were that she was born male. If that had been so, even though she is your junior by two floodings, we would unhesitantly pass over you, Born of Djehuty, in favor of her as Horus-in-the-Nest and Heir to the Double Crown.

"Check those tears, boy. No Horus-in-the-Nest is above reprimand. And you, daughter, wipe that smirk off your face. Now, be gone, all of you! We would be alone with our great grief for poor Asar Born of Amen. That is, except for you Brother of Mut. We desire your attendance on another matter."

The two children and several adults filed out of the brazier-illuminated large tent into the orange-hued dusk, the Barque-of-Re-in-Wawat about to slip behind the western horizon. Senenmut had stepped to one side to let the others pass. Once the last of the commanders and sprinkling of courtiers had departed, the broad-shouldered tall youth, in a linen tunic, stepped in front of the seated Son of Re, bowing forward ever so slightly.

"Your Majesty."

"Relax and bring a stool." Djehutymes gestured towards a number of such pushed back against the perimeters of the tent. He then doffed the bulbous leather war crown he was still wearing and placed it on a table beside his field chair.

Senenmut retrieved one of the camp stools and brought it to

where he had been standing. He then sat on it without further leave to do so, making eye contact with his master. He smiled, uncertainly.

"Were we too hard on the boy? You may speak candidly to Our Person, as always."

"He will only hate you more than he already has up 'til now, Your Majesty. If I may say so, the prince has always been a most-cheerless child, is my observation. Perhaps because he never knew the love of his birth mother. But also perhaps — forgive me for being so blunt, Your Majesty — because Her Highness, the Great Royal Wife, acts towards him as if he doesn't exist, showering all maternal attention and favor on young Noblest Woman and, before, on late Asar Beautiful Bee, as well — as only is natural, of course, the girls being of her body. The role of stepmother isn't a normal condition." Senenmut cleared his throat, twisted the leather band on his wrist.

"God's Wife Moon Born has never cared for the boy, we grant that, although she has always been favorably inclined as stepmother to his brother, the Heir-Deceased. She found the eldest prince engaging and fully worthy of the Double Crown, we know, from her own private remarks to Our Person."

After he was certain that the Son of Re had finished his thought, Senenmut continued: "Again, if I may speak bluntly, Your Majesty, I fear that Princess Noblest Woman may take fully to heart what you have said today, publicly, as it were. She already clearly dislikes her half-brother and immensely enjoys besting him at everything from script lessons to pulling the bow. Now her self-pride at being Your Majesty's openly declared favorite may cause further problems between them. Which will make for a most unhappy marriage union in the future."

"Always thinking ahead," mused Djehutymes aloud. "So, shall we now add *seer* to your many talents, Brother of Mut?"

Mighty Bull's personal scribe bowed his head — to hide the smile on his full lips.

THIRTY-EIGHT FLOODINGS LATER, INUNDATION 10
THE MAATKARE/MENKHEPERRE COREGENCY
THE RESIDENCE, WASET

Chief Steward of the Estates of Amen-Re Senenmut stood watching in the milky light provided by the clerestory windows high above, arms folded across his tunic-clad broad chest. He watched as his body-servant and aide-de-camp, Minmes, finished spreading the large sheets of linen on the painted floor of the columned audience hall of the Residence, these rectangular panels arranged directly in front of and facing the throne dais.

The young man then made small adjustments here and there, so that the charcoal cartoon-sketches on the sheets aligned properly. Minmes also stood up and stepped back, to appraise the end result.

"Perhaps the second one from the bottom on the outer row there could be straightened even more," suggested the Chief Steward, pointing where he meant. In addition to his plain mid-thigh linen tunic, he was attired in an overlaid sheer ankle-length skirt tied at the waist, and wore gilt-leather sandals. On his head was a black wig of several tiers of short braids that brushed his wide, if slightly stooped, shoulders.

The shortish, swarthy, quite beautiful youth — wearing a much simpler wig and pleated kilt that showed off his tightly muscled lean torso and hard thighs, knelt where Senenmut had indicated and adjusted the large linen canvas just a hair. Minmes was a native of the far-off island kingdom of Kheftiu in the Great Green, but had resided in Kemet since he was a very young child, brought there by his recently widowered merchant father. He had long ago forgotten how to say his Khefti birth name.

"That's about as perfect as we can make it, Master." He looked up at the pointed, creased face of the much older man.

Which was perfect timing, inasmuch as at that moment the high, wide double doors at the far end of the hall were heard opening. Minmes rose upright quickly, moving to alongside and just a pace behind Senenmut; and the two men looked in anticipation towards the imminent arrival of the sole person for whom this unusual display was intended. As a matter of fact, the exact same sort of event had occurred a dozen or more times before in recent seasons.

Two armed Medjay guardsmen stepped into the hall and quickly flanked the doorway, facing inward. After a long moment, a diminutive figure resplendent in white and gold advanced through the opening, followed immediately by a body of others also attired in white garb with gold embellishments: the four prophets of Amen-Re and at least a dozen favored male members of the court of Mistress of the Two Lands Maatkare, Daughter of Re Hatshepsut — who was the small figure in the lead. A bewigged, tallish, quite fat female brought up the rear.

As the ruler and her entourage came to the perimeter of the arrangement of linen panels, Senenmut and Minmes bowed slightly in unison. The Chief Steward spoke.

"Greetings, Your Majesty."

"Greetings in return, Count Brother of Mut." The ruler replied, moving around the large rectangular composition and stepping onto the dais. She positioned herself on the gilded throne and Nine Bows low footstool there.

The entourage fanned around the perimeter of the display, which was wide and deep enough that everyone had an unobstructed view of the huge design, albeit most were looking at it upside down, others from the sides. Only Nurse In Sitre stepped onto the dais and went to stand at one corner of the throne.

"So this is what you have for us today?" Hatshepsut was attired in her usual white plain knee-length strapped sheath, worn with gilt sandals and a gold-bead collar of several connected strands. She also sported the Lord of the Two Lands' *Nemes* head-covering of heavily starched pleated white linen with shoulder lappets, held in place by a sheet-gold headband fronted by an inlaid-gold rearing cobra. She carried no scepters or other regalia.

"Yes, Your Majesty," replied the Chief Steward from his position at the left front corner of the dais. "I have here for approval the master design of one key portion of the north wall of the middle colonnade of the Holiest of Holy Places Mansion for Eternity, the decoration program of which, as Your Majesty will recall, is the Coronation and events leading up to it. This portion for Your Majesty's consideration is the initial scene depicting Great Soul of Re, Born of Djehuty when he declared Your Majesty his successor."

"Your artists have gotten it all wrong," was Hatshepsut's quick terse judgment. She was leaning forward, elbows on her knees.

"Surely not, Your Majesty. How so?" replied Senenmut, frowning.

The Mistress of the Two Lands sat rigidly upright again.

"We were not *facing* our father when he made his declaration of our selection as the Living Horus's chosen Heir. We should be facing out, *towards* the courtiers. Are we to presume these three rows of figures behind the text represent the courtiers?"

"They do, Your Majesty."

"Then, we were *facing* them at the time."

"I remember that Your Majesty was standing facing the seated Lord of the Two Lands, and behind Your Person were the assembled notables. I was there — at the time." Senenmut had folded his arms across his chest, a subtle gesture of defiance.

"Nurse Fish, Daughter of Re, you were also there that day. Were we facing our father or away from him?"

The elderly woman seemed clearly uncomfortable. "Well, I, ah, honestly don't recall, you know, it was so long ago. But I am also certain you were facing whichever way *you* remember." Only In Sitre dared publically refer to the Mistress of the Two Lands so familiarly.

"So, Count Brother of Mut, instruct the artists to reverse our figure to face outwards with the notables facing us. And there are other problems. First, we were not wearing the Sidelock of Horus, but rather the *Khepresh* helmet. And our father was attired in his Renewal Festival robe and the *Khat* head covering, not an apron-kilt and the war-helmet, as here. Have those corrections made, as well, and Our Majesty will be satisfied."

Hatshepsut stood and stepped off the Nine Bows footstool. The presentation was concluded. In moments the Mistress of the Two Lands and her entourage had departed the audience hall. When the Medjay guards closed the doors behind them, Senenmut ordered young Minmes to begin folding up the cartoon panels. He knew very well that the artists had gotten every detail right, since he had instructed them on these himself. Point of fact was that Lord of the Two Lands Akheperkare had not declared the King's Daughter Hatshepsut his Heir on that long-ago occasion, but merely stated he would have done so had she been a prince instead of a girl. Not that it really mattered, Senenmut supposed. So much of the decoration of Djeser Djeseru was pure fiction.

THIRTY-EIGHT FLOODINGS EARLIER, INUNDATION 2
REIGN OF AKHEPERKARE DJEHUTYMES
REGENCY OF GOD'S WIFE AHMES
THE RESIDENCE, WASET

Three women sat in a colorfully painted garden pavilion of the Residence at the southern capital, Waset. Two were elderly, the third somewhat younger. They were Dowager Great Royal Wife Ahmes Nefertari, King's Mother Senisonbe and Great Royal Wife, God's Wife of Amen Ahmes, Acting Regent of Kemet in the prolonged absence of Lord of the Two Lands Djehutymes. They had just been joined by the sole surviving son of Ahmes Nefertari, lame Prince-Count Siamen. He took the fourth chair in the pavilion.

"Greetings, Your Highnesses." The bewigged count accepted a goblet of wine offered by a young serving-girl, who had followed him through the garden and onto the pavilion, and he raised it in a silent toast to each of the women. "Thank you for agreeing to meet with me this beautiful morning, great ladies."

"It is our pleasure, Cousin, inasmuch as we see you so seldom," replied the Regent. "How is country life in the Delta treating you and your family, especially young Prince Tao?"

"'Country life' is routine, if always pleasant enough, Your Highness. And my boy is very well, very soon to be shorn of his Sidelock. He sends greetings to you all, particularly the grandmother whom he very much misses." He nodded towards his mother.

"Never had much time for me, as I recall," replied Ahmes Nefertari tartly.

Siamen let the remark pass. He had learned as a young boy that there was no point in contradicting the former King's Great Royal Wife and God's Wife. Since he found making small talk, especially with the women of his family, tedious at best, he turned the conversation immediately to the reason he was there.

"So, Your Highness," speaking directly to Regent Ahmes, "has any word come from the South as to when Lord of the Two Lands and the Army of Kemet will be returning from the policing campaign in wretched Wawat?" He sipped his wine.

"Nothing for several weeks now," Ahmes replied. "The last messenger reported the terrible accident which took the life of Crown-Prince Asar Born of Amen, and that the young Namesake had been elevated to Horus-in-the-Nest. Also, that all hostilities had ceased and the expedition would be sailing north in due time."

"I'd heard a rumor to the effect that Crown-Prince Born of Amen had tragically died, fully unexpectedly, and of the last Son of the King's Body had been designated successor. Which is why I am here today, Your Highnesses." He sipped more wine and continued. "It greatly worried me when our cousin, Son of Re Born of Djehuty, decided to take all of his living offspring with him on campaign to Wawat, a most unhealthy place, as we all know. Especially the Heir, but the 'spare', as well. And the Yellow Land is no place for a juvenile King's Daughter, not even a tomboy one, I feel."

"We couldn't agree with you more, Cousin," replied the regent. "But the Son of Re was adamant. Our several pleas feel on deaf ears. The Hidden One, Lord Amen-Re, would keep all the children safe, His Majesty was confident."

"A confidence misplaced, so it would seem" inserted Ahmes Nefertari.

"Frankly, Your Highnesses, I am personally uncomfortable with the prospect of the Namesake one day, sooner or later, donning the Double Crown. But more so," Siamen continued, "that he is still a minor — perhaps not in the best health, I've heard reported — and should, the gods forbid, something dire happen to him as well, where would that leave the House of Tao and the Horus Throne?"

"Our husband is still vigorous, Cousin. His Majesty would just have to produce himself another Heir. By one of his harim, as we are now barren, following our miscarriages," stated the Great Royal Wife matter of factly, but smiling.

"What of my son, Prince Tao?"

"What *of* him?" asked the Dowager Great Royal Wife, waving her fly whisk.

"He is Blood of the Line."

"*Out* of line," Ahmes Nefertari chuckled. She reached for her beer tumbler.

"I may have been passed over — when my dear brother, Asar Sacred Soul of Re, Amen is Satisfied, flew to ride the Barque of Re without issue — in favor of our also 'out of line' cousin, now the Living Horus, presumably because of my, well, handicap," he looked accusingly at his withered leg and then his mother. "But Tao is fully vigorous and will be taking a wife soon and producing his own heirs — my spy tells me he has already lain with at least three of my *female* slaves," he looked at his mother, "at only twelve floodings!"

"We have lost *you*, Son of Amen," interrupted the Regent. "What point are you attempting to make?"

"Simply put, that our Prince Tao should be regarded — if not actually formally named — as potential Horus-in-the-Nest, should anything, gods forbid, happen to Heir Namesake before he, the gods willing, is capable of procreating the next generation of princes of the Blood. Certainly *that* if the Namesake should fly to heaven prematurely and our beloved cousin, Son of Re, is suddenly without an Heir of his own body."

"All of this is way far premature, if not bordering on seditious," stated the Dowager Great Royal Wife. "I think you have once again clumsily overstepped yourself, Son of Amen. Pun intended! This interview is concluded. Have a nice voyage back to your farm. And his grandmother does *not* send your young Min our regards!"

Count Siamen stood and nodded at just the Regent and her mother-in-law, Senisonbe. He then turned, stepped down from the pavilion and limped across the garden.

"One to keep an eye on," stated Ahmes Nefertari dryly, tapping the fly-whisk handle on the arm of her chair, sipping beer.

"Son of Amen?" asked the regent, looking to the old woman.

"Prince Tao," was the reply.

LATER IN INUNDATION 2, REIGN OF AKHEPERKARE DJEHUTYMES
A REMOTE WADI IN THE WEST OF WASET

L ord of the Two Lands Akheperkare, Son of Re Djehutymes reigned his chariot to a halt several cubits behind the already stopped vehicle which bore Royal Architect Ineni and his charioteer. In several moments a third two-steed vehicle driven by King's Scribe Senenmut pulled up in the airborne dust and reigned to a stop in tandem with the other conveyances and horses. It carried not only the tall bureaucrat but also King's Daughter Hatshepsut, freshly shaved head with sidelock visible alongside her tutor. Ineni stepped down from the first chariot and quickly strode back to where the Son of Re still stood at the royal vehicle's handrail, lax reins in hand. Next to the ruler was young Horus-in-the-Nest, whose shaved head and sidelock came only to his father's bare shoulder. Son of Re wore a cap-wig, simple kilt and sandals, but was otherwise unadorned with jewelry or regalia. A sheathed dagger hung from the belt of his kilt, however. The Crown-Prince wore only a short tunic and was barefooted.

Chariots and passengers had halted at the base of a rugged soaring cliff-face in a mountain-rimmed desert canyon some long distance from their point of departure Riverside. A contingent of half a dozen unarmed soldiers had been awaiting the vehicles' arrival, having run well ahead to clear the canyon's rough natural trail of the largest rocks and moveable boulders. Standing with the soldiers in the narrow band of shade provided by the cliff were two tall Medjays and their lances.

"This is the place, Your Majesty," a dusty stout Ineni smiled up at his sovereign, gesturing towards the cliff-face behind the advance guard.

"Which is just as well, as it doesn't seem the chariots could have gone much further," replied Son of Re Djehutymes, pointing towards the apparent end-point of the sun-blasted valley, the soaring cliffs forming a very high barrier. He looped his horses' reins around the chariot handrail and stepped down onto the gravely surface. The Crown-Prince remained standing in the chariot, clearly uncertain whether he wanted to disembark in this formidable place. However, as Djehutymes moved around the vehicle to stand face to face with the royal architect, young Princess Hatshepsut came running up to her father. She was trailed at a few paces by Senenmut, who halted at a respectful distance. The girl also wore a short tunic and was barefooted like her half-brother. The young scribe/tutor's head was covered by a cap-wig in style similar to that of His Majesty, and as dusty as his linen tunic.

"That was *fun*, Papa!" Hatshepsut enthused, taking one of Djehutymes's hands in hers. "This is a very strange place, stranger even than Wawat. Are you really *sure* this is where you want to live someday?"

"That's what we've traveled all the way here to decide," Son of Re replied, patting the small shaved head affectionately with his free hand. He turned back to his chariot. "Come off your perch, Namesake," he ordered the Crown-Prince.

The boy let go of the railing which he still had been clutching tightly, and reluctantly stepped down from the vehicle, coming alongside his father parallel and opposite his half-sister. He was brushing dust from his tunic.

"I...t is un...unpleas...antly d...d...dirty here, Your Ma...jesty." Since his elevation to Horus-in-the-Nest only a few months earlier, Crown-Prince Djehutymes had begun referring to his father formally rather than familiarly. "And I'm v...very hungry and e..s..specially thir... thirsty."

"There's a canteen on the chariot to solve the latter problem. And we think you could well miss a meal now and then," the ruler said of his son, who had begun to grow obviously pudgier since the return from Wawat.

"*I'm* not hungry *or* thirsty," offered Hatshepsut, looking around their father and sticking her tongue out at young Djehutymes, who immediately turned and clumped through the dust to step back onto the chariot, retrieve the canteen there and relieve his parched throat with several noisy gulps.

Meanwhile, His Majesty had gestured for his personal scribe to advance. When the young man came up immediately, Son of Re instructed: "Brother of Mut, take these two troublemakers and go exploring about, while we and our architect tend to serious business. But not too far, and keep all eyes out for Lord Set's dangerous sand minions."

Princess Hatshepsut immediately released her father's hand and stepped over to clasp the cool palm of her tutor. The two of them, tall and very short, turned and began walking away in the direction from which they had come. Horus-in-the-Nest Djehutymes had no choice but to step down off the royal chariot again and follow — shuffling, several paces behind — in their dust. At a hand gesture from Lord of the Two Lands, one of the armed Medjay began trailing the trio, at a distance. Akheperkare Djehutymes then turned back to Royal Architect Ineni.

"All right now, Master Builder, all that bothersome child-business addressed, what do you have to persuade us? We trust it's well worth the long ways out here to this scorching middle of barren nowhere."

"Your Majesty," Ineni began, "After very much reflection, and then myself tirelessly searching all through the expansive desert wadis west of Waset — and even well beyond — I've at last determined that the Mansion of Millions of Years of Your Majesty should be located very far away from where all people see and hear. Since the beginning of eternity, your great royal predecessors have chosen to impress subsequent generations by locating their eternal abodes in obvious places, marked by even more unmistakable visible monuments to themselves — which indeed succeeded in serving their intended purpose of drawing all eyes to them, but also always unintentionally prompted rumors of what vast hidden riches they marked."

"And we know that most of those great 'eternal abodes' long since have been plundered, at least in some part, by belly-crawling worms who thieved such 'vast riches' for their own misspent gain," interrupted the Son of Re, smiling matter of factly.

"Exactly, Your Majesty!" grinned Ineni. "Which is why I have devised an ingenious — if I may say so — thieves-proof plan for your own Mansion of Millions of Years. Rather than site it out in open view — there where your immediate ancestors of the houses Tao and Inyotef are abiding eternity at the edge of the flood plain, with their walled courtyards and miniature mud-brick Mountains of Re — we shall secret your mansion out here in the desert, at this very place, hidden from every eye for all eternity. No one shall ever hear rumors of Your Majesty's burial riches — because their location won't be known!"

"No monument, then, will mark our resting place?"

"Only this grand *natural* Mountain of Re which rises above us from this very spot!" Ineni gestured up towards the towering peak, that did, indeed look very much like a rugged Mountain of Re. "Note this great cleft which runs down from the peak, Your Majesty? There, at its bottom, we'll cut your mansion directly into the bedrock. Here are the plans." As he was speaking Ineni had taken a rolled papyrus out of the leather cylinder-case suspended from his belt. "If I may approach, Your Majesty?"

"Of course."

The architect came alongside the Son of Re and unrolled the scroll, holding it so Djehutymes could look at the ink draft of a floor plan.

"See, after a deep shaft there will be rock-hewn steps down to a doorway (which will be well sealed, of course) and beyond that will be a corridor leading to the Antechamber, in the center of which will be another staircase leading down to the large Resting Chamber itself, the star-painted ceiling of which, as Your Majesty sees, is to be supported by a massive column. Off the Resting Chamber we can hew smaller rooms as treasuries for your provisions and riches. Your Majesty will note that the Resting Chamber will be shaped in imitation of the royal name-oval, a real innovation, if I do say so! And its walls will be plastered and painted ceiling to floor with texts and scenes of *The Book of What is in the Underworld* — for Your Majesty's reference in the Afterlife."

"And the sealed first doorway is all that will keep the wretched thieves out?"

"Oh, no, Your Majesty. I should've explained that the deep shaft here will be filled to its very top with large boulders and other desert debris, completely hiding and totally disguising its location for all time."

"So," said Son of Re Djehutymes, stroking his stubbly chin, "if we are to rest hidden away out here in this desert canyon, where are our cult offerings to be made? That's the purpose, as you well understand, architect, of the chapels marking the very locations of our ancestors' Mansions of Eternity."

"And Your Majesty's Double shall have its daily offerings, too. We shall erect an elaborate chapel for that purpose also at the edge of cultivation, something not unlike the Great Mansion of the Hidden One directly across the river, only more modest in scale," he chuckled, "so as not to make Lord Amen-Re, well, jealous." Ineni tilted his head to scrutinize the somber beaked face of the Lord of the Two Lands, who was still studying the plan on the scroll.

Suddenly a loud, lengthy, high-pitched scream echoed off the canyon walls, startling the three teams of horses and bringing the six soldiers and single Medjay — who had been hunkering a ways off in what little shade was available — collectively to their feet. Instantly the Lord of the Two Lands was off running at a full gait down the chariot trail in the direction which Senenmut, the royal children and the Medjay had gone earlier. Ineni, not a young man, was uncertain whether to follow. While pondering that decision, he was quickly passed by the soldiers and Medjay, all dashing away in the Son of Re's wake.

Calling out their names, Djehutymes, his dagger unsheathed, came around a large rock outcropping — and upon a curious scene. The tall scribe/tutor was standing to one side with his arms folded across his chest in his usual fashion. The Medjay guard stood even taller beside him, his bronze-tipped spear at ease. The crown-prince squatted on the ground, forehead on his knees, arms over his head. He was sobbing. The princess was upright a few paces from and facing her half-brother, feet braced apart, arms stiff at her sides, fingers of her small hands rigidly straight. On the sandy gravel between them was a large squashed scorpion, beside which was a sizeable rock. Senenmut turned, dropped his arms to his side and nodded his head, as his royal master came running up.

"Greetings, Your Majesty," he said calmly.

"What by Amen's blue balls goes on here?" Son of Re Djehutymes sharply demanded, as the other running men rounded the outcropping and halted abruptly.

"It seems young Horus-in-the-Nest got himself cornered by one of Lord Set's vile creatures," he pointed to the very dead arachnid, "and little Noblest Woman bravely came to his rescue, slaying the thing."

An impulsive deed she would come to regret.

TWO FLOODINGS LATER, INUNDATION 4
REIGN OF AKHEPEKARE DJEHUTYMES
ATOP A GEBEL IN THE WEST OF WASET

The cobra glided gracefully across the sand, raised itself and began slowly moving up the large sun-blasted white boulder. When it reached the flattish summit, the female serpent lifted its oval flat head and looked about with faint vision. This was lowered and the sleek long body began forming itself into a large coil. Just minutes later a wide shadow passed over the boulder and its new occupant, which did not register with the heat-seeker. But when an overly large black vulture, with a flurry of flapping, dropped onto a close-by other rock outcropping, the brown cobra suddenly raised a cubit of herself off the sunning spot, patterned hood flared wide, a hiss escaping the fanged open mouth, forked pink tongue rapidly flicking. The great bird fanned out her heavy wings and then repeatedly beat the hot desert air, a long piercing screech coming from the hooked yellow beak. Wadjet the cobra and Nekhbet the vulture were arrived together for the interment rites of Dowager Great Royal Wife Asar Ahmes Nefertari. A large portable funerary pavilion and many white-garbed humans could be seen in the middle distance, had either goddess's embodiment chosen to notice. The reptile's and carrion-eater's focuses were, however, only on challenging one another. Wing feathers and hood remained fully spread.

The harsh alarm of the bird screech did not register with the gathered mourners under the large painted-linen canopy, with the single exception being ten-inundations-old King's Daughter Hatshepsut, who twisted on her low stool to stare out into the brilliant desert light, in the direction of the faint disturbance. She could just barely make out the distant perched black creature with flared wings. But her attention was quickly snatched back to the ritual underway, when God's Wife Ahmes — seated beside Hatshepsut on an ebony armchair and resplendent in the Great Royal Wife's gilded vulture cap-crown, tripartite wig and gold modius with tall ostrich feathers — sharply elbowed her young daughter's bare upper arm.

Also elaborately wigged and bejeweled, King's Son, King's Brother, Prince-Count Siamen was just finishing the incantations of the Opening of the Mouth of his deceased mother. The old woman's linen-wound shrunken husk was encased, of course, in her now standing-upright gilded inner coffin inlaid with colorful feather-patterning. Various peculiarly shaped sacred implements had been applied with great ceremony to the large golden visage on the coffin, by both old Uncle Son of Amen and the shaved-bald First Prophet of the Hidden One, who was draped with a stiff leopard skin. This serene face bore absolutely no resemblance to her cranky old great aunt, was Princess Hatshepsut's private thought. The wrinkled, withered crone had been dead so long — well, seventy days — the girl could barely recall how Osiris Moon Born, Beautiful Companion had always negatively dominated every family gathering since she herself had memory, and — stories told — way long before then.

Little there was now of the once-large family of Asar Ahmes Nefertari left to attend her long-awaited departure for the Afterlife. Enthroned to the right of his wife was Lord of the Two Lands and Son of Re, Akheperkare Djehutymes, that day attired in his full regalia — red and white Double Crown, strapped on False Beard, Crook and Flail, the emblems and implements of his kingship. He was the deceased's nephew, son of her long-dead eldest brother. And it was because of the wilful personal decision of Dowager Great Royal Wife Ahmes Nefertari that he had been handpicked to follow on the Horus Throne the youngest of her sons, Asar Djeserkare Amenhotep. She thus, for a second time, had bypassed her last surviving offspring, the same Prince-Count Siamen who was now performing his filial duties towards the deceased. Son of Re Djehutymes had never felt any personal affection for his often difficult aunt, but was deeply indebted to her for his unanticipated good fortune.

To Lord of the Two Lands' own right sat — on a small plain chair rather than a stool — Crown-Prince Djehutymes, whom his father more often insensitively called just "Namesake." Young Horus-in-the-Nest had recently passed twelve floodings in age and so still wore his child's Horus Sidelock. That day the latter was concealed under a short wig — which made his round cheeks appear even fuller than usual, had been his half-sister's barely contained mean thought. Djehutymes was the youngest son of his father's first marriage, and he'd never known his mother, inasmuch as she had flown to heaven upon giving birth to him (a fact his father seemed to hold against the boy). His three older brothers were also variously deceased, the sole reason for his now being Crown-Prince. Djehutymes was what might be thought of as a "momma's boy" without a mother. Awkward and without coordination it seemed, he shunned the playing field in favor of his toy soldiers and pet cats; but he also was not studious, in fact very much slower at his lessons than half-sister Hatshepsut. A stammerer and loner by nature, and often petulant in the company of his elders, the Crown-Prince's serious shortcoming, however, was gluttony. He was always nibbling some sweet or else complaining of being hungry. And, on the verge of his teenage years, it was becoming all too apparent that Namesake's "baby fat" was probably going to be a permanent condition. Petite Hatshepsut, in fact, never missed an opportunity to poke fun at his less-than-impressive appearance.

In the row behind the immediate royal family sat Prince-Count Siamen's pride and joy, Prince Tao, now fourteen floodings old and already the father of a new infant son — named Amenhotep — by the commoner girl whom he had married and who sat demurely by his side, her head modestly bowed. Although his father had been born lame, one leg severely stunted, Prince Tao was the picture of physical good health, if not especially handsome (as most males of the House had not been, either). That day he wore a fully adult wig and a bead broad collar adorned his otherwise bare leanly defined torso. Tao's ambition — or so Siamen bragged — was to be a soldier (or a commander of soldiers, more likely). Because he lived with his new family at the Delta country estate of his father, the young prince was nowadays mostly a stranger to his younger cousins and one-time playmates, Djehutymes and Hatshepsut. The King's Daughter found Cousin Tao, however, to be everything her half-sibling regrettably was not.

Except for a pair of quite elderly unmarried sisters of the deceased, who also were seated in the second row of mourners, that was all there was surviving of the House of Tao. The several others in attendance that day were the other three prophets of Amen-Re and titled notables from the court of Lord of the Two Lands Akheperkare Djehutymes, including, of course, the two viziers of Upper and Lower Kemet. Royal scribe and tutor Senenmut had a place in the very back row. Asar Ahmes Nefertari herself almost certainly would not have invited the young bureaucrat, however.

The last of the incantations were being recited before the upright coffin by First Prophet of Amen-Re Hapusenub, who was waving a smoking censer in front of the deceased's idealized gilded nose. He now stepped back, turned and handed off the implement to an acolyte priest, then bowed stiffly to the enthroned Lord of the Two Lands, effectively concluding the funeral rites. Several necropolis pallbearers immediately came under the canopy and carefully lowered the coffin to its backside, in preparation for taking it into the tomb, the gaping black entrance to which was visible a short distance away in the bright sun. Asar Ahmes Nefertari's massive outer coffin had been deposited inside well before the arrival of the funerary procession, where it had been laid, lid off, alongside the large wooden sarcophagus of the sepulcher's sole present occupant. The earthly personal possessions which she had chosen to take to the Afterlife already had been added to the earlier provisions there. The late Dowager Great Royal Wife had been adamant that she was not to be put to rest in the place which her long-deceased husband had prepared for her years before, but rather that she was to share the Mansion of Eternity of the son who had flown to heaven four floodings before, Lord of the Two Lands Asar Djeserkare Amenhotep. The present Son of Re, Djehutymes, saw no particular reason to go against his late aunt's wishes — however very unconventional a double interment of a royal mother and Lord of the Two Lands son would be. He had been assured that Asar Ahmes Nefertari's several-cubits-long outer coffin would not have fit that original sepulcher, in any case.

Once her gilded second coffin was hefted to the shoulders of the pallbearers, a large group of bare-breasted professional female mourners — who had been crouching close by throughout the rites — rose collectively to their feet and began the loud wailing, hair pulling and dust tossing for which they had been paid from the royal coffers. They had come with the procession from the river and now followed after the pallbearers as far as the tomb entrance. When the coffin had disappeared inside, their demonstrations immediately ceased, and they began walking quickly away.

Meanwhile, under the pavilion canopy, the gathered mourners had risen and were quietly talking among themselves — during which interlude seating was being rearranged by servants and low tables introduced, in preparation for the formal simple funerary banquet to follow. And none too soon was the thought of at least one individual present.

* * *

<h1 style="text-align:center">4</h1>

Her pair of Medjay doormen stepped wide, allowing Mistress of the Two Lands Maatkare to pass with a flurry into the antechamber of her personal apartments of the Residence. She strode quickly across that dim, columned space and pushed open with some force the door panels to her sleeping chamber. It was nighttime and the room was minimally illuminated by a single brazier. Nurse In Sitre shuffled along in her wake, doggedly trailing at many paces.

Hatshepsut sat abruptly on one of the cushioned armchairs available, pulling off her starched-linen headcovering, gold cobra headband and all, slinging these onto a nearby low table. She raised a slender arm, snapping her fingers loudly, then leaned forward, elbows on knees, interlaced fingers cupping her high forehead. In the deep shadows a serving maid slipped through a side doorway, off to seek wine.

Ancient One In momentarily came shuffling up, huffing, and broadly gestured, with resignation, a "Well, what?"

Hatshepsut had looked up at In's approach. "*Well*, it's taking forever! She's been on and off and on again the bricks for hours. We have no more patience playing sidelines midwife, Nurse. No, better, a *spectator*, as if our birthing assistance was actually in any way required. They will come for us when she's finally dropped her bastard."

"It is a most difficult delivery, Your Majesty. *The* most difficult. Her narrow hips. And the head should be first, not the feet."

"Like Beauty of Re to get it *backwards*!"

"King's Daughter's life is very threatened."

"So, one spreads wide her thighs for a god, one suffers the divine consequences. As if God's Wife thought anyone, *anyone* at all believed that wild fantasy she spun about the Hidden One Himself impregnating her! More likely Captain Nebet. Captain Nebet we could understand. Not approve, but *understand*. If the bastard's black, that will be the dead give-away. Though, you know as well as we, it could have been *anyone* with a stiff Min. Why, even Brother of Mut. Beauty could have seduced even that aging *boy*-lover! Then, there's the pet dwarf, gods forbid!"

Nurse In shrugged her massive rounded shoulders. At the same moment, one of the midwives came up to the Medjays at the outer doorway, who, of course, blocked her entrance. She began calling out rather than pleading or negotiating passage.

"Your Majesty! It's happened! The delivery has happened!"

Hatshepsut was immediately on her feet, across the bedchamber and through the antechamber in a flash — just as the serving maid came out of the shadows, bearing a tray with a single faience goblet. Nurse In gestured for the girl to approach anyway. The crone took the elegant vessel from the tray and drained it, then followed, as always.

When the Mistress of the Two Lands entered the Residence's specially devised birthing chamber, it was the scene of extravagant blood letting. The mud-brick stand in the center of the semi-darkened space — where the delivering mother traditionally squatted for eventual expulsion of the newborn — was awash in wet crimson. The plaster floor was violently splattered red all around, as well. Two midwives knelt or squatted in the birth debris, one having pulled off her Heket frog mask, the other a big-snouted cartonnage Tawsret head. They silently wept, nodding, swaying. Off in the shadows, alongside a column, turning his humped back to the tableau, the green-painted naked dwarf Khawi was rapidly masturbating, still wearing his grotesque Bes-lion hood. To one side, on a low bed, deeply sunk into several supportive cushions, lay Neferure, King's Daughter, King's Sister, God's Wife, Divine Hand. Soaked with perspiration, she was covered to her chin by several fine-linen sheets, widely stained brilliant scarlet where her huge belly had been. Several servants knelt or hovered. Neferure was still alive, just hovering at consciousness, but clearly not for long.

Hatshepsut stepped gingerly through the slick mess and stood looking down at her one surviving child, misbegotten embodiment of all her grandiose dreams. Her only thought was that Beauty of Re should now be spared of any more pain, should fly up to heaven as quickly as possible. As if that thought had divine will, the purged young woman looked directly at her mother, the Female Horus, as if to speak, pink bubbles escaping her parted lips, instead. Then her *ba* sped out and soared away. The attending women began keening, pulling hair, without being cued to do so."

"Where is the bastard?" demanded Her Majesty.

"The girl-child was without *ankh*, Oh Mistress," replied an older woman among the mourners.

Nurse In had entered the chamber and now stood filling the doorway. Dumbfounded. Or not.

"So, let us see the little body that killed our daughter," demanded Hatshepsut, throwing her arms wide.

"It, *she*, is gone. Taken away, immediately, Your Majesty," replied the dwarf Khawi, who had sprayed his release and pulled off the grotesque disguise. "A monster. Terrible. Terrible. Two heads. Two! Scorpion pinchers for hands. Taken away, utterly destroyed by now. Gone. Gone. Our Beauty, too!" He began to weep theatrically, grinding both eyes with clenched small green fists.

The Mistress of the Two Lands knew she had totally lost control of the present situation. But, in this case, did it matter, finally? She crossed to the bed and bent to kiss the clammy brow of the dead princess. She stood upright again.

"Take her to the House of Beautification. We personally shall inform Lord of the Two Lands Djehutymes of this tragedy."

She strode from the room, In Sitre at her heels, more or less.

Eighteen Floodings Later, Inundation 29
Sole Reign of Menkheperre Djehutymes
The Residence, Waset

Advancing along the cool, dim Residence hallway, following as quickly as her years permitted on the heels of her guide, the Dowager Great Royal Wife and teenage Prince Amenemhat rounded a corner and abruptly halted, Hatshepsut coming alongside him. A small group of bureaucrats were advancing towards them, chattering among themselves. When these several white-garbed men came up to the old woman and youth, arm to shoulder, effectively blocking their passage, they, too, stopped in their tracks. The short, scrawny individual in the delegation's front rank, wearing the peculiar long bulbous garment of the vizier, nodded his shaved head and spoke officiously.

"Greetings, Prince Amen at the Head. Greetings Dowager Great Royal Wife Noblest Woman. What brings you both to the Royal Apartments this fine morning?"

"W...W...We've c...c...come for an audience w...with my f...f... father," stammered the prince. A full wig hid his jug-ears. His knee-length white kilt was simple, his feet unshod.

"You have an appointment?" was Rekhmire's challenge, pointed chin tilted up.

"None is ever needed by *us*," was Hatshepsut's curt response. Dressed as usual in a strapped white long sheath and gilt-leather sandals, her only adornment was the small inlaid-gold cobra emerging above her forehead from within the black depths of the heavy tripartite wig she wore. "Step aside, notables, so that we may pass." It was a command rather than a request.

"His Majesty is fully engaged this morning, Your Honored Highness." Rekhmire ran the palm of one thin hand over his bald pate. "We have just concluded our own daily council with him, we ministers. Mighty Bull Lasting Manifestation of Re is now in conference with the new First Prophet. You simply will have to return another time, I'm afraid."

"We are certain you *are*. Afraid, that is." Hatshepsut motioned for the half-dozen officials to step aside, so that she and the prince could pass. "We shall just see if Horus dares refuse us admission."

Five of the bureaucrats backed against the wall, to open up the narrow passageway, bowing their heads. Only Vizier Rekhmire remained unbudged. That is, until he realized his fellows had been cowed by this imperious old woman who still fancied that she was mistress of all Kemet.

"As you will, Your Highness." He, too, stepped to one side, chin dropped to his bony clavicles.

And Prince Amenemhat continued leading his new grandmother towards the inner sanctum of the Mighty Bull.

While his recent appointment prattled on about estates and endowments and cattle counts, Menkheperre Djehutymes sat back in his cushioned armchair, hands tented per habit on his tunic-covered chest. He was silently assessing the newly named First Prophet of Amen-Re Menkheperresenub. A fresh man. Just recently Second Prophet of Ptah at Mennufer. No allegiances here in Waset. So, hopefully with only one loyalty, to Lord of the Two Lands who had just advanced his fortunes. Menkheperresenub had proven a capable — if unremarkable — administrator of Lord Ptah's vast business in the northern capital, so was a proven veteran of priestly politics. Retired ancient Hapusenub had been First Prophet of the Hidden One for so long — appointed to that position in the reign of Son of Re Amenhotep — that corruption in the ranks here at Ipet Isut was inevitable. Old captains command lax vessels had been Menkheperre's experience. He was certain that elderly Second Prophet Bekenamen was furious at being passed over, that his superior had been brought in from another, rival priesthood. But he would soon enough come to realize that he was perfectly suited to be Number Two, Menkheperre was certain. Nuances of liturgy was Bekenamen's forté, not cattle counts.

Lord of the Two lands was just returning from his musings, to tune in again to what the new First Prophet was now pontificating, when there was a disturbance at the outer entrance to the royal apartments. Sitting bolt upright, he, of course, recognized the sharp female voice calling his name from afar.

"Born of Djehuty, we would be admitted!" his aunt/stepmother demanded. "We have urgent business that will not wait!"

"You need excuse us, First Prophet, the Past is present," chuckled Son of Re Djehutymes. "It seems our former coregent and now guest under this roof requests an instant audience. We shall continue your orientation at a later time. Even tomorrow, perhaps. We shall send word to Mansion of the Hidden One. You will exit by the side door, please." Lord of the Two Lands gestured to somewhere beyond the shadowy forest of slender brightly painted wooden columns off to his left.

First Prophet Menkheperresenub realized his abrupt dismissal, immediately rose from the armchair he had been occupying and bowed from the waist.

"Of course, of course, Son of Re, Son of Amen. I am always at your disposal."

"Indeed, you are. Indeed, you are, First Prophet. *Always.*"

The lean middle-aged man with shaved head and long white kilt moved off in the direction that had been indicated. The shrill demand came again:

"Nephew, we *will* be heard! Hawk Beak, let us in!"

Djehutymes bridled at the old nickname, but remained seated, fingers tented again, playing the "wait game" with the proud woman who had so often kept him tapping his own bare foot over the years.

But suddenly, there she was, standing in the open doorway to his personal audience chamber, having somehow breached his Medjay doormen. Visible behind her was poor bastard Amen at the Head, and behind him the frustrated Wawat team. Instantly he knew what was about to transpire. And Lord of the Two Lands, admittedly, had orchestrated it himself.

B efore Dowager Great Royal Wife Hatshepsut could launch her presumed inquisition, Son of Re Djehutymes ordered that drink and refreshments be brought to the three of them seated now around the low table in their midst. Prince Amenemhat slouched on a straight-back chair occupied just previously by the First Prophet. His grandmother, hands clasped on her lap, was rigid in her chair with arm rests. And Lord of the Two Lands relaxed, with tented fingers still, as usual. Diversionary small talk about dedication ceremonies of the Hidden One's new barque-shrine the day before filled the gap, with His Majesty the chief commentator. Once golden goblets with the current finest Delta vintage had been delivered by serving women, along with a tray heaped with bunches of grapes, Hatshepsut's pent-up fury finally spilled forth.

"Well now, where to begin, Nephew?" began Hatshepsut."We have just spent some considerable time this morning reviewing with young Amen at the Head, here, the circumstances of his birth..."

"Of which he can have absolutely no personal memory, you will agree," inserted the Son of Re.

"Of course! But a storehouse of the memories of *others*, all of those related to him again and again since his young childhood. He knows...fully well understands... that he was violently brought forth into this Black Land from the ripped womb of King's Daughter, King's Sister, God's Wife of Amen Beauty of Re, Justified."

"That was never an unknown fact."

"Except by *us*!" Hatshepsut barked. She forcefully slammed the arm of her chair with her small flat palm.

Déja vu for Son of Re Djehutymes.

"We were told that our daughter had delivered a still-born *girl*!"

"And so she did, Aunt. *And* our prince here. There were doubles, girl *and* boy, one dead the other, obviously living." Son of Re gestured towards Amenemhat.

"You didn't say there was a sister, Prince!" Hatshepsut turned on the youth.

"I di...di..didn't know th...that until th...th...this moment. I w... w...as never t... t...told of a dead sis...sister. Never told."

"And he was not. It was our decision, Aunt. As well, that you were not to be told of *him* until we decided the time was right. It never was until, well, now. Our prince was raised at the oasis harim where you now reside, brought to live in the Mennufer Residence at the time of your installation at Wer-Mer."

"'Our Prince'? You claim him as Son-of-the-King's-Body?" Hatshepsut snorted.

"We do because he is."

"But not Crown-Prince. Eldest son but not Crown-Prince."

"He is not son of the Great Royal Wife. Namesake Heir Lasting Manifestation of Re is that son. Amen at the Head, not born of a Great Royal Wife, is now the spare, which he realizes." Son of Re nodded towards the teenager. "Spare, that is, until there are further sons from the Great Royal Wife. Which there will be, of course, though Sitiah has miscarried several times now." Son of Re looked to his bastard offspring.

"Would you excuse us, Prince? The mother of your mother and Our Person have further private matters to discuss."

Amenemhat stood and without formality turned to depart the chamber. He muttered as he went, "Th...this family has t...t...too ma...ma...many d...damn secrets!"

Hatshepsut sat silently glaring at her nephew/stepson until her newly revealed grandson was out of hearing.

"We don't believe that you ever laid with Beauty of Re, Hawk Beak."

"And why not? She would open her thighs to *any* ready Min, and you well knew that, Aunt." Djehutymes smiled at his former coregent's obvious discomfort with this bluntness.

Hatshepsut would have assaulted him with her fly whisk, had she thought to carry it with her that morning.

"Simply because God's Wife despised *you*, Hawk Beak, a callow boy of, what?, only, say, fourteen, fifteen inundations! Even had that been our desire, our plan, she would never have agreed to marriage with you, to be your Great Royal Wife. She told us that herself, far more than once. She, we, had other plans for her promising future."

"That is why we had to deceive her. Brother of Mut arranged it, of course. It was his quite ingenious plan. We would have never thought of it ourself." Djehutymes bent forward and lifted his wine goblet. He savored the aroma before sipping.

"*Him*, always sticking that pointed nose into where it had no business!" Hatshepsut gripped the arm rests of her chair with bony fingers. "Even that gilt tongue of his could not have persuaded Beauty of Re to lay with you."

"Not his tongue, Aunt, but the potion added to her wine," he raised his goblet, "made Beauty of Re believe she was dreaming. Of course, the blue Brother of Mut painted our head and neck helped delude her that we were the Hidden One made flesh. We remember that the masquerade excited us sufficiently to quite easily perform as Amen-Min."

"And you impregnated the God's Wife so that she would agree to be your Great Royal Wife?" The Residence guest plucked a fat grape from a bunch on the tray before her and sucked it before pushing the whole fruit into her thin-lipped mouth.

"That was not our intention, ours or Brother of Mut's, to sow her with our royal seed. All we intended was to go between her thighs, just to prove that it could be done by us. We had not lain with females until then. Only with Brother of Mut, and that after a matter of speaking."

Hatshepsut swallowed the chewed grape, sighed and rubbed the bridge of her nose. "Was our father, Asar Great Soul of Re, the only Born of Djehuty never seduced to that sinister one's bed?" Ignoring the roll of her nephew's eyes, she continued, "Which takes us directly to the secondary purpose of this interview, Hawk Beak. We did recognize the old one who went directly into the jaws of Amam at the banquet last evening."

"He still draws breath. Not for very long, likely. Brother of Mut's deathbed wish, so we have been told, is to see you again, face to face." Djehutymes sipped his wine.

"He was supposed to have been Amam's lunch inundations ago. We were told he *had* died, while in his exile, sent by us. Sometime soon after our retirement from the Horus Throne." Hatshepsut likewise tilted her goblet.

"Pardoned by then *sole* Lord of the Two Lands, instead. Count Brother of Mut's many talents were too great to have been lost to us through a pique of blind fury by True Soul of Re. He was, of course, never restored to his many official positions — those that really mattered had, you will remember, already been refilled by Her Majesty — but he has served as Our Majesty's personal counselor these intervening inundations. If less so of late, regrettably, as his thoughts have become often fogged. Do swallow great pride and force yourself to go to his bedside, Noblest Woman. Seek peace with the one who was so instrumental in making True Soul of Re even possible for so long."

When a tempered Hatshepsut finally departed the impromptu audience with her former coregent, she was thinking that, yes, she would, indeed, have final words with Lord High and Mighty of This and That. And, with any luck, spit on his still-warm corpse!

FIFTY-TWO FLOODINGS EARLIER, INUNDATION 6
FINAL DAY OF THE REIGN OF AKHEPERKARE DJEHUTYMES
A DESERT PLAIN IN WESTERN ASIA

S enenmut sat cross-legged on a flat cushion, bent over a low narrow table in the wide wedge of light from the hatch of the royal tent. He was reviewing his several design sketches for the *What is in the Underworld* decoration of the resting chamber of Lord of the Two Lands Akheperkare. Teenaged Crown-Prince Djehutymes lay prone in the shadows at the far side of the tent. He was sprawled naked on the campaign cot of His Majesty, snoring, one bare arm hooked across his face. He was clearly sated by the just-concluded oral copulation between himself and the King's Chief Scribe. A linen kilt and loincloth lay crumpled on the mat-covered ground by the cot, with abandoned sandals alongside.

Senenmut tilted his uncovered, close-sheared head and listened carefully. There seemed to be a commotion approaching, far-off shouting that was growing in intensity. In moments he could make out faint calls for the army physicians. Then there was the distant pounding of hooves and the thundering of several speeding chariots. The tall scribe quickly unfolded himself, rose and went to the tent hatch, peering out. At the far end of the encampment of the Army of Kemet, half-a-dozen vehicles and teams of horses were reigning in their oncoming charge. Soldiers began pouring from the rows of tents lining the approach to Lord Akheperkare's campaign dwelling. Two Medjay guards came running up from wherever they had gone off to, after being dismissed by Senenmut in His Majesty's absence.

The wide-shouldered red-haired man turned back into the royal tent. "Prince Djehutymes," he directed loudly towards the now-stirring youth. "Get up, up, and wrap yourself. Your father's hunting party is returning far *sooner* than expected!"

The chubby teen sat upright, swung his bare feet to the ground, rubbed his eyes and bent to retrieve his loincloth. Senenmut returned his own attention to the action beyond the tent. In a cloud of dust some several paces off, the lead chariot had been pulled to a halt by its driver, the lathered team tossing heads and snorting, pawing at the ground. It was His Majesty's war chariot, but Akheperkare Djehutymes was not at the rail. The king's driver renewed his frantic call for the army's two physicians. The other chariots had come to a halt, as well; one also seemed to be occupied only by the driver.

Senenmut dashed to the royal vehicle, followed on his heels by the Medjays. When he came around behind the chariot, it was immediately clear what was wrong. The Lord of the Two Lands sat in a crumpled position on the floor, his head in the high blue war-helmet slumped forward onto his chest, his scaled-leather corselet and short kilt completely soaked in wet blood. An arrow shaft protruded at an upward angle from below one clavicle, having penetrated the protective corselet.

"Ambush," shouted the driver, whose own kilt and legs were red with the royal blood. "A single bowman hidden at a high position. He loosed two arrows in rapid succession, both finding their marks in His Majesty and General Gold of Amen."

A throng of soldiers and camp personnel was massing around the two lead chariots. The second in the short file had conveyed the wounded General Nebamen. Senenmut shouted above the commotion at the stony-faced Medjay guards, "Quick, quick, take His Majesty to his tent."

By now one of the army physicians had forced his way through the onlooking soldiers and come alongside the King's Chief Scribe. An assistant was immediately behind him, a wooden case suspended from his shoulder by a wide strap: the medical kit. "Take care how you move Horus," he ordered the Wawat pair, who were beginning to pull Lord of the Two Lands forward to the edge of the chariot deck, quickly becoming bloodied themselves nearly to their ebony elbows. One Medjay grasped Akheperkare's wet bare legs behind the knees, shifting the limp unconscious man around until the other guard could get a grip under each armpit. When they lifted His Majesty off the chariot, the king's head fell backward between his up-slung shoulders and the bulbous blue-leather war crown slipped off, dropping to the ground. Senenmut immediately bent to snatch this royal regalia up from the dust. The dense crowd parted as the tall black men began shuffling with their heavy weight across several cubits to the royal tent, in the door hatch of which stood a fully reattired Crown-Prince Djehutymes, looking stunned, as if having just suffered a heavy blow to his youthful fleshy chest.

Waving his hapless royal charge aside, Senenmut rushed into the large linen-walled pavilion, closely followed by the Medjay pair with their unresisting weight draped between them — and, close on their heels, the visibly anxious physician and his assistant. The King's Chief Scribe crossed to the campaign cot so recently occupied by the Crown-Prince, and quickly pulled this closer to the broad triangular slice of daylight coming through the hatch, alongside the low table and cushion he himself had previously been occupying. The Medjay positioned themselves to lower Ahkheperkare onto the narrow surface, when the physician, wildly waving his arms, abruptly interceded.

"The *arrow*!" he indicated, pointing. "I must cut the shaft coming out His Majesty's back!" He looked helplessly about. "Who has a blade?"

The assistant sat the medical case on the ground to open it, but the Medjay positioned at the Lord of the Two Land's legs quickly lowered these onto the royal bed, drew the long curved dagger at his waist, moved forward a step and, in a single swipe downward, neatly sliced through the slender wooden length of the Asiatic sniper's arrow. There was no reaction from Akheperkare, as his bloodied torso and bare head were then gently lowered onto the thin cushion of the cot.

The physician moved alongside His Majesty and gripped the remaining arrow shaft protruding from Lord of the Two Land's left upper chest. He pulled this quickly forth and cast it behind himself, onto the ground. The cleared wound now oozed yet more fresh blood through the small hole in the corselet. "Cloth, water!" he ordered. One of the king's body servants, among those who had forced their way into the royal tent, quickly left to find same. The crowd of soldiers outside parted so he could pass.

Senenmut knelt on one knee by the cot and lowered his ear against Akheperkare's gaping red maw. After several long moments he stood again. "No need for further ministrations, physician, Lord Horus has flown," he pronounced, running a palm over the coppery bristles on his head. He reached down and lifted one dangling arm of the deceased ruler of Kemet and repositioned this across the wet broad chest. "Horus-in-the-Nest Born of Djehuty is now Lord of the Two Lands." He turned and looked towards the youth of fourteen floodings, who stood to one side of the tent hatch, mouth gaping, shoulders slumped.

MONTH 3, INUNDATION 1
REIGN OF AKHEPERENRE DJEHUTYMES
THE PRIVATE RESIDENCE OF ROYAL STEWARD SENENMUT, WASET

When the double doors quietly closed behind his dalliance of the hour before, Senenmut sat up on the wide, low bed, still naked. He swung his long legs over the side, placing bare feet on the cool painted-plaster floor and standing. Listing forward ever so slightly, as always, he then crossed the sleeping chamber to relieve himself in the adjoining latrine space. Returning to the sparsely furnished ample room, still naked, he sat again on the edge of the bed, deciding whether or not he was hungry or thirsty enough to go seeking refreshment elsewhere in his residence. Once again his thoughts segued instead to reflecting on how things had changed since returning with the Army of Kemet from the ill-fated campaign in the wretched mountainous North.

His royal benefactor, Lord of the Two Lands Great Soul of Re, Son of Re Born of Djehuty, had led his forces there on an annual routine policing action, and without warning had been struck dead in his prime by a cowardly sniper's well-placed arrow. This had happened while the king was lion hunting with his generals — one of whom was also a hapless victim at the same time, but who had survived to tell the tale. The soul-empty Son of Re's mortal shell had been summarily treated on the spot by the funerary priests who always accompanied the army in the field. This had been sufficient enough to allow the hurried overland transport of the royal remains back to Kemet. The king's corpse had then been taken by river vessel to the southern capital at Waset, where it had undergone the full procedure necessary to assure Asar Great Soul of Re's revival in the Afterlife.

The seventy days of preparation and mourning were nearing an end, and a revivified Horus-Flown-to-the-Stars would soon be laid to rest in his secretly located Mansion for Eternity. This, alas, was still unfinished but deemed adequate to receive its owner. The *What is in the Underworld* scenes that Senenmut had designed to decorate the resting chamber's walls would now never be painted. By default Royal Architect Ineni had gotten his way; he had despised the King's Chief Scribe's unorthodox images, dubbing them "unsuitable, childishly crude stick figures." Son of Re had found them "quite commanding" — or so he had confided to Senenmut — but now was not there to order that they, in fact, be used. Thus the resting chamber's curving walls would remain unadorned, except for a wide band of *kheker* motifs near the high ceiling.

Senenmut looked across the dim space to a sizeable calcite jar placed on a low table by one wall. This was elegantly inscribed on its cylindrical side with Asar Great Soul of Re's, Born of Djehuty's prenomen and nomen name-ovals. He had commissioned this vessel as his personal donation to his late master's Afterlife furnishings. Perhaps this very day he finally would take it to the Residence, to place it with the other objects to be deposited in the Mansion for Eternity prior to the Opening of the Mouth ritual and interment. Or perhaps another day, soon enough.

Throughout the present period of royal mourning, Senenmut had been to the Residence only occasionally, summoned or otherwise. His role there had changed considerably. On the return journey to Kemet, he had turned aside the clumsy sexual advances of the new Lord of the Two Lands, teenaged Akheperenre Djehutymes — for the reason that their previous occasional intimate oral exchanges were no longer private indiscretions, now that the awkward youth wore the Double Crown. As might have been expected, the insecure, petulant Djehutymes had taken Senenmut's rebuff as a personal rejection. In retaliation he had arbitrarily named another as his King's Chief Scribe, appointing Senenmut instead as Steward of the Estates of the God's Wife of Amen-Re, Dowager Great Royal Wife and Regent, Ahmes — as well as of the estates, such as they were, of King's Daughter, King's Sister Hatshepsut.

Mistress of the Two Lands Ahmes reportedly was taking her new authority as governing regent for her underage stepson quite seriously, so probably had little time now to deal with the management of her sizeable and complicated God's Wife estates. Besides surely having absolutely no interest in any such mundane matters, the twelve-floodings-old princess was almost certainly otherwise distracted just then, in any case. She had taken her father's recent sudden demise very badly and was reported to be totally withdrawn and ill tempered of late. It was perfectly fine that Senenmut's attentions weren't required, inasmuch as the girl's sometime-tutor had very little patience with most females, generally, and with difficult ones, none at all.

Deciding that, indeed, he actually was hungry that morning, the red-haired bureaucrat put on his loincloth, wrapped and tied a long pleated-linen kilt around his narrow hips and went prowling the premises barefooted, seeking something to munch on.

* * *

5

King's Regent Ahmes was beginning to regret that she had granted a private audience to her distant House of Tao cousin, Prince-Count Siamen. When he had requested such in a general audience with the court present, she had not been quick — or experienced — enough to do other than grant his seemingly innocuous request. That was before the funeral rites and interment in his Mansion for Eternity of her late husband, Asar Ahkheperkare Djehutymes — those particular events being now some crossings of Re in the past. Almost immediately upon publically inviting the lame count to dine at the Residence, however, Acting Mistress of the Two Lands Ahmes realized her cousin's agenda in achieving a private face-to-face meeting with the sole individual who, for all practical purposes, ruled Kemet. And now for several long, long minutes, she had been enduring his polite harangue that his now-adult son, Prince Tao, be named forthwith as Horus-in-the-Nest to his cousin, her stepson, Akheperenre, the not-yet-in-his-majority new Lord of the Two Lands.

When Count Siamen retrieved his wine goblet and sipped from it, Regent Ahmes grasped the opportunity to interrupt the Delta dweller's droning monologue.

"Cousin Son of Amen, we understand your sincerely expressed concerns for the future of our great house, you and ourself being the last surviving members of the Tao line of our generation. We, too, have given much thought to the present situation, with His Majesty being a minor still, without issue, even without a Great Royal Wife to produce same. But previously there was no immediate reason to marry off young Crown-Prince Born of Djehuty when he was Horus-in-the-Nest, given his youth. Our late Lord of the Two Lands was still vigorous and likely would have produced additional sons, had he not been struck down so unexpectedly. That is why..."

"Exactly my point, Mistress Moon Born!" Count Siamen interrupted, sitting his goblet on the table between them with some force. "Fate is unjustly fickle. Great Soul of Re should have flourished many, many more inundations — as hopefully we both shall, as well. More sons of His Majesty's body fully would have been forthcoming, certainly. And Crown-Prince Born of Djehuty would certainly have taken a wife in due time and produced his own heirs. But that is future past. And now the Throne of Horus is occupied by a callow, retiring youth, whose health is perhaps not the best — or so it is whispered in some quarters. He easily enough could, gods forbid, be struck down — well, not literally, of course — but by some terrible malady that would suddenly shoot him off to the stars. And where would that leave the House of Tao? The Horus succession would be in total flux. That is, unless a recognized Heir could legitimately don the Double Crown without challenge. The best candidate for that position is, I repeat, Mistress, none other than the only living grandson of The Liberator and Asar Moon Born, Beautiful Companion. Prince Tao is fully an adult now, vigorous of body, father of one boy, Amen is Pleased, and soon a second child, very likely another boy. Tao alone can with certainty assure continuance of the line of the great Liberator and his revered ancestors of our house before him. A third Tao on the Horus Throne! Think of it."

Siamen reached for his goblet again, and once again Regent of the Two Lands Ahmes saw her chance to terminate this unwelcomed long lecturing. "You are like a bored hound chasing its bony tail, talking in circles, Cousin, very much repeating yourself, as if you regarded us as not quite bright enough to have understood you the first time. You will remember, surely, that you've made this exact case before, when Asar Holy Soul of Re, Amen is Pleased flew to the stars several inundations ago. At that time your own revered mother said your succession proposition bordered on sedition and she sent you lurching back to the Delta. We regard it totally the same today."

"That last remark was beneath you, Mistress," Siamen countered.

"We *meant* offense, Cousin. You have offended *us*." Ahmes picked up her goblet for the first time, sipped and continued. "By absolutely no choice of our own, we are now the temporary caretaker of Kemet. In that role we are consulting almost daily with Lord of the Two Lands Great Form of Re. As you noted at the formal audience yesterday, he sits on the dais with us, beside us. But what even His Majesty doesn't yet know is that we have made a decision today, this very hour, regarding His Majesty's personal future and that of Kemet" She sipped again. "What, Cousin, you have *not* taken into your manipulations, into your calculations for the future of the Horus Throne, is our *daughter*, also Daughter-of-the-Body of Asar Great Soul of Re — King's Sister, now God's Wife,

Noblest Woman! She's only recently bled and so thus shall bear soon enough. Therefore, it's our decision that she quite quickly will be Great Royal Wife to the new Lord of the Two Lands, her beloved half-brother. And within the next flooding, consequently, there shall be a Horus-in-the-Nest — who is totally of the House of *Djehutymes*! Thus, We've no need for a warmed-over Tao prince sitting by, playing board games, idling away his days 'til whenever. You're dismissed, Cousin, Prince-Count Son of Amen."

With that, Regent Ahmes drained her faience goblet and returned it to the table, rose and dismissed herself by walking briskly from the room. She, after all, did indeed have at least two large wrinkles to smooth.

EIGHT FLOODINGS LATER, INUNDATION 8
REIGN OF AKHEPERENRE DJEHUTYMES
THE RESIDENCE, WASET

Nurse In Sitre sat on a stool beside Great Royal Wife Hatshepsut's bed. She was spooning a thick lettuce broth into her patient, who had eschewed a headrest during her postpartum convalescence in favor of down-filled pillows, several of which she now sat upright against. The new mother's glossy jet long hair was somewhat duller than usual, and pushed informally behind her ears, held in place by a simple linen fillet. She wore no makeup and was fully naked, the bed sheet covering her to the waist. Her small brown breasts showed no evidence of lactating; she, of course, was not nursing. That was being left to a harim professional.

The very full-breasted Sitre, in her fashion, had attired herself that morning as if going to a party. To complement her otherwise linen sheath-dress, she was wearing both her very best wig and bead collar, as well as paired inlaid bracelets. As usual the eye kohl and lip rouge failed to glamorize her coarse features, a fact she seemed to not realize. In Sitre was just sixteen floodings older than her mistress and twice a widow (bad luck, marrying soldiers). Her own several babes had been stillborn or died in early infancy. Thus her total devotion was to her royal charge's physical and mental well-being, as it had been since she was selected as Hatshepsut's wet nurse some twenty floodings earlier.

The God's Wife swallowed a final spoonful of the broth and raised her hand to signal "no more." "That is quite enough of cook's gruel for this morning, Fish. We need something solid at midday," Hatshepsut, stated, wiping her mouth with the back of her small hand. "Fruit would be good, we think. Figs. Yes, we have a craving for figs at the moment."

The petite royal lady had delivered her first living offspring one week earlier. Three previous pregnancies had ended in two miscarriages and a stillbirth, all males. Her fourth and finally successful effort was a female, however. Which, needless to say, did not please the healthy infant's father, Lord of the Two Lands Akheperenre, Hatshepsut's own despised (by her at least) half-brother. A girl Child of His Body was still no Horus-in-the-Nest. Djehutymes Junior — as the Great Royal Wife disdainfully referred to her husband — had worn the Double Crown for eight floodings without an heir. The twenty-two-floodings-old Living Horus laid full blame for this lack of a Son of His Body to his sister-wife. Hatshepsut, of course, faulted her spouse, who undertook his marital duties infrequently, clearly reluctantly and, well, somewhat ineptly. If he was so anxious for an heir, she had confided to Nurse In Sitre, there were always the harim concubines, whom he never visited, or so her spies in those quarters reported.

In Sitre placed the wooden broth bowl on a side table and clapped her hands loudly. In moments a serving girl entered the Great Royal Wife's bed chamber and bowed for instructions.

"Take this back to Cook," In pointed to the bowl, "then go to the nursery and tell Wet Nurse Rai to be prepared to bring King's Daughter Beauty of Re to Her Majesty, when word comes shortly."

The girl crossed, picked up the bowl, bowed towards Hatshepsut and departed.

"Shall you arraign yourself for the interview, Your Majesty? Don a wig, certainly put on a sheath?"

"We need not show our best face to our steward, Nurse. He even has seen us unclothed, you know. These do not excite him," she said, indicating her small breasts, cupping and uplifting them with her palms. "Rather Count Brother of Mut is made clearly uneasy by exposed female flesh, we have often noted. Bare those great udders of yours in his presence, Fish, and he'd dash from the room, mumbling excuses."

"You've not shared why you've sent for him this morning, Your Majesty. Surely you do not desire to go over accounts at this time."

"Of course not. Brother of Mut ably manages our God's Wife estates — and those many we inherited from our late mother, as well — without any supervision from us. We've summoned him to our presence because we wish him to meet our daughter, finally."

Many minutes later a servant woman slipped into the sleeping chamber from its anteroom, closing the door panels behind her and bowing from the waist towards God's Wife Hatshepsut — still sitting upright on the bed, still nude to the waist — and Royal Nurse In Sitre, who had moved to by her mistress's shoulder at the head of the bed.

"State your business, Tje," commanded the nurse, folding fleshy arms over her bosom.

Tje raised upright. "Her Majesty has a visitor in the person of her Chief Steward, mistress," the servant responded to In.

"Tell him we are awaiting his attendance," replied Hatshepsut, smoothing the linen bedsheet over her lap. "He may enter."

The woman bowed again and slipped back through the barely parted door panels. In a few long moments there was a light knocking on one of these.

"Enter," commanded the God's Wife with a strong voice.

The doors opened inwards, framing a tall man in a formal, shoulder-length layered wig, attired in a full-sleeved tunic, around the waist of which was tied a long sheer kilt reaching to his ankles. He affected no jewelry and his sandals were of plain reedwork. Chief Steward of the Estates of the God's Wife Senenmut sported a small, short goatee now in vogue at court (in his case dyed black to disguise its natural orangish hue and thus match his wig) and his small eyes were enhanced with a triangle of kohl at the outer corners. Chin tilted up a bit, as if looking down his long, pointed nose, the steward then bowed just his head.

"My Lady," he addressed the Great Royal Wife with an informality she permitted from him in private.

Welcome, Count Brother of Mut," Hatshepsut responded, smiling. "Come forward." She gestured with one hand.

Senenmut raised his head, also smiling. "Good morning this beautiful day, My Lady, Noblest Woman." He advanced to within three cubits of the foot of her bed. "You are looking, ah, refreshed."

"My strength is returning, finally, Steward. Perhaps this very afternoon we shall attempt a stroll in the garden. Convalescence is boring. Most matters of importance cannot be attended to from this bed. We're certain that governance of the Two Lands has been suspended in our absence from the High Council Chamber and the Audience Hall," she laughed, only half-jokingly.

"I wouldn't know if that is so, My Lady. His Majesty does not seek Brother of Mut's counsel." The chief steward moved to change this touchy subject. "But, I must ask, how is the new princess? I've heard that she is vigorous and, well, really quite vocal."

"Yes, a howler, to be sure. We are told she also bites her wet nurse's nipples." Hatshepsut noted that Senenmut's fairish complexion visibly darkened at this remark. "Would you like to meet her, Steward? The Princess has been asking after you," the God's Wife laughed.

"That would be a great pleasure, My Lady. An honor, indeed."

Hatshepsut twisted at the waist so that she could direct her order to the royal nurse. "Fish, take yourself off to the harim nursery and escort Wet-Nurse Rai and our daughter back here, so that the First Born may be properly introduced to her tutor."

In Sitre departed the bedchamber on her mission.

"My Lady," Senenmut looked at his smiling mistress. "Did I hear you correctly?"

"Which part of what we said?" she toyed with him.

"'Her tutor'. Have you chosen *us* to be tutor to the God's Wife's daughter?"

"That I have, Brother of Mut. I remember you served quite well in such capacity for ourself, many inundations ago now. Of course, it will be some while before the First Born is old enough to benefit from your wise instruction. But soon as she has become a toddler, it is our desire that you spend time with her daily, molding her character, even before giving her first lessens. In order to be always available for that, we've instructed that a suitable apartment here in the Residence be readied for your occupancy. You'll doubtless want to retain your present quarters beyond the Residence, for entertaining and other, ah, *personal* activities. Your recompense shall be well increased, of course. And you'll continue as primary manager of our estates, with the new title Great Steward."

Before a taken-aback Senenmut could get his usually glib tongue around a response, Royal Nurse In reentered the Great Royal Wife's bedchamber. She was trailed by a large-breasted, naked-to-the-waist young woman cradling a linen-swaddled bundle, from which loud bawling emitted. In moments, the Great Steward of the God's Wife met tiny Neferure for the first time. And his life changed forever, once again.

EIGHT FLOODINGS EARLIER, INUNDATION 1
REIGN OF AKHEPERENRE DJEHUTYMES
THE RESIDENCE, WASET

Young Lord of the Two Lands and his sister-bride, the even-younger King's Great Royal Wife, sat side by side in armed chairs towards one end of a semi-darkened columned chamber of the Residence often used for private audiences. Several cubits in front of them was a rectangular dais, on which the Horus Throne was usually positioned. On this low platform was an empty ebony bed with headrest, such as to be found in the Residence's sleeping chambers. A tall floor-brazier neart each corner of the dais provided the only illumination in the large space. Unseen to one side, in the shadows behind the double row of columns, a blind harpist was quietly plucking his instrument.

Earlier that same evening, Horus Akheperenre and King's Sister

Hatshepsut — in the presence of witnesses that included God's Wife and Regent Ahmes, both viziers and a select dozen courtiers — had exchanged brief vows and a pair of linen-wrapped hair-balls fashioned from their own sheared-and-saved Horus Sidelocks of Youth. These were then placed together in a small casket with a vaulted lid, which was next presented by Akheperenre to the King's Chamberlain (who would later deposit it in the Treasury of the Mansion of Amen-Re for safekeeping). With that simple ritual — at her mother's command, very much against her own will — Hatshepsut became her half-brother's King's Great Royal Wife. A formal banquet had followed, hosted by the new couple; and now the two of them — thickset teen and petite pubescent — were about to be instructed for their marriage bed.

Both youths were nervous at the prospect of physically consummating their union. While Hatshepsut's smoldering anger steeled her for what would eventually happen, her brother-husband was now obviously shaking in his chair beside her. They had been led to this space and their seats by the King's Chamberlain, who had withdrawn, but would return later, he had said, to lead them on to Akheperenre's personal sleeping chamber. The pair were still attired in their regalia, he the Double Crown, she the Vulture Cap-Crown with modius and double plumes, worn over a tripartite wig. Crook-and-Flail and Fly-Whisk scepters had been handed over to their care keepers before the banquet, however. Lord of the Two Lands and Great Royal Wife sat staring straight forward, contemplating the lonely bed for what seemed like an eternity. Then the string music ended.

Suddenly two persons dashed from out of the columned shadows. They ran hand-in-hand to the illuminated dais, stepping onto it simultaneously. Hatshepsut recognized one of her handmaidens, perhaps a half-dozen inundations older than herself. And the man, probably in his twenties, was her brother-husband's charioteer, she thought. The girl wore only a simple white sheath and was barefooted, her long hair swinging loose. The closely shorn driver was attired in only a short linen kilt and was likewise unshod; his bare torso, in contrast to that of Hatshepsut's young husband, was trim and muscular. Without speaking or at any time glancing towards their royal audience, the two began their pantomimed marriage-bed "instructions."

First they embraced, kissing with evident enthusiasm. Then he knelt before her and, taking the hem of her sheath, began working the tight-fitting garment up her shapely calves and full hips, to her narrow waist and — first freeing her generous breasts — finally over her head, the girl having raised her arms straight into the air to let the fabric pass.

He dropped the garment and she shook her head several times to rearrange her mussed jet tresses. Standing face to face, he now fondled the melon-sized breasts, dipping his head to suck on one dark nipple, then the other, and back on the first again.

A fascinated Hatshepsut sensed her brother-groom shifting uneasily beside her.

After more of this fondling and sucking — with the handmaiden's head thrown back so that her hair fell between bare shoulders — the charioteer knelt again on both knees and began nuzzling the dark triangle of the girl's crotch, rubbing one shaven cheek and then the other against the thatch, then clearly lapping at its center with his tongue.

More shifting by Akheperenre, with heavier breathing apparent to Hatshepsut.

The charioteer finally stood. His mid-thigh kilt was obviously tented at his own crotch. The fully naked handmaiden reached out and untied the short sashes at her partner's waist, then he himself unwrapped the garment, letting it drop to the dais floor. The young man was not wearing a loincloth so now was also totally nude, his fully gorged long member standing out from his hips at a decidedly upthrusting angle.

Hatshepsut instantly was reminded of the several depictions of Lord Amen-Min, which she only recently had seen carved on the walls of the Holy of Holies chamber in the Mansion of the God, where she was beginning to perform her daily sacerdotal duties as God's Wife and Divine Hand, roles only just abdicated in her favor by Regent Ahmes. These involved — besides recited invocations, incense offerings, and the drinking and pouring of a lettuce broth — the new royal supplicant stroking several times, with her small right hand, the carved horizontal rigid phallus of a just-under-life-sized golden statue of Amen-Min, temporarily removed from his Holy of Holies shrine. All of this being very alien — and even, frankly, somewhat distasteful — to a girl of just over twelve floodings!

As if Hatshepsut's rush of thoughts had inspired her handmaiden, that teenager now grasped near its base the apparently offered, greatly exaggerated member of the King's Charioteer in her right hand. She immediately began to stroke the just-up-curving thick shaft of flesh, very tentatively at first, then more and more rapidly. Akheperenre's driver repeatedly thrust his naked hips forward, back and forward again, to counterpoint his performance partner's movements. Crossed forearms rested atop his head. His eyes were tightly closed, the novice God's Wife noted. She also saw in her peripheral vision that husband young Akheperenre beside her was leaning forward now, both his own forearms still along the chair arms, however.

This rush of manual activity suddenly halted, when the naked young woman sank to her knees, so that she was quite literally face to face with the charioteer's "Min." She grasped that thick pole again, then took its knob-finial into her wide-open mouth, the driver uttering an audible gasp. She then began fellating, something the God's Wife had never conceived of ever being done, required or even being possible. She could hear her new husband's heavy breathing.

After some minutes of this, the serving girl pulled off the charioteer, stood, turned and climbed onto the low bed on her hands and knees, positioning herself so that she was parallel with her spectators. The very erect man also knelt on the bed, directly behind his instructional partner's offered buttocks. Without any preliminaries, he pushed his phallus downward and entered her from the rear, paused, adjusted his kneeling position, grasped the narrow teenage waist with both hands and then began thrusting his hips back and forth, at first measuredly, then with increasing rapidity. His partner seemed to be enduring their coitus passively, any expression hidden by the long hair which draped her profile.

Hatshepsut was beginning to grow bored, wondering how long this dispassionate mounting — not unlike what she had often enough observed her late father's hunting dogs doing — when, without warning, Akheperenre suddenly rose from his chair, pulled off the Double Crown — which he thrust at his startled bride — and dashed away into the shadows. In moments Hatshepsut could hear him violently vomiting behind a column. Soon the door panels to the audience hall opened and closed. Which did not bode well for the royal wedding-night.

The charioteer and handmaiden apparently were unaware that they had been abandoned by one of their pupils and were still determinely giving and stoically receiving. The Great Royal wife continued studying their performance, relieved rather than disappointed by the unforeseen turn of events. Perhaps some morsel at the banquet had given her brother-groom a bad stomach. She was tempted to pull off her own regal headgear and try on the Double Crown resting on her lap — but did not dare to do it, finally. Instead she placed the joined Red and White crowns on the empty chair, to stand-in for fled Horus-in-the-Flesh. The conjugal instruction continued, unabated, for several more minutes.

When the pair — or at least the man — finally accomplished the purpose of this coupling and dashed away hand-in-hand, the King's Chamberlain emerged from the shadows and came to stand in front of the still-seated Great Royal Wife, bowing from the waist. Without an exchange of words, Hatshepsut was led from the audience hall and escorted back to her personal suite. It would be some long while before she and the

Lord of the Two Lands finally managed a first awkward reenactment of that evening's demonstration of marriage-bed procedure.

EARLY AFTERNOON, THE NEXT DAY
STABLES OF THE RESIDENCE, WASET

King's Driver Bek had just attached a leather feed bag to the bridle of his favorite stallion of the royal team, and was patting the all-black steed on his snout, when he realized that the chatter of the grooms and other charioteers who were then in the Residence Stables had ceased. The stallion snorted and tossed his head in agitation, eyes wide. Bek turned around and was startled to see His Majesty standing not three cubits away, arms folded over the tunic covering his barreled torso. Akheperenre Djehutymes also wore a short kilt without the royal apron, and plain reed sandals. A close-fitting wig of short curls emphasized his plump cheeks. He was without adornment other than the small inlaid-gold cobra on his forehead, protruding from the wig.

Quickly glancing towards the doorway of the long horse barn some ways off, Bek could make out the silhouetted tall figures of the pair of Medjay bodyguards who always shadowed the Lord of the Two Lands.

"Master, you gave me a start," Bek bowed from the waist and rose immediately upright again. "No word came that you desired to travel this afternoon." The charioteer realized that his own appearance was something less than expected of him, inasmuch as he was wearing just a loincloth, was barefoot and even without the close-fitting green-linen cap that was part of his King's Driver livery. "Pardon my unpreparedness, Your Majesty." He self-consciously brushed at the odd bits of straw clinging to his damp brown chest and flat belly.

"We s...suppose you g...got a late s...s...start this m...morning, charioteer, s...s...sleeping in as y...you must have," Akheperenre spoke barely above a whisper, "following la...last evening's s...s...strenuous ac.. ti...vity. Which, you m...may have noted, physically *sick...sickened* us, s... so that we had to m...m...miss the f...finale and any en...encores."

"I was told Your Majesty had become suddenly ill, probably something eaten at the wedding banquet," Bek hung his handsome shaved head, crossed his wrists behind his buttocks.

"Wha...what si...sickened us was the s...s...sight of *you* ram... ming that fe... female's vile hi...hidden place. Of *her* hand and m...m... mouth on your p...prod! We were cer...certainly not expecting tha...t our little mar...marriage-bed pantomi...mime would be performed f...for us by our own King's Driv...Driver, of all the pos...sible p...p...persons, considering."

"It was not my doing, Your Majesty Born of Djehuty" Bek looked again at the teenage Horus. "I was summoned before the Regent only yesterday morning and instructed what was required of me. Her Highness did seem to realize my hesitation, and smiled much throughout the interview."

"Yes, our s...stepmother, for all of h...her pu...pu...put-on honey s... sweetness, is wickedly de...devious, just l...like our M...Min-envying si...ster-now-w...wife, her much so...so-pamp...pampered daugh...ter. It would p...p... please her to...to make us u...uncomfortable."

"Then the Regent knows about...*us*?"

"Very most p...p...probably. And the cur...cursed c...court, as well. There aren't any s...s...safe se...crets in the Hou...se B...Born of Dje...huty. But no m...matter. We are the L...Lord of the Two L...ands and may do exact...ly as we p...p...please. And what p...pleases us these d...days is being 'dri...driven' by our King's D...Driver, when the r...right m...mood s...trikes us. As it ha...has this af...afternoon. C...Come to our apart... ments in one hour. The Med... Medjays, as u...usual, will admit you th... through each ch...checkpoint. And yes, c...come to us ex... exactly as you are th...this mo... mo... moment, Charioteer B...Bek. We rather l...l... like our st...stallion with 's...s... stable' on his glos...glossy hide."

With that young Mighty Bull turned and walked back to his ebony bodyguards and out of the horse barn. Leaving the charioteer wondering just how much longer he could keep up the charade.

SIXTEEN FLOODINGS LATER, INUNDATION 16
REIGN OF AKHEPERENRE DJEHUTYMES
THE RESIDENCE, WASET

With eight-inundations-old naked King's Daughter Neferure skipping beside her, Great Royal Wife Hatshepsut entered the area of the Residence housing the Harim. King's Daughter's Tutor Senenmut trailed them at several paces; behind him waddled the omnipresent dwarf Khawi, Neferure's playmate; and nearly bringing up the rear was Royal Nurse In Sitre, shuffling along as best she could. The rear guard was just that, Hatshepsut's personal Medjay pair. This motley entourage was paying an impromptu visit that morning to toddler Horus-in-the-Nest Djehutymes, and, unavoidably to his mother, King's Wife Iset.

Word had been sent ahead, so their arrival en masse was anticipated; and they were awaited and lavishly greeted at the entrance to the Harim apartments by the rotund eunuch Ruru, chamberlain of the place.

Hatshepsut impatiently interrupted his flowery officiousness with a wave of her hand. "Yes, yes, Ruru. Enough, before I have you demoted for exaggeration. Now lead us to Harim Mouse."

"The creature may not enter, Your Majesty." He was still filling the doorway with his considerable width, pointing at Khawi.

"May not *enter*? And who says so? Not *you*, I hope."

"Orders of Lady Iset, Your Majesty. It may, she feels, frighten little Horus-in-the-Nest." The eunuch was wringing his dimpled hands.

"Nonsense! More likely frighten Harim Mouse! Dwarf Khawi is with us. *He* shall enter with us. Now, either lead on or stand aside, butler."

The Great Royal Wife took a step forward, and Chamberlain Ruru had no choice but to pivot his bulk and do as ordered: lead them to his mistress and her little son. The Medjay took up their post outside the Harim portal, and Senenmut paused to close the door panels after Nurse In had wheezed her way through.

This women's-and-children's quarters consisted of a large rectangular chamber with porticos of brightly painted tall columns running two deep around all four sides. It was illuminated in the daytime by two sets of clerestory windows, at the ceiling of the four outer walls and rimming the higher ceiling over the smaller central area, which served as a common work and recreation space. Doorways opening in three walls gave access to individual sleeping chambers, baths and storerooms. There were several current adult residents of the Harim: nearly a dozen of the Lord of the Two Lands' never-called-upon concubines — younger daughters of high-status families from throughout Kemet, and two foreign princesses — plus King's Wife Iset, who, by virtue of her now-married status, was the senior of the entire lot (and therefore occupied the largest apartment with its own bath facility and private garden, at the far end of the common area, directly opposite the entry). The Harim was at this time home to only a single royal child, however: two-floodings-old King's Son, King's Heir, Horus-in-the- Nest Djehutymes. He and his wet-nurse shared his mother's quarters. Well before he reached puberty, the crown-prince would be assigned his separate personal spaces elsewhere in the Residence. By all rights, because of her young age, King's Daughter Neferure should now be living in the Harim, as well. Hatshepsut had seen to it, however, that the First Born had her own Residence quarters, in the immediate vicinity of the Great Royal Wife's suite of chambers.

At this time of the day, late morning, the common area would ordinarily be alive with gossiping or relaxing or casually working Harim residents. Several looms were arranged helter-skelter, with partially completed weavings. These had been abandoned, along with other everyday objects, including musical instruments and game boards, scattered about on the plastered floor painted with foliage-trimmed pools populated by various colorful River fish and brightly plumed water fowl. The space was furnished with half-a-dozen simple armless chairs and even simpler stools, and as many low wooden tables. A few cats slept or prowled. With advance warning by Chamberlain Rudu, all the concubines had retreated to their individual sleeping chambers, likely taking any servants with them. Some perhaps were afraid of the squat, bow-legged Bes demon, who was always tagging at the naked heels of the King's Daughter. All were cowered by the indomitable Great Royal Wife!

The eunuch wended his way through the domestic flotsam, leading the procession of Harim visitors. When he came to the closed double-doors centered on the far wall, he quietly knocked. Midway through the chamber, King's Daughter Neferure had broken ranks to chase after one of the felines. She was ordered to cease her pursuit by the Great Royal Wife, who had now come up behind Rudu. The princess rejoined her mother, taking her hand. Hatshepsut did not hear a response from beyond the door panels, but the chamberlain's hearing apparently was attuned to Royal Wife Iset's tiny voice. He pushed the doors open, stood to one side and gestured for the Great Royal Wife and entourage to enter. Which they did.

Iset's space was not overly spacious, but did have doors in the wall opposite its entrance, which stood open, revealing a columned loggia and garden greenery beyond. As if holding an audience, Akheperenre's secondary wife now sat on an ebony armchair centered on a small dais positioned in the middle of the chamber, so that she was backlighted by the garden view. She wore the enormous braided wig she favored and which emphasized her childlike small size; in fact she was only a very little larger than Princess Neferure. Her simple white-linen sheath garment was accessorized with a beaded collar and two inlaid bracelets on each arm (gifts of Akheperenre? Hatshepsut wondered). As always, "Harim Mouse" wore too much eye makeup, making it appear as if she was peering out through dark holes in her small oval face, dominated by a beaked nose. As if signaling her possession of him, the King's Wife had taken her three-floodings-old son onto her lap. He was naked and wore a small Horus Sidelock of youth. Clearly uncomfortable, his back was arched and he appeared to be sliding between her knees towards the floor. Crown-Prince Djehutymes's wet-nurse stood off to one side of the chamber.

Hatshepsut advanced to within four cubits of her "enthroned" rival. "Greetings, Iset. My thanks for receiving us on short notice."

The Great Royal Wife's companions arranged themselves more or less in a row behind her. The little naked prince now succeeded in slipping off his mother's lap, and once on the floor he dashed to his wet-nurse, Itbet, peeking out wide-eyed from behind her ample thighs.

"My pleasure, Sister Noblest Woman," pipped Lady Iset. "Greetings to both yourself and Princess Beauty of Re, and the others brought along. Except that I did request the awful creature not be admitted. See," she pointed at the cowering boy, "it has clearly frightened Prince Born of Djehuty, as I knew it would."

Dwarf Khawi grinned widely, revealing his yellowed buck teeth. He placed his small hands, palms out, on either side of his wide face, wiggling the stubby brown fingers and repeatedly thrusting his long pink tongue at the King's Wife, a taunt that Hatshepsut could not see. But Neferure giggled.

"Nonsense. Our little amusement is quite harmless, else we would not trust Khawi alone in the company of our daughter," the Great Royal Wife retorted. "We have come to the Harim today to check on the progress of our nephew, little Hawk Beak, and to introduce him to his future tutor, Count Brother of Mut, also already tutor to Beauty of Re." Hatshepsut twisted enough to indicate Senenmut with a hand gesture, the former King's Scribe slightly bowing his head towards Lady Iset. "Step forward, Tutor," the Great Royal Wife commanded, indicating the open space beside herself. "Tell Hawk Beak to come from hiding, Lady Iset, so that he and the Count may properly meet."

All eyes in the room now on him, the royal toddler squealed and ran giggling twice around the wet-nurse, then peered out from behind the other side of her.

"Born of Djehuty, these people came here to see *you*. Stop acting like a silly little baby and go there, to in front of this tall man. Right now!" Iset pointed to a spot near where Senenmut was standing. "I said, right *now*! Before I have to discipline you."

Clearly embarrassed by this scolding in front of strangers, his lower lip jutting, the small brown boy reluctantly came from behind the wet-nurse and slowly crossed to where his mother was still pointing. When he passed Khawi, the dwarf contorted his face and the Crown-Prince squealed and ran to stand facing, looking up at, Senenmut towering high above him. Small hands were clenched alongside his naked hips.

The tutor, who was attired in his usual tunic and long over-kilt with reed sandals, and sporting his usual close-fitting cap-wig and squared-off short goatee, squatted so that he was nearly eye-to-eye with little Horus-in-the-Nest.

"Greetings, Prince." He offered his open palm for a handshake, and the toddler placed his brown fist on it without hesitation. Senenmut closed his hand and gently pumped the short arm. "My name is Brother of Mut." The tutor looked towards Lady Iset. "Does he speak yet?"

"A few words. Just a few."

Looking again to the wide-eyed round face intently staring at him, he asked, "Can you say, Brother of Mut?" At the same time he released the boy's still-clenched fist.

"Nose!" Prince Djehutymes squealed, reached out with the freed hand and gripped the big man's long pointed one.

Senenmut laughed. "You've got quite a nose, yourself, Prince! He tweaked Hawk Beak's "beak," eliciting another squeal, before the boy pulled away, ran to the dais, stepped up onto it and moved to stand, narrow shoulders pushed back, by his mother still perched in her chair. The tutor rose to his full height again, leaning forward slightly.

"Off to a good start, I would say," Senenmut directed his remark to Hatshepsut.

At that moment, another person walked into the King's Wife's chamber and stood akimbo behind the others. It was Lord of the Two Lands Akheperenre.

"And w...what in the Ne...Netherworld is go...ing on here?" he barked.

Hatshepsut and her entourage all turned to face the stout balding young ruler, hands on his hips.

"Papa!" Neferure exclaimed and ran to grip him around his thick waist.

"We are introducing Hawk Beak to his new tutor," the God's Wife replied calmly, indicating Senenmut. "The boy shall begin his lessons very soon, we think."

"With *him*? Not o...over my dead b...body!"

A Few Weeks Later, Inundation 16
Reign of Akheperenre Djehutymes
King's Apartments, the Residence, Waset

Senenmut had calmly whispered to Hatshepsut what had happened, but spared her any details. She was totally stunned, therefore, when she entered her brother-husband's sleeping chamber and witnessed the carnage there. The Great Royal Wife was accompanied by her chief steward and daughter's tutor, as well as the First and Second prophets of Amen-Re, Vizier of the South Amenwashu, Royal Treasurer Irterau, Chief Chamberlain Minnakhte and perhaps a dozen others of the High Council, which had been in its weekly meeting with Hatshepsut that morning, discussing mundane matters of tax collection and revenue dispersals. The Great Royal Wife was first through the wide-open double doors.

What confronted her and the several men at her back was horrifying. Lying just inside the door was the supine nude body of one of the King's Apartments Medjay guards. Blood smears on the plaster floor indicated that the corpse had been pushed to where it now lay by the forced inward opening of the door panels. That the dead man of Wawat had been stabbed several times in the chest was apparent, but additionally it was very obvious that his penis was missing, although the large scrotum was intact. The naked guard had apparently fallen dead directly in front of the closed doors, meaning that no one could have left the chamber through that portal.

With a visible shudder, Hatshepsut hiked her sheath and stepped over the man's mutilated body, followed in turn by Senenmut and several of the others. Most of the stunned nobles opted to gawk in disbelief at a distance from the doorway. The royal bed had been shoved or thrown from the low dais in the middle of the space. The room's two chairs and single low table were also overturned. A broken faience goblet and a shattered ceramic bowl and the bunches of grapes it had held were scattered about. Blood had been splattered everywhere. Clearly there had been a violent struggle. Walking around the sleeping platform, Hatshepsut came to an abrupt halt. Hidden from initial view by the broad bed on its side, widely sprawled, also supine in a slowly spreading blood pool on the floor, was the totally naked and clearly very dead body of her brother-husband.

With a loud gasp, the Great Royal Wife quickly covered her mouth with both hands, to suppress the bile surging up her gullet. Like with the Medjay, Akheperenre Djehutymes evidenced several deep cut-wounds about his thick torso. But the full horror was that a severed large black penis had been forced into — and now protruded obscenely from — his mouth. And his own genitalia, both penis and scrotum, had been sliced completely away, leaving a massive raw lesion. Hatshepsut's projected vomit sprayed the royal corpse.

Scarlet barefoot prints led away through the open doors to the loggia. The assassin — or perhaps an avenging lover? — seemingly had exited by that route, escaping over the garden wall. Lord of the Two Lands' manhood would never be found. Nor would the absent other Medjay guard.

* * *

6

King's Wife Iset sat on a cushion, playing a third-in-a-row game of *senet* with Horus-in-the-Nest's young wet-nurse, Itbet. She had won the previous matches, but was wondering if the girl was purposely making wrong moves so that her mistress would win. Through the open doorway to the loggia and walled garden, Iset could hear the squeals of young Djehutymes, as he romped with the hunting-hound pup that his father had given him for his recent third birthday. The chamber's other closed doors shut out the buzz of the women working and relaxing in the common room of the Harim.

But suddenly there was a commotion there — even panicked shrieks from the concubines or their serving women. As Iset started to get to her feet, the door panels to her quarters were thrown open. Itbet screamed, as she too rose to her knees. Into the room burst half-a-dozen near-naked Wawat savages with bronze-tipped spears — actually, Medjay royal guardsmen. They parted and stood in facing ranks as Dowager Great Royal Wife Hatshepsut strode into the space as rapidly as her tight sheath-dress permitted. Immediately behind her was the tutor Senenmut, followed by waddling Harim Chamberlain Ruru, wringing his hands.

Iset, standing now, bowed her head. "Your Highness, what is happening?"

"Where is the boy?" Hatshepsut demanded, clearly distressed.

"In the garden, with his puppy."

"Get him, Brother of Mut," Hatshepsut ordered, pointing towards the loggia.

The tutor crossed the room to the loggia in several long strides, disappearing into the garden.

"There's been a tragedy." The God's Wife laid her cool hand on Lady Iset's shoulder. "The Living Horus has been murdered in his bed! Horus-in-the-Nest is now Lord of the Two Lands! We're taking the boy with us, for his protection. There may be a plot to wipe out the House Born of Djehuty!"

The new widow began to sob, covering her mouth with both hands, as she struggled to comprehend this sudden loss of both husband and son. At that moment childish screaming was heard in the garden, and all heads turned in the direction of the loggia doorway. A few seconds later, Senenmut reentered the King's Mother's apartment with a kicking and screaming Living Horus held tightly to his chest. The hound pup was tagging along, anticipating a new game.

Iset started to move to the tutor and his frightened burden, but Hatshepsut restrained her rival, clasping both shoulders from behind.

"Please, give my son to me!" Iset thrust her thin arms towards the still-kicking and now-bawling toddler.

"More importantly, *only* Son of His Father's Body, so now — however ridiculous it actually may be — ruler of the Black Land, lady, on whom you no longer have any claim. As Dowager Great Royal Wife, we are taking full responsibility for the third Born of Djehuty, whose throne name shall be Lasting Manifestation of Re, as his father once confided to us was his wish." Hatshepsut released the new widow's shoulders.

Small face streaked with tears and kohl, Iset turned away from the boy, whose bawling and kicking were quieting some — the tutor shushing him. She faced the older woman, who was only a little taller than herself. "Am I now to be Regent for my son?" she asked meekly.

"Don't be ridiculous, Harim Mouse. Of *course* not! *We* are now Regent. In any case, we've long been governing the Black Land on our late husband's indifferent behalf, and so will continue doing so on the unrealizing behalf of our new Lord of the Two Lands, who," Hatshepsut smiled, "shall have to be lifted onto his throne for the foreseeable future. Nothing changes, except one Born of Djehuty has been replaced by a newer version."

"Will I be permitted to see my son?"

"Most certainly! You are now King's Mother. We shall have an apartment prepared for you, near the one he will occupy. It would be, well... unseemly for the King's Mother to reside here in the Harim. Since Living Horus is still at the nipple, you will come with us this very morning." Hatshepsut directed her remark to the trembling Itbet, who had slowly backed away as far as she dared.

"Bring the infant, Brother of Mut," Hatshepsut directed at the tutor. "We shall secure little Lord of the Two Lands and then call together the High Council, to strategize. It must be determined if our country cousin is behind my brother-husband's violent end." She turned to leave the chamber, privately certain that Siamen could in no way be implicated.

When Senenmut carried his light burden past King's Mother Iset, the sobbing toddler began screaming again, reaching out to her. With his free hand, the bureaucrat brushed aside the small woman's attempt to intervene and followed in the wake of the regent's Medjay escort. Ruru gestured for Nurse Itbet to go along as well. When she had passed through the doorway, the eunuch looked towards the forlorn figure of the new King's Mother and shrugged his shoulders, pulling the doors closed.

Standing alone in the middle of the insulated world she had known for four floodings, young Iset listened helplessly, as the cries of her son faded away.

SEVEN CROSSINGS OF RE LATER
ESTATE OF PRINCE-COUNT SIAMEN, THE DELTA

The last surviving son of The Liberator, Asar Nebpehtyre Ahmes, and Great Royal Wife Asar Ahmes Nefertari, was just finishing lunch in the small garden pavilion of his walled country estate overlooking a quiet branch of The River. Seated with Prince-Count Siamen were his wife, Lady of the House Teyit, their sole offspring, Prince Tao, and teenage grandson, Prince Amenhotep. Two female servants were clearing away the leftovers of the summer repast, and conversation had turned to fowling in the marshes, a favorite pastime for these few survivors of the House of Tao. Young Amenhotep was describing the performance of a new throw stick he had personally fashioned, when the distant sound of a chariot rapidly approaching along the lane leading to the isolated estate captured their attentions.

"Someone is in a hurry," dryly remarked Tao, before draining his wine.

"Perhaps word from the Residence at Waset," offered Teyit, raising her cup for a refill of beer from a third servant with a pitcher. "They are all still up south, are they not?"

"Maybe the bloated deviate who wears the Double Crown has finally choked himself on a quail bone — or, more likely, a *prick* — and you are being invited to assume the throne, grandfather," suggested Amenhotep, laughing.

"Or he's sending for me to lead the Army of Kemet in his place, to quell some new feuding by the wretched Wawats," joked the count, also sipping from his goblet.

Conversation continued in this vein until the estate's butler came scurrying through the garden. Bowing, he announced, "Count, there is a messenger from the Residence at Mennufer. He says he must speak directly to you, most urgently."

"Send him here. No, no, better, Nepu, we should receive him properly in the audience hall." Siamen stood, as did his son and grandson.

"Do you desire our attendance, father?" asked Tao.

"Yes, when dealing with tiddings from the Residence, verifying witnesses certainly are in order."

Lady Teyit remained in the pavilion, while the three generations of House of Tao men crossed the garden to the sprawling villa, followed by Butler Nepu. The eldest of the men, in the lead, moved with a lurching limp.

A quarter-hour later, when the messenger from the Mennufer Residence was finally admitted to Prince-Count Siamen's private audience chamber, the trio had donned formal wigs and the patriarch was quite literally enthroned on a low dais in an expensive chair rivaling those used at the Residences (in fact, an heirloom, once belonging to The Liberator himself). Son and grandson, standing, flanked the count.

The messenger and his driver came forward and bowed from the waist. When greeted and commanded so by the count, they stood upright again.

The messenger then spoke with haste. "My lord, I bring word from the Residence at Waset. There's a new Living Horus and his name is Lasting Manifestation of Re, Born of Djehuty. You, sire, are commanded to present yourself in Waset within sixty days, for the funeral of the late Horus and the immediately following coronation of the new Horus in the Mansion of the Hidden One, Lord Amen-Re. Provisions for you, sire, and your entourage of no more than six persons total, will be provided at the Residence, for the duration of the festivities."

"An explanation, please," responded a taken aback Siamen. "Who's this 'Lasting Manifestation of Re' and what of Great Form of Re, Born of Dejhuty?"

"He's recently flown to the stars," answered the messenger, "and his infant son occupies the Horus Throne. Now Regent of the Black Land, on his young lord's behalf, is Dowager Great Royal Wife Noblest Woman. Lord Amen-Re and his four prophets are satisfied, and all's well with *Maat* in the Two Lands."

Or perhaps not, was Count Siamen's disturbed private thought at that moment.

"Did the late Lord of the Two Lands suffer a short illness or some accident?" asked lord of the estate. "We'd not heard that he was in, well, ill health."

"It's just rumor, my lord, but it's being said that Asar Great Form of Re was murdered in bed by one of his Medjay bodyguards. In a jealous fit. Another Medjay was slain, as well, it's being said."

"A hot-tempered bunch, the Medjays!" barked Tao. "I never understood why grandfather chose to make those half-savages the police forces of Waset and Mennufer, not to mention the royal bodyguards."

"It's being said, my lord," offered the messenger, unprompted, "that the new regent fears a conspiracy against the House Born of Djehuty, and so she quickly secured the throne for the infant Heir."

"House Born of Djehuty!" Tao scoffed. "That lot are but upstart bastard relatives of the House of Tao. My father here should have succeeded Asar Holy Soul of Re, not his out-of-the-line uncle! Grandmother erred badly in that."

"Silence, Tao! We do *not* air family linen in front of others' servants." Prince-Count Siamen turned back to the messenger, forcing a smile. "Our gratitude for this bad news — and the *good* news, as well. Convey to the Residence that we Taos shall attend both last rites and coronation, as 'commanded' — My wife and I, our son and grandson, and two servants." With a hand wave, he dismissed the messenger and his driver.

When those two had departed the audience hall, Siamen turned again to his son. "That careless outburst from you, prince, soon enough will be heard word for word in Waset by the bitch Noblest Woman. This is a delicate situation and the House of Tao must not call attention to ourselves. With the bastard infant son of an incompetent stepped-up half-royal now on the Horus Throne — and yet one more wilful female Regent deciding matters — our time may still come. Perhaps sooner than we might've dared imagined only this morning. Exercise patience, if you or your son ever hope to don the Double Crown."

Several Weeks Later
The Residence, Waset

R ehearsal for state events was not unique. Every new Lord of the Two Lands had to commit to memory the blocking, gestures and spoken lines of ritual, until these finally were second nature. Kemet was a land of highly formalized religion, and its sovereign was the chief officiant at great state ceremonies. What was unique, at this time at least, was the rehearsal of a three-floodings-old Lord of the Two Lands, for the occasions of the interment rites of his predecessor and his own formal elevation to the Horus Throne— that is, his coronation as the Living Horus in the presence of Lord Amen-Re, the Hidden One. Improvisation clearly was in order.

Gathered together for this initial rehearsal process, in the private audience chamber of Regent Hatshepsut, was the Regent herself; the infant ruler; Vizier of the South Amenemopet; First Prophet of Amen-Re Hapusenub; the Fourth Prophet Pairi; recently appointed Great Steward of the Estates of Amen-Re Senenmut; and His Majesty's newly assigned tutor, Senimen — plus several others of the court. Hatshepsut and little Menkheperre sat enthroned side by side on the dais, he on a gilded chair scaled to his small size (although his feet still did not touch the accompanying footstool). The others occupied armchairs randomly arranged in front of the dais.

Off to one side was the upright gilded coffin that would soon house the mortal form of Asar Akheperenre Djehutymes. This was still undergoing its lengthy preparation in a tent across The River. The boy-king was just then clicking together the miniature Crook and Flail scepters he clutched awkwardly. Hatshepsut indicated that Menkheperre should lower these to his lap. She also put a finger to her pursed lips to signal that he should remain quiet. Then she turned back to the others.

"Our thanks, notables, for assembling today to help us determine how best to deal with the reality that the principal participant in both the interment of our late husband and then his own official donning of the Double Crown is but a young child — whose speech is only just beginning. Needless to say, perhaps, is the additional problem of his very short stature. Are there any suggestions as to how these double limitations of the Lord of the Two Lands may be overcome?"

The men were silent.

"Come, speak up. We shall entertain even the most improbable solutions," Hatshepsut cajoled. Even as Great Royal Wife she had often referred to herself in the ruler's plural first person.

Vizier Amenemopet finally responded, "I notice that His Majesty has new scepters today. Will the rest of his regalia be similarly scaled for him?"

The Regent nodded towards Senenmut.

"Yes, Vizier. A suitable Double Crown is being fashioned in the royal workshop," the new Great Steward of Amen-Re answered. "Individual Red and White, the Double and Blue crowns, as well. His Majesty will need all four in the two different ceremonies, the Blue during the Opening of the Mouth rite, and the others for his coronation."

Hatshepsut inserted, "Regalia's not the problem, rather stature and speech."

Menkheperre had begun to squirm on his throne. The Crook scepter clattered to the dais.

"Tutor Brother of Amen, come here to His Majesty and distract him for us," the regent instructed. "He must sit quietly, or else be dismissed for his nap."

The short handsome young man stood and went up to the dais. He squatted beside the boy-king's seat, picking up the Crook and handing this back to his charge. He patted the small shaved head, even tugging the short Horus Sidelock playfully. He then whispered into Menkheperre's ear. The child giggled, pipped "Yes!" loudly and twisted to whisper into his tutor's ear. Senimen intercepted the two scepters sliding off the royal lap.

"How will His Majesty say his lines and, in the situation of the funerary rites, reach our husband's coffin?" Hatshepsut persisted, indicating the golden anthropoid container.

Fourth Prophet of Amen-Re Pairi stood and responded, "Since it is I, as lector, who will be officiating for Opening of the Mouth, perhaps I could speak for His Majesty, prefacing with, 'Lord of the Two Lands Lasting Form of Re utters...', and then reciting the lines myself. With His Majesty at my side, or standing in front of me, of course."

"Will you also lift him up so that he may apply the *pesesh-kef* blade to the coffin mouth?" asked the Regent.

"If he would permit it, Your Highness," replied Pairi.

"Well, let us see, shall we? Did you bring a *pesesh-kef*, Fourth Prophet?"

The elderly priest bowed his shaved head. "I did not, Your Highness, not anticipating such would be required today."

"Who has something that may substitute for the blade?" Hatshepsut asked, to no response. "Well? What about the pendant you're wearing, First Prophet?"

Hapusenub reached up and lightly touched the emblem of his office on his bare chest, then glanced down at it. Looking at the Regent again, he said, "I suppose, Your Highness, but a poor stand-in for the sacred implement, certainly." He pulled the thin gold chain with the pendant over his head, handing these to his associate beside him.

"Fourth Prophet, come forward, to be introduced to His Majesty," Hatshepsut commanded. She twisted to Senimen. "Brother of Amen, tell the boy exactly what is going to happen, then lead him to the priest."

Senimen immediately whispered into the ear of young Menkheperre. The boy-king grinned widely, shaking his head affirmatively. The tutor grasped the toy scepters, which their holder easily surrendered. He then impulsively thrust these towards the Regent, who received them, as unthinkingly. The Lord of the Two Lands scooted forward on his throne.

The young tutor lifted him under the arms, then lowered him to the footstool, where the small boy stool very upright, chest forward, shoulders back. Senimen squatted, wrapped his arms around the young ruler's hips and pulled him to his own chest, the child clasping his neck. Then he stood again, stepped off the dais and walked a few steps to the waiting priest.

Speaking to his charge, Senimen said, "Your Majesty, this is Lord Amen-Re's Fourth Prophet. He'll hold you so that you may touch the object he'll hand you to the mouth of the golden statue there," pointing to the coffin. "Understand?"

Menkheperre shook his head that he did. Clasping the pendant, the priest held his arms to receive the boy, who was then passed into his bony embrace. The child placed both of his widespread palms against the old man's bare chest and pushed his arms straight, so that he was looking the Fourth Prophet directly in the face.

"Greetings, Your Majesty," Pairi smiled, his yellow teeth large.

Menkheperre's expression was very somber. The priest held up the inlaid-gold pendant, its chain dangling. The child reached out and grasped the latter. "Not yet," said Pairi, attempting to pull the pendant and chain away. But Menkheperre would not release his tight grip. Senimen stepped to behind the boy and whispered into his ear. The chain was let go. The Fourth Prophet turned with his small burden and walked to in front of the coffin, the large face of which was higher than the priest's head.

"When I hand you this object, Your Majesty, you'll hold it up to the mouth of the statue, like this." Pairi reached out with the pendant and touched it to the sculpted lips. "Do you understand?"

The boy-king shook his head vigorously up and down. "Nose!" he squeaked, pointing at the golden face with the large inlaid eyes.

"Yes, a big nose," agreed the priest. He held the pendant in front of the child. "Now take hold of this and reach up with it to the mouth, just as I did."

Menkheperre grabbed the object, which the fourth prophet released. Then, without warning — squealing "Nose!" — he threw the pendant so that it hit the coffin face squarely and fell noisily to the plastered floor, bouncing once. Senimen immediately squatted to retrieve it.

"Hawk Beak! Behave!" erupted Hatshepsut, rising. The small assembly began murmuring. And the boy-king forcefully pushed himself away from the priest, screaming, squirming and kicking his bare feet.

"Brother of Amen, take His Majesty to his quarters," ordered the Regent, "even put him to bed. Early nap-time today!"

"Your Highness," Senimen nodded towards Hatshepsut and then

lifted the squalling boy-king from the Fourth Prophet's released grasp. Once in his tutor's arms, the child's outburst tempered into sobbing and the kicking ceased. Senimen handed the dented pendant back to the priest and quickly strode from the audience chamber. The departing Menkheperre, peering over his bearer's shoulder, stuck out a pink tongue in the direction of his stepmother.

"Well, this definitely needs rethinking," stated the Regent, matter of factly.

Two Floodings Later
The Holy of Holies, Mansion of Amen-Re, Waset

Mistress of the Two Lands Maatkare, Daughter of Re Hatshepsut stood rigidly four cubits from the bolted gold-plated double doors to the innermost shrine of the deity, his Lord Amen-Re's Holy of Holies, wherein he dwelt. She wore the bulbous Blue Crown — studded with gold bosses and with a golden cobra on the brow — her long hair totally hidden. An elaborately beaded collar and enameled-gold pendant adorned the sheer tunic covering her otherwise bare torso; a pleated kilt was fastened around her waist; from the inlaid golden girdle was suspended a starched triangular apron; centered on this was a long, narrow rectangular second apron of hinged inlaid-gold plates, the bottom corners each being decorated with a rearing golden cobra. Her feet were bare. Crossed on her narrow chest were the gold-and-lapis Crook and gilded Flail scepters. Small pointed chin thrust high, she waited.

Arrayed behind Maatkare Hatshepsut in the dim chamber sweet with incense, shoulder to shoulder, were the Second, Third and Fourth prophets of the god, their totally shaved bodies attired only in ankle-length kilts. All were barefooted. Each held before him a fuming censer. Behind them was a double file of lesser priests, several of whom bore ritual implements and a ewer, one with a rolled towel, two holding large trays heaped with breads and fruit. In front of the ruler, facing the shrine doors was First Prophet Hapusenub, attired like the other priests, except for the pendant of his office on his smooth-shaven chest. He carried a gilded baton and — after muttering an inaudible prayer — the high-priest lightly tapped its rock-crystal finial on one doorjamb. He then leaned forward, an ear tilted towards the doors.

Apparently hearing a command from within, Hapusenub drew the bronze bolt to one side, then slowly pulled the high panels outwards, exposing the shrine interior with its large gilded model barque supporting a gold-plated naos shrouded with a sheet of scarlet linen. The god's First Prophet bowed from his waist, rose and stepped to one side of the opening. Immediately part of the force of *wab* priests swarmed with their para-phernalia around the unmoving three prophets and Maatkare Hatshepsut. They ceremoniously undraped and folded the naos shroud, then one priest unbolted and opened the doors of that smaller shrine. Standing inside was the golden figure of ithyphallic Amen-Min, less than half human-size. A miniature pleated scarlet kilt attired the cult statue, from which jutted a generous rigid male-member. Two gilded hawk tail-feathers rose side-by-side from the flat top of the god's cylindrical short crown. One of the priests lifted the image by its legs and carried it to a waist-high granite altar situated in front of the barque's bow, setting it there so that it faced towards the Mistress of the Two Lands and the three prophets. The kilt was untied by the same priest and removed from the god's now-naked image.

At a nod from the First Prophet, Maatkare Hatshepsut handed her scepters to Hapusenub, stepping forward into the shrine and to in front of the golden figure. She bowed her crowned head and measuredly intoned, "Hail to thee, Lord Hidden One. We trust last night's voyage through the Twelve Gates saw victory over Dark One Apep, and that we may offer thee refreshing lustration and renourishment."

In moments a low, sonorous voice from the deep shadows at the back of the shrine responded, simply, "Which you may, Daughter of Our Limbs."

With that the priest holding the ewer stepped up to the Mistress of the Two Lands and handed the silver vessel to her. Maatkare Hatshepsut lifted this and poured a stream of water over the statue's body. This ran off the altar and fell into a catch basin. The priest with the scroll of towel stepped forward and the ruler took this, unrolled it and wiped the god's figure dry. She handed the damp fabric back to the priest and took a fresh half-sized kilt from yet another officiant. She placed this around the im-age's mid-section and tied the red sash above the protruding phallus. Next she turned around and received the gold tray loaded with upright small cones of baked bread, then turned back to the image again. Now the Second, Third and Fourth prophets entered the shrine and came around her. With the Fourth Prophet chanting an incantation, the three waved their censors over the bread offering. This was repeated with the fruit offering.

And within minutes the cult image was returned to its naos, the latter was reshrouded and the officiants backed out of the shrine, bowing as they exited. First Prophet Hapusenub handed her scepters to the Mistress of the Two Lands, then slowly pushed the door panels closed and slid the bolt in place. In reverse order of their entrance, the assistant priests, three prophets, ruler of Kemet and high-priest processed out of the inner sanctum of the God's Mansion of Lord Amen-Re.

As always following this daily ritual, Maatkare Hatshepsut was thinking that, regrettably, it would be some long time before her five-inundations-old Coregent would be capable of fulfilling on his own this particular tedious duty of ruling the Two Lands.

INUNDATION 2, REIGN OF MENKHEPERRE DJEHUTYMES
THE RESIDENCE, MENNUFER

K ing's Daughter, King's Sister Neferure, age eleven, placed her scribal palette to one side of the low table at which she sat cross-legged on a cushion. She picked up the rectangle of papyrus on which she had been copying the lines of glyphs that her tutor, Count Senenmut, had given her for the day's writing lesson. Why, she was wondering yet again, were there so many bird signs, and so many of these so really similar? She was concentrating on the script and did not notice the clicking approach of canine nails on the plaster floor, and so was startled when a soft wet tongue licked her ear.

"Oh, *stop!*" Neferure squealed and pushed at her half-brother's gangly hound, which began barking in response, its long tail wagging excitedly. At that moment young Menkheperre himself came running into the chamber.

"User!" He shouted at his pet, which immediately went to him, tail tucked.

"Hawk Beak, take that stupid pest and go play somewhere else. Can't you see I'm very, very busy with lessons?"

"That's not our name!" The five-floodings-old boy folded his arms over his bare chest.

"It's what *Mother* calls you — 'Hawk Beak' — because your nose is so *big*." She made a gesture in front of her own snub nose. "Just lucky she doesn't call you 'Ibis Beak', since you *are* 'Born of Djehuty' and he's got a *really* big nose," the princess laughed, extending her slender arm full length from her face.

Before the boy-king could reply, his tutor, Senimen, came rushing through the doorway. Hard on the young man's heels was a Medjay with the omnipresent spear.

"*There* you are! Your Majesty must *not* dash about the Residence, chasing after that dog. I turn my back for *one* minute, and you're off!"

"User runs off, I follow and catch him." The Lord of the Two Lands responded defiantly, petting the animal's narrow head, then hugging its neck.

"Perhaps we shall have to tie User on a rope, so he won't get away," suggested Senimen, taking the boy's hand.

"Better to keep Hawk Beak on a leash," laughed Neferure. "Mother will be really, really mad when she learns Baby Lord of the Two Lands has been running around without his bodyguard. She says bad people could hurt him. Even *steal* him. Especially here in Mennufer, where lots of very bad people are, Mother says."

"They are everywhere, Your Highness," corrected the tutor. "Bad people."

"They take away Hawk Beak and *I* shall have to be the ruler with Mother," asserted the king's sister proudly. "*That's* why I'm learning to read and write!"

"Enough, Beauty of Re!" ordered Senenmut. He had come up alongside the Medjay. "No more nonsense."

From behind the count's hips, the dwarf Khawi stared bug eyed at the girl. He grinned broadly and then thrust out his long tongue, wagging it. Neferure giggled.

ONE WEEK EARLIER, THE RESIDENCE, MENNUFER

Sitting cross-legged on the mussed sheets of her bed, a fully nude Hatshepsut could hear the loud flow in the lavatory adjacent to her sleeping chamber, which was weakly illuminated by a single brazier. She ran hands through her thick shoulder-length tresses, then vigorously shook her head.

Moments later another stark-naked person was walking through the shadows, returning to the bed. Prince Tao — wide-shouldered, stockily muscular, head close-cropped, pubes shaved away — smiled confidently as he came up and sat on the low surface. He then swung his hairless legs so that he was also cross-legged and facing his kinswoman. His former erection was no more, not particularly a disappointment for Hatshepsut.

"Well, that's better," he whispered. "Now where were we, Cousin?"

"Finished with our 'business', it would seem," Hatshepsut gestured towards his limpness, smiling.

"Oh, in minutes, I'll be mighty Min again." Tao reached out to fondle Hatshepsut's small breasts.

She pushed the grope away. "We are much out of practice, Prince. Our late brother-husband rarely fulfilled his marital duties, especially once he found Harim Mouse much more to his perverse tastes than ourself."

"Not to mention endowed charioteers and the occasional Medjay, or so went the court rumors," chuckled Tao, running a spurned palm over the bristles on his pate.

"Rumors kept from our ears at the time. In any case there was never anything like sibling affection between us. Full contempt, rather. We truly despised each other from childhood. Born of Djehuty Junior never forgave us that our father publically said *we* were a more deserving prince than his last son, and would have been his successor save for our... well, lack of one of those." She gestured toward's Tao's crotch.

"Asar Great Form of Re was but half royal, at best, whatever his many personality deficits," replied Tao. "And when a stepped-up mongrel ruts a Harim bitch, the result is another cur. Our new Lord of the Two Lands is not only a pup, but just a fraction royal, as well."

"And — except that she also is without the requisite organ — our Beauty of Re would have been her father's better Horus-in-the-Nest than little bastard Born of Djehuty Three. But enough of this talk, Cousin. What is *is*." Hatshepsut swung her legs off the bed and stood, swinging tresses brushing her narrow shoulders. "Lasting Manifestation of Re *is* the Living Horus, plain and simple."

"*Living* is the key word, is it not, Regent Noblest Woman?" With the space now clear, Prince Tao stretched out his legs, supporting himself on his elbows. "What if something should change that status to 'flown to the stars', before Lord Cur Pup has made himself his own Heir? Since that prospect is as many as a decade of floodings off, the Horus Throne *is* and will continue to be in peril, you must agree."

"Where are you going with this, Cousin?"

"The Black Land is most capably governed by yourself, to be certain. Which does not mean that there would not be a great succession crisis should anything...ah, *unforeseen* happen to our sprout of a sovereign. *Maat* requires the boy-king to have a Horus-in-the-Nest, sooner rather than later."

Hatshepsut already thought she knew what Tao had in mind, but wanted to hear it from his own lips. "So, Prince?"

"*So*, Noblest Woman, one of the House's bloodline should be named Heir, 'plain and simple'. As a safeguard, only, of course." Tao now also stood and retrieved his loincloth from the floor, and began wrapping and tying this in place.

"And by 'House' we presume you mean that of the Taos. And your candidate for standby Heir would be your esteemed father, Prince-Count Son of Amen?"

Actually, Cousin, I rather had *myself* in mind. Father will see only a few more floodings, to be frankly candid. Whereas, I am still young and, well, most vigorous — as Your Highness may now personally attest," he chuckled, retrieving his discarded pleated kilt from the floor and wrapping this around his waist. "I have a son now into his majority, whose own young wife is very much with child. No shortage of Horuses-in-the-Nest! Since we ourselves are now both without spouses, you and I could swear vows, exchange hair and start our own great line of Heirs!"

"And you would have us as your Great Royal Wife when you are finally Lord of the Two Lands." It was a statement, not a question.

"Exactly!" Reattired Tao stepped to Hatshepsut and leaned forward, his arms wide for an embrace.

Instead, the Regent slapped his cheek with all the force she could manage.

"*Out*, you plotter, before we have our Medjays arrest you!"

"But — ?" Tao stood half upright.

"Take yourself back to the fetid swamps you crawled from. You and your kin are now — and for all time — aliens to the Residence. Perhaps you all should book passage to Kheftiu, if you know what's wisest for the whole lot of you. Out of our sight, *now!*"

The prince plucked his wig from the chair where he had tossed it. Pulling this on, he quickly exited the regent's sleeping chamber, without even a backwards glance at the woman with whom he had been so intimate just shortly before.

Still naked, she crossed to her bed, sat on it, laid down, positioned the headrest and pulled the crumpled sheet to her chin. It was still several hours before the god Re emerged from the Underworld.

Regent Hatshepsut dreamed. Royal Nurse In Sitre was heaped on the painted floor, sobbing. Given no other choice, the Regent placed one wrist over the other and the Medjay guard bound her arms together in front of her, using a soft strip of tanned gazelle hide. She stared past him at the seemingly indifferent young man in court dress and carrying a baton of some sort. She did not recognize him. She could not make eye contact either, as he seemed focused beyond her shoulder, perhaps on the contingent of five other Medjays who were waiting to escort her. To where she could only guess. She wished she had been given some warning, so as to have at least had herself made presentable. The courtier had denied her permission to don even a wig. Her own glossy hair fell smoothly to her narrow shoulders. At least she had been fully clothed when the bunch of them arrived at her apartments. Brandishing his baton of authority, the courtier had ordered her personal Medjays aside and then entered her spaces, interrupting a game of *senet*.

"Your name, again, young man?" she directed at the courtier. "We didn't catch it when you introduced yourself."

"I did not give it, Noblest Woman. My name is of no importance, in any case." He still was not looking directly at her. "This is about *you*, not me."

"Where are you taking us, bound like this? You know, we are Regent for Lord of the Two Lands. We could have you perched on a stake by nightfall."

"Not if you're on one yourself *before* then, lady."

As the Medjay escort — the Regent barefoot in their midst — followed the haughty courtier from the chamber, Hatshepsut said loudly, "Get control of yourself, Fish. We *will* return!" The mound of nurse continued sobbing.

The dream continued. She had passed this way innumerable times, usually with her personal Medjays following close behind, sometimes with the Lord Chamberlain just in the lead. This particular escorted walk through the passageways of the Residence was a first for Hatshepsut, however. As she had suspected, she was being taken to the Royal Audience Hall, where she was almost daily the auditor, but never the petitioner. The courtier-led group entered the hall's antechamber, and to Hatshepsut's surprise, it was quite crowded with bewigged persons in court finery, men and women alike. She recognized none of them, however. Their murmuring ceased and the group parted down its middle, to allow passage of the bound Regent in the midst of her guards.

In several strides Hatshepsut was standing before the tall double doors of the hall itself, the confident young escort just in front of her (the Medjays, however, seemed to have fallen away). The Regent felt scores of disapproving stares at her back. The courtier raised his baton and knocked its gold finial three times against a bronze plate in the middle of one of the panels. In several long moments, the doors swung slowly inward, revealing yet another parted crowd. At the end of the chamber, the dais supported several occupants. Resting on a low bier in front of the dais was a quite small, all-black anthropoid coffin. Hatshepsut followed her escort through the two flanks of strange, somber faces, to stand in front of the ominous container. The young courtier now backed away, bowing towards the persons on the dais and moving behind the Regent's peripheral vision.

Seated side-by-side on gilded thrones with footstools were three individuals whom she did know. In the middle, wearing the Double

Crown and False Beard, and clasping the crossed Crook and Flail against his wide chest, sat His Majesty, Khakheperre Tao (Hatshepsut somehow knew this). To his right was none other than His Majesty elderly Menphetyre Siamen (which she magically knew, as well), wearing the Blue Crown (no beard) and also holding the ruler's scepters to his scrawny breastbone. And the third throne was occupied by His Majesty teenage Sehkemre Amenhotep (again, this throne name was already known to her), in the ruler's *Nemes* striped headcovering with lappets and the False Beard, with the same identically displayed Crook-and-Flail regalia. Arrayed behind this unique kingly trio were several individuals whom the Regent recognized only by their distinctive attire: the bald Four Prophets of Amen-Re and the viziers of Kemet's North and South, in their billowing long kilts. Off to one side was a tall middle-aged man with a pointed nose, wearing a wig of short coppery curls, who seemed very familiar, but lacked a name.

In moments the middle one of the enthroned three began speaking, but Hatshepsut was deaf to whatever was being said. In turn the other two also spoke, but still the Regent only saw moving mouths without sounds coming forth. When Sehkemre Amenhotep finished whatever it was he had been saying, all three extended at arms' length their hands holding the Crook scepters. At first Hatshepsut thought they were pointing these at her. Then she realized that it was towards the miniature black coffin in front of her instead. Two funerary priests suddenly appeared and the lid of this was lifted from its head and foot ends, then placed on the floor near the Regent's feet. Within the interior was a red shroud covering the coffin's contents. As the Lords of the Two Lands trio continued pointing their Crooks at the coffin — shouting silently in apparent unison — one of the funerary priests pulled away the shroud with a dramatic flourish.

Hatshepsut gasped and reflexively raised her bound wrists to her mouth. Side by side in the basin were three decapitated heads — which she instantly recognized. Two were withered and darkened, eyes closed, thin lips in grimaces: on the left that of her father; in the middle her brother-husband's. The third on the right was the fresh, still bloody small head of none other than the boy-ruler for whom she was Regent, his glassy black eyes staring back in pure terror, his wide-open mouth an O of astonishment. The Audience Chamber quickly dimmed to total blackness.

The dream ended. Hatshepsut sat upright so suddenly that the bed's headrest toppled over behind her. Her naked torso was soaked with perspiration, her loose hair damp. The small hands on her sheet-covered lap trembled. Dim light afforded by the sleeping chamber's one brazier revealed the heap of Nurse In, snoring away on her own low bed in the deep shadows across the room. She obviously had returned, following Prince Tao's departure. Hatshepsut's only thought was that she had to summon her counselors, immediately. Or at least very first thing in the morning.

SEVERAL HOURS LATER
THE RESIDENCE, MENNUFER

It was actually early afternoon by the time the High Council had assembled in the private audience chamber of the Regent's apartments. She could not tell them that this impromptu gathering was the result of her nightmare just hours before, itself prompted by her very real visit from Prince Tao. Not a large group, those present were: First Prophet of Amen-Re Hapusenub, First Prophet of Ptah Paneb, Great Steward of Amen-Re Senenmut, Vizier of the North Amenneferu, Chief Treasurer Khaemhet, Generalissimo Besenmut, Chamberlain of the Northern Residence Minnakht and Captain of the Royal Guard Nebet. Hatshepsut sat on her throne centered on the small dais, the others in armchairs arranged informally before the latter, there being no particular order of the counselors' rank (which really only existed in the Regent's head). Two female servants were passing out goblets of the best Delta vintage. When all were served, the acting ruler of Kemet began her meeting.

"It has come to our attention — in which manner it is not our choice to say — that there is a present danger to the Horus Throne and its young occupant. Because this concerns Living Horus Lasting Manifestation of Re personally, he should by all logic be here this afternoon. Owing to his tender age, however, it is not likely that he would add anything meaningful to the discussion of his own welfare, or even understand our concern.

"To be direct about it, most of you are all well aware that the accession of our late father to the Horus Throne some years ago was rather an anomaly. When it became apparent that Asar Holy Soul of Re would in all certainty fly to the heavens without having fathered a Son-of-His-Body to succeed him, it fell to his mother and stand-in-consort, the Great One, to ensure a smooth transition of the Double Crown when the time came. She then had one still-living son besides Holy Soul of Re, his older sibling, Prince-Count Son of Amen. For reasons known only to her, the Great One decided to bypass this elder son — as he previously had been bypassed in favor of his junior brother as successor to The Liberator — and instead named her nephew, our father, Generalissimo Born of Djehuty, as the Heir and Horus-in-the-Nest. At that time he had two surviving sons, although his wife was already deceased. So he was soon joined to his cousin, our mother, Asar Moon Born, with the prospect of fathering yet more potential heirs. And so, when Lord Holy Soul of Re did finally fly up, it was our father who became the next Living Horus, as Great Soul of Re — to the tireless rejoicing of all the gods and of the people of the Black Land, as well.

"For reasons known only to those great gods, however, our half-brother, the Heir Born of Amen, died tragically while campaigning with our father in wretched Wawat. Thus Lord of the Two Lands' youngest son was elevated to Horus-in-the-Nest at a tender age. Equally tragically, our father's time on the throne was cut short when he was slain on campaign in the land of the filthy Asiatics. And so our young half-brother became Lord of the Two Lands, as Great Form of Re. Because he'd not reached his majority, it fell to the Dowager Great Royal Wife, our mother, his stepmother, to assume the responsibility for the day-to-day governing of the Black Land.

"It was at this time — although we understand he had made a similar proposal to the Great One years earlier — that Prince-Count Son of Amen approached the Regent with the plan to have his only son, Prince Tao, named as Horus-in-the-Nest, inasmuch as the new Lord of the Two Lands of course had neither Great Royal Wife nor any issue. He argued to our mother that this would be the only way ensure the certain continuance of the House of Tao, should something happen to young Lord Great Form of Re, before he produced an Heir of his own body. Our mother later told us she had responded that the ruling family of the Black Land was now the House Born of Djehuty and that the new Lord of the Two Lands would very soon be taking us, his half-sister, as Great Royal Wife, and that we would be bearing the Heir. Thus there was no pressing need, she said, for Prince Tao to be standing idly by.

"Of course, you all know that — after failed attempts — we gave the Living Horus our daughter, Beauty of Re. Great Form of Re also celebrated a Son-of-His-Body, whom he named the third Born of Djehuty, and who was, well, automatically Horus-in-the-Nest. What no one foresaw, of course, was the unexpected assassination of our brother-husband in his prime, which we have always suspected was the result of plotting by persons not directly involved with actual commission of the crime — but had no hard proof of that.

"And so, the infant Born of Djehuty was suddenly Lord of the Two Lands Lasting Manifestation of Re. And we are now Regent of the Black Land, governing — with benefit of the wise counsel of you all — on his behalf. But since it will be some many floodings before the young

Lord will have his own issue, we hear confidential reports of murmurings that the Two Lands would be better attuned with *Maat* if someone of much greater maturity was wearing the Double Crown. We understand it is being said that His Majesty should willingly step aside. Failing which, that he should be *put* aside, so that the House of Tao may be restored. This would be by elderly Prince-Count Son of Amen. Or — far more practically — by his son, our cousin, Prince Tao, who is himself father of a son at his majority. We understand that, though still young himself, Tao is soon to be a grandfather, as well. It's being whispered that the Taos have no 'shortage' of potential Horuses-in-the-Nest.

"This, need we say, is wholly unacceptable to us, as present guardian of the House Born of Djehuty — and, of course, of the best interests of our young nephew, who is *fully* the legitimate occupant of the Horus Throne.

"Thus, notable ones, we have called you here today to advise us on what we may do to fully secure what already *is*. Besides, of course, increasing our young Lord's personal safety by guarding him more fully. Which we have already ordered." Hatshepsut drank deeply from her goblet.

There was a long pause. Generalissimo Besenmut was the first to respond. "Arrest and impale all the surviving male Taos. Sever the serpent at its head. That seems simple enough."

"With all due respect," the Regent placed the goblet on the table beside her throne, "that would be the desperation of a tyrant, General. There is no hard evidence that these rumors of sedition are actually true. To every present appearance, all the Taos are living in retirement on their vast Delta estates. Their most recent *public* presence — at Waset — was for our brother/husband's Opening of the Mouth and the coronation rites of our nephew."

"Would it be of use to bring Prince-Count Son of Amen here to Mennufer, to question him, before the High Council, as to his aspirations for the House of Tao?" asked Vizier Amenneferu.

"He'd only profess full allegiance to Hawk...that is, to His Majesty," replied Hatshepsut. "Our country cousins are ambitious, but not stupid. Prince-Count Son of Amen would never admit to his family's private aspirations. He would never be so foolish as to say, 'Why, yes, we do want Baby Lord of the Two Lands gone, so we, the Taos, may fill the void'."

"Does the count have present support for his 'cause', from some faction at court," Vizier Amenneferu leaned froward in his chair, looking left and right at his colleagues, "or from the military?" directed at Generalissimo Besenmut.

"He couldn't muster a single company of the Army of the Two Lands! Who'd follow an old cripple?" barked the general.

"But the Army *is* loyal to a toddler?" asked Great Steward Senenmut, leaning forward to make eye contact with the military man.

"The Army's allegiance is always to the *legitimate* Lord of the Two Lands, and Lasting Manifestation of Re, toddler or not, *is* the Living Horus," asserted Besenmut. "You all heard him cheered by the troops when he reviewed them, wearing his miniature Blue Crown and corselet, carrying his miniature bow and arrows."

Hatshepsut interrupted, "We are not concerned at this time about an actual armed insurrection against the Throne. We do not believe the Taos could rally an attack on the Residence. The threat is not from outward force but inward guile."

"Then you are saying, Your Highness, that there are those at *court* who would prefer a Tao — old, young or younger — on the Horus Throne?" asked First Prophet Hapusenub. "None present, I dare say."

Senenmut spoke up. "The reality that Her Highness is getting at, I believe, is the obvious lack of a Horus-in-the-Nest, and the prospect that there'll be no new male of the Born of Djehuty bloodline for many floodings, at least. This may be perceived by some at court as a serious vulnerability, even a dangerous situation for *Maat*. In the distant past, so my researches have revealed, if a potential problem with the succession loomed, the ruling Lord of the Two Lands would associate himself with a Coregent — usually his eldest son or, lacking that, a brother — who then was no longer merely the Heir but full-and-equal Living Horus. Thus there was a Double Throne as well as a Double Crown. And so, should one Lord fly up prematurely the other merely continued ruling without any disturbance to *Maat*. Perhaps the present situation calls for a similar solution."

"Except," replied Chief Treasurer Khaemhet, "Our present young Lord has *neither* son nor brother."

"I said a *similar* solution," responded the Great Steward. "Clearly the problem is not that the Black Land is without governance. Certainly Her Highness is actual ruler of the Two Lands until His Majesty comes of age, some floodings in the future. But regency has always been intended as a temporary solution, never a long-term one. What the present situation calls for — even what *Maat* requires — is not a governing Regent but a reigning Coregent. Kemet again needs a Double Throne."

"But again, there are no candidates for a second Lord of the Two Lands, Great Steward," retorted the Vizier. "Unless you're thinking of Prince Tao, or even Prince Amenhotep, after all."

"Of course not. That would create great problems, when Lord Lasting Manifestation of Re does reach his majority and produces, as he certainly will, his own Heir. Are you by chance a Taoist, Vizier?" returned Senenmut, smiling. "No. The sole candidate sits with us today." He gestured towards Hatshepsut. "Her Highness Noblest Woman could rule the Black Land far more authoritatively as Mistress of the Two Lands rather than as a very young boy-king's stand-in."

"A *female* Horus?" questioned First Prophet of Ptah Paneb.

"Actually, there *is* precedent," inserted fellow cleric Hapusenub. "Perhaps 300 floodings ago, a female Horus wore the Double Crown: Soul of Re Sobek, last ruler of the great House of Amen at the Head. And there were other female Horuses in the mists of time far past. Lord Hidden One Amen-Re would have no problem with such a resolution of the present circumstance, this I'm quite certain. In fact, I can assure you, He greatly favors Noblest Woman."

The counselors were murmuring among themselves, when Hatshepsut spoke again, having drained her goblet.

"*We* have not been consulted regarding your present proposal, Great Steward. This is not a solution which *we* are putting forth, we'd make that *perfectly* clear. We have absolutely no ambitions to share Lasting Manifestation of Re's *throne*. Simply to govern on His Majesty's behalf as long as needed is quite enough, we think."

"With all due respect, of course, Your Highness," returned Senenmut, "Your High Council is pleased then to hear what the Regent herself has in mind."

"If we *had* a proposal, but of course, we would've made it in the first place." She turned again to Hapusenub. "You're absolutely certain, First Prophet Hapu is Well, that Lord Hidden One would permit a 'Double Throne' solution, which Great Steward of the god's estates has outlined?"

"In fact, Your Highness, this is *exactly* the divine desire," replied the god's chief officiant, bowing a shaved head towards Hatshepsut. "Lord Amen-Re, greatest of the Great Ones, *invites* his God's Wife to be Mistress of the Two Lands — as soon as possible."

"Well then, we can't very well resist what is the expressed will of our Divine Father, can we now? So be it," declared the Regent.

Hatshepsut stood, stepped off the dais and quickly departed the chamber. The High Council briefly conferred among themselves, then also went their separate ways. Senenmut and Hapusenub were the last to leave, whispering together. Their plan had worked. Kemet would not be the same for another twenty floodings.

* * *

7

M istress of the Two Lands Maatkare crossed the large apartment to the exterior doorway. She had left her Medjay escorts at the antechamber's entrance, presumably to pass time with the two Wawatmen posted there. She stepped out into the columned space and seated herself in one of several chairs, including a miniature version of the others. She was amused by the scattering of wooden soldiers and horses hitched to a tiny chariot that populated the painted floor of the Lord of the Two Lands' private loggia. The toys' owner, the five-floodings-old Living Horus, was presently in the walled garden beyond, engaged in a game of catch-the-ball with his tutor. A third player was the boy's young hunting hound.

Maatkare Hatshepsut had not come to pay a social call on her juvenile Coregent that afternoon, however. Rather she was there for the purpose of engaging attractive young Senimen, the King's Tutor, to inform him of his additional new duties in the royal household. Intent on their ball tossing, the man and small boy in the bright sunlight had not noticed her presence in the roofed, shaded space. The gangly dog was too busy romping and barking to have spotted her.

In moments a serving girl came through the doorway carrying a tray with two faience goblets of Delta wine, exactly as she'd been instructed by the Daughter of Re on the latter's arrival. She sat the refreshments on the low table in front of the seated woman, bowed her head, murmered "Your Majesty," and backed away, turning and going back inside.

Hatshepsut picked up the closest goblet and sipped the bittersweet vintage. She would wait until she was noticed. It pleased her to watch, unobserved, Senimen in physical exertion. He wore only a short kilt and his muscled bare torso and nicely biceped arms were lightly glossed with perspiration.

His Majesty was, of course, totally naked, as usual with young boys in private; he didn't seem to have broken a sweat, however. But he was apparently thoroughly enjoying the activity, shouting his pleasure each time he caught the small leather ball and didn't fumble it. His throw back was surprisingly strong — and straight — for one so young. Senimen called out encouragement to the boy each time little Djehutymes's catch was successful. Her Majesty rather liked the melodious baritone.

Several minutes passed. Hatshepsut's goblet was nearly drained when the ball bounced off Son of Re's hands and landed a few feet from the loggia platform. He ran across the clipped grass, barking pet at his heels, and squatted to recover the small sphere. Standing upright, he spotted the spectator in the shadows, pointed at her and called to his tutor, "She's here!"

From his position several cubits away, Senimen shielded his eyes with one hand as he looked towards the loggia. It took him a moment to recognize the Mistress of the Two Lands seated there, who, after all, was attired very informally, devoid of any regalia, not even wearing a wig or jewelry. When he realized who the visitor was, he immediately bowed from the waist.

"Your Majesty."

"Relax, Brother of Amen, and come in from under Lord Re."

The shortish young man stood upright and approached the loggia, clearly uneasy. He mounted the two steps, moved a pace into the shade and stood with arms straight at his sides. Young Son of Re Djehutymes followed on Senimen's heels and mimicked his tutor's rigid stance.

"Hello, little Hawk Beak. You are becoming quite the ball player. Soon you may be even better than Beauty of Re."

The dog scrambled up the steps and bounded awkwardly onto the platform, slipping on the smooth plaster surface. He recovered his stance and, nails clicking, ran up to the seated human, pink tongue drooling. Before he could put his paws on the inviting thigh, Hatshepsut sharply ordered,

"Get away, stupid beast!"

"His name is User," stated the little Lord of the Two Lands, "not 'Stupid Beast'."

"*User!*" Senimen ordered, pointing towards the loggia's doorway, "Inside, inside. Now! Right *now!*"

Bony long tail tucked, the cowed brown-and-tan young canine reluctantly exited the loggia. His brief presence had served to relax the situation, however. Hatshepsut spoke first, after a few moments.

"Doesn't His Majesty need a bath and nap?" she asked his still-rigid tutor.

"No nap!" asserted Djenhutymes, stamping a bare foot.

"With Your Majesty's leave," stated Senimen, nodding towards Hatshepsut. He quickly moved across the loggia to the doorway. "Itbet!" he called loudly. "Come here. His Majesty is ready for his bath."

As if she'd been waiting just within, the full-breasted young wet-nurse immediately came into view. Senimen moved to one side and she stepped onto the loggia, holding her arms open towards Djehutymes still standing formally at the platform's edge, barely out of the sunlight. She seemed unaware of Hatshepsut's presence. Itbet knelt down, her arms still wide, and the young boy crossed to her and let himself be enfolded, putting his arms around her neck, wrapping his legs around her waist. When she stood with her burden and turned to depart, the young woman saw the seated Mistress of the Two Lands and halted abruptly.

"Oh, Your Majesty!" She attempted to bow. Djehutymes used the opportunity to detach himself from her grip and stood on the floor, turning to face his Coregent again. Itbet quickly took his hand.

"Be on your way with Hawk Beak, Nurse," Hatshepsut waved them off.

Itbet immediately left the loggia, towing Djehutymes. Senimen continued standing in place, however.

Hatshepsut spoke first, smiling. "Brother of Amen, come, take a seat." She gestured towards one of the empty chairs.

"Forgive me, Your Majesty, I'm not properly attired to be in your presence. And I'm wet from Lord Re's heat."

"Nonsense. You're overly modest, Son of Amen. And the sweat's already drying. Must we order you to sit down and refresh yourself?" She pointed to the goblet on the table, still holding her own.

The tutor came forward and stiffly sat in a chair opposite Hatshepsut, the low table between them. Nodding at her he reached for the goblet, brought it to his mouth and sipped the wine, then returned the vessel to the table. There was a long pause.

"You may speak if you wish," Hatshepsut broke the silence.

"I've never spoken directly to you, Your Majesty. Have never been alone with you, in fact. It's unnerving. I'm not worthy...."

"You're," Hatshepsut interrupted, "'worthy' enough to be entrusted with the care and education of the Lord of the Two Lands. We'd say that's also worthy enough to have a private conversation with Our Person, Brother of Amen." She smiled.

"Thank you very much for your confidence, Your Majesty." He retieved the goblet.

"What's your story, King's Tutor?"

"I'm not certain I understand what you're asking, Your Majesty."

"We know you came recommended for your post as tutor by Count Brother of Mut. Are you one of his minions?"

"Minions? I don't know...."

"Are you or have you been *intimate* with him?"

"'Intimate'?" Senimen took another sip of wine.

"Don't be coy. Has he, well, *used* you...sexually?"

"Oh, no, Your Majesty! To be sure I've heard the rumor that he lays only with men, particularly young men, but never with me. Perhaps I should be, well, *insulted* that he's never even propositioned such." Senimen chuckled, shrugged and tipped the goblet again. Finishing off the contents, he sat the empty vessel on the table, and ran a palm over the bristles of his closely cropped hair.

"Well, we can't imagine why he never made at least the *effort*. You're certainly physically well-favored by the gods." Hatshepsut drained the last of her own wine, returned the goblet to the table and clapped loudly. "So, if you're not one of Brother of Mut's whore-boys, who *do* you relieve yourself with, tutor? Which one or ones of Our Majestys' servants?"

At that moment the serving-girl who had delivered the wine earlier came back onto the loggia, again carrying a tray with two faience goblets. At a gesture from Hatshepsut, she approached the table and exchanged the drained vessels with the full ones. Nodding towards Her Majesty, she turned and departed the loggia.

"Have you had that particular one, Brother of Amen?" Hatshepsut asked bluntly.

"She rebuffed my advances. Seems she's actively sexing with one of the groomsmen in the royal stables here. Ah, well..."

"Perhaps she prefers brutes to intellectuals."

Senimen shrugged. "I'm certainly not 'intellectual', Your Majesty."

"We've been led to believe you're a highly talented scribe, Brother of Amen. In this place, the ability to read and write makes you intellectual enough. But we digress. Who *are* you 'sexing' with?"

"Presently with no one, Your Majesty, if by 'sexing' you mean taking to bed. My current circumstances," he gestured towards the loggia doorway, "don't exactly lend themselves to privacy, inasmuch as I share the same sleeping chamber with His Majesty. And Nurse Itbet sleeps the next chamber over. We never know when Dowager King's Mother Iset may show up unannounced, to visit young Born of Djehuty."

"By 'we' is meant you and Nurse Itbet, presumably. Have you had *her*?" Hatshepsut persisted.

"Not really, Your Majesty. Only some quick, ah...casual fondling on occasion. Nurse finds me, well, too, ah, 'large', and she is not my... how should I say it? I'm not attracted to Itbet in any way sexual. I prefer less buxom females, and ones not so, well, generous in the hips as she is. We're just colleagues, playing out our assigned roles as substitute parents to His Majesty." Senimen picked up the goblet closest to himself and gulped from it.

"Stand up Son of Amen," Hatshepsut ordered. She retrieved her own goblet.

Looking puzzled he returned the vessel to the table and rose to his full height, arms at his sides as before.

"Take off your kilt."

"But, Your Majesty, I'm not attired with a loincloth just now!"

"Then that won't have to be discarded, as well. Remove your kilt, tutor, we want to see how 'large' you are for ourself."

Reluctantly, as evidenced by how slowly he moved, Senimen undid the narrow ties at his waist and unwrapped the linen rectangle. It fell away, but not to the floor, as he gripped the fabric in one hand. Reflexively he held the garment in front of his crotch.

"Move your hand aside," the seated woman ordered and took another sip of wine.

Senimen let his hand drop to along his thigh and stood totally exposed to the Mistress of the Two Lands. Approving of what she saw, Hatshepsut smiled and said, "Recover yourself, Brother of Amen. Itbet hasn't overly exaggerated."

The King's Tutor quickly rewrapped the kilt, further embarrassed that it was slightly tented by his nascent erection. He continued standing, looking somewhere over Hatshepsut's head, avoiding eye contact.

"Take your seat. We've further business with you." Hatshepsut sipped more wine. After a pause, while Senimen sat in the chair again, she continued, "It would seem, from what we've been told, and by what we've witnessed just this afternoon, that you and little Hawk Beak have bonded nicely. Since you're now more of an adult playmate for him than a teacher, your role here in the Residence isn't as demanding as it'll become in due time, when daily lessens actually begin. In other words, Tutor, your talents aren't, presently, being utilized to the fullest." She took another sip from the goblet. "Therefore, we've decided that, in addition to functioning as King's Tutor, you shall now also be King's Scribe."

When Senimen frowned, indicating he did not understand, Hatshepsut continued, "And that 'King' is ourself. Since our acceptance of the Double Crown, we've relied on a number of scribes from the

Residences' staffs for our dictations. But now it's time, we've decided, that a single King's Scribe is required. Great Steward Brother of Mut recommends you for that trusted position. And now we concur. Starting today you shall be available to us when we require your...ah, *scribal* services.

"Since we wouldn't want Hawk Beak left unattended on those occasions — yes, we realize Nurse Itbet still will be here — we've decided to find him an appropriate playmate nearer his own age, some boychild to come here daily as his companion. We don't have a present candidate, but there must be royal servants who live beyond the Residence that have suitable male children from which to choose. When such are identified, they'll be brought here for you to make the final selection. Perhaps you'll even want to let Hawk Beak assist in that, indicate who *he* likes. Then it will fall to you to organize and supervise their daily amusements."

There was a pause while Hatshepsut drank again.

"Well, Brother of Amen, do you have any questions?"

"Will I still continue to reside here with His Majesty, share his bed chamber?"

"We see no reason for that to change, for the present, at least." She placed her empty goblet on the table. "So, that concludes our afternoon's business, King's Tutor now also King's Scribe." Hatshepsut rose, as did Senimen simultaneously. "We've in mind to do some *dictation* this very evening. So come to our apartments the first hour after Re's barque has gone behind the western horizon. The Medjays will've been instructed to allow you to pass into Our Person's presence. Be sure to bring papyrus and your writing...um, tool."

With that the Mistress of the Two Lands smiled, turned and was quickly gone from the loggia. The young scribe stared after her, then looked down to the still-evident hint at one of his "talents" which had gone underused — perhaps, that is, until now.

SOME HOURS LATER, THE SAME DAY AND PLACE
MISTRESS OF THE TWO LANDS' BEDCHAMBER

Hatshepsut waited for King's Scribe Senimen to return from the lavatory adjoining her sleeping chamber, much as she had waited for Prince Tao in the same circumstance two seasons before. She was not regretful of her personal decision to create this present situation, however, as she had been almost immediately in the Tao instance. Senimen had proven to be all that she'd hoped for — and even surprisingly more so — in a sexual partner, obviously without the personal-ambition baggage of her cousin. But she now had to clearly draw perimeters for young

Senimen, if there were to be further secret liaisons of this nature.

The Mistress of the Two Lands had left her sheet-tangled bed and was now seated, fully nude, in an armchair nearby. In short moments the naked figure of the awaited young man emerged from the shadows into the golden glow afforded by the brazier floor lamp. He was totally flaccid but still most impressive nonetheless. He came up to Hatshepsut and seated himself in the chair opposite hers, without asking or being instructed to do so. There was a long silence as the two locked gazes. Hatshepsut was the first to speak.

"So, Brother of Amen, that was, well, really quite enjoyable. For you too?"

Bare forearms resting on the chair arms, he leaned forward and hung his head for a few moments, then looked up at the petite older woman less than three cubits away. "May I be honest and admit I had to imagine that you were just a kitchen maid, Your Majesty. Otherwise being on you, in you, would've been too, well, overwhelming for me to have sustained as Min."

"So tonight we were your scullery slut? Well, I suppose that is comparable to us having imagined you as a sweaty plow-pusher from The River's west bank, with cow dung between your toes!"

"Your fantasy is far, far closer to the truth than my poor one. I *am* the son of dung-toed farmers in the Delta," he chuckled.

"And now you've just been laying with the Mistress of the Two Lands."

"Unless today has been a long, incredible dream, Your Majesty."

"No dream, beautiful young Brother of Amen, unless we both are having the same dream. Be assured, you *are* now our King's Scribe. And you continue, for now, as King's Tutor to our little Coregent. And you *shall* be invited to join us here, as this night, at *our* discretion. But...and it's a very large 'but', you must understand, this aspect of your relationship to Our Person is *totally* between Brother of Amen and Noblest Woman. No one, absolutely *no one* must know of it. And if it should become even the smallest hint of court gossip, well, that shall be your total undoing. Understand?"

Senimen again bowed his head briefly, then looked Hatshepsut directly in her eyes. "Understood fully. Now, am I expected to stay the night?"

"Absolutely *not*! Exit as you entered. Return to sleeping Hawk Beak. We shall summon you again Young Min, sooner or later, when we've further evening 'dictation'."

Hatshepsut smiled and casually dismissed Senimen with a wave of her hand. He retied his kilt, pulled on and adjusted his wig, slipped into his sandals and departed confidently, without a glance back. Perhaps a glance back would have been in order. Or perhaps not.

THREE FLOODINGS LATER, INUNDATION 3
MAATKARE/MENKHEPERRE COREGENCY
ESTATE OF PRINCE-COUNT SIAMEN

L ady of the House Teyit had made her husband as comfortable as possible. Panels of linen were now hung over the clerestory windows of Prince-Count Siamen's bedchamber, to soften the daylight which burned his eyes. Several down-filled bolsters had replaced the headrest on his bed and two wool blankets kept off the winter chill of *Peret*. The only surviving offspring of Ahmes The Liberator had begun to fail several weeks before and had not left his bed in a dozen transits of Lord Re, sleeping most of each day and night. He had taken no nourishment, save sips of wine, for the last several of those.When he chose to speak, it was in a raspy whisper.

Lady Teyit feared the end was nearing. Thus — without her son, Prince Tao, knowing — she had sent word to the Residence at Mennufer, specifically to Mistress of the Two Lands Maatkare, informing the female ruler that her great uncle was close to breathing his last, and that she might wish to pay him a final visit. She had not expected that would happen, however. So it was a great surprise when a Residence messenger appeared at the estate with notification that the Female Horus would be arriving with her entourage around midday the next day. Today.

When Teyit had timidly informed Prince Tao of the pending arrival of their royal relative, he was furious, shattering against a wall the faience tumbler from which he'd been drinking. He had stomped out of his mother's bedchamber, slamming the door panels behind himself. Young Prince Amenhotep, who was also present, kept his seat, however, and broke the silence after several awkward moments.

"Father seems somewhat displeased by your invitation to our vile cousin, Grandmother. You really should've conferred with him before asking his arch enemy to flaunt her illegitimacy here in our presence, especially as Grandfather is about to embark on his journey to the Field of Reeds."

"True Soul of Re is your father's grandniece, Amen is Pleased, and should be accorded the opportunity to pay her respects while he is still drawing breath, was my reasoning. I didn't suppose she'd actually *come* here. Do you think your father will boycott Her Majesty's visit?"

"Oh, you know, Grandmother, I rather imagine he's secretly relishing the opportunity to confront the bitch again, on our own territory."

The royal entourage arrived at the gate of the walled Tao estate almost exactly at the pinnacle of Lord Re's daytime voyage. It consisted of a large escort of soldiers and several Medjay of the Royal Guard, including its captain, Nesbet. There was a curtained ebony palanquin borne by eight black-skinned porters, in which rode the Female Horus, whose only regalia was the cobra on the gold brow-band of her pure-white kingly *Nemes* headcovering, worn with a figure-hugging linen sheath and gilded sandals. There also were two chariots, and their passengers were the surprise of the day. One bore none other than the eight-floodings-old Lord of the Two Lands, driven by his youthful tutor (later introduced to the Taos as Senimen). Stepping down from the other conveyance was slender teenage God's Wife of Amen-Re Neferure, accompanied by her own tutor, none other than Great Steward Senenmut. His Majesty Menkheperre wore a cap-wig with a Horus Sidelock, fronted by the royal cobra; a simple white kilt and reed sandals completed his attire. His half-sister was without a wig, her close-cropped hair adorned by a simple gold fillet; she was clothed in a form-fitting linen sheath like her mother's and was barefooted.

After being assisted from the palanquin by the hand of Captain Nesbet, Maatkare Hatshepsut was immediately joined by the young Co-regent and her daughter, and the three walked together — Her Majesty in the lead, Djehutymes and Neferure side by side a pace behind — through the gateway and along the paved path to where the members of the Tao family were waiting to greet their royal visitors on the columned entrance porch of the villa itself. The pair of tutors and two of the Medjay guard followed at a discreet distance.

The Taos were few in number. The somewhat-stout Lady of the House Teyit, wearing a simple long wig and loose sheath dress, was flanked on one side by her widowered son, Prince Tao, and on the other by her grandson, Prince Amenhotep, and his young wife, who held their toddler son. Nothing adorned the shaved head of Tao, though both Amenhotep and wife Bastet were bewigged and simply attired, as was Tao as well. The group bowed their heads in unison when the co-rulers and God's Wife came within a dozen cubits of the porch platform. The trio stopped and, before anyone else could, Maatkare spoke.

"Greetings, dearest cousins. It is our pleasure — and His Majesty's and the God's Wife's, too — to accept your kind invitation to this lovely country home, to pay respects to our ailing great uncle, whose recovery is imminent, surely."

Teyit raised her head to speak, but was preempted by her son.

"Welcome Your Majesties — and Mistress of Amen-Re. The House of Tao is honored that your highnesses would travel out here to our humble abode. I, *we all*, are especially pleased to unexpectedly welcome His Majesty, Son of Re Born of Djehuty, whose acquaintance it has never been my — our — good fortune to make. Special welcome to you, Lord of the Two Lands Lasting Manifestation of Re! You are the image of your grandfather as a youth." (Tao, in fact, had been born well after Lord of the Two Lands Asar Akheperkare's boyhood.)

Maatkare looked down at the prepubescent Coregent at her side and ordered in a stage whisper, "So, *say* something, Hawk Beak."

The boy-king glanced up at his aunt/stepmother, then, chin raised, looked back at Tao, who was smiling. "Are you the one who wants our throne? You don't look all that evil."

Neferure snickered, covering her mouth with a small hand.

Before the suddenly frowning prince could respond, Maatkare took charge. "Well, there's certainly no need to rehash the past, is there now? And our schedule is very full back at the Residence, so perhaps we might be shown into the presence of The Liberator's last surviving son, our beloved great uncle?"

Enraged Tao would have had his say on the spot, except that he was restrained with a tight grip on his elbow by Prince Amenhotep, reaching behind his grandmother. Lady Teyit then led the royal trio, pair of tutors and Medjay guards through the villa to her dying husband's bedchamber. Princes Tao and Amenhotep followed.

Count-Prince Siamen began his journey to the Field of Reeds only a few crossings of Re after his audience with Kemet's co-rulers. Whether he had realized who his deathbed royal visitors were, Teyit doubted, as her husband fell into his final deep coma soon after their departure — and he'd not responded to any of what had been said to him by Maatkare Hatshepsut, merely staring blindly into the space above her head.

Those remarks — expressing the Female Horus's condolence that The Liberator's clearly ablest son had been passed over for succession to the Double Crown only because of his lameness — Prince Tao was quick to damn after the royal delegation's departure, as absolutely hypocritically insincere. To be sure had eldest-surviving royal son Siamen actually been Asar Nebpehtyre Ahmes's chosen successor those many years ago, he would only now be dying in the Residence as a very aged Lord of the Two Lands; Hatshepsut and her bastard nephew would be anonymous commoners; and Tao himself would be planning his own coronation. Most importantly the House of Tao would still be ruling Kemet, not the illegitimate so-called House of Djehutymes!

Although invited, the Lord and Mistress of the Two Lands did not attend Prince-Count Siamen's funerary rites. In fact the Coregents and their court had already sailed up The River to the southern capital at Waset well before the seventy days required to prepare the deceased for Eternity had passed.

Many floodings earlier, some decades actually, the default doyen of the House of Tao had prepared himself a Mansion of Eternity in the necropolis of Mennufer, no mean abode, rather a rock-cut arrangement consisting of a vertical shaft and short passageway leading to three squared-off subterranean chambers — as had become the fashion for elites in those years following the Reunification of the Two Lands by The Liberator. Painted-plaster decoration of its antechamber had been completed more recently and depicted the deceased making an offering to his enthroned royal father and mother, as well as seated with his own family before a table heaped with a banquet meant to renew for all time, and at work with his wife in the Field of Reeds, supervising gathering in the flooding harvest of early *Peret*.

The tomb was outfitted just prior to Siamen's funerary rites with furnishings from the Delta estate, as well as personal goods and objects which had been placed in storage for that purpose over the years. His wooden mummiform coffin with gilding had also been prepared well in advance (as had that of Teyit, for her interment at his side, when the time came). In his will Siamen had provided an endowment to ensure that actual food-offerings would be left in perpetuity for him (and Teyit) in the small block-built surface chapel which marked the site of the underground Mansion itself.

Prince-Count Siamen's funeral was a low-key event. Few persons besides the immediate surviving Tao family were in attendance (except for an all-but-forgotten couple of collateral-line ancient aunts, who somehow materialized). Secretly bribed to do so, First Prophet of Ptah Paneb officiated as lector-priest, and Prince Tao performed the Opening of the Mouth ritual — traditionally the reserved responsibility of the deceased's eldest son. Widowed Lady of the House Teyit wept copious genuine tears, and a dozen hired morning-women tore at their hair and tossed dust on themselves, wailing all the while. Amenhotep's toddler son bawled loudly throughout the ceremony as well, although certainly not for his great-grandfather's sake. A tall onlooker with a pointed nose arrived late, stood at the seated group's back, and left early, unremarked by the family or mourners.

(Regrettably for the kas *of Siamen and Teyit, the endowment for their eternal sustenance was exhausted by the time grandson Amenhotep died a very old man early in the reign-Inundations of the third Lord of the Two Lands of the same personal name. During the subsequent reign of the Heretic, their offering chapel itself was dismantled and the stones carried away for recycling. Some time after that, their Mansion for Eternity was discovered by robbers and thoroughly plundered of its contents, their bodily remains generally crushed into dust at the same time. It was not until the first decade of the Second Millennium AD that a team of Japanese archaeologists relocated their final resting place and published its avant-garde wall decorations, thereby resuscitating their identities and giving them some small measure of the millions of years they had sought so long before.)*

FIFTY-FOUR FLOODINGS EARLIER,
NEXT TO LAST INUNDATION OF THE REIGN OF NEBPEHTYRE AHMES

The Liberator entered his personal apartments of the Residence at Waset, closely followed by his sister-spouse, Great Royal Wife and God's Wife of Amen-Re Ahmes Nefertari.They were returning from the funerary rites for their second son and Crown-Prince, Ahmesankh, who had died seventy days earlier while hunting hippopotami in the Delta marshes, violently slain by one of those ponderous spawns of Set. The Heir had been but seventeen floodings at the time and was the third of the seven children of Lord of the Two Lands Nebpehtyre, Son of Re Ahmes and his sibling-wife. The eldest and first Crown-Prince, Ahmesnahkt, had died in his early twenties of a fever only a few floodings earlier, leaving a childless young widow. The Liberator's grief at this sudden loss of a second Crown-Prince was so great that he had refused to consider naming Ahmesankh's replacement as Horus-in-the-Nest until after the youth's interment — the choice being limited to his two surviving sons, Prince Siamen who was fifteen floodings and Prince Amenhotep, only eight.

Ordinarily the appointment of next-in-line Siamen would have been a foregone conclusion. However, the youth had been born with a withered left leg and consequently was a cripple, who now — although fully ambulatory — walked with a very pronounced lurching. Ahmes Nefertari had always despised her offspring's obvious imperfection and, since Ahmesankh's death, had privately lobbied her brother/husband to bypass Siamen in favor of younger Prince Amenhotep — who also happened to be Ahmes Nefertari's favorite of her several children (the youngest of whom, Prince Remes, had died in infancy). The Great Royal Wife's argument against choosing Siamen had been simple enough: her third son's severe physical handicap was incompatible with what the people of Kemet expected in their Living Horus. Even so, The Liberator had tended to favor the young teenager; despite his unfortunate birth-affliction, he was clearly the brightest of the royal brood, and already accomplished in his studies, or so Nebpehtyre had been told. And Lord of the Two Lands was also informed that sniffling little Amenhotep seemed to prefer playing with his sisters' dolls over more suitable boyish amusements. But the fact was that Lord of the Two Lands Nebpehtyre, Son of Re Ahmes most often succumbed, finally, to the wishes of his strong-willed Great Royal Wife, and always had since their own childhood.

The short, still-slender ruler had devested himself of his Double Crown and scepters regalia immediately upon entering the Residence and was now simply attired in a knee-length white kilt and gilded sandals. He crossed his spacious sleeping chamber to an arrangement of elegantly carved wooden armchairs and a low table near the double doors opening onto the loggia and walled garden. Pouring himself wine, he tilted his closely cropped head back and drained the silver goblet, while standing facing away from Ahmes Nefertari. Still wearing the Great Royal Wife's Vulture Cap-Crown with golden modius and two tall embossed sheet-gold feathers, she came up behind her brother-husband and laid a small hennaed palm on his shoulder. He flinched ever so slightly and turned to face her.

"Wine?" he asked, indicating his empty goblet.

She merely nodded affirmatively and seated herself on one of the chairs, without leaning back, hands folded atop her linen-sheathed thighs.

Ahmes placed his goblet on the table, then picked up a silver ewer of Asiatic design and poured his spouse a drink. He handed her the goblet and refilled his own. Returning the wine vessel to the table, he sat in the chair furthest from that of Ahmes Nefertari, his own arms resting on those of the ebony seat with gilded decoration. There was a long silence as Lord of the Two Lands Nebpehtyre stared into the empty space beyond the paired imitation feathers of his sister-wife's crown.

Ahmes Nefertari sipped from her goblet, then finally spoke over its rim. "Well?"

Son of Re Ahmes lowered his blunt chin and made eye contact with her.

"We were just thinking what an excellent Horus-in-the-Nest Living Moon Born was. He'd've made a fearless Mighty Bull."

"Fearless and *foolish*." The Great Royal Wife sipped more wine. "Fearless enough to go hunting river horses, perhaps, but also foolish to do so, that recklessness resulting in his being crushed in the pegged jaws of one of those Set monsters. It's small wonder enough of him could be recovered to sufficiently restore for his eternal existence!"

Again, silence, until Ahmes Nefertari asked again, "Well?"

"What?"

"Which of our two remaining sons have you decided on to fill the empty Nest?"

"Both have their shortcomings."

The Great Royal Wife laughed. "Prince Son of Amen, to be sure, if you were referring to his withered limb!"

The Liberator stood and began pacing. "He is far the more capable, we believe. A sound mind, if a game leg. Amen is Pleased is a more Daughter-of-Our-Body than youngest son, so we are told by our spies in the Harim. The prince certainly was not cut from the same tough cloth as his late elder brother — or Son of Amen, for that matter."

"He is young still. But a boy. All little boys play with dolls. You certainly did, we remember."

"Not when I was eight floodings old!" Ahmes took a deep swallow of wine and retraced his steps.

" Amen is Pleased shall put aside the dolls once he has left the Harim for the apartments of Horus-in-the-Nest and isn't bound to play his sisters' games." The Great Royal Wife drained her goblet, returned it to the table and continued, "It simply isn't feasible, Brother, that the next Living Horus would go hobbling about in public, making a mockery of the sacred rituals by his imperfect presence. Living gods do not *hobble*, simple as that."

Nebpehtyre Ahmes returned to the table, placed his empty goblet there and, still standing, faced his sister and wife, arms folded across his narrow bare chest.

"So, as usual Moon Born, Beautiful Companion you've made up our mind for us. Amen-Re and the Holy Ones doubtless will look more favorably on a presently little sissy Horus-in-the-Nest than on a forever crippled one. Youngest Son-of-Our-Body is the new Heir, then. Shall we send for the two princes now, so they'll be the first to hear the good and bad news?"

INUNDATION 3, COREGENCY OF MAATKARE/MENKHEPERRE AGAIN
TWO CROSSINGS OF RE AFTER THE INTERMENT
OF PRINCE-COUNT SIAMEN
STABLE OF THE DELTA COUNTRY ESTATE OF THE TAOS

Young Prince Amenhotep adjusted the feedbag of his chariot horse and patted the animal's forehead. It snorted, as did its harness mate in the next stall. Sensing he was not alone in the dim stable, the young man quickly turned and confronted Prince Tao standing only a few cubits away.

"You gave me a start, father!"

"You've been gone all day, left before dawn Cook Mai reported, and it's now nearing time for the Barque of Lord Re to sail behind the horizon," the older man stated matter of factly. "Your wife has been worried for your safety."

"I was driving in the desert. Old Mai fixed me lunch, as I asked her to last evening. I needed to get away, to mourn Grandfather by myself, is all. He used to take me driving out there when I was a boy, you'll remember."

"You should have left word as to your intention. If you'd been thrown from your chariot and cracked your skull, no one would've known and you'd've been a hyenas' banquet this night."

"I was thinking of death, Father, but not of dying myself. I'm truly sorry. It was stupid of me, I can see now."

"Are you finished here?"

"Yes, I think so. No, I am."

"Then come with me, Amen is Pleased," said Prince Tao as he turned away and began walking across straw to the stable entrance. Looking back, he added, "I want you to stroll with me in the gardens, where we can speak without any chance of being overheard."

A few minutes later father and son were standing shoulder to shoulder at the edge of the estate's large fish pond, their reflections extending across the coppery still surface towards a large cluster of water-lily pads.

"I was seething with anger, you must know, and would have confronted our illegitimate ruler face-to-face regarding her outrageous blasphemy against Maat, had you not secretly grabbed my elbow that afternoon months ago, when she, the bastard's bastard and the bogus God's Wife — accompanied by their tutor toadies — came to gloat over your grandfather on his deathbed. Cousin Noblest Woman's audacity exceeds even that of my villainous grandmother, The Liberator's manipulative sister-wife!"

"She did seem to speak with the forked tongue of Wadjet when she lamented that Prince-Count Son of Amen had been bypassed for the Double Crown solely because of his lameness." Amenhotep tossed a pebble into the water, obliterating their mirror images, then continued, "But the usurper was *invited* here by Grandmother Tiyet, wisely or not. The surprise is that the bitch came at all, with her husband's bastard and her own brat in tow — not to mention the stepped-up Great Steward of Amen-Re himself, and the rather handsome other one, whose name I've conveniently forgotten. I suppose that we should be relieved that at least she had the decency to miss Grandfather's funeral itself — though I suppose she wouldn't have brought the court back down river from Waset, simply in order to have attended. And this was the second week of the Opet, in any case, at which the two false Horuses officiated."

Prince Tao turned away from the pond and began walking across the clipped lawn. Amenhotep was quickly at his side again.

"The question is, Son, whether we last heirs of the House of Tao, bloodline grandson and great-grandson of The Liberator himself, mutely accept the corrupted status-quo and continue living our uneventful, comfortable country lives; or whether we take the brave initiative to restore our pure Tao legitimacy to the Horus Throne and thereby return the Two Lands to *Maat*, to how things *should* be rather than how they now are — and, doing so, fulfill our beloved Prince-Count Son of Amen's longtime dream."

"It would seem that we, you and I, are, well, rather powerless to affect any change, Father. We don't even have positions at court, where we might, at least, cultivate a Taoist faction."

"True, of course. But I've a plan which makes that not necessary. Now, here's what I have in mind...."

* * *

8

Royal Nurse In Sitre sat off to the side, sipping wine, while one of the Residence handmaidens finished winding Mistress of the Two Lands Maatkare's long locks into a tall coil atop her head, held in place by intertwined red-linen ribbons. Next, another serving girl lowered the bulbous blue-leather helmet-crown over the cone of hair and carefully adjusted the *Khepresh*'s gold brow-band on the ruler's broad forehead, making certain that the rearing golden cobra was perfectly centered. This done, she stood back and a third maiden handed Maatkare Hatshepsut a highly polished silver mirror with an inlaid-gold handle depicting the cow-eared goddess Hathor. Sitting rigidly upright in her gilded armchair, the Female Horus regarded her reflection only briefly, handing the mirror back to its presenter. She turned her head slowly towards Nurse In Sitre.

"We should probably be relieved, Fish, that the Double Crown isn't required for this processional event. But there will be a stiff neck again this evening, in any case." Hatshepsut snapped her slender fingers, the signal for wine.

Yet a fourth young woman stepped forward with a silver tray bearing a chalice in the form of an open water-lily. She handed it to Her Majesty, who immediately sipped the sweet-sour beverage and returned the calcite vessel to the tray. The second maid approached again, holding out a bead collar for Hatshepsut's approval. The royal head nodded, ever so slightly, and the accessory was held in place, then draped over the Female Horus's shoulders. The hairdresser hooked its end-finials together, centering the counterweight between the ruler's shoulder blades. The mirror was offered again and the reflection checked. Hatshepsut briefly raised hennaed finger-tips to the gold and carnelian tube beads, then handed the mirror back.

Her unique Mistress of the Two Lands attire was complete. The linen tunic covering her slender torso was sheer enough to hint at the bare flesh beneath, but not actually reveal her small breasts. A pleated man's kilt reaching to the knees was fronted by a heavily starched triangular linen apron secured by an inlaid-gold belt. Suspended from this was a narrow, jointed sporran-apron, also gold with inlays and framed at its bottom sides by paired rearing golden cobras. Practical leather sandals with gilt detailing shod the royal feet.

"Well, Our Person is ready it seems," stated Maatkare Hatshepsut, matter of factly. "Let us go then, Fish, and rendezvous with young Hawk Beak at the appointed place. Presumably he's already there and awaiting us."

But as both Her Majesty and the elderly In Sitre rose from their seats, there was a slight commotion in the Female Horus's antechamber. All the women looked towards the closed double doors separating that space from her bedchamber. In moments these were pulled wide and two armed Medjays entered, then stepped to each side of the opened portal, at attention. In moments the nine-floodings-old Coregent Lord of the Two Lands Menkheperre, Son of Re Djehutymes, strode in with an air of confidence. He was dressed almost identically to Her Majesty, except his brown torso was bare, the triangular apron seemed a bit too large, and he carried his *Khepresh* helmet-crown under one arm, balanced against his narrow hip. His own head was covered with a tight-fitting linen skull-cap, concealing his doubtlessly unbraided, rearranged Horus Sidelock. His Majesty stopped a couple of paces into his aunt's bedchamber, and immediately the figure of his court-attired tutor, handsome young King's Scribe Senimen, was framed by the doorway. Maatkare Hatshepsut smiled: both at the pompous attitude of little Hawk Beak and at seeing her secret lover again, so soon. The boy-king bowed slightly, but stiffly, towards his coruler. He clearly enjoyed the dress-up aspect of his role. The serving women bowed towards him, Nurse In Sitre merely nodding her head.

"Your Majesty," he addressed his Coregent, chin jutting.

Maatkare Hatshepsut merely nodded towards him. "And *Your* Majesty. You take Our Person by surprise. We were expecting to meet you at the assembling point, just inside the main entrance to the Residence, for our collective transfer by carrying chairs to the Mansion of Lord Hidden One, Amen-Re."

The youth looked up and at his stepmother-aunt. "We've been waiting exactly there for you for some long time, Your Majesty. We — ourself and our Brother of Amen — finally were concerned for you and so came directly here to learn the cause of your delay."

"Well, our sincere apology, Your Majesty," Her Majesty responded. "We did not realize that our preparations had taken so much time as to make you wait on Our Person more than is usual. But we are all ready now, so let us proceed to the Hidden One's abode and get this parading underway."

Maatkare Hatshepsut moved to the doorway, followed by the Royal Nurse. The boy-king stepped aside to let the Coregent pass, but immediately inserted himself between her and the old woman, who stopped in her tracks. King's Scribe Senimen moved to one side, so that the two rulers could pass into the antechamber, one leading, the other following. When Nurse In came up to the portal, Senimen offered the heavy-set senior his forearm for support. She smiled at him from within the large wig framing her face, and winked. Not surprisingly, she did know of his frequent late-night visits to the very space they were now exiting. But her lips were as sealed as those of a royal lion-effigy.

A SHORT WHILE LATER, IPET ISUT, THE MANSION OF AMEN-RE

The wide, high cedar-wood double doors sheathed in gilded bronze slowly swung open, each panel shoved at arms' length by three acolyte priests, and the vanguard of the Opet processional was revealed in place, waiting to begin moving into the bright noon-hour light of Lord Re. At the very front, side by side, were two of the three leading civil officials of the Two Lands: Great Steward of the Estates of Amen-Re Senenmut and Vizier of the South of Kemet Amenemopet. The two men, one tall, the other somewhat shorter, dressed in full finery (the vizier in his billowing ankle-length garment) slowly advanced in unison through the newly completed side portal of the god's mansion and onto the smooth paving stones of the long processional way leading to the Mansion of Lady Mut, Mother Goddess and heavenly consort of Lord Amen-Re. Lining both sides of the wide avenue immediately beyond the portal were two score of white-kilted soldier-drummers, who fell into rank and file behind the bureaucrats and immediately began beating a cadence on the tubular tambours they each carried on a strap slung across their bare torsos. As soon as the musicians had advanced enough, a contingent of spear-and-shield-bearing soldiers stepped in measured unison onto the avenue from both of its perimeters and followed in formation.

An interval of space opened and then a dozen acolyte priests with shaved heads and long kilts emerged through the portal, each swinging smoking censers. They were followed several long moments later by two other acolytes, leading between them on a pair of gold leashes a very large black ram, its massive curling horns and four hooves fully gilded, an embroidered and bead-encrusted blanket across its back, reaching nearly to the ground on both sides. A gold modius was affixed to the crown of the snorting beast's head, from which rose a tall pair of sheet-gold feathers, quivering with the wearer's plodding movement. This was the sacred animal of the Hidden One, and Amen-Re's sometime manifestation. It seemed resigned to this parading, having done it dozens of times before.

Amen-Re's ram had advanced several dozen cubits along the avenue before the god's chief-priests walked through the tall portal, with First Prophet Hapusenub a few steps in the lead, his three colleagues side by side behind him. All four clerics carried their batons and staves of high office, wore their priestly white finery and were wigless, their shaved heads gleaming in the bright sun as if oiled — which they doubtless were. After another short interval, the prophets were followed by a rank and file of *wab* and lector priests, some two dozen in number. Each wore a white-linen sash tied around their bald heads. Then four more acolytes came through the portal, swinging smoking censers.

In several moments, that day's procession principals emerged from the portal's shadow into the bright light of Lord Re: side by side, one half a head taller than the other, were Mistress and Lord of the Two Lands, Maatkare Hatshepsut and Menkheperre Djehutymes, the Double Living Horuses. The boy-king now wore his *Khepresh* helmet (which had been scaled to fit him properly) and the joint-rulers each bore a long gilded staff and carried at arm's length along their sides the chisel-shaped *Kherp* scepter, gripping in the same hand a gilded *ankh* device. Menkheperre's regalia were all slightly smaller than Maatkare's, in other words were boy-sized. The Female Horus counted a whispered "one, two, three, four," and the royal pair stepped forward in unison, trailing the censering acolyte priests by some twenty cubits. A dozen Medjay royal guards stepped onto each side of the avenue as the rulers passed and moved forward in two parallel files, flanking them at a short distance.

After another brief interval, drumming could be heard again, coming from within the god's mansion. Then the Hidden One himself appeared — or rather his gold-plated barque, on which he rode, unseen within the tall golden shrine at midship, this draped in an ample shroud of bright-red linen. The barque itself was borne on the shoulders of two-dozen shaved junior priests in short white kilts, walking in practiced unison under their heavy burden.

Once the god in his model river-vessel had moved a ways down the pavement, the additional drummers emerged into the sunlight, trailed by a dozen or more half-naked female acrobatic dancers, who moved along with a wild abandon of cartwheels, hand-flips and swinging long hair. Immediately behind them followed a single row of shaved-headed temple-women shaking sistra in tinkling accompaniment to the drumming cadence. And in moments the God's Wife of Amen and Divine Hand advanced through the portal, the last of the Opet Procession's chief participants.

This was seventeen-floodings-old King's Daughter, King's Sister Neferure, successor to her mother, Hatshepsut, in the inherited sacerdotal role. The slender-hipped teenager was attired in a simple, tight-fitting low-cut linen sheath which exposed her small breasts beneath a gold-bead collar; and tied around her waist was a tightly braided narrow red-linen sash-girdle, emblem of her God's Wife status. A similar narrow band encircled her close-cropped head. She carried, clasped in each hand, the God's Wife's mace at arm's length by her side and her wedge-shaped gilded scepter — the latter resting on one narrow bare shoulder — as well as a golden *ankh* emblem pendant from the same hand as the mace. As was always the case with the God's Wife in public, she walked barefooted. Doubtless the fresh paving stones were quite uncomfortably warm at this time of day, with the princess anxious to reach the first barque station midway along the route to the really not-so-far-distant Mansion of Lady Mut.

En Route to the Southern Harem

Each gripping a wine goblet, Maatkare and Menkheperre were seated side by side on portable thrones centered under the temporary canopy which had been erected adjacent to the God's Barque Station that stood alongside the new processional way, within sight of the dwelling of the Hidden One's divine spouse. Although the coregents were enjoying the refreshment, the real purpose of the halt was to give the twenty-four bearers of the god's boat-borne shrine a deserved brief rest. The divine vessel sat shaded on a stone pedestal in the middle of the stone-built way-station, the priestly porters squatting around the structure's exterior perimeters.

Murmuring among themselves, the Great Steward of Amen-Re, Vizier of the South of Kemet and the four prophets of the Hidden One were likewise taking advantage of the canopy's shade. The rest of the procession participants, however, were simply stopped in place, still under the midday sun. The God's Wife had, of course, left her place in line, going forward to join the other principals; and she was now seated on a stool in their midst, also sipping wine.

Suddenly His Majesty announced, "Our Person has to piss."

He unceremoniously handed his goblet to Maatkare and stood up from his smaller-than-hers throne. The group of dignitaries parted down the middle, so the boy-king could move to the back of the canopy, where a cloth-paneled booth was located. He pushed aside the length of linen that covered the entrance and disappeared inside.

The murmuring resumed, but the opened space remained. In less than half a minute, the booth's door flap was pushed aside again and Menkheperre emerged, adjusting his sporran apron.

"Don't you think they've rested enough? he asked, returning to his seat.

LATER, THE MANSION OF LADY MUT

From his hidden vantage high atop the left wing of the pylon gate fronting the Mansion of Lady Mut, the kneeling archer watched the slow approach of the Opet procession down the recently finished paved avenue that led from the distant Mansion of Amen-Re. While the populace of Waset turned out in force to watch the divine parade each year, the chief concentration of cheering onlookers was always along the vast stretch of avenue between the dwelling of the Mother Goddess and the Opet, or Southern Harim, itself, with the crowds greatest in the immediate vicinities of the two divine mansions and the procession's riverside destination. Thus, looking down, it was apparent to the unseen bowman that people were especially massed on each side of the processional way closest to the pylon towers. Somewhere in that crowd, on which side of the avenue he didn't know, was his single cohort, another disgruntled discharged soldier of the Two Lands. Together, today, they would play their recruited roles in returning Kemet to the right order of *Maat*. His own part would be the greater one, however.

After several long minutes, the procession's vanguard neared the Mansion of Mut. The archer didn't recognize the two men in the lead, but supposed the short one was a vizier, judging from his billowing long gown. They were immediately followed by a company of military drummers, who set the cadence for the walkers; and behind them was another company of armed soldiers. The two men passed out of the archer's sightline, as they went through the opened gateway. The drummers did not follow, however, but divided into two files and moved to the perimeters of the avenue, turning about face shoulder to shoulder, and continuing their percussion. The soldiers did not enter the goddess's abode either, but fell into two files that marched through the parted crowd, heading no doubt to the back of the divine precinct, where another, smaller gateway beyond the sacred lake opened onto the continuation of the processional avenue that led the rest of the distance to the Southern Harim.

Now a large gaudily bedecked black ram, being guided by two priest-types, drew near the pylon. The archer notched an arrow in place on his Asiatic composite bow, as the awaited moment was almost upon him.

He again scanned the flanking crowds closest to the gateway, but could not spot his ally. Several cubits behind the ram walked four white-clothed men with shiny bald heads, priests to be sure. And close after them came his easily recognizable targets that day. He selected a spot on the narrow bare chest of the shorter of the two individuals, whom he'd been instructed to strike first.

Just as the ram and its attendants were about to pass out of the archer's view, the large animal suddenly lurched and then fell onto the knees of its forelegs, before toppling sideways onto the pavement. His dagger-wielding co-conspirator's aim had been as true as he'd promised it would be! A collective gasp of disbelief went up from the paired crowds, the front ranks surging forward some, and the four shiny-headed men broke into a run towards the downed ram. Most of the drumming ceased.

Almost at the same moment, a cry could be heard further up the procession and everyone stopped in their tracks. A petitioner had stepped onto the avenue and approached the god's barque, which had come to an abrupt halt. While the four priests knelt helplessly around the prostrate animal, its legs twitching, the archer's two targets turned around to stare back towards the no-longer-moving portable shrine of Lord Hidden One a ways off. He stood fully upright, looked down the arrow shaft, to the now-even-easier mark he sought, pulled the bowstring taut and let fly.

Just Moments Before

Lord of the Two Lands Menkheperre leaned towards his Coregent and asked, "What's happening, Aunt? Why is the drumming stopped? Is something wrong? What are we supposed to be doing?"

Before Maatkare Hatshepsut could respond, the boy-king tried to rub his beaky nose with the back of the hand holding his long staff, and he let go of the gilded rod in the effort, so that it fell with a clank to the pavement. Menkheperre dipped quickly to retrieve his regalia and suddenly a thin shaft embedded the upper back of his *Khepresh* helmet with a loud thunk, the sudden force throwing him off balance and forward, so that his bare knees struck the paving stones of the processional way.

Instantaneously, instinctively, Mistress of the Two Lands shrieked "Hawk Beak!" and bent sideways towards her crouching Coregent, and as she did so, an arrow grazed her left shoulder, then smacked into the avenue surface beyond and shattered. She also dropped to her knees, but with blood spurting. In moments the two files of Residence Medjays had rushed forward from their sidelines positions and they surrounded the pair of downed royal figures with a defensive ring of very tall humanity.

At a quiet command from the priest in charge, the barque bearers carefully lowered the god's conveyance to the ground. All acrobatic dancing and sistrum shaking had ceased, and the barefooted Neferure hiked her sheath and came dashing forward, mace and scepter unceremoniously dropped where the God's Wife had stopped. Amen-Re's four prophets likewise abandoned the dying sacred ram and hurried, quickly as their collective dignities allowed, to add to the gathering crowd. Finally, Great Steward of Amen-Re Senenmut and Vizier of the South of Kemet Amenemopet reemerged through the Mut pylon gate and, forgetting their dignities, sprinted to the sizeable knot of persons in the center of the processional way.

All the while two would-be assassins made their getaways, a bow and quiver of arrows abandoned on the narrow roof of the Mut pylon tower, only to be discovered there some while after the fact.

A FEW HOURS LATER, THE RESIDENCE

Seated on her gilded throne in the ruler's private audience chamber, shoulder elaborately bandaged, Maatkare Hatshepsut was holding court informally. On a similar-though-smaller throne alongside the Female Horus hunched her coregent, the boy Son of Re, young Djehutymes. Both rulers were divested of their ceremonial attire: Her Majesty wore her natural hair hanging loose to her shoulders, and His Majesty's rebraided sidelock was all that adorned his shaved head. She wore only a simple sheath and he a plain kilt; both were barefooted.

Seated in chairs arranged informally before the throne dais were the members of the joint-rulers' High Council, which included, of course, among several others, Great Steward Senenmut, Vizier Amenemopet and First Prophet Hapusenub. King's Scribe Senimen sat off to one side, cross-legged on the floor, behind a low table on which a sheet of papyrus was spread, his writing kit at hand. Royal Nurse In Sitre and His Majesty's nurse, Itbet, were perched on stools well behind the dais, should their services be required for any reason. God's Wife Neferure was not present; her mother had determined she would have nothing useful to contribute to the topic to be discussed, and was, in any case, still so distressed about the day's events that she had taken to her bed.

"Well, then," Hatshepsut spoke first, as was expected, "we are indeed pleased to be able to confer with you this early evening, notables. What occurred today was extraordinary, perhaps almost unique in the annals of the Two Lands. Count Senenmut," she nodded towards him in the front row of seats, "informs us that his quick search in the archives showed that — while there were individual failed efforts to strike down two or three of the hated Foreign Rulers, finally ousted from the Northern

Black Land by our illustrious ancestor Asar Strength of Re, The Liberator — there apparently has not been an act such as this afternoon's against a legitimate Living Horus since the first Amen at the Head, Satisfied Heart of Re many, many generations ago.

"That our Coregent," she gestured to him, "and Our Person escaped death at the hand of an assassin is nothing short of a miracle, one determined by Lord Hidden One himself almost certainly. Had not a petitioner of the god caused us both to turn around, we would have been facing the assassin when he struck. It might be said that Son of Re Born of Djehuty was saved by his nose," she smiled, "since, if he had not suddenly rubbed it and doing so dropped his staff, the assassin's arrow would have found its mark in His Majesty's exposed back. And had we not bent to him impulsively when the shaft imbedded his *Khepresh*, our own back would have taken the second arrow meant for us, which only grazed our shoulder consequently." She touched the bandage gingerly.

"What is unknown is whether this was the act of a lone madman — well, *two* madmen, as the slayer of the Sacred Ram was surely in league with the bowman — or whether it was a coordinated assault on the Horus Throne itself, in the persons of its current occupants. Are there opinions on that?"

After an awkward silence, Senenmut rose and spoke. "Your Majesties, since the would-be assassins made good their escapes, and so can't be held to account as to their purposes or allies, whatever might be offered here is just that, opinion, and...

"So what is *your* opinion, Brother of Mut," Hatshepsut interrupted. "We especially value your opinions, as they are most often the correct ones." She smiled.

Senenmut continued, "Well, it seems highly improbable — not impossible, but improbable — that the pair who stuck together this afternoon were madmen. Madmen do not work in pairs and act with coordination. Thus, it's likely that they were merely the failed agents of another, or others, who did have distinct motives for undertaking such a heinous act as to slay a living god...that is, *gods*."

"*Our* opinion, exactly, Brother of Mut," responded the Female Horus. "And have you an *opinion* as to who that other or others with 'motives' might be?"

"Well, Your Majesties, it need only be asked what would have been the consequence if the bowman had found his marks and the resulting wounds would have been fatal. Especially, if I may be wholly candid, had Lord of the Two Lands Lasting Manifestation of Re been, well, slain. To state the obvious, due to his tender age, His Majesty has not yet produced an heir of his body and the Horus Nest consequently is empty."

"Well, that is not exactly so, Brother of Mut," Hatshepsut interrupted. "There is, of course, God's Wife Beauty of Re. If one Female Horus, why not two?"

"Absolutely unprecedented!" asserted First Prophet Hapusenub.

"We digress," continued Senenmut. "Hopefully Her Majesty's question will never have to be answered. It is obvious that the vile assassin meant to slay both Lasting Manifestation of Re and True Soul of Re one after the other, which had he succeeded would have left the Two Lands without either Lord or Mistress. Neither does Her Highness King's Sister, God's Wife Beauty of Re have offspring, thus the currently reigning House Born of Djehuty would be defunct, effectively no more.

"So what then would be the obvious solution to reoccupying the empty Horus Throne? To return to the House of Tao, of course, which does have plenty of viable males, starting with Prince Tao himself, direct descendent of The Liberator, followed by a son of his body, Prince Amen is Pleased, who, I understand, has two sons of his own, and is young enough to produce another or even several others, as well. Thus, the persons who would most benefit from the sudden, simultaneous deaths of the present Living Horuses are the Taos. Princes Tao and Amen is Pleased are Your Majesties best *circumstantial* candidates for today's villainy. That, at least, is my *opinion*."

Senenmut nodded his head towards the Coregents and sat down.

Again an awkward silence followed, finally broken by Hatshepsut, again.

"So, are there other opinions? Or has our Great Steward of the Estates of Amen-Re spoken the truth, as most always?"

"What is 'circumstantial'" asked young Son of Re Djehutymes, breaking his own silence. "And are we talking about those cousins we visited in the country, to see the very old man who was nearly dead?"

"Yes, Born of Djehuty, those people," replied Hatshepsut. Looking at Senenmut, she asked, "Could you explain the word to His Majesty, Great Steward? And please, keep your seat and be brief in your response."

"Well, My Lord, the word 'circumstantial' means what appears to be true but without factual — that is, *actual* — evidence or proof of it. Even if something *seems* so, it may not *be* so. One should not be judged guilty simply because one *ought* to be guilty. That would go against Maat. Do you understand?"

Menkheperre shrugged his narrow shoulders. "I suppose. So, these evil cousins *might* be guilty, but there's no *proof* that they tried to kill us is what you've been saying?"

"Yes, My Lord."

"Too bad the bowman got away. And the one who killed the Sacred Ram. We're sure the god is very angry about that."

"Indeed!" Offered First Prophet Hapusenub.

"Why don't we bring our cousins here to Waset and just ask them if they were the ones who tried to have us killed?" The young Son of Re questioned, simply enough. "If they say 'yes,' we can find them guilty then. If they say 'no,' they won't be, and that's it, and someone else is the villain, and we may never know who."

"Thank you for your innocent wisdom, Born of Djehuty," replied Hatshepsut, patronizingly patting her Coregent's arm. "But since the court shall be returning north once the Opet is concluded — and the processional will have to be redone, are we not right about that, First Prophet? — we shall invite our country cousins, Tao and Amen is Pleased, to come visit Our Persons at the Mennufer Residence, to protest either innocence or guilt — as if there is any question which it will be. Personally, we would rather have both arrested as soon as an order to do so might reach the northern capital, and them perched on stakes before Re sails west that very same day!"

Mistress of the Two Lands Maatkare stood, once more lightly touching fingertips to her bandaging. "So that, Our Person believes, concludes this evening's business, notables." She stepped from the dais and quickly left the audience chamber, followed by shuffling Nurse In Sitre and striding King's Scribe Senimen, rolled papyrus under one arm.

Fourteen Crossings of Re Later, Delta Estate of the Taos

Prince Amenhotep was tossing bits of bread to fish in one of the large water-lily ponds on the family estate, when his father came striding into that part of the gardens. The prince's youngest son, Ahmes, age four floodings, squatted naked at the water's edge, trying unsuccessfully to touch the colorful darting swimmers with a thin, long stick.

"There you are, Amen is Pleased!" Prince Tao called out as he approached. "Bastet said I would find you here."

"Greetings, Father. How were things in Mennufer? Any news?"

Arms wide, little Ahmes went running to his grandfather, who picked the boy up.

"Only bad, I'm afraid. The royal fleet returned from Waset just yesterday, bearing the court and, it grieves me to say, the False Horuses, too, both of them. And in good health, apparently. It seems we failed.

"I wasn't able to get much information at the docks, speaking to just three or four of the royal sailors, since I didn't want to be obvious in my curiosity. There *was* an attack during the Opet processional, as planned, but the Hidden One intervened — or so one sailor claimed — and only the Sacred Ram met its fate. Neither of the Horuses were seriously injured, the bastard's bastard not at all, in fact, and the usurper only a grazing flesh wound on her shoulder.

"The good news is that the assailants both escaped, in the confusion, and, being from the North, neither was identifiable by those Wasetans who noticed them. Several days after the incident, two crocodile-mutilated stabbed male bodies were found together on The River's bank just south of Waset — as we arranged, success or failure. Thus, we shall never be implicated through tortured confessions." He put his grandson on the ground and Ahmes ran back to the pond and his poke-the-fish game.

"Surely, Father, we can't suppose that we are above suspicion. Were I Noblest Woman — gods forbid! — the Taos would be the *only* obvious instigators of any attempt on my life and the boy-king's. Perhaps we should be booking passage to Kheftiu this very day, Father!"

"We discussed the very real chance of failure, Amen is Pleased." Tao took the loaf from his son and tore off a small piece, tossing it onto the pond's surface. "Until such time as we are accused, we shall do nothing that suggests we even have any awareness of what happened in Waset. And, of course, should there be a charge of complicity with the assassins, then we plead our complete innocence. As blood descendents of The Liberator, our sworn word counts a great deal, believe me. We are the Taos, after all, not common criminals." He tossed another small piece of bread and handed the loaf back to Amenhotep.

"But criminals, nonetheless, father, however lofty our motives."

Later that day a royal messenger arrived at the estate, with a written command from the Two Horuses that Tao and his son appear at the Residence in Mennufer in two crossings of Lord Re, for an audience with the Coregents. They were instructed to bring with them Amenhotep's wife and two sons. Which did not bode well, to be sure.

Twenty-one Crossings of Re Later, the Docks, Mennufer

Leaning on the railing at midship, Tao watched as Khefti sailors carried export cargo aboard the foreign-looking, sea-going sailing vessel. The plain cedar-wood chest on one of the naked shoulders contained some clothes and a few other earthly possessions that he — until recently a prince of Kemet and master of the Two Lands' former ruling house — was being permitted to take into exile. When he arrived at Kheftiu fourteen crossings of Re from now, he would effectively be an expatriate pauper. But he still had his gold signet ring, an heirloom from his father, with the bezel name-ovals of his grandfather, Asar Nebpehtyre Ahmes, The Liberator. Perhaps it would gain him an audience with the ruler of that island nation in the Great Green, and thus possibly some servile position at the legendary Court of Minos. His revered grandfather, after all, had forged very good relations between the reunited Two Lands and the short, slender brown people who wore outlandish costumes that never failed to greatly amuse the citizens of Kemet — relations which continued to the present day. Clearly the Khefti were indifferent as to who actually sat on the Horus Throne — or exactly how many so-called " Living Gods" shared it at one time.

That fatal confrontation not so long before, between himself, his son and the Double False Horuses, had obviously not transpired in Tao's favor. When he, Prince Amenhotep, Bastet and the boys arrived at the Mennufer Residence as commanded, they were taken by the Kings' Chamberlain — with a Medjay escort — directly to the informal audience chamber of Mistress of the Two Lands Maatkare. She and the boy-king Coregent were seated side by side on the throne dais, attired in formal regalia, the White Crown on her head, the Red Crown on his. Behind the two rulers, also on the dais, were the Great Steward, Vizier of the North and First Prophet of Ptah. Off to one side, documenting the proceedings was the King's Scribe. The Great Steward acted as master of ceremonies and initially did all of the talking — which had to be over the wails of little Ahmes, until his mother succeeded in quieting him.

The pompous Great Steward informed the Taos of what they, of course, already knew (Amenhotep had told Bastet of the attack on the Coregents at Waset), but pretended was news to them. He went on to say that the would-be assassins had made good their escape, but that two unrecognizable murdered male bodies — badly chewed on by sons of Sobek — were later recovered, which were presumed to be the villains, dispatched (prior to their crocodile encounter) to ensure their silence — this arranged by the person or persons who had recruited the pair for the unholy business of regicide.

The long-winded bureaucrat then waxed philosophical about who or whom would have most benefited had the double assassinations succeeded. He finally got to the point that this would have been none other than the Taos, father and son, cousins of the Coregents and in the direct bloodline of Asar Nebpehtyre Ahmes, The Liberator. However reluctantly, it had therefore been concluded by the Two Living Horuses that their own relatives had attempted to have them sent prematurely flying off to the stars, so that one of those blood kin — most probably Prince Tao, being the senior — would be the obvious next wearer of the Double

Crown of Kemet, the redundant House of Tao thereby fully restored.

His recitation concluded, the Great Steward had directed Tao to respond to the royal charge that he and Amenhotep had plotted to murder together the Mistress and Lord of the Two Lands. And the prince had of course expressed shocked disbelief that his beloved cousins would even dream that he and his son would want to strike them down to further personal ambitions. Such an act would have been against *Maat*, would have violated the very order of the universe, he had protested, even raising his voice.

At that point Maatkare Hatshepsut had interrupted, reminding Tao that his deceased father, Asar Prince-Count Siamen, had repeatedly made the case that one of the surviving Tao line — himself or, better, his son, Prince Tao — should be named as "standby" Horus-in-the-Nest, inasmuch as Asar Akheperenre and Menkheperre had both ascended the throne in their minority. And lest he forget, she continued, he, Tao, had personally made the same argument to herself as Regent: that Prince Amenhotep should be Horus-in-the-Nest until Menkheperre produced an heir of his body. Since those arguments had failed to persuade, she'd concluded, it was obvious that, once their doyen was no more, the surviving Taos had decided to finally take the matter of Horus Throne succession into their own hands.

The prince had attempted to protest his and his son's innocence of any wrong-doing, but the Great Steward had cut him short, announcing that Their Majesties had already made an irreversible decision regarding the fate of the adult Tao males. They were both believed to be very much guilty of treason by way of attempted regicide, a capital crime requiring impalement. However, because their guilt could not be proven absolutely, through witnesses or damning evidence, the Mistress and Lord of the Two Lands had decided mercifully to spare their cousins' lives.

But the consequence was that Tao would be stripped of his title as prince and immediately go into exile to a destination of his choice, never again to return to the Two Lands. Amenhotep would likewise be titleless for the rest of his days, which he would spend in guarded confinement on the Tao estates, in the company of his grandmother, wife and sons, the latter permitted to inherit the property on his death. Their Majesties, said the Great Steward, were being so generous out of deep regard for The Liberator and familial love of their cousins.

With that Tao had been permitted to emotionally embrace his family one last time, before being led away by Medjay guards, to temporary incarceration in the Residence until the details of his deportation could be arranged.

From his vantage on board the Kheftian vessel, Tao could see the distant tall figure of the Great Steward standing on the wharf in conversation with the ship's captain, and beyond them, at attention, the four Medjay policemen who had accompanied him and the pompous bureaucrat to the riverfront from the Residence, and seen him delivered on board. Angry though he was, of course, the former prince had finally resigned himself to his uncertain future. Although he had failed in his desire to restore the Two Lands to *Maat*, by attempting to right the present wrong-order-of-things — because the Lord Hidden One had not come to his aid, perhaps even had confounded him (or at least his ill-fated agents) — Tao supposed he should be thankful that he still had his own life, as did his son, and that his young grandsons would not spend their lives as paupers, begging on the streets of Mennufer.

In time all the cargo had been loaded, the gangplank was taken on board, and the wiry Khefti sailors were bending their bare backs over the oars that moved the sailing ship into the River's current, headed to the Great Green. As the vessel slowly pulled away from the dock, the small figure of the Great Steward raised his arm and waved. To his own surprise, Tao realized he was waving back.

Sixteen Kheftian Years Later, Palace of the Minos, Kheftiu

Bent over the game board, Taotios contemplated his next move against his fourteen-year-old son, Ahmesti. The clean-shaven older man was attired in a brightly patterned short, sleeveless tunic befitting his years and wore his receding gray hair long, hanging down his back, in the Kheftian fashion. The teenager, his thick raven hair also very long, was bare to his slender waist, which was wrapped around with the elaborate, colorful short kilt that all younger Khefti males affected. He was very good at this game, and leaned back, arms folded across his nut-brown chest, to smile at his father's intensity at trying to decide which game piece of his to move next. The two sat on benches opposite one another at a stone pedestal-table, on the low-walled balcony of their comfortable mural-decorated airy apartments in the royal palace, Knossos.

Taotios was, of course, the former Prince Tao of the royal house of Kemet, a land that worshipped animal-headed gods far off across the Great Green. He had arrived at Kheftiu some sixteen years earlier, an exile banished from his homeland by the female "king" who wrongfully co-occupied the so-called Horus Throne, sharing same with her stepson/nephew, the presumably legitimate ruler of Kemet, but then still a young child. These two were Tao's blood relatives, whom he'd been accused (rightfully) of attempting to have murdered. There had been no actual proof of his presumed guilt, so he'd escaped impalement and instead had been sent forever away from the Black Land (as Kemet was called), having been allowed to choose Kheftiu as his destination.

Being a clever individual, who had managed to master some of the Kheftian tongue during the lengthy sea voyage to the island nation, Taos had soon enough charmed his way into Knossos and been given an interview with the ruling Minos (as all kings of Kheftiu were named). The latter had accepted Tao's claim that he was the grandson of the legendary warrior-king who had driven the occupying Asiatics out of Kemet in the time of the Minos's great grandfather, Minos, and was known even across the Great Green in Kheftiu as "The Liberator." Tao had shown the Minos his solid-gold signet ring with the name of the latter (the Minos could not read the little glyphs, of course, but accepted the foreigner's confident assertion).

So, because the Minos — who was younger than Tao by a few years — believed he could benefit from the sage counsel of a prince of Kemet, exile or not, he invited him to stay at Knossos and assigned him a small apartment there. In time, as his proficiency in the Kheftian language increased, Tao began calling himself Taotios, which at least sounded less foreign to the island dwellers. By the end of his first year as resident counselor to the Minos, he had wooed and wed the latter's maiden elder sister, Minatis. And nine months later, their son was born and given the foreign-sounding name of Ahmesti. All in all, life for Tao-now-Taotios was happier and far more comfortable than he could have ever hoped it to be again when he'd boarded, in disgrace, the sailing ship bound for Kheftiu those several years before. He had become an avid worshipper of the Mother Goddess and rarely ever thought of the Two Lands, never sought news from there, so was totally unaware that the situation had recently changed in Kemet, regarding who now occupied the Horus Throne.

Taotios finally made his game move and young Ahmesti, laughing brightly, immediately trumped it. Just then Princess Minatis came onto the balcony. As a woman of middle years, she now wore an embroidered bodice that did not fully expose her generous (sagging) breasts, although there was still plenty of bare cleavage. Her colorful ankle-length skirt of tiered flounces and hair fashion of very long spiral-curls (admittedly dyed jet black) replicated what all the high-born women of Knossos wore. Taotios looked up from the game board, towards her.

"Yes, my dear?"

"You have a visitor, Tio" This was her pet name for him. "An emissary from Kemet, he says. He requests to see you regarding important business from across the Great Green."

"Oh? I suppose I should be curious what that is, but am not. 'Though it would be rude to turn him away, certainly. Where is he?'"

"Waiting in the antechamber. I've had wine brought for him."

Taotios had decided to keep the man from Kemet waiting a bit, and so continued playing the game until his son beat him, soon enough, as nearly always. When he finally walked barefooted into the antechamber of the apartment's sitting room, the emissary was seated on one of the masonry ledge-benches that lined the walls of the elaborately painted but sparsely furnished space (wooden furniture was scarce in largely treeless Kheftiu). His head bowed, he clearly was dozing. An octopus-decorated beaker sat on the surface by the visitor's thigh, very probably well drained. Taotios cleared his throat and the other man's bewigged head jerked up.

"Oh, My Lord, I must have dropped off!" He stood in his not-so-fresh linen tunic and wraparound kilt. "It's been a long voyage."

"You must have me mistaken for someone else. 'Though I am married to the sister of the Minos, I'm not a 'lord' here."

"But you are Prince Tao, are you not?"

"Was. I've not been a prince since being expelled from the Black Land, several years now, or 'floodings', as is said there."

"Well, perhaps that will've changed. I've been sent all the way here with a message for you, for Prince Tao, from the Living Horus." He turned back to the bench-seat and picked up a leather carrying tube that had been laying behind him. He handed this to Taotios.

"Which one? Which 'Living Horus'? True Soul of Re or Lasting Manifestation of Re?" He pulled the cap from the tube.

"There's only one Living Horus these days, My Lord, and that's Lasting Manifestation of Re, Born of Djehuty. He rules alone."

"Then, the usurper is dead?"

"Not dead, but gone into retirement. At least that's the official word. Her Majesty, that is, Her *Highness* is residing at Wer-Mer, lakeside in the oasis, Ta-She. When necessary, she's now referred to as Dowager Great Royal Wife Noblest Woman."

"I would've never imagined she'd relinquish power, just step aside." Taotios tapped the tube against his palm, then extracted the papyrus roll. He crossed to one of the masonry benches, one with a cushion, sat and began unrolling the narrow sheet. He read in silence.

Greetings, beloved Cousin, from Lord of the Two Lands Menkheperre, Son of Re Djehutymes. Life! Prosperity! Health! We are writing to tell you that we have rescinded your exile from Kemet. You are hereby invited by Our

Person to return in haste to your family estate, joining there your son, our beloved cousin Prince Amenhotep, and his now-grown sons, and to resume your own title of Prince-Count of the House of Tao. We trust that when you arrive back you will come quickly to whichever Residence Our Person is then at and be received by us, to hear our pledge of lasting friendship. Should you have not learned it as gossip across the Great Green, the former Coregency is no more. Maatkare is no more. Hatshepsut still lives, however, but rules not. Our Majesty is eager to see you again, grandson of The Liberator, our mutual ancestor. Eternal Life! Eternal Property! Eternal Health!

Taotios let the scroll snap closed, then crushed it in his hand and tossed it to the floor painted with stylized wave patterns and naturalistic sea life. He sighed and rubbed his brow, finally hanging his head. After a few moments, he stood and then looked towards the foreigner in the wig and boring clothes.

"Convey to His Majesty Lasting Manifestation of Re my thanks for his pardon. It comes sixteen of the Black Land's floodings too late, however. I prefer to be the happy brother-in-law of the Minos than the dis-contented country cousin of the Living Horus. And I'll take my chances with Eternity."

* * *

9

The elderly woman accepted the hand of one of the porters, rose and, after a pause, stepped from the carrying chair which had been provided by the royal Residence, where she was staying during her brief visit to Waset. She smoothed her sheath dress and adjusted her full tripartite wig, then turned to await her companion. She was, of course, Dowager Great Royal Wife Hatshepsut; and now walking slowly towards her, was the even more aged Royal Nurse In Sitre, whose great weight had required an additional four porters for her carrying chair. Hatshepsut never went anywhere without her lifetime companion. The nurse was attired similarly to her mistress, except that she wore more makeup and jewelry, as dictated by her personal vanity.

They had arrived at their day's destination, which was the entrance gateway to the small urban estate of Count Senenmut, once the most powerful man in the Two Lands, and Hatshepsut's confidante for many inundations, from the time she was Great Royal Wife of Lord of the Two Lands Asar Akheperenre Djehutymes, through her short regency for Lord of the Two Lands Menkheperre Djehutymes, and well into her own Coregency with the latter, when she shared the Horus Throne as Mistress of the Two Lands Maatkare, Daughter of Re Hatshepsut Embracing Amen.

Because of grievous offenses against the Double Crown — in the form of commoner Senenmut's personal usurpation of strictly royal prerogatives — committed (or at least discovered) some floodings before Hatshepsut's retirement, she had found it necessary to banish him from Kemet. He had selected to take refuge in the Great Green port city of Gubla, and she had been told that he died there in obscurity some years before. In fact, she now knew that he had been recalled from exile shortly after she stepped down from the Horus Throne, by her former Coregent and present Lord of the Two Lands Menkheperre. Senenmut had not resumed his former many titles, except for the honorary designation as "Count"; but he was awarded the small estate she was standing at the gate of at the moment; and he'd been functioning as sometime advisor to the Son of Re, when the court was in residence at Waset. Only a few evenings earlier, the now-quite-elderly Senenmut had suffered a massive seizure during the retirement banquet of First Prophet of Amen-Re Hapusenub. It was doubtful that he would live much longer, and Menkheperre personally had urged his former Coregent to call on the dying man and make her peace. And so this she reluctantly was doing that day.

When In Sitre came up, Hatshepsut rhetorically asked, "Now where is the prince? I would have thought he'd have beaten us here in his chariot."

She was referring to Prince Amenemhat, whose very existence she had learned of only since arriving on her present visit to Waset. He was the teenaged bastard son of her late daughter, God's Wife of Amen-Re Neferure, who had died very soon after delivering the boy and his still-born twin sister; thus Amenemhat was the grandson Hatshepsut never knew she had. And the youth's father, or so he now claimed, was none other than Hawk Beak himself, Menkheperre, who had sewn his seed in his half-sister through the duplicity of trusted advisor Senenmut. The newborn infant had been sent away to be secretly reared by nurses at the same oasis royal residence, Wer-Mer, that Hatshepsut had occupied since her retirement. Because teenage Menkheperre and his half-sister Neferure were not married, Amenemhat was technically out of the line of succession, the position Horus-in-the-Nest (the Heir) thus being held by his pre-teen half-brother, another Menkheperre, only son of Lord of the Two Lands and Great Royal Wife Sitiah. Amenemhat was a homely, jug-eared youth and had a stammer; he reminded Hatshepsut of his grandfather, her brother-husband Asar Akheperenre Djehutymes, who also was homely, jug-eared and stammered.

Before In Sitre could do more than shrug her massive shoulders in response to her mistress's question, a chariot rounded the corner of the walled city lane running in front of Count Senenmut's estate, and came towards the women at a faster-than-necessary approach. Prince Amenemhat reigned in his team only several cubits from where In Sitre's porters were grouped, ready to leap for safety if horses and vehicle kept coming. The teenager jumped off the chariot, walked the horses forward and tossed the reigns to one of the chair-bearers. He then approached Hatshepsut and her companion, brushing dust off his kilt as he came.

"Gr...eetings Grandmo..mother and N...urse Fish! Have I k... k... kept you w... waiting?"

"Not very much," Hatshepsut replied, as the youth took her narrow bare shoulders in each calloused hand and kissed her lightly on both cheeks. He simply shook In Sitre's plump hand.

"Something c...c...came up as I was a...b...bout to leave the Re... sidence s...s...stables, which re...quired my atten...tion," he grinned and flexed his brows. "B...But here I am now! Sh...all we g...go in?"

Hatshepsut ordered the head porter to get the attention of whoever tended Count Senenmut's gate; and very soon the trio was being led towards the modest house by the butler of the former Great Steward of the Estates of Amen-Re.

S enenmut's smallish bedchamber was only dimly illuminated by a single floor lamp. To filter the bright daylight, red-linen panels had been hung over four high clerestory windows. The count reclined supine amid numerous bolsters, his bed raised on a wide dais that took up most of the room between the double row of painted-wood columns flanking the central space. He was bare-chested and covered with only a sheet pulled to his waist, exposed arms resting along his sides. For a man who in his prime was taller, more robust than most, he seemed shrunken, his sharp-featured face definitely gaunt. His closely cropped hair was now white rather than coppery red, as Hatshepsut remembered it. He appeared to be sleeping as she and the prince and nurse came into the room, shown through the doorway by the butler, who then immediately departed.

Senenmut was not alone, however. Seated on a stool at the head of the bed was Minmes, the count's Kheftiu-born body-servant, aide and — it had been a poorly kept secret — male lover for some twenty floodings now. He had even accompanied the disgraced bureaucrat into exile (Senenmut would have preferred Kheftiu over Gubla as his destination, but had deferred to Minmes, who did not want to return to his childhood homeland). Hatshepsut remembered him as an exceptionally beautiful, small-boned, slender young man (as youthful male Kheftis often were); now, however, Minmes, though still slender, was well into middle age, his raven long hair grayed some and receded, his refined features definitely blurred, as well. He held an unrolled scroll on his lap, and had been reading to Senenmut — or possibly only to himself.

Looking up, but not in any way startled, Minmes smiled broadly (his perfect teeth were still exceptionally white). He let the papyrus roll snap closed.

"Your Highness and Prince Amen at the Head, Nurse Fish, greetings. Welcome to our humble dwelling. The Count will be pleased you have come — finally."

Hatshepsut approached the foot of the bed and could see that Senenmut's eyes were closed, his mouth slightly open and noticeably drooping on one side. His breathing was audible.

"Does he slumber? We can come again."

"He does sleep mostly, and very deeply. But I'll waken him. He would be most disappointed, Highness, were he to learn you'd been here and he'd missed your visit."

Minmes bent towards the sleeping man, laid a brown hand on bare shoulder and spoke close to Senenmut's ear.

"Master, awake. You have visitors. Someone you'll want to see."

Senenmut did not stir. After a moment or two, Minmes spoke again, louder, the same words.

"I heard you the first time," the old man responded in a slightly slurred croak, his eyes still closed. "No need to shout! And I recognize the voice, though she sounds like an old woman, which I suppose she is, now." He suddenly blinked several times, then raised one hand in a weak salute. "Welcome to my deathbed, Noblest Woman. Thank you for coming. I doubted you would, unforgiving as you always were. Why are you standing? I won't have you standing in my presence. Chair. Get her a chair, Born of Min. And another for fat Fish." He awkwardly flapped the hand that had saluted.

Prince Amenemhat quickly moved an armless chair from against the wall with the door and placed it behind his grandmother, who carefully sat. He pulled another one to In Sitre and she sank onto it in relief. There was a pregnant silence. Senenmut's eyes were closed again and his visitors each silently thought he may have slipped back into sleep. Then he suddenly spoke, but his eyes remained closed.

"Well, Noblest Woman, say something. Or have you satisfied your morbid curiosity and left already?" His speech, though strong, was definitely slurred.

"You have become quite cantankerous in your great old age, Brother of Mut." Hatshepsut folded her bony hands on her lap. She paused. "You're correct. We very nearly didn't come today. It was quite a shock to us to learn that you still lived, at the banquet, when you were carried out. We had been told that you died in Gubla some floodings ago. Lasting Manifestation of Re was quite duplicitous in pardoning you, recalling you. Your oversteppings, in our view, were unpardonable affronts to the Double Crown, and thereby to the Black Land itself, treasonous even."

"Still speaking as if you're wearing the Double Crown, I see, with your grand plurals, 'we,' 'our', 'us'. But then old habits die hard, as is said, I suppose." He opened his eyes and turned his head towards Minmes.

"Do our guests — and I mean mine and yours — have refreshments yet, Born of Min?"

"No, Master, they've but just arrived and I wasn't expecting them."

"Well, go then and have Butler bring something." He looked back to Hatshepsut. "Wine? Beer? Water?"

"Nothing, *I* think, we — the *three* of us — won't be staying long," Hatshepsut replied. "It would appear you aren't so close to setting off for the Field of Reeds as Lasting Manifestation of Re seems to think. Hawk Beak will doubtless be thrilled to benefit from your wise counsel again, soon enough."

"Highly unlikely, Noblest Woman. I shall never leave this bed again. One half of me's stone dead already." He gestured to the arm which he hadn't moved, then lifted it with his good hand and let it drop like a palm log. "The leg, too. *And* face." He pointed to the side which, indeed, was drooping, the mouth even drooling a little.

"So, Brother of Mut, since you're resigned to departing this realm sooner rather than later, where will you be spending the rest of time in your Mansion for Eternity? If memory serves, we — that is, Mistress of the Two Lands Maatkare — made certain that the *two* of those that you were preparing at the time of your banishment were totally nullified: work on the one you'd so recklessly caused hewn deep beneath the sacred precinct of our own Holiest of Holy places ceased, the entry sealed; and work on your other fully proper one terminated, as well, and the coffin box you secretly had already made — in red stone, in imitation of the sacred royal name-oval — smashed into uncounted pieces. So, unless our former Coregent has blindly also given these relics back to you for restoration and completion, where do you expect to rest your bones for all time?"

Senenmut did not respond for several moments.

"And it was said *I* bored all to tears with my long windedness!" Senenmut passed the good hand over his closed eyes, then let it fall at his side. "Worry not — as if you would — old friend. With Lasting Manifestation of Re's *blessing*, as it were, I've made myself another place for Eternity — albeit one far more modest than those two which you recount. And I'll be joined there by my beloved Born of Min, when his time comes, some long while from now."

There was another long pause, before Senenmut totally changed subjects, as the very old and terminal often do near the end.

"Hum, you've, ah, made the acquaintance of our dear Prince, it would appear."

That was all, followed by another long pause. Then Hatshepsut broke the silence.

"Even more shocking than the discovery that you still live, Brother of Mut, was the almost simultaneous realization that we've had a grandson for the past eighteen floodings, whose very existence had been kept from us by both you and Lasting Manifestation of Re — that poor Beauty of Re delivered doubles, which we also never knew, and that one of them, Amen at the Head here, lived and was claimed by our teenage Coregent as the Son-of-His-Body, albeit illegitimate. Son of Re has confessed to us now that you arranged for him to lie with his half-sister, and that she was impregnated as the consequence."

Senenmut rubbed his forehead and rested his hand across his eyes, covering most of the large pointed nose.

"Ah, yes, my quite clever personal joke, which went very wrong. I really should've made certain that Beauty was not ripe when I duped her into letting teenage Born of Djehuty lose his virginity with her. Painting his head and shoulders blue worked wonderfully; in her delirium she really did believe she'd lain with the god himself, whereas she never would've parted her thighs for the little brother she so despised."

He let his arm drop along his side and continued with his eyes closed.

"Of course, when her pregnancy became evident, I assumed that she finally was growing the seed of that Medjay captain...what was his name? Nefu? No, Nebet, I think. It was known by everyone — except apparently you, Noblest Woman — that that handsome black-skinned man of Wawat was her ongoing lover. Of course there was a host of other candidates, as well, including a Residence charioteer, an acolyte or two of the Hidden One, your own King's Scribe, the unfortunate Brother of Amen — or so he once confided to me himself — even that dreadful bandy-legged dwarf bragged about that he'd lain with her! Your beloved Beauty of Re was *not* discriminating, Noblest Woman. I swear she even repeatedly tried her very best to seduce her tutor, once she'd started to bleed." He laughed. "*Me*, of all people, unapologetic devotee to the shaft of Min that I've always been!"

"Enough of the filth from your old man's mouth, Brother of Mut. We didn't come here to listen to you sully the memory of our only child. We don't suppose that Amen at the Head wanted to hear that his young mother was a common whore."

The prince, who was still standing, shrugged his narrow shoulders and broke his silence. "W...W...What I've al...always b...b...been t...told, Grand...mo...ther. Also t...hat I am the mi...mi...stake of a t... trick."

There was another long pause, until Noblest Woman stood, saying, "Well, we'll almost certainly never see you again, Brother of Mut. We don't suppose that this meeting has brought the grand reconciliation that Hawk Beak sought, but we did make the effort. True Soul of Re owed you a great deal — Noblest Women, nothing at all. May the Devourer not choke on your black heart, when it tips the balance, as it surely will. Farewell."

She turned and walked to the door. Prince Amenemhat assisted Nurse In to her feet. And the three of them departed the premises. Senenmut indifferently waved a listless hand at their backs and immediately fell asleep again.

Hatshepsut never learned that her former Great Steward was standing in the Hall of Judgment just two days after the royal yacht, *Arrow of Re*, had begun riding the current north, returning her and In Sitre to Wer-Mer, the retirement villa in the She-Ta oasis.

TWENTY-SIX FLOODINGS EARLIER, INUNDATION 2
COREGENCY OF MAATKARE/MENKHEPERRE
WEST BANK OF THE RIVER, WASET

The speeding chariot slowed then came to a halt in a cloud of dust several cubits from the temporary sunshade erected in the Great Bay of Meretseger, very nearly in the shadow of the ancient mortuary temple of Nebhotepre Montuhotep. It had been in the lead of several other vehicles which arrived in a dusty cluster, as the first chariot's passengers stepped down onto the sand, the driver, Great Steward of the Estates of Amen-Re Senenmut, offering his hand to the passenger, Mistress of the Two Lands Maatkare, Daughter of Re Hatshepsut. He passed off the horse reins to a groom who'd approached from the group of men standing in front of the sun shade. Additional grooms were dashing to secure the other chariots' horses.

"Well, Brother of Mut, that was nearly as thrilling as the time we drove quite a lot further many floodings ago, to see that lonely site where our father would make his Mansion for Eternity," enthused the Female Horus, brushing at her sheath dress, then adjusting the linen *Khat* concealing her natural long hair. She had worn no adornment that morning, except for the small rearing cobra affixed to the gold brow-band of the head covering. Senenmut was simply attired in a linen skullcap and knee-length tunic and also was without any adornment. The pair turned to greet the approach on foot now of First Prophet of Amen-Re Hapusenub, who'd been a passenger in one of the other chariots. Close on his heels came Hatshepsut's Coregent, seven-floodings-old Lord of the Two Lands Menkheperre, Son of Re Djehutymes, who walked hand-in-hand with his tutor, Kings' Scribe Senimen.

"I must say that I've never been here before," said Hapusenub, who also wore a linen skullcap to protect his shaved head from the sun. "This setting is really quite spectacular, Great Steward. Is that the shared offering-temple over there of Asar Amen is Pleased and his mother, the Great One?" He pointed towards a modest plastered mud-brick structure with a smallish pylon gateway some distance closer to the dramatic cliff face, which was surely well over three-hundred cubits high.

"It is," responded Senenmut, "and regrettably it's exactly where we'll be building the platform for Her Majesty's monument. It shall have to be taken down, another place for them built elsewhere."

"Or, being a sacred structure, might it not be incorporated within the new one, the platform, in some way?" the priest asked.

"We'll certainly take that option into consideration, First Prophet Hapu is Well," was the noncommittal response.

"What's that?" asked the young Coregent, pointing towards the closer-by massive stone temple-tomb of the "Unifier," who had ruled a newly reunited Kemet some five-hundred floodings earlier. "It looks old."

"And it is, Your Majesty," replied Senenmut. "It was built as the combined offering place and Mansion for Eternity of a distant ancestor of yours, a Lord of the Two Lands who ruled many hundreds of floodings in the past."

"It would seem to have rather fallen into disrepair," remarked Hatshepsut. "If we're going to build our own monument so near to this, it'll have to be renewed a great deal, will it not, Brother of Mut?"

"It was no doubt totally neglected during the dark time of the Foreign Rulers, like so many mansions of the gods here in the South of the Black Land. But to answer the question, Your Majesty, yes, it's the plan to make necessary repairs to this unique monument of Asar Montu is Pleased. It's this ancient structure, in fact, that's been my inspiration for the design of your construction, which'll be far grander, however. We're here today not only so you can you see the building site itself, but also to look at the plans for Your Majesty's undertaking, and a small model of it, as well. The sun shade is for this, for viewing these." Senenmut pointed towards the nearby large linen canopy. "Shall we go there now?"

After studying Senenmut's ink sketches on several large sheets of papyrus, detailing the plans for Maatkare Hatshepsut's memorial, as well as viewing the small wooden model of it which he'd personally made, showing how the structure would actually look (but only if seen by the Horus hawk from on high — or else looking down on it from the cliff top), Hatshepsut offered the suggestions — requirements, actually — that there be two platforms or terraces with fronting porticoes, so that her structure would be significantly higher than its ancient neighbor. She also wanted one of the top-level's two areas flanking the central court with Amen- Re's chapel — especially that one with offering chapels dedicated to her father and brother/husband — to have an open-air altar for royal offerings to Lord Re. These responses (demands) voiced, the Female Horus then asked to visit Senenmut's nearby ancient inspiration up close.

This literal site-seeing had not been part of the Great Steward's well-thought-out scenario for the day, even so he had no choice but to acquiesce to Her Majesty's expressed desire. Thus the royal party trudged from the sunshade across the sand to the foot of the very long ramp leading up to the huge platform supporting the deteriorating memorial temple of the mostly forgotten Lord of the Two Lands Asar Nebhotepre, Son of Re Montuhotep.

Once on the temple's high base, the group crossed to the interruption in the square-columned portico running around the structure which surrounded on all four sides the base of a small pyramid, the core of the monument. Through the tall portal a dense forest of square pillars could be seen receding into the total darkness of the building's interior. Because no torches had been brought along that day — Senenmut had not anticipated Her Majesty would decide to go exploring — it was thought best to not enter the doorway, but to continue walking under the exterior portico (and so out of the bright sun) to the rear of the temple.

But once there it was discovered that the only access to the rest of the monument beyond the platform and built against the cliff face was by actually passing through the temple structure they had decided to not attempt to navigate because of the darkness inside.

Pointing to the empty small porticoed courtyard just below where they stood on the platform's edge, Senenmut drew Their Majesties' attentions to the narrow ramp that descended into the bedrock, remarking that it lead to Nebhotepre Montuhotep's violated tomb chambers. The actual offering chapel for the tomb was the structure abutting and bored into the cliff base, he said. This had not functioned in many generations; but inasmuch as the earthly remains of the king seemingly had been destroyed long ago, his grave furnishings thoroughly plundered, there would have been no point in continuing his funerary cult.

"Well, our curiosity is satisfied, Brother of Mut," Hatshepsut replied. "We were unaware that our distant ancestor had caused such a grand monument to be raised in his day — to futile purpose, if his eternal rest was terminated by vile thieves. But the memorial planned for Our Person nearby is not meant to include our Mansion for Eternity, as here, if My Majesty understood your explanation of its design."

As Senenmut and Hatshepsut walked together, in the vanguard of the rest of the party, back through the long portico to the front of the monument, he explained that Her Majesty's Mansion for Eternity would be well hidden in the same remote desert valley where her father and her husband had both gone to their rests for millions and millions of floodings.

"That desolate place lies just beyond these high cliffs — so, secretly located there, your own resting chambers will be in immediate proximity to your very visible offering chapel here, but not physically part of it." They were now back in the sunlight and moving towards the platform ramp. "So, there is absolutely no chance that Your Majesty's eternal peace will be terminated, as was that of this ancient Lord of the Two Lands."

Hatshepsut could only take the Great Steward at his word.

SIX FLOODINGS LATER, INUNDATION 8
COREGENCY OF MAATKARE/MENKHEPERRE
THE COAST OF PUNT

Chancellor Nessi stood in the prow of the expedition flagship and shielded his eyes with one hand, as he surveyed the shoreline still some distance away. The great vessel was close enough to its destination, however, that he easily was able to make out the curious dwellings of the local natives nestled among the tall palms and other more exotic trees beyond the wide beach: These structures looked like great inverted grain baskets elevated on tall stilts and accessed by long narrow ladders. The approach of the fleet from Kemet had already brought scores of the villagers streaming out onto the white sand, many of them standing at the water's edge or even ankle deep in the gently lapping surf.

These were a brown-skinned people attired vaguely similarly to the inhabitants of the Two Lands: The men and male youths in just wraparound colored kilts with pointed aprons; the women and maidens in simple sheath dresses of various solid colors; the children of both sexes totally naked. Many of the adult males sported long, braided goatees, their flowing wavy hair secured with headbands; and the females pulled their natural black hair behind their ears so that it hung in thick masses down their backs, also secured by cloth fillets matching their sheaths.

The arrival of the five immense sailing vessels from afar was apparently non-threatening to these people, many of whom were waving greetings and shouting welcomes in their tongue. Several of the men and older youths had pushed slender long canoes into the water and were rowing towards Chancellor Nessi's vessel. No weapons were visible, so their approach was not an attack; in fact they merely paddled this way and that around the great ship, waving, smiling and shouting happily.

After the huge canvas sail was furled, it took some long while for the ship's thirty oarsmen to maneuver the craft sideways so that it could moor in the shallows parallel with the shoreline, just opposite the peculiar houses of the village. Several sailors jumped into the sea and waded with the thick mooring lines to the shore, where long stakes were driven into the sand and the ropes secured. Throughout this operation these sailors were surrounded by excited naked children, who jumped and clapped and squealed.

The four other ships of the expedition remained dead in the water at a distance from the shore. One by one they slowly would duplicate the flagship's actions, until in time all five vessels lined the beach, parallel in a single row.

Before the second vessel came close, furled its sail and began its sideways maneuvering, Chancellor Nessi ordered the long gangplank of his ship lowered to the footprint-pocked dry sand. Several white-kilted soldiers debarked, carrying spears, battle axes and large cowhide-covered shields. Once on the ground, they formed two facing files. Preceded by a sailor carrying a low wooden table on which were heaped an assortment of gaudy bangles and baubles, daggers and axes, Nessi himself next walked down the plank carrying his long gilded staff of office. He was attired in a mid-calf length white tunic and wore a tightly curled short wig.

When he reached the sand, Nessi followed the sailor with the table down the narrow corridor formed by the two rows of shield-bearing soldiers. The table bearer stepped to one side and the Chancellor approached the crowd which had gathered to greet him, sailor and table following. Before he came up to the front ranks of the latter, it parted down its middle and along the created aisle of humanity strode a middle-aged, bare-chested, tall, thin male with a plaited gray goatee, wearing a bright-red felt skullcap and a white kilt with the pointed apron sported by the other men. What set him apart was a necklace strung with several large cowrie shells and the unsheathed bronze dagger tucked into his kilt's waistband. Additionally, he carried what clearly was an engraved-ivory baton of authority.

Immediately behind this individual — the local chief was Nessi's thought — waddled one of the most grossly obese females the Chancellor had ever laid eyes on. She was attired like the other adult women, but her enormous sheath was white rather than colored, as was the cloth band tied around her head. She also wore a cowroid necklace and bracelets and anklets which appeared to be fashioned from seashell. It was impossible for Nessi to tell where the woman's incredible bosom ended and her belly began. Her back was greatly swayed and her thrust-out buttocks were positively enormous; as were her upper arms, thicker than a grown man's thigh; and her own thighs were triple those in size. She would prove to be Ety, wife of the local ruler, the man she followed; and he would be identified as Pererhu — or how it sounded to the foreign visitor.

Closely following this odd couple was another adult male, attired like the others, and bearing a large wooden platter piled high with some sort of orangish fruit that Nessi didn't recognize. When he later braved biting into one, he found it both sweet and sour and not particularly to his liking. At least he didn't try a second one.

Inasmuch as it had been generations since a trading expedition from the distant Two Lands had visited this place — which was called something sounding like "Punt" to the dwellers of Kemet — there was no one who could speak both the local tongue and that of the foreigners, so interpretation was impossible. Realizing that communicating their wants to the locals would not be possible through verbal language, several sheets of papyri had been prepared by a scribe back in Waset which contained drawings of the objects and products that were being sought. After incomprehensible mutual introductions were made, Chancellor Nessi selected one of the scabbarded bronze daggers from the table brought ashore and presented it to the chieftain, whose grin communicated his pleasure. He next gave him a bronze axe, which seemed to be even more well received. And Nessi hung several strings of beads around the non-neck of the chief's spouse. A toothy smile creased her wide fleshy face.

The expedition remained in hospitable Punt — the soldiers and sailors pitching their tents and building their cooking fires on the beach, the chancellor given sparse accommodations in one of the "basket" huts on stilts — for three long weeks, while the goods depicted on the papyri were assembled by the locals. Most important of these were living myrrh and frankincense trees, the root balls of which were wrapped in coarse linen by the soldiers and encased in large reed baskets brought along for that purpose. These would be replanted back in Waset, in the gardens of the Mansion of the Hidden One, Amen-Re — gifts to the god from his daughter, Her Majesty Maatkare Hatshepsut. Then there were huge quantities of lumpy incense resins and gums, brought to the assembly point near the beach by the scores of basket loads. These later would be burned in sacred rituals for the many gods of Kemet. Gold dust and nuggets by the basketful were smelted on the spot into more portable large rings.

Elephant tusks were piled high on the sand, along with stacks and stacks of animal skins (especially leopard, favored by the high-priesthoods of most of Kemet's deity cults), and countless planks of ebony. Row upon row of upright amphorae containing precious and exotic unguents and oils rested in the beach sand. And there were numerous caged living mammals and birds, as well, destined for the menageries that His Majesty, young Lord of the Two Lands Menkheperre, had established at the Residences in Mennufer and Waset. There was so much product and produce that Chancellor Nessi wondered how, once it was loaded on the ships, there would be room on board for all the soldiers, as well. The long voyage back to Kemet would be a cramped one, indeed!

And it certainly was. Sailing north again — rowing all the way, actually — the fleet finally docked at the seaport of Sawu, where the reverse procedure of the outbound trip occurred: all five vessels were unloaded and completely dismantled. Then the cargo and ship parts were transported by an immense donkey caravan through the lengthy desert wadi leading to The River port of Guft, where the vessels would be reassembled, reloaded and sailed south against the current, the wharves at Waset their destination.

Relayed word reached the Residence at Mennufer that Chancellor Nessi fleet had reached Sawu and the ships were being taken apart for the overland transport to The River. So the Mistress and Lord of the Two Lands immediately set sail with the court principals for the Southern Residence at Waset, to be on hand for Nessi's triumphal return with the precious cargo from the Land of Punt. One month after the court's arrival, the five ships of the fleet were seen to be making their approach to the southern capital. Thus, when the heavily laden vessels finally tied up at the wharves of Waset, the local populace had turned out in force to cheer the return. For his tremendous success, Their Majesties awarded Chancellor Nessi the Fly of Valor, usually reserved for military victors. Perhaps the most amazing thing about the whole Punt venture was that a bizarre very tall, spotted animal with an unbelievably long neck and long tongue somehow survived the water and land voyages and became the centerpiece of young Menkheperre's private zoo at Waset. For a few months at least, until it did suddenly die, unfortunately.

Inundation 9, Coregency of Maatkare/Menkheperre, Waset

The River spectacle had awed all who observed it between Swenet and Waset. Surely no larger vessel had ever moved on water — or land, for that matter. It was not the first time that obelisks hewn at the granite quarries of Swenet had been floated north to the southern capital, and even as far down the River as Mennufer, the northern administrative center, and nearby Iunu, site of the great mansion of the sun-god, Re — whose special monument the obelisk was. This had been accomplished many generations earlier and as recently as during the reign of Asar Akheperkare Djehutymes, some thirty floodings before. But the two needles of stone ordered by Mistress of the Two Lands Maatkare for her current additions to the Mansion of the Hidden One, Amen-Re, were the longest — nearly seventy-five cubits — and thickest ever attempted. To transport these unfinished monuments to their destination at Waset had required the most amazing water-borne vessel ever constructed. And it was now slowly approaching from upstream.

Seated side by side in the elevated royal viewing-pavilion, especially erected riverside for the occasion, raised ever so much higher by the throne dais, Their Majesties, Maatkare and Menkheperre, strained to see the distant flotilla, both shading eyes with hands at their brows. The co-rulers wore identical *Khepresh* helmet-crowns. At fourteen floodings of age, the Lord of the Two Lands had grown taller than his stepmother/aunt and his throne was now fully adult-sized. Positioned on a stool forward but off to one side of the dais was King's Daughter, King's Sister, the God's Wife of Amen, Neferure, in the simple regalia of her sacerdotal office.

Arrayed standing in the pavilion behind the coregents were prominent members of the court, the most prominent being Great Steward of the Estates of Amen-Re Senenmut. The cutting and transporting of the twin obelisks had been his proposal, plan and responsibility. In a real sense, the arrival that day of the massive stone shafts at Waset was the tall bureaucrat's shining hour in his long service to five different wearers of the Double Crown. While neither a stonemason nor an engineer, and lacking any maritime experience (other than being a passenger on The River, of course), the Great Steward had nonetheless overseen the entire operation of hewing the largest obelisks ever attempted, their removal from the quarry and difficult maneuvering onto the mammoth barge he had redesigned from plans of the earlier — but long ago dismantled — example used to transport the less-ambitious spires of the first Son of Re Djehutymes. Senenmut had also devised a new method of towing the barge using a flotilla of thirty rowed vessels. He had also designed the wide short canal dug into the bank of The River, which would receive the barge and its cargo, then be filled in, burying the floating platform so that the twin obelisks subsequently could be hauled on sledges the rest of the way to the Mansion of Amen-Re, for eventual erection there. In fact, this gaping raw wound in the riverbank was only a short distance from the viewing pavilion.

Lord of the Two Lands Menkheperre was whispering something into the ear of his squatting tutor, King's Scribe Senimen, so Maatkare Hatshepsut indicated she wanted to speak privately to Senenmut. He came alongside her throne and bent so that his head was level with hers.

"We don't understand, Brother of Mut, how this monstrous vessel can be brought from the middle of The River and into the canal there. You've said that it has no power of its own aside from the four long rudders designed to keep it on course in the water."

"It won't be easy, Your Majesty, to be sure." Senenmut spoke softly. "There, of course, has been no opportunity to rehearse the maneuvers, but the admirals assure me that they'll work. See, even now the far rank of ten towing vessels has cast off their cable attaching them to the barge. Soon the middle ten will do the same. Finally, the last ten will reverse course towards this bank and..."

A collective gasp had gone up from the crowds lining the east river bank upstream. Senenmut stood fully upright, looking in the direction of the tripartite flotilla and massive trailing barge, which now was close enough to the viewing pavilion that the pair of red-granite needles easily could be seen laying lashed side by side on the vessel's open-work "deck." What caused the reaction on shore was the fact that the four sailors manning the huge rudders at the stern of the barge seemed to be struggling with some sort of unseen change in The River's current, so that, when the guiding cable of the outermost towing fleet was detached, the stern of the barge began drifting towards the far shore, causing the increasingly taut thick hawser connected to the ten towing vessels closest to the east bank to suddenly snap with a loud cracking noise. This release of tension on the barge made it totally impossible for the rudder men to stop the huge floating platform from beginning to turn in a circle, with the third, middle tow-line snapping, as well, so that the vessel was now fully adrift and continuing its slow rotation, as if trapped in some unseen gigantic whirlpool.

To the horror of all watching, this slow spinning motion apparently was affecting the stability of the two obelisks, which seemed to be shifting together from their flanking-centerline position towards one side of the open wide deck. Suddenly the weight of one of the pair pressing against the uprights forming the framework for the barge's hogging-trusses caused these to begin shattering with loud poppings.

Both Maatkare and Menkheperre were on their feet when the shifted weight of the obelisks resulted in the unbelievable happening: the barge itself began to list to the side that now bore the incalculable weight of both spires of granite. And very slowly, accompanied by human moaning and wailing on the riverbanks, the immense platform capsized, sending its sacred cargo, quickly one after the other, to the depths of The River, never to be seen again.

Undaunted and determined, Great Steward Senenmut tried again and that time succeeded in getting a pair of obelisks from the Swenet quarry downstream to Waset and ultimately standing tall before the entrance to the forecourt of the Mansion of the Hidden One. As was the way in Kemet, the catastrophic incident on The River that day went totally unrecorded for posterity.

INUNDATION 10, COREGENCY OF MAATKARE/MENKHEPERRE
THE RESIDENCE, WASET

As always the God's Wife reached her climax before the King's Scribe, arching her back and lifting her hips, so that she pushed him fully into her, at the same time gripping his head by the ears and pulling his opened mouth onto her jutting tongue. After a shudder or two, Neferure lowered herself back onto the bed mattress again, withdrew her tongue, released the head grip and moved her hands to pinch Senimen's nipples. His pumping motion continued only a few moments longer, then he lifted his sweat-drenched torso off hers and raised fully upright on his knees, so that he pulled free, almost immediately lobbing his seed onto her abdomen. As always the King's Scribe was very careful to not climax within the God's Wife. Their affair did not allow even the risk of a pregnancy. Especially since he was also the longtime secret lover of Her Majesty Maatkare, Neferure's mother. Because she was barren, he didn't have to take the same precautions with his orgasm.

Senimen sat back on his well-muscled haunches, straddling the God's Wife's legs, breathing heavily. Neither the petite teenager nor the solidly built handsome man fifteen floodings her senior made eye contact. Theirs was a physical relationship, not a romantic one. They rarely made even an effort at conversation, either as prelude or follow up to their always-nocturnal couplings. Senimen found the young woman to be frivolous and fully self-focused; for her part Neferure thought him to be a tedious intellectual; in short, they had nothing in common but satisfying each other sexually. He'd not seduced her, rather the opposite; he'd succumbed finally to her persistent coquettishness, her relentless blatant invitations to come lay between her thighs, whispered when no one could overhear.

Senimen swung his thicker leg over her slender ones and rose off the low bed. He crossed to the armchair where earlier he'd deposited his kilt and loincloth and, with his back to Neferure, reattired himself, slipping into his reed sandals. He'd not worn a wig that late warm evening. Without uttering a word or even looking back, he left the God's Wife's bedchamber, closing the double-door panels. Crossing the dimly lighted antechamber, he let himself through its unattended doors into the passageway. He'd not noticed the figure lurking in the deep shadows of the room's rows of columns; nor did he hear the doors open quietly again when he was several cubits down the passage illuminated only by a tall brazier at its intersection with a perpendicular corridor.

The King's Scribe rounded the corner there and had gone a ways along the second passage when he suddenly felt an intensely cold sensation in his solar plexus, bringing him to an abrupt halt. He reached to his lower back and sensed warm wetness. Returning the hand forward and opening the palm, he saw it was dark with what was clearly blood. Suddenly there was another inserting coldness in the opposite side of his lower back. Senimen spun around and found himself looking into dim emptiness. When a third sharp, this time painful, intrusion immediately penetrated his flat abdomen below the navel, he looked down and, to his horror, beheld Neferure's grinning pet dwarf holding a bloody dagger poised to strike yet again.

"Khawi!" Senimen gasped and took a step backwards, slipped in his own blood and, arms flailing, fell backwards to the now-wet plastered floor. Before he could raise himself on his elbows, the dwarf had come up and begun stabbing the blade again and again into the King's Scribe's broad bare pectorals. Senimen's last momentary thought was of the leering face of the god Bes, long pink tongue flicking.

When his contorted rigid corpse was discovered by Medjay guards before dawn the next morning, lying in a massive pool of congealed blood, no one seemed to notice — or at least paid any official attention to — the pigeon-toed small footprints leading away from the scene of the crime. The foot tracks of others had obliterated these by the time coregents Maatkare Hatshepsut and Menkheperre Djehutymes arrived to view the sheet-covered remains. Of course she was outraged by her...ah, King's Scribe's murder — which, even so, went uninvestigated and consequently unpunished.

* * *

10

Mistress of the Two Lands Maatkare, Daughter of Re Hatshepsut sat playing the board game *senet* in a poolside sun-shade with Nurse In Sitre, her companion of so many years. As usual she was winning, as In always let her. Soon they were joined by Great Steward of the Estates of Amen-Re Senenmut, who took a chair with the women, after the appropriate greetings. He had requested a private audience with the Female Living Horus.

"So, Brother of Mut, we've not had the pleasure of your company for some little while now," remarked Hatshepsut, dryly. Her Majesty had a way of asking a question by making a statement.

"I've been very busy of late, even more so than usual, with overseeing progress on your Holiest of Holy Places. I'm pleased to report that the work is going forward on schedule, even ahead of schedule, and soon it will be time for another inspection tour by Your Majesty. I trust you'll be particularly pleased by the now-painted second-court portico relief scenes of the great expedition to Punt. They're really quite stunning, in my view."

"Although we realize it's not your personal project, rather that of First Prophet of the Hidden One, but have you any latest news on the status of our Mansion for Millions of Years?"

"When I saw First Prophet Hapu is Well at the abode of Lord Hidden One just a few days ago, he remarked that hewing of the second passageway had begun. He offered little more information, I'm afraid." Senenmut took a faience goblet of wine from the tray presented by a serving girl who had come onto the sun-shade platform. The two women had helped themselves while he was speaking.

"You've requested this meeting, Great Steward. So what do you have to discuss with Our Person?" asked Hatshepsut after a sip of her wine.

"A matter of state, Your Majesty, so I was hoping we might speak privately."

"In other words, you're asking that My Majesty dismiss the Ancient One here." Another statement-question.

"I think it best if what will be said is strictly between Your Person and myself," replied Senenmut.

"So, dearest Fish, perhaps now would be a good time for your afternoon nap."

Without having uttered a word, the heavyset old woman stood with effort and made her arthritic way down the paved garden path, heading back to the apartments of her mistress. She took her full wine goblet with her, of course. After she was well out of hearing, Senenmut spoke.

"Since, Your Majesty, Coregent Lasting Manifestation of Re reaches his majority in a few months, it's high time, in my humble view, that he take a Great Royal Wife and get about the business of producing a Son-of-His-Body. The Two Lands have been far, far too long without a Horus-in-the-Nest."

Hatshepsut placed her goblet on the low table holding the *senet* board and captured playing pieces. The way she gripped the arms of her ebony chair signaled her displeasure with the topic raised by the Great Steward.

"Hawk Beak has never indicated to *us* his interest in taking a wife any time soon. Have you raised this matter with him, or he with you? Behind Our Person's back, we might add?"

"We, His Majesty and I, have, yes, discussed it, privately, Your Majesty. I didn't presume we were speaking together inappropriately, however. The subject of marriage came up in another context and segued into looking at his own options. Which are decidedly few, I might add."

Hatshepsut pinched the bridge of her nose. "And those are?"

"Well, speaking frankly, just one, Your Majesty: his only sibling, the God's Wife, Divine Hand Beauty of Re. It was established tradition in the House of Tao, and now in the House Born of Djehuty, for the Heir to marry his sister or half-sister. At the present time, that means Beauty of Re, there simply being no one else." Senenmut sipped his wine.

"Traditions are made to be broken, as Our Person is living proof, Brother of Mut. Even if she were anxious to marry Hawk Beak, add Great Royal Wife to her titles — which, let us assure you, she decidedly is *not* — we've quite different plans for the God's Wife. In case you've forgotten, and it would appear you have, at the time of our elevation to the throne of the Two Lands, it was privately shared with you and the First Prophet that it was our desire Beauty of Re would succeed us as Female

Living Horus and Coregent with Hawk Beak, when the time came. That wouldn't be possible if she was Great Royal Wife."

"If Your Majesty is indeed of a mind to continue a line of Female Living Horuses co-ruling alongside the Lord of the Two Lands, I fail to see how this will be accomplished, if the former are to be virgins," Senenmut suppressed a smile, "Well, at least unmarried and presumably childless."

"Simple enough, Great Steward." Hatshepsut recovered her goblet and drank it dry, then returned it to the table. "The Female Living Horus always will be the sister or half-sister of the Living Horus, as we were our husband's half-sister and Beauty of Re is Hawk Beak's. The Female Living Horus after Beauty of Re will be Lasting Manifestation of Re's eldest daughter, by whichever wife, as the eldest son by his Great Royal Wife will be his successor as Living Horus."

"By 'whichever wife', is Your Majesty implying that Lords of the Two Lands should have multiple *simultaneous* wives?"

"Which has always been the reality, if not the fact. Harim Mouse, as a case in point, was never a King's Wife, though she, by happenchance, mothered the Heir. If Iset had been a recognized spouse of our brother, rather than only a harim concubine, Hawk Beak's legitimacy would never have been questioned by the noisome Taos."

"When you became the Female Living Horus, Your Majesty relinquished the role of God's Wife to Beauty of Re. So is it Your Majesty's plan that when she, your daughter, eventually succeeds as Mistress of the Two Lands, Beauty of Re would do likewise? Relinquish her God's Wife, God's Hand roles to another?" Senenmut frowned.

"Of course. To Hawk Beak's eldest daughter, the one who would become the next Female Living Horus and coregent with her brother. She first would be God's Wife and Divine Hand, until she eventually donned the Double Crown and abdicated her sacerdotal roles to a younger sister or, better, to the eldest daughter of her brother and Co-ruler."

Senenmut shook his head incredulously. "With all due respect, Your Majesty, have you discussed any of this with the First Prophet of Amen-Re?"

"Not yet, but shall, in due time."

Before their conversation could continue, Hatshepsut and Senenmut were suddenly joined under the sun-shade by none other than God's Wife of Amen-Re Neferure herself, who had approached through the garden unnoticed by her elders.

"Greetings, Mother and ex-tutor, Brother of Mut. I hope I'm not interrupting something serious and *boring*," the young woman said cheerfully. She took an empty chair. "Is there more beverage?" She clapped her hands loudly, signalling for the serving girl.

"Nothing more 'serious and boring' than your personal future, Beauty," replied her mother. "The Great Steward here has one thing in mind for you and My Majesty has something else, quite different."

Neferure looked, smiling, to her former mentor. "And what would *you* have me do, Lord High and Mighty of This and That?"

"Be respectful, Daughter."

"Simply enough, God's Wife Beauty of Re," Senenmut, smiling hard-lipped, replied, "I was suggesting to Her Majesty that it very soon will be time for Your Highness to exchange hair with your half-brother and become Lasting Manifestation of Re's Great Royal Wife and then mother of his Heir."

The serving girl had come up to the trio.

"Beer for me. More of what you two are drinking?" Neferure ordered and inquired.

Both Hatshepsut and Senenmut shook their heads in the negative. The girl left.

"So, Hidden One's Great Steward, you want me *married* to little half-brother Hawk Beak." Like her mother, Neferure often asked questions with statements.

"Not what *I* want, Your Highness, but what *tradition* requires. More so, you are, as you very well know, the only royal female of the House Born of Djehuty available for His Majesty to marry."

"But I *despise* Hawk Beak. Always have. Always will."

"Just as Her Majesty despised her half-brother, your father." Senenmut drank the last of his wine. "Personal feelings don't play a part in royal marriages, Your Highness."

"Have you forgotten, Great Steward, that I'm *already* married — to none other than the Hidden One Himself. I'm God's Wife *and* Divine Hand. I'm the one who pleasures Him by stroking his Min! What would Lord Amen-Re think if I also had to stroke Hawk Beak's?" She shuddered. "If I could even find *it!*" she laughed and took the beer tumbler now offered by the serving girl, downing a large swallow.

"Since previous God's Wives have all been simultaneously Great Royal Wives, I don't believe Lord Hidden One would suddenly be jealous of *you*, Beauty of Re. Your *marital* relationship to Him is, well, fully mystical rather than, well, *physical*. But the First Prophet could explain theology to you far better — at least with more authority — than this lowly servant, who only manages His vast estates."

"Well, manager, no one knows better than *me* that Lord Amen-

Min visits my bed regularly, however many of His cows *you* may count!" Tossing her closely cropped head back, Neferure drained the ceramic tumbler, then sat it with some force on the table. "So, to be simple and direct about it, 'lowly servant', inasmuch as Her Majesty wishes for me to one day reign over the Black Land from a throne *alongside* Hawk Beak, what makes you think I'd ever entertain the idea of making a successor for him — in his *bed*?"

King's Sister, God's Wife, Divine Hand Neferure rose and strode on her slender legs out of the Mistress of the Two Land's private garden.

Not many minutes later, Great Steward of the Estates of Amen-Re and "High Lord and Mighty of This and That" left as he had arrived, as well, but with an idea already sprouted in his fertile mind.

JUST LATER THAT SAME DAY
THE RESIDENCE, WASET

Immediately upon leaving the private garden of Mistress of the Two Lands Maatkare, Great Steward Senenmut went to the other side of the sprawling Residence, to the personal apartments of teenage Lord of the Two Lands Menkheperre. At the Medjays-guarded entrance, he was met by Renna, His Majesty's portly middle-aged personal steward, and was informed that the Living Horus had gone fowling before midday, in the marshes upstream from Waset, with a small party of younger male courtiers. Renna had no certainty about when they would return, but supposed it would be by late afternoon. It was then mid-afternoon. Senenmut told the steward that he would come back in two hours; and, if His Majesty arrived before then, to inform him that Count Senenmut had requested a few minutes of his time regarding an urgent matter. The tall man with the pointed nose had busy work in the archives of the nearby Mansion of Lord Hidden One, Amen-Re, which could occupy him in the interim.

When Senenmut was met a second time by King's Steward Renna, the latter informed him that, yes, the Living Horus had returned to the Residence only a short while before, but had gone directly to his private zoo and presumably was still there, inasmuch as he had not yet appeared at his apartments. This information had been conveyed by a messenger sent ahead by His Majesty, so, no, Renna had not had a chance to inform his master of the Great Steward's request for a private audience. Senenmut thanked the officious servant and headed for the Royal Menagerie at the far rear of the Residence.

At the gateway to the walled compound where Menkheperre Djehutymes kept the animals brought back by the Punt Expedition three floodings earlier, and even more creatures acquired since, Senenmut was, of course, halted by the armed Medjay guards, who — although they very probably recognized him — would not let him pass. The Great Steward finally persuaded one of the tall natives of Wawat to go into the Menagerie and inform the Living Horus that Count Senenmut was at the gate and would like to speak privately with His Majesty on a matter of importance. In only a few minutes, the lean muscular black man returned and, in the heavy accent of Wawat, informed the bureaucrat that he could find the Living Horus at the very rear of the compound — which Senenmut knew was where the aviaries were located.

The Royal Menagerie was actually a small park of carefully tended shrubbery and flower gardens, with a number of mature acadia and palm trees, as well. There were also several water-lily ponds stocked with additional water flora and well-fed colorful fish. What differentiated it from the other walled gardens adjoining each of the royal apartments of the Residence was both its extent and the sizeable animal population: numerous gazelles and other small antelopes grazed on the lawns at will; there were several uncaged hares and at least one large tortoise; a wide variety of monkeys and a few neutered baboons were also unrestrained, chattering or screeching from the larger trees; a number of brightly plumed geese and equally colorful ducks occupied the environs of the ponds; several larger antelopes and two or three ibexes were confined to pens; and scattered about under the trees were the large cages housing animals of prey, including three cheetahs, a black leopard, a pair of hyenas and their pups, several jackals, and even a young male lion. This is where the very strange long-necked spotted animal with hoofed pole-like legs had been housed, dying a few months following its arrival at Waset, after having miraculously survived the sea and overland trip from distant Punt. The Menagerie also had several scantily clothed humans present, caretakers and gardeners engaged in their various work, who cast suspicious glances towards him as Senenmut passed by on the gravel path leading to the aviaries area.

The latter consisted of several large flight cages built against the high back wall of the compound, elaborate tent-like constructions of poles and specially woven nettings — within which were confined a staggering variety of smaller song birds, and larger ones with brilliant plumage of the sort the Great Steward had only seen in this one place. There were also several ibises, guinea fowl, quails, a couple of pelicans and, in a pen, a solitary ostrich. Secured by individual cages were a vulture, several hunting falcons and even a very large owl.

When Senenmut came up to the central grouping of flight cages, he spotted His Majesty inside of one, kneeling on the ground along with an attendant: their bare backs to him, he was unable to see what they were occupied by. The bureaucrat watched until both Lord of the Two Lands and the other young man stood and separated, so that a tall heron could struggle, wings flapping, to its feet. One of its long legs was tightly bound with a reed splint. The young ruler said something to the other youth that the Great Steward couldn't hear, then he turned towards his observer.

"Brother of Mut!" called the Living Horus, raising his lean bare arm in greeting. He crossed to the weighted flap of netting that secured the entrance to the flight cage and pushed it aside so that he could exit. "It has been a long time since you visited our little collection of animals and birds."

"Too long, Your Majesty. This is a very special place. I know of none other quite like it."

Menkheperre Djehutymes came up to the much older, somewhat taller man and offered his hand. Which Senenmut took and shook quickly. He was always somewhat unsettled by the Lord of the Two Lands' informality — in private, at least.

"So what brings you here this afternoon?" The broad-chested, perspiration-damp youth was attired in only a short kilt, somewhat rumpled, with a greenish stain on one hip. His closely cropped head was uncovered and he sported no emblems of his kingship. Without headgear or wig, his prominent nose was "beakish," indeed, was Senenmut's thought.

"Is there somewhere in the menagerie that we can speak privately, Your Majesty? I have an important matter to discuss with you."

"Follow me, Brother of Mut. There is a viewing bench near one of the fish ponds," he said as he walked away from the aviaries.

In a few moments Son of Re Djehutymes and Great Steward Senenmut sat on opposite ends of a long reed-work garden bench, youth and older man facing towards a large pond with pale-blue water lilies in full bloom at its center. After a pregnant pause, the bureaucrat began.

"Earlier today I had a private — well, almost private — audience with Her Majesty True Soul of Re, to present to her the matter of which we, you and I, have spoken recently."

"About Our Person taking a Great Royal Wife, when we've reached sixteen floodings in a few months? That we marry Beauty of Re? That we father our Heir by her?"

"Exactly. As Your Majesty and I expected, however, the Coregent was very much unreceptive to that idea. As I thought she likely would, Her Majesty countered that she had distinct *other* plans for your half-sister. As I warned you, Living Horus, your aunt/stepmother intends that the

God's Wife succeeds *her* as your co-ruler, as another, the second, Female Living Horus. She has in mind to establish a line of females to rule co-equally alongside future Lords of the Two Lands. This clearly would be absolutely contrary to *Maat*, to the correct order of things as they've always been since Lord Atum masturbated the universe into existence on the Mound of Creation."

Menkheperre smiled and Senenmut, who was staring into the depths of the pond and the fish darting there, continued.

"When the High Council agreed to secure your throne for you — save it from the defunct Taos — by allowing then God's Wife and Regent Noblest Woman to assume full co-kingship at your side — so that the fact of your extreme youth and the obvious lack of a Horus-in-the-Nest could be overridden by the irrefutable reality of there being *two* co-reigning Horuses, not just a single juvenile one — it was seen by us as a temporary measure, at best, not one that the self-named True Soul of Re would subsequently mean to make a permanent arrangement for the governance of the Black Land."

Menkheperre asked, "So, what does she, our Coregent, have in mind for us to do, regarding a Great Royal Wife and Heir?" The youth ran both hands over the dark bristles of his hair, then cradled his chin on clasped hands, elbows forward on his knees.

Senenmut stood and walked a pace or two away, stopping with his back to the young Lord of the Two Lands.

"Before that subject could be even opened, we, Her Majesty and I, were interrupted by none other than Beauty of Re herself. Her appearance at that moment was wholly coincidental, of that I'm certain. In any case, at her mother's allowance, the God's Wife immediately inserted herself into our conversation. In short order she made it vividly clear that she has *always* 'despised' — her word — Your Majesty, since your birth, and would never lay with you now, let alone bear you any offspring." He turned back to Menkheperre. "It seems, Your Majesty, that she harbors the illusion that Lord Hidden One Himself takes her God's Wife role quite literally, and — would you believe as Amen-Min — regularly visits her bed and intimately lays with her."

"We've always regarded our beloved big sister as a bit lacking in her grasp of reality, not to mention in simple intelligence, too. That she 'despises' Our Person we've known since we were old enough to be aware of anything.

"Frankly, Great Steward, we would rather *not* have Beauty of Re as our Great Royal Wife, although we do shudder at the prospect of her sharing our throne as co-ruler. Her mother, at least, is highly capable, if sometimes, well *often*, overbearing — although never to us personally. What she says of us out of Our Person's hearing, we've certainly never had anything reported in the negative. Of course, there's her mean nickname for us, but we've heard that from her mouth for so long that we don't take real offense any longer. At least she refrains from calling Our Person 'Hawk Beak' in public!"

The slender teenager also rose and stepped to the edge of the pond. After a few moments of staring into the green depths, he looked towards Senenmut and continued.

"You are correct though, of course, that there should be a Horus-in-the-Nest, very much sooner than later. Would that could happen without us having to sow our seed in the necessary manner. As you well know, Brother of Mut, we've no experience that way, with females. My Majesty isn't even confident that we could perform as required in that regard."

"Every young man's fear. Practice makes perfect, Your Majesty, as the old saying goes," replied Senenmut, who'd sat on the bench again during Menkheperre's holding forth. "When I heard Beauty of Re confidently claiming that Lord Hidden One actually comes to her in the flesh and engages in physical coupling, an idea came to me which I wanted to share — which is why I sought out Your Majesty this very afternoon."

Senenmut then proceeded to present to the young ruler his plan to have him, Menkheperre, impersonate the Hidden One so that he could, in fact, lay with his sister, who would otherwise never consent to spreading her legs or going on hands and knees for him. This could be accomplished, the bureaucrat proposed, by him secretly putting a potion in Neferure's wine that would dull her immediate sense of reality and at the same time greatly heighten her imagination. He suggested that Lord of the Two Lands' head and face, even shoulders, might be painted blue for the charade and that he could wear a headband with double-plumes, imitating the unique crown of Amen-Min. And His Majesty might even chew on a small lump of myrrh before entering his sister's bedchamber, the Great Steward suggested, so as to have exotically sweet breath like the god.

Being a teenager, Son of Re Djehutymes was immediately receptive of this preposterous great joke on his hateful half-sister. He'd repeatedly heard court whisperings regarding her considerable — and wholly indiscriminate — coupling experience, so she very well might prove a far better teacher for him in the ways of marriage-bed performance than whatever nobleman's virgin daughter he'd eventually end up taking as his Great Royal Wife. And if his make-believe impersonation of Amen-Min finally wasn't equivalent to Neferure's fantasy expectation, well, certainly the God's Wife would never dare tell negative tales on the Hidden One!

"This is a great plan, Brother of Mut! Yes, we're up for it — in a manner of speaking," the third Djehutymes laughingly replied.

SIX FLOODINGS LATER, INUNDATION 17
COREGENCY OF MAATKARE/MENKHEPERRE
THE RESIDENCE, MENNUFER

Great Royal Wife Sitiah sat up propped by pillows on her bed. While her maid held a polished-silver mirror, she pushed a few strands of her own hair behind the edges of the heavy wig framing her pale oval face. She motioned that she was finished with the mirror and held her arms out to receive the small bundle being held by her mother, Nurse of the God Ipu. Sitiah cradled the weeks-old infant to her small bosom and lifted the flap of linen which covered the tiny sleeping face. If only this one will live was her first thought on staring at the wrinkled, pinched countenance. Here was the second son and fourth child she had given her young husband, Lord of the Two Lands Menkheperre, in three floodings time, and the earlier three infants had all died in childbirth or soon after: one of the twin girls had been stillborn, more accurately. The teenaged Great Royal Wife had gone on the bricks weeks early with the present son and she had bled profusely. In fact, she had nearly departed for the Field of Reeds. That the infant had survived even this long was just short of miraculous.

Sitiah, eighteen floodings old, had been made Great Royal Wife when she was only fifteen and Lasting Manifestation of Re, Born of Djehuty nineteen. It was His Majesty's first marriage, and hers too, of course. There had been no romance or courtship involved in their union. She had, in fact, only seen him from a distance prior to their introduction, which was not all that long before the ceremony took place wherein they'd exchanged linen-wrapped balls of their own hair, signifying their married status. (Son of Re Djehutymes's hair had been from his saved Horus Sidelock, inasmuch as nowadays he kept his head closely cropped, periodically fully shaven.)

Plain-featured teenager Sitiah had come to the notice of Lord of the Two Lands only because of her mother's purely symbolic sacerdotal capacity of Nurse of the God. Inasmuch as there had been no God's Wife of Amen-Re since the tragic death (from complications of childbirth) of King's Sister Neferure several floodings earlier, the "nurse" role as Lord Hidden One's human-female companion had been created by Mistress of the Two Lands Maatkare; and Ipu — a niece of Royal Nurse In Sitre, the Female Living Horus's lifelong companion — arbitrarily was selected to fill it, even though she'd never served as a Royal Nurse herself. Sitiah's father was long deceased, but had been a high-ranking officer in the Army of Kemet. Thus, fully a commoner by birth, young Sitiah now had a spacious apartment in the Residence (at Mennufer but not Waset) and spent her days playing board games, working at her loom and chatting with her female attendants (occasionally visited by Ipu). Only rarely did she enjoy the marriage-bed attentions of her Living Horus husband. In short, her sole responsibility was to produce the Heir and, with any luck this time, she finally would be mother of Horus-in-the-Nest, and in due distant time King's Mother. Her fertility was not in question, only the vitality of her offspring.

Menkheperre had waited this long before recognizing the infant boy as Son-of-His-Body and thus the next Living Horus, and giving him a name, Sitiah presumed, because Lord of the Two Lands wanted to be certain that the child would not die right off, as the first boy-baby had, soon after being declared Heir and named Djehutymes like his father. Menkheperre had not, in fact, yet laid eyes on this second son — again, Sitiah presumed — because he wanted to feel confident that the infant would indeed survive before he acknowledged his very existence. Apparently reports that all was going well had prompted this afternoon's visit by her husband, for which she was now ready, babe in arms.

The maid departed and Sitiah and her mother were left to whisper together (so as to not awaken the infant). It was not long before the Great Royal Wife's elderly steward came to the door of the bedchamber and announced the arrival of Lord of the Two Lands and other visitors, including Mistress of the Two Lands herself. As if on cue, the boy began to cry loudly.

"Tell my husband and Her Majesty to come in," Sitiah replied, jiggling the now squirming bundle cradled in her thin arms.

As the steward departed, Nurse of the God Ipu seated herself on the armless chair beside her daughter's bed — so that she could appropriately rise when Their Majesties entered. Which happened in mere moments. Accompanying Menkheperre and Maatkare were Great Steward of Amen-Re Senenmut and, of course, Royal Nurse In Sitre. The Coregents — who advanced to stand side by side at the foot of the bed — were both dressed informally, Maatkare in a plain sheath-dress, her only royal emblem being the inlaid cobra rearing from the gold brow band of her tightly curled short wig. Sitiah's husband, as typical for him in the privacy of the Residence, was without any head-covering and his attire was a simple kilt without an apron; he was barefooted, as usual. The other visitors were in more formal court attire, and the elderly nurse wore both excessive makeup and too much jewelry. Senenmut, in his familiar curled cap-wig and tunic worn with a long sheer kilt, lifted a chair from its position beside the doorway and placed it so that In Sitre could rest her very considerable weight.

The infant continued crying.

Menkheperre spoke first. "Take your seat again, Nurse of the God. Greetings, Sitiah. You are looking, well, very much improved from our last visit. The wig really wasn't necessary, though. We prefer your natural hair, in any case." He came around to the side of the bed opposite where Ipu sat. "So, it sounds as if his lungs at least are strong. Or is he bawling because he's ill?"

"Oh, no, no, Your Majesty, he rarely cries. Almost never. He's a very content infant, with a hearty appetite, his wet nurse repeatedly assures me," the Great Royal Wife replied, defensively. "He's perhaps just excited to meet, finally, his father."

Son of Re Djehutymes stretched out his opened hands. "May we hold him?"

Sitiah laid the small bundle on her lap, unwrapped the linen swaddling and lifted the kicking tiny brown body — grasping the infant around his narrow torso, under his arms — towards her husband, who took him somewhat awkwardly, having almost no experience handling infants (except for his short-lived first son, and then only on a couple of brief occasions). Cradled in the bare arms of Lord of the Two Lands, the naked little boy suddenly stopped crying and kicking, his tiny fists remaining tightly clenched.

Touching a finger to it, Menkheperre remarked, "Well, at least he has Sitiah's nose." He turned, grinning, towards his Coregent — who rolled her eyes and thrust her pointy chin higher than usual. "Would you like to hold him, Noblest Woman?" he asked.

"Holding *you*, Hawk Beak, in a similar circumstance — all those many, many floodings ago — was quite enough, thank you, no. Is there a chair Our Person might sit on?"

Immediately Senenmut pulled up another armless seat and Mistress of the Two Lands lowered herself, folding bony hands on her lap.

Lord of the Two Lands sat on his wife's bed, near its foot end, and brought the again-content infant against his own chest.

"Well, by coming down between the bricks well ahead of time, it would seem that our little one here has gotten a head start on this life, and is grabbing ahold of his destiny. Thus, we take the risk, yet once gain, of presuming he'll, indeed, succeed us one day, so that it should be declared now — before the two witnesses of our Coregent and the Great Steward of the Estates of Amen-Re — that he's indeed the Son-of-Our-Body and thus the Heir, the new Horus-in-the-Nest. And his name shall be — after much careful reflection — Lasting Manifestation of Re."

"So, you're breaking with tradition," said Maatkare in her statement/question manner.

"And which 'tradition' is that, Aunt?" Menkheperre responded.

"Simply that, as the next male ruler of the Black Land, he should be named Born of Djehuty, like his father, grandfather and great-grandfather before him. To honor the House Born of Djehuty. Lasting Manifestation of Re is more properly a throne name, or so it seems to us."

"Indeed, we considered Born of Djehuty, Aunt, but since his short-lived brother was given that personal name, we decided repeating it would be inappropriate, perhaps even unlucky," replied Lord of the Two Lands Menkheperre, who stood and handed little Horus-in-the-Nest back to his mother, which prompted another outburst of crying.

"Shall we be going then?" asked Maatkare, rising. She had no patience for infants, Crown-Princes or not.

One Flooding Later, Inundation 18
Coregency of Maatkare/Menkheperre
The Residence, Waset

First Prophet of Amen-Re Hapusenub let the large scroll of papyrus close upon itself. He had just shown Mistress of the Two Lands Maatkare sketches for how the stone sarcophagus which had originally been cut for her use would be recarved now to accommodate the nested pair of coffins of her father, Asar Akheperkare Djehutymes. With the hewing of the resting chamber of her Mansion for Millions of Years nearing completion, she had made the decision to transfer there — from the more modestly scaled Mansion for Millions of Years he had made for himself many floodings before — the burial of the first Djehutymes. This, so that he would lie directly beside her for all eternity and more immediately benefit from the offering chapel already dedicated to him in her Holiest of Holy Places. Hapusenub had also shown her the plans for the sarcophagus which would now be carved for her own future use. The Female Living Horus had approved both the alterations and the new design — which, to be clear, was not all that different from the original.

"Do you think, First Prophet, that we should visit our Mansion for Millions of Years in person, to view the work completed so far?" Maatkare asked, crossing from the high table where she'd been standing with Hapusenub and sitting in the elaborately carved armchair which had been provided for her.

"Frankly, the very long passageways descend into the mountain at such a steep angle that it'd be most unsafe, in my judgment, for Your Majesty to enter. I've been all the way to the resting chamber only once myself, and the great heat and very thin air down there are most uncomfortable, practically unbearable. Whats more, ascending back to the surface is very difficult and wholly exhausting. I wasn't certain, at my advanced age, I had the strength to see the light of Re again. As has been reported to Your Majesty, a great many workmen hewing the passages and chambers have expired over the floodings construction has been underway."

"And their families were compensated by our largess for their loss, we remember."

"Four bushels of emmer wheat are used up rather quickly, Your Majesty," the priest replied, but bowing his shaved head.

"Perhaps those who gave their lives in our service will have the good fortune to be our Answerers in the Next Life. That would be a more-than-suitable reward, we think. Is there anything in your sacred books which suggests that might happen?"

Just then the Great Steward of the Estates of Amen-Re Senenmut came into the chamber. He had been listening at the door for a few moments.

"Having a profound theological discussion, Your Majesty and First Prophet?"

"Actually, we were discussing our Mansion for Millions of Years, Brother of Mut. Join us, of course." Senenmut advanced into the chamber. "We understand the hewing of the resting chamber is almost complete," stated Maatkare. "We therefore suppose the decorating of the walls is the next phase."

"Well, there is some problem in that regard, Your Majesty," Hapusenub responded. "The chief of the masons informs me that the quality of the rock where the resting chamber lies is too inferior to allow much smoothing and therefore plastering for decoration."

"So, you'd have Our Person spend eternity resting in a plain, even rough, chamber. We understood that the walls were to have Brother of Mut's charming stick-figure renderings of the *What is in the Underworld* texts — which were planned for the resting chamber of our late father, but never executed there."

"There's a way that, yes, that's still possible, Your Majesty," the Great Steward offered. "I've discussed this at length with the First Prophet and he agrees that the chamber easily enough could be fully lined with specially cut blocks of the local white building stone, and that the figures and texts could be painted on these, as if on plastered walls. Perhaps we might even plaster the blocks in place to receive the images, although it would be far easier on the scribes to have the drawings done directly on the smoothed blocks, before they're taken down into your Mansion for Eternity and assembled."

"Well, well, very well, let you two and the masons and artisans resolve how it is to be accomplished. But, remember, both of you, we will not be bored throughout eternity with nothing to look at and read." Maatkare stood and moved towards the doorway. She then turned and said, "And, First Prophet Hapu is Well, despite your dire warnings, we still do expect to see in person where we'll spend eternity."

Mistress of the Two Lands left the chamber. Hapusenub shook his shaven head. The Great Steward merely shrugged.

SEVERAL WEEKS LATER
ON THE GREAT GREEN, ENTERING THE HARBOR OF GUBLA

With Minmes close at his side, their bare arms actually touching, Senenmut rested his elbows on the midship railing of the Khefti merchant vessel, taking in an amazing sight he'd never expected to see. The sea-going sailing ship was entering the vast bay of the harbor of Gubla, the coastal port known in far off Kemet as the City in the Cedar Groves. The harbor was busy with water-borne traffic, trading ships from all over the Great Green arriving with their cargos, or departing with new ones. Soaring, darting, diving sea gulls populated the faience-blue sky, their chorus of screechings very alien to the two men's ears. In the distance the white-washed architecture of Gubla was coming into focus. Beyond the sprawling city were lush green slopes of cedar trees and, in the far distance, dazzling white peaks, which brought to Senenmut's mind those great man-made mountains near Mennufer, sacred tombs of the ancient rulers of the Two Lands.

The middle-aged tall man's head was uncovered, his closely cropped hair bright-coppery in the midday sun. The salty sea breeze repeatedly blew shorter Minmes's shoulder-length raven hair in thin veils across his face, so that he had to finger-comb and push it behind his ears. Senenmut wore a linen tunic with long kilt and reed sandals, his familiar attire. The Kheftiu-born somewhat younger man sported just a short wraparound kilt and was barefooted.

The two were newly exiled from the Two Lands and Gubla was their destination of choice. Technically, only the former Great Steward of the Estates of Amen-Re was the exile. His body-servant, aide, confidante and bed mate had freely chosen to accompany his intimate companion of several floodings in the latter's banishment. Senenmut would have preferred the island nation of Kheftiu as the alien place to live out his remaining years; but Minmes had been reluctant to return to the exotic homeland he hadn't known since a very young boy, and the fallen bureaucrat had deferred to his friend's preference for Gubla (which a young Minmes had visited on one occasion, when en route to Kemet on his father's trading ship, quite a few floodings before).

On Kheftiu Senenmut might have encountered Prince Tao, whose own exile he had engineered, once upon a time — that is, if the scion of the no-longer-viable House of Tao still lived. But Gubla apparently harbored a sizeable community of expatriate citizens of Kemet, so settling in there would probably prove less stressful, ultimately. Unbeknown to the Mistress of the Two Lands — whose sudden fierce animosity had sealed his fate — her sympathetic Coregent had provided Senenmut with a royal letter of introduction to the tribute-paying vassal princeling who ruled the City in the Cedar Groves. Thus, perhaps the man who so recently had been the most powerful commoner in all of Kemet might find some sort of employment in this busy trading hub — at least a task even slightly up to his considerable bureaucratic talents.

Without looking towards his shipmate of ten risings and settings of Re, Minmes finally spoke. "I really detest these squawking birds. I've seen them before in Mennufer, at the wharves, but usually only one or two at a time."

"Lost, those," replied Senenmut. "I hope their collective loud nastiness here doesn't forebode our official welcome in Gubla."

"Well, you *know* what the scroll says. At any rate, there seemingly won't be our ordered beheadings on arrival, as Her Majesty might've wanted. But perhaps the ruler of this place is literate in the Kemet language and will guess that you've read Son of Re Born of Djehuty's private letter before presenting it to him."

"The chance of that is far smaller than small, beloved Born of Min. Even so, he certainly won't know that the official stamped seal of the Lord of the Two Lands has been replaced by that from our own signet ring."

The extensive wharves of Gubla drew ever closer. Dark pinpoints of human activity there could be made out by both men.

Minmes turned completely around, resting his elbows and bare lower back against the ship's smooth hand-railing. He then brushed the fanning hair out of his eyes, yet again. "Why do you suppose Son of Re Born of Djehuty gave you the letter of introduction?" he asked his fellow exile. "Perhaps a quiet defiance of the Coregent?"

Senenmut continued leaning forward on the railing, gazing towards Gubla in the distance. He was silent, as if lost in his own thoughts.

After several long moments he looked at Minmes.

"That possibly was the case. My relationship with the younger Born of Djehuty was much closer than Noblest Woman ever knew. That their Coregency arrangement works so well has amazed me, frankly, especially since there's never been any real familial love between those two. That he's never defied her openly, now that he's fully adult, escaped my understanding. She's a truly formidable woman, as I should know, cut from the same cloth as the Great One, Moon Born, Beautiful Companion — who terrorized everyone in the House of Tao, the harridan. But Born of Djehuty is not his father's son, figuratively speaking. He isn't cowed by Noblest Woman as the second Born of Djehuty was. Rather he just smiles that enigmatic smile of his, tents his fingers on his broad chest and precedes to do as he personally wishes, quietly, without her ever suspecting — as in the case of the letter of introduction in question. He's just biding his time, I think."

"Waiting for her to die? Or for a time to rid himself of her?"

"The first, to be certain. Time is on his side. I very much doubt that he'd ever depose True Soul of Re or otherwise dispose of her. That would go against his own character. He understands that she very likely saved him his throne, from possible usurpation by the Taos, and has definite gratitude for that, I'm sure. His stepmother/aunt will be gone one day, alas, then Lasting Manifestation of Re will come fully into his own, mark my word. He's a good enough ruler now and will be a truly great one in time."

Senenmut looked towards looming Gubla again and resumed contemplating his own very uncertain future.

SEVERAL WEEKS EARLIER
THE RESIDENCE, MENNUFER

S enenmut, Great Steward of the Estates of Amen-Re, and possessor of a plethora of other grand titles, stood two arms length from the closed cedar double doors of the principal audience hall in the Residence of the Lord and Mistress of the Two Lands in the northern capital, Mennufer. Sporting a growth of white-flecked coppery whiskers, his bare head was uncustomarily bowed and his wrists bound together below his bureaucrat's ample belly. Barefooted, he wore a soiled simple tunic and was flanked by a pair of lance-bearing Medjay royal guards, both only a little taller than himself. Immediately in front of him, his back to him, was Vizier of the North Amenuserhat, a portly aging man with a shaved head, who was rapping his baton of office against a polished bronze plate centered on one of the door panels.

The most powerful individual in Kemet — after the two Living Horuses, of course — was still at a loss to why he was standing there at that moment, unkept, bound and guarded like some criminal. How it had come about, he knew well enough.

Over seven crossings of Re before, shortly after dawn, he was just awaking alongside his still-snoring bed companion, Minmes, when there had been a loud disturbance in the antechamber to the sleeping space of his country estate, just outside Waset, the southern capital of Kemet. Suddenly the double doors had burst open, with half-a-dozen armed Medjay police rushing into the dimly illuminated room with a wider-than-usual bed on the low platform at its center. Senenmut had sat bolt upright, as he and the just-stirring younger man were surrounded by the half-naked black mercenaries from Wawat. Both of them were then roughly dragged off the bed by the intruders, who seemed greatly amused to have found the two fully nude males together, and laughed loudly, pointing to the slender Khefti's impressively erect state. In a thick accent, the captain of the team had ordered the two to attire themselves; and Senenmut wrapped on his loincloth, pulling the previous day's tunic over his head, while Minmes simply wound on his discarded short kilt, having eschewed a loincloth the evening before.

With all the authority he could command — and he'd been decidedly shaken by what was transpiring — Senenmut had stood at his full height and demanded an explanation of the captain, even as his hands were being tightly tied behind his buttocks with a green-hide thong.

"See, soon," was all the grinning captain had responded.

After being allowed to step into their sandals, the bureaucrat and his somewhat-younger companion had been led away to a donkey cart waiting outside the estate gateway. Forced to sit on the plank floor of the conveyance, they'd been escorted by the trotting Medjay on a bumpy ride back into Waset and the police headquarters there. They'd been subsequently untied and then shoved together into a dank, grimy cell with only a small grilled window near the ceiling in one wall and musty straw on the floor, but without a bench or stools for sitting, or even a pot to piss in. That day had slowly passed without further interference from their jailers — nor the presentation of any food or drink.

When the cell was completely dark, except for vertical pale slivers of moonlight emitted through the high window grille, Senenmut and Minmes had been jerked from their slumberings by the sound of bolts being drawn on the heavy-plank door. When it had finally swung open, both prisoners were standing again. Just a backlighted silhouette to them, the Medjay captain had ordered the two men to follow him; and, when they'd stepped one after the other through the cell door, the upper arms of each of them had been tightly gripped by two pairs of spear-toting black guards.

Still without being told why this was happening, Senenmut and Minmes had been allowed to urinate onto the ground, were bound again, blindfolded that time, and made to climb onto a cart — probably the same one which had brought them into Waset. Another bumpy ride had ended at The River wharves of the southern capital, where they'd been taken on board a vessel, freed of their bindings and blindfolds, and confined in a small midship cabin with sealed windows and no furnishings.

The downstream sail to Mennufer had taken the usual several crossings of Re. The moldy bread and soured beer they'd been afforded through a door slot was consumed in darkness — save for what little daylight leaked through the walling of the cabin — sitting on the plank floor. There'd been no reason not to, so, as was their habit anyway, the two men satisfied each other sexually several times during The River voyage.

Upon arriving at Mennufer's docks, the pair had been taken off board at night — again blindfolded and wrists bound — to further imprisonment, presumably in the local Medjay station; but that time Minmes had been put in a separate cell. Senenmut had sat alone in his own cramped space, which did at least have a stool, a piss pot and a smelly straw-filled mattress of sorts to recline on. Again, the single window was so high in the wall, it had been impossible to look through it. At least two risings and settings of Re's barque had occurred before he'd found himself standing before the familiar doors to the main audience hall of the Mennufer Residence. Senenmut had not bathed during his confinement, of course, and was well aware of his personal appearance and pronounced stench.

Those tall doors swung inwards and Vizier Amenuserhat passed through. The Medays' grips on his upper arms indicated that Senenmut was to follow. He raised his bristly head and looked straight forward. Many cubits away, over the bureaucrat's rounded bare shoulder, he could see the Lord and Mistress of the Two Lands seated side by side, elevated on the throne dais at the rear of the hall. The two rulers were attired in formal regalia, Menkheperre wearing the Red Crown, Maatkare sporting the counterpart White Crown, as was usually her choice.

Two facing double rows of armchairs were arranged perpendicularly to the dais, a few cubits separating the files, and seated on these were members of the High Council and other notables of the royal court at Mennufer, including the First Prophet of Ptah and Hapusenub, First Prophet of Amen-Re, who only rarely traveled to the northern capital. Placed between these arrayed spectators, facing towards the enthroned Double Living Horuses was an empty three-legged stool. Senenmut was led to this by the Medjays, and instructed to sit on it by Amenuserhat, who then untied his bound wrists, and took one of the empty chairs to the Great Steward's right, alongside Vizier of the South Merymaat. The Medjays retreated to the hall's double doors, closed these and took flanking positions there alongside a fellow pair of guards. In the space between Senenmut's stool and the front edge of the dais was a low table on which rested a chunk of red stone, that he did not immediately recognize.

The prisoner avoided eye contact with either of the rulers, looking instead at the soiled hands folded on his thighs. It seemed interminably long moments before the Female Living Horus addressed him.

"Look at Our Person, Brother of Mut."

He raised his chin and stared straight at his benefactor of so many floodings.

"You do realize *why* you're here, in these humiliating circumstances."

Her typical statement/question, he thought.

"Precisely, no, Your Majesty." His voice was hoarse, but then he had not spoken to anyone in a very long while.

"Well, in part, because of that piece of stone there. You recognize it, we assume."

"Again, no, Your Majesty."

"So, pick it up and examine it. Perhaps then your memory will uncloud."

Senenmut leaned forward and lifted the object, sitting rigidly upright on the stool again. It was obviously a broken fragment of something, the corner edge of two flat, smoothly finished surfaces. It had almost certainly originated from the red-stone quarries of Swenet, at the First Cataract, gateway to Wawat. Still it did not dawn on him what exactly it was — or had been — and what its relationship was to him, seemingly a cause for his arrest and imprisonment.

"I'm at a loss, Your Majesty. I don't recognize what this is — or used to be, since it's obviously a broken part of something."

"Would it surprise you then, Brother of Mut, that is was until just recently a part of the grand coffin-chest that you'd secretly installed in the resting chamber of your grand Mansion for Millions of Years on the west of Waset?"

"If Your Majesty says so, it must be, but I wouldn't know that myself. I must presume that the object to which you refer has been destroyed." Without asking permission to do so, Senenmut leaned forward and placed the heavy fragment back on the table, sitting upright again.

"*Totally!* Smashed into countless pieces by Our Majesties' agents. This, we are told, is one of the larger bits, brought to us as proof of its destruction." There was another long pause, while Maatkare held the Great Steward's unblinking gaze. "You realize why Our Person ordered that done, Brother of Mut." To his silence she brittlely replied, "Because it was an abomination to us, this coffin-chest which you secretly ordered fashioned in blatant imitation of those chests of our own, of our father, our husband — in the very shape of the *shenu*, the royal name-ring! What's more, fashioned in the sacred red-stone, the use of which is the exclusive prerogative of wearers of the Double Crown — *exclusive!*"

Senenmut let his receded chin drop, breaking eye contact with his interrogator.

Maatkare continued, "Do you have any explanation for this blasphemy, Brother of Mut? Or did you rationalize that your oh-so-elevated position in the Two Lands — 'Lord High and Mighty of This and That', as our beloved Asar Beauty of Re dubbed to you — entitled Lord Amen-Re's bureaucrat to rest for all eternity as if he'd actually ruled the Black Land instead of being only its most favored — and, we would add, most *trusted* — servant?"

After another pause, Senenmut looked up again, replying, "My pride betrayed my better judgment, Your Majesty. I dared presume you would never know of my overstepping. I humbly offer my apology."

"Not accepted." Another pause. "As if this particular 'overstepping' was not unforgiveable enough, you've offended us in a far, far more *blasphemous* way, Brother of Mut. And you very well know what that is."

"You've been informed of my cenotaph, I imagine."

"Another of your secrets kept from us! Had you personally requested it of us, we might've — no, *would* have — permitted you to make yourself a modest memorial in the vicinity of our Holiest of Holy Places, in our appreciation of all your many services to us and the Two Lands. But it was reported to us, and now confirmed by our investigating agents — who included none other than First Prophet of Amen-Re Hapu is Well, present today — that this 'secret' monument of yours has been tunneled so that it intrudes on and violates the very space of My Majesty's sacred precinct itself. We can only imagine that you purposely did this so as to audaciously share in, benefit from, the eternal blessings which we're intending for Our Person, our father and our husband alone!"

"I did not realize, Your Majesty, that it reached as far as the perimeters of the Holiest of Holy Places. Its length was never measured, at least that I was told of."

"Be that as it may, Brother of Mut — and we believe you do dissemble in this regard — your monumental transgression is no more, or will be very soon. As we are speaking, our agents are filling it in, burying it, so it will never be looked upon again."

"Once more, my sincerest apology for offending Your Majesty." Senenmut hung his head. He supposed he should be thankful that, apparently, the relief images of himself he'd caused to be carved behind the doors of several chapels in the Holiest of Holy Places had not been discovered — yet.

"Apologies fall on deaf ears. Our Majesty's confidence and trust in you has vaporized, like spent incense smoke drifting skyward. Were yours the dark offenses of a lesser person than Brother of Mut, we'd likely have him sitting on a stake by the time Lord Re sails over the horizon this evening.

"But no, rather than cutting short your vile life and having your miserable corpse fed to the sons of Sobek, we shall show you our very greatest generosity and send you far away from Our Person and the Two Lands, banished to go into the jaws of Amam one day in a wretched distant foreign place of your own choosing.

"You must be on your way, Brother of Mut, by the time the Barque of Re returns over the eastern horizon tomorrow. If he chooses to do so, we'll allow your Khefti whore-boy to accompany you into your great disgrace. Now, be gone forever from the Living Horuses' divine sight!"

As Senenmut slowly rose to leave the audience hall, bowing his head towards the paired sovereigns, he supposed that his grand Mansion for Millions of Years would remain forever unfinished, since he'd never dwell there now. He couldn't know, of course, that it had already been visited by the hammer-stones of Maatkare's "agents."

* * *

11

Thanks to Lord Amen-Re, someone had the foresight to put up this sun-shade, thought Royal Nurse In Sitre, as she fanned herself where she sat shielded from the late-morning desert glare by a small roofed canvas pavilion hastily erected against boulders jutting out from the base of the high cliff face rising above the dark rectangle that marked the entryway to her mistress's Mansion for Eternity. From this vantage point, In could also look towards the spot down the gravel-strewn slope where the entrance to her personal final resting chamber was just visible. Mounting roughly-hewn steps, sweat-slick, stark-naked workmen would emerge up from that dark gash in the bedrock at intervals, balancing large baskets of whitish stone flakes on bent backs, to carry these away around a rock obstruction and out of In's view, presumably to dump the excavation debris — inasmuch as each would return after a bit with his rush-work basket empty and then descend again out of sight. The nurse had not, in fact, actually seen this subterranean place being prepared for her, so that she would lie for all time close by the woman to whom her entire adult life had been devoted. In, of course, had been shown the plan for the simple chamber with a single side-room; but she had no desire to visit there while still drawing breath — even had her great girth and shuffling gait not been basic issues mitigating against any personal inspection tour.

Such as was at this very moment being undertaken by Mistress of the Two Lands Maatkare Hatshepsut in the third kingly Mansion for Eternity to be hewn in this isolated, rugged, lifeless gorge — the others belonging to her father and husband, both gone for many, many floodings. Although counseled by the First Prophet of Amen, her Coregent Menkheperre and others of her closest advisors against a visit to the site beyond its entrance, the Mistress of the Two Lands — in her wilful fashion — had waved aside the difficulties and even dangers involved in descending all the way to the resting chamber, which lay deep in the bedrock, at the end of a pair of very long connecting corridors and then beyond a large antechamber, positioned — as best estimate could have it — directly behind the central offering chapel of the Holiest of Holy Places, her grand memorial mansion nearing completion on the other side of the high mountain-range.

The present visit had required considerable preparation — such as the building of the temporary pavilion wherein Nurse In was awaiting now her mistress's return to the surface — and the expedition this day from the Residence at Waset, the southern capital, had included a small army of royal retainers. Lord of the Two Lands Menkheperre had not accompanied the royal party to Waset, electing to remain instead down river at Mennufer, in order to oversee pertinent army matters there. But most of the High Council had sailed south with Her Majesty and so had no intervening option but to accompany the ruler across The River and on the very long, plodding trek through flood-plain cultivation and into the inhospitable mountain-rimmed canyon — where some decades before Asar Akheperkare Djehutymes had decided to break with royal tradition and locate his unmarked Mansion for Eternity, hidden somewhere deep within the bedrock there.

While Mistress of the Two Lands Maatkare and her companion, Nurse In, had been transported all the way aloft within their individual roofed, curtained palanquins, the several male courtiers (plus First Prophet Hapusenub and Vizier of the South Merymaat) had traveled by chariots — the horses at walking pace — with numerous royal attendants of both sexes and a six-man force of Medjay bodyguards trailing behind on foot. Once the ruler and her parched counselors finally reached the remote site, liquid refreshment awaiting them there had been partaken within the pavilion; then Hapusenub — as putative architect of Maatkare's Mansion for Eternity — preceded by several torch-bearers, led Her Majesty down into the bowels of the soaring mountain, followed in single file by the royal-counselors contingent.

While the others descended on foot, Maatkare Hatshepsut herself had disappeared through the rectangular entryway sitting fully erect on a carrying chair borne at arms' length by four muscular black men of Wawat, who'd been called out from the two palanquin teams of royal porters. Thoroughly forewarned about the very great heat she would experience once within the mountain depths, the co-ruler had eschewed a wig or crown that morning, her grey-streaked shoulder-length hair held in place by a simple gold fillet fronted by the rearing royal cobra. Attired in a sleeveless plain sheath-dress, she carried on her narrow lap a fan of trimmed ostrich feathers and an embossed-leather flask, containing water with which to refresh herself, as it might very well prove necessary.

After a short time, In Sitre grew bored by her lonely vigil — although she certainly wasn't alone, inasmuch as the male and female attendants and Medjay bodyguards squatted, chattering among themselves, in what spots of shade from boulders existed in the near vicinity of the resting pavilion; and the palanquin bearers and chariot divers and grooms were posted some distance away, out of the nurse's view. Rather than sheer boredom, it was more probably the quantity of wine In had continuously sipped that finally brought her bewigged head forward, as much as the double chin permitted. Her snoring doze was interrupted, however, by a sudden commotion from within the Mansion for Eternity's entrance.

In's head jerked up and she saw Vizier of the South Merymaat emerge from the black rectangle, quickly followed by another High Council member, whose name she couldn't just then recall. Their linen tunics and kilts wilted and stained with perspiration, both men were feebly shouting to the royal attendants — who were all now on their feet — both babbling simultaneously that a strong man was needed within, immediately. One of the carrying chair's porters had collapsed into unconsciousness on the steep return ascent, Merymaat rasped, consequently nearly dumping Her Majesty in the nearly airless corridor; and the grounded Mistress of the Two Lands was now complaining of short breath and faintness herself.

Instantly all half-dozen of the Medjays were scrambling up the gravel incline to the entryway, the two exhausted nobles stepping aside so that the lean tall black men could crowd inside, disappearing from In Sitre's view. The attendants murmured together anxiously; and one of the Residence men dashed off downhill, to alert the palanquin teams and charioteers.

It seemed like an eternity to the now fully awake nurse, before the royal counselors began emerging one by one into the daylight, all looking very much the worse for their experience in the mountain's heated bowels. Several more long moments passed before two spears-burdened Medjays in the lead came out, followed immediately by their four comrades bearing the carrying chair with its royal passenger — who was upright but slumped, her head bowed. Hard on their heels followed two porters, carrying their inanimate squad-man slung between them, the fourth of their number close behind. Hapusenub and others of the High Council staggered into Re's glare, one after the other, all with their linen attire drenched by sweat.

In Sitre had raised her bulk out of the armchair she'd been occupying, but didn't move to step off the low platform of the pavilion —

which was now occupied by Residence serving women, busily pouring wine and water into glazed-ceramic goblets from numerous amphorae lugged there for the very purpose of provisioning the royal expedition on completion of the inspection tour. With effort the nurse bent to pick up one of these from the low table holding the goblets, one with wine, to have it ready for handing to her mistress. As the carrying chair was brought into the pavilion's shade, Maatkare Hatshepsut slowly lifted her damp head and smiled weakly towards her old companion.

"That really was quite like going into Lord Asar's dark realm, Ancient One," the ruler addressed In Sitre in a hoarse whisper, wiping her sweat-beaded brow with a thoroughly soaked handkerchief and reaching out for the offered drink, even as the chair was being carefully lowered to the floor planking. Her small hand visibly shaking, Maatkare tilted her head back and downed the tepid wine in several unregal gulps. In Sitre had once again taken the space's single seat, which had been brought there solely for the ruler's use. The latter, however, clearly was intending to stay put on the carrying chair, until being returned to her waiting palanquin.

The four Medjays had stepped away in unison and then off the pavilion, returning to their waiting cohorts, to recover the spears they had handed off when relieving the chair porters. Hapusenub, Merymaat and the other High Council members began coming under the sun-shade, accepting in turn the goblets of refreshment held out by the servers. The several palanquin porters had by now come running up the hill and were gathered around their prostrate mate, who had not yet responded to having a jug of water poured over his head and bare chest. One kneeling porter laid his ear on the man's glossy ebony pectoral and said something in Wawish to the others, who began shaking their shiny shaved heads negatively. The fellow was no longer breathing, it appeared.

"Well, First Prophet, for our poor porter's sake, we perhaps should have listened to your foreboding about seeing in person exactly where our mortal bones and those of our beloved father, Asar Great Soul of Re, shall spend eternity," Maatkare addressed Hapusenub — who, not being even middle-aged any longer, was still laboring with effort to bring his seriously aggravated breathing under control.

She held out her goblet for a refill, then directed her remarks to the High Counsel members in attendance. "But, by visiting there today, Our Person now has a great appreciation for all of those brave workmen who've given their lives to make this very demanding place ready for us. It's a wonder that even a great many more of them haven't expired under their baskets of rock chip or even with mallet and chisel in hand!

"The suggestion by him whose name we no longer speak — that

the veneering blocks for the resting chamber's walls and its columns be decorated with *What Is in the Underworld* texts and images *prior* to being taken down for installation — makes perfect sense to us now, although we previously had favored having them plastered and painted once in place. Our talented royal scribes are few enough as it is, so we can't very well have those quick-tongued, thick-waisted fellows gasping their last desperate breaths down there, can we?"

Mistress of the Two Lands Maatkare, Daughter of Re Hatshepsut drained her goblet a second time — and accepted yet another refill. After she'd downed that, the royal entourage made the tedious long trek back to The River, crossed over and returned to the Residence, with the First Prophet of Amen-Re, the Vizier and other notables then going their separate ways. The aging co-ruler of Kemet would never again in life return to her penultimate resting place.

FOURTEEN FLOODINGS EARLIER, INUNDATION 4
COREGENCY OF MAATKARE/MENKHEPERRE
FORTRESS OF BUHEN, SECOND CATARACT, WAWAT

Her Majesty Maatkare Hatshepsut was still wearing her bulbous blue-leather war crown as she approached the spacious audience chamber of the commandant of the Fortress of Buhen. (She couldn't remove the *Khepresh* in the manner of a male ruler, inasmuch as her long natural hair had been coiled and tied into a cone atop her head by Nurse In Sitre, and would've therefore been unpresentable beyond her personal apartments — which she had not yet been taken to in the fortress's residence area.) She was preceded into the space by Commandant Unnefer, who, once through the doorway, immediately stepped to one side, bowing at the waist and gesturing for the Female Horus to enter. Maatkare was followed by Generalissimo Besenmut and five other of her general officers, plus Unnefer's second-in-command, one Captain Mentu, young King's Scribe Senimen and — bringing up the rear — elderly Royal Nurse In Sitre, of course.

A number of armchairs and straight-back seats, plus a few stools, as well, were clustered in a semi-circle in the middle of the columned chamber, facing a small, low dais from which Unnefer usually conducted interviews and like business. He indicated that the sovereign should take the armchair positioned there. Once Maatkare was in place, the others seated themselves, Senimen and In Sitre selecting stools at the rear of the assembly, as was suitable to their civilian stations in this otherwise-military company. Senimen carried his scribal palette and several small sheets of papyrus for note taking. Almost immediately three serving women entered the chamber, bearing trays loaded with plain ceramic tumblers and a single gold chalice, which Unnefer took, stood and presented the elegant vessel of refreshment to the sovereign, Maatkare.

The Female Horus and her generals — and Senimen and In Sitre — had arrived at the huge riverside fortress only shortly before, in advance of the Army of Kemet, which that morning had defeated a sizeable ragtag force of rebellious local wretches — most of whom had fled the battlefield in complete disarray. Her Majesty had not physically participated in the brief skirmish — nor Besenmut and the other general officers, for that matter — but rather observed the action at a remove, from a temporary sun-shade erected on a low rise overlooking the desert plain where the dirt eaters made their pathetic assault on the superior assembled, ordered ranks of Kemet infantry. She had, however, personally visited the battlefield immediately after the departing rebels disappeared over the barren horizon, walking among the numerous befeathered black corpses there, picking up a few souvenirs (a bow, a throw stick, even a small, round spotted-cowhide shield) to take back north to Waset, for presentation as war trophies to her young Coregent, Lord of the Two Lands Menkheperre, Son of Re Djehutymes.

He, being only seven floodings old, had, protesting, remained behind at the Southern Capital, to "govern" Kemet in her absence (which, in fact, was being taken care of quite ably, she was certain, by Great Steward Senenmut and First Prophet of Amen-Re Hapusenub). Her High Council — which included those two, as well as Generalissimo Besenmut — had strongly counseled against Maatkare personally leading the Army of Kemet in a policing expedition to distant wretched Wawat; but she'd overruled those objections and thus now had satisfied her secret ambition to return one day to the Yellow Land, where she'd visited once as a mere child, in the company of her campaigning father, the great warrior-king Asar Akheperkare Djehutymes. It was in Wawat, after all, where Lord of the Two Lands Akheperkare had declared "Prince" Hatshepsut his successor — at least as she'd chosen to remember the occasion. And she also wanted to see the impressive Fortress of Buhen again, inasmuch as she had decided to build a mansion there for the god Horus.

After general brief sipping of the beverage by everyone — which was local beer, not wine — Maatkare spoke first, as was protocol.

"Well, now, congratulations are in order to Generalissimo Besenmut and the other commanders, for our decided victory this morning over the poor Black Devils." She raised the gold chalice in a salute to the officers.

The others lifted their humble tumblers with murmers of assent.

"And Commandant Unnefer," she continued, "We thank you for your hospitality here at the Fortress. Our stay will be brief, overnight only, as Our Person must be on the way back down The River to the First Cataract and Senwet, where the royal fleet awaits the Army's and our victorious return to Waset."

"Your Majesty is most welcomed to linger here at Buhen, for as long as Your Majesty would like," Unnefer replied. "Our accommodations are rough but clean, provisions plain but plentiful, thanks to the always generous largesse of the Double Horuses."

"Before we are shown to those accommodations, Commandant, it is Our Person's desire to walk about within the walls of the Fortress, so that we may determine exactly where to build an abode for Lord Horus, which shall be known as the Mansion of Horus of Buhen. It was the intention of our father, Asar Akheperkare Djehutymes, to raise this; but, as all know, he suddenly flew to heaven prematurely, and so it is our present plan to fulfill his wishes accordingly."

"The personnel of Buhen will be most honored to have Lord Horus dwelling here among us!" Unnefer responded, beaming, obviously pleased.

"Before we depart to make our tour of the Fortress grounds, Commandant, Our Majesty must ask a question," said Maatkare. "Your second-in-command," she pointed to where he sat in the second rank of chairs, "Captain Menna, is it? You seem familiar to us, although we haven't been able to think why that's so. Please rise. Why should the Mistress of the Two Lands know you?"

The tall young officer stood up.

"It is *Mentu*, Your Majesty. And I am both greatly pleased and very embarrassed that you should perhaps recognize me in this place, Buhen, where my chief duty is overseeing provisioning of the garrison and relations between we military personnel and the sizeable settlement of wretched locals round about the Fort."

"Yes, a challenging job, second-guessing those half-savages, who will say one thing today and do something quite else tomorrow. But you've not answered our question, Captain. Again, just why should Our Person recognize you, and from where?"

"Well, Your Majesty, it's *your* doing that I'm here. I'm banished here to Buhen by Your Majesty's personal order." Mentu's handsome countenance had darkened to a deeper bronze. He hung his head, then raised his chin again.

"Explain."

"Yes, Your Majesty. Two floodings ago I was stationed as a marine officer at Waset. My responsibility was directing the flow of passenger barges which daily ferried workers at your glorious Holiest of Holy Places, from the east bank of The River where they lived to the west one for their labor.

"One unfortunate day three of these heavily loaded barges were simultaneously swamped by a herd of river horses and a score or more of the passengers perished from drowning or else in the jaws of the sons of Sobek. I was not myself present when this disaster happened, but nonetheless was charged with having permitted the ferries to cross when a herd of those spawns of Set were occupying the mid-River at the time.

"I appeared very briefly before your Majesty in audience at the Residence, for your final judgment of my case, which was rendered as as 'guilty' and banishment for five floodings to here, Buhen. I was, *am*, most grateful, to have been spared the stake."

"Thank you for that, shall we say, most-thorough explanation, *Mentu*. Frankly, we don't recall your case, only your face. Perhaps My Majesty was so lenient because, well, your face *pleased* us." Maatkare caught the eye of King's Scribe Senimen, who had looked up from his note taking. She smiled at him. He winked back.

"We would commute your sentence here and now, captain, except that you are surely most indispensable to Commandant Unnefer. When your remaining three floodings are completed, and you return to Waset or Mennufer, make your presence known to whichever Residence and we certainly shall be able to find something for you in our personal service."

Maatkare rose, and the others quickly stood as well.

"So, now, let us go see where to build that new Mansion of Horus of Buhen."

Stepping off the dais, she strode from the chamber, her entourage following single file, Senimen and In Sitre bringing up the rear.

LATER THAT EVENING, MAATKARE'S GUEST QUARTERS, BUHEN

The impromptu banquet hosted by Commandant Unnefer for Her Majesty and the Kemet generals in the modest dining hall of his Buhen residence had proven predictably provencial, the food and drink "plain," indeed, if "plentiful" enough. The company had been as boring as would be expected on the frontier, consisting of the Fortress's several junior officers and their native wives — as well as handsome bachelor Mentu — plus a very few dignitaries from the sprawling small town beyond Buhen's high walls — local chieftains who, although they affected the attire of Kemet, were still very much primitives at the core. The banquet's mercifully brief entertainment had been local, as well, of course: half-a-dozen near-naked Wawat men in dyed feathers and body paint, writhing and contorting to the loud rude accompaniment of drums and rattles. Pleading fatigue and an early departure in the morning, Her Majesty had excused herself from the festivities as soon as it was polite to do so, knowing that having dined, however briefly, with the Female Living Horus in person would prove to have been the all-time high point in the dull lives of those Buhen rustics present.

Captain Mentu and four Medjay guards had escorted Maatkare Hatshepsut back to her modest Fortress guest quarters — from which they had collected her earlier — and she'd been sorely tempted to toss protocol and caution to the desert wind and invite in the charming young officer, whose most-attractive face — and obvious hard-lean fitness — were "pleasing" her anew. A temptation resisted, however, as other plans for the rest of the Daughter of Re's evening were already firmly in place.

Nurse In Sitre was lifting a broad collar of gold and carnelian beads from Hatshepsut's bare chest, when a light knocking sounded at the chamber's single cedar door. The old nurse carefully placed the elaborate piece in an open drawer of a small inlaid jewelry chest on the table beside her mistress's armchair, then shuffled across the room to admit the expected visitor. Hatshepsut shook her shoulder-length raven hair, the formal wig and cobra band she had worn to the banquet having been removed just earlier. She sipped a Delta vintage from her expedition's provisions.

When the single panel was unlatched and pulled inward, King's Scribe Senimen walked right in, patting Nurse on her fleshy forearm as he passed. The pair of Medjays guarding the entrance were from the Waset Residence and so had not challenged Her Majesty's well-familiar evening caller. Handsome Senimen, wigless, attired in just a knee-length fresh kilt and reed sandals, carried his scribal palette and a roll of papyrus, maintaining what had long been his personal charade.

"Dearest Fish," Hatshepsut unnecessarily addressed In still at the open door, "we've some private dictation for our King's Scribe. Could you be a sweetheart and find something else to occupy yourself with? Until you observe Brother of Amen depart?"

Without responding the old woman closed the door and was gone — but to where in this foreign place? Hatshepsut's brief thought was that perhaps her old confidante had already caused a chair to be positioned in a dark alcove, so that she could watch for the young scribe returning finally to his own assigned sleeping space. Or nodding off, more likely.

In no time two sweat-glossed naked bodies were interlocked on the narrow bed of the guest chamber, goldenly illuminated by the flickering wick of a single brazier.

A Few Weeks Later, the Residence, Waset

Young Lord of the Two Lands Menkheperre had stepped down from the loggia into his co-ruler's private garden, accompanied by his tutor, King's Scribe Senimen, to try out the bark-inlaid throw stick just presented to him by Mistress of the Two Lands Maatkare Hatshepsut, one part of the "trophies of war" which she'd brought back as his gifts from the expedition she'd recently led to that reportedly desolate far-off place way up The River, which was originally home to the tall black-skinned men who stood with spears outside the doorways of royal apartments in the Southern and Northern Residences. He'd left the long bow (much too long for his still-short arms) and strange-looking spotted small shield with dangling green feathers laying on the low table where Her Majesty and his pubescent half-sister, God's Wife of Amen Neferure, were seated in armchairs. The seven-floodings-old ruler threw the curved weapon with all of his might, and it wobbled through the air, to disappear in dense shrubbery against a garden wall. Neferure laughed loudly.

"*I* could do better than *that*, Hawk Beak!" the girl with the budding bare breasts piped from the loggia shadows. "You throw like a *baby!*"

"Enough of that, Beauty," chastised her mother. "Hawk Beak *is* still a young boy, after all. Even you couldn't have done any better when you were only seven floodings. A throw stick takes practice."

Changing the subject, Neferure cheerfully demanded, "Tell me again, Mother, how you bashed out the bloody brains of the naked monkey-men!"

"We did *not* say that *we* did that, Beauty. What we *did* say was that it's long been the tradition for Lords of the Two Lands to ritually club to death enemy chiefs captured in battle, as gratitude offerings to Lord Hidden One. Unfortunately, or fortunately for them, none of the Wawat rebels were captured alive." Maatkare reached for the faience goblet on the table in front of her and sipped its contents. "Very many died by the blades and arrows of the Black Land's stalwart foot soldiers, to be sure; but most of the poor primitives proved just frightened cowards and dashed away instead, as fast as their long legs could carry them, shitting down their thighs as they ran."

Maatkare had not actually witnessed that herself, so was only reporting third or fourth hand what her front-line soldiers had claimed later.

Neferure laughed loudly again. "That must have been very, very funny, the monkey-men shitting themselves, I mean." She reached for a bunch of grapes from a fruit platter on the table, popping one, two, three in her mouth. "And the walls of this old fort-place where you stayed overnight were the highest you've ever seen, you *did* say."

Like her mother, Neferure often asked questions as statements.

"Yes, Beauty, much higher than those around the Mansion of Lord Amen-Re, with many even taller towers at the gates and numerous other places. It must have taken a very long time and much effort to construct. It was first built by our ancestors of the House of Amen at the Head, countless floodings ago. The commandant of the place — which is named Buhen — told us it has been altered and enlarged several times over many generations"

"I remember Brother of Mut going on and on and on about them, the Amen at the Heads, that they were the last powerful rulers of the Two Lands until our not-so-distant ancestor, The Liberator. He made it really very *boring*, though. But Brother of Mut is always really *very* boring, as I'm sure you well know, Mother."

"I am, am I?"

Senenmut had come onto the loggia.

"Great Steward, welcome." Hatshepsut twisted in her armchair to look back at him. "Please join us. Have a seat." She gestured to one of the empty armchairs at the low table. "Beauty of Re was just talking to hear herself talk, which is her habit, as *you* well know."

"Well I was a *pupil* of Lord High and Mighty of This and That, Mother," Neferure responded, plucking more grapes and popping them one after the other into her mouth, all the while batting her kohl-rimmed eyes at the tall bureaucrat, who had taken a seat opposite her.

She had been shorn of her Horus Sidelock upon reaching twelve floodings the previous year and now wore her hair closely cropped, as was the practical fashion for the God's Wife of Amen — which the princess had been since her mother became the Female Horus four floodings back and relinquished that sacerdotal role. However, she donned a sleeveless sheath dress appropriate to her age only when performing the God's Wife rituals; otherwise her attire while in the Residence was a man's-style short kilt that she wore topless, even though her brightly rouged nipples were now supported by the hint of incipient breasts.

"We were talking about Mother's just-completed grand expedition to put down the wretched monkey-men way up The River," Neferure continued, talking while chewing her mouthful of grapes. "She was telling me how she bashed out all their brains and hung their ugly, shit-stained naked dead bodies from the really high walls of the big fort."

Hatshepsut shook her head as she looked towards Senenmut.

"We said no such thing, did no such thing. Beauty of Re has a way-too-vivid imagination, as you've frequently reported to Our Person, Brother of Mut."

"Oh, telling tales out of school were you, Tutor?" Neferure spat some grape seeds onto the plastered floor.

Before Senenmut could respond, young Lord of the Two Lands Menkheperre stepped back onto the loggia, followed at his heels by King's Scribe Senimen, who was carrying the retrieved throw stick.

The Coregent plopped into an empty armchair immediately next to his half-sister. Nodding to both Her Majesty and the Great Steward in turn, the youthful tutor-scribe pulled out the straight-back chair on the other side of Neferure and likewise sat down. Both boy and man wore a sheen of perspiration on their naked torsos above sweat-stained white short kilts. Senimen laid the throw stick on the table and lifted the faience goblet he'd been drinking from before accompanying his young charge into the garden.

"Did you master the Wawat throw stick, Hawk Beak?" Her Majesty asked.

He shook his head in the negative. "Some of the little bark inlays fell out. It's not very well made."

Senenmut offered, "It was probably only meant to be thrown once, in battle."

Looking sideways at her sibling, holding her small nose, Neferure remarked to him, "Phew, you do stink like a shity monkey-man, Hawk Beak!"

She then turned to Senimen seated to the other side of her, reaching out and running an index finger down the length of his hard brown bicep. "So does Brother of Amen," she added, holding the damp finger to her nose and then licking it, "but in a very much nicer way!"

"God's Wife! You're dismissed! Leave Our Person's presence now." Hatshepsut barked. "Go directly to your apartment and stay there until you're sent for."

The princess immediately stood, hands demurely folded on her narrow bare chest, below the scarlet nipples.

"House arrest again. *However* shall I amuse myself?" She put the guilty finger to her pursed lips and sucked its tip. "I think I know!" And she darted off the loggia through the doorway opening onto to her mother's sitting chamber.

Hatshepsut shook her head. Senimen self-consciously bowed his. Senenmut tried not to smile. And the Living Horus giggled and clapped approval.

Four Floodings Later, Inundation 8
Coregency of Maatkare/Menkheperre
The Residence, Waset

God's Wife of Amen Neferure walked into the smallish antechamber of her apartment in the Waset Residence, already pulling over her freshly shaved head the simple linen sheath she'd been wearing. She dropped the garment and its red braided-linen girdle on the floor and crossed the sparsely furnished space barefooted, headed for her bedchamber, the double doors of which stood wide open, as if greeting her.

She was returning from having spent the entire long day on the west bank of The River, participating in the tedious annual Beautiful Feast of the Valley rituals orchestrated by the Amen-Re priesthood and conducted by her mother, Mistress of the Two Lands Maatkare, Daughter of Re Hatshepsut, and by her little half-brother, Lord of the Two Lands Menkheperre, Son of Re Djehutymes — or "Hawk Beak," as she preferred to call the prepubescent Coregent. By the time the teenager walked into the bedchamber, dimly lighted by four braziers, she was totally naked, except for two plain-gold bracelets, one on each wrist, part of her sacerdotal regalia.

As she crossed to the dais-elevated bed in the middle of the space, Neferure's personal handmaiden emerged from the latrine doorway in the far wall. Meket was only a couple of floodings older than the princess, the grandniece of her mother's fat old companion, Nurse In. The young woman's bewigged head was down as she came back into the bedchamber, attention focused on readjusting the long plain skirt she wore. She was topless, as Neferure required in the privacy of the apartment. Meket looked up and saw the princess by the bed.

"Oh, Mistress! You startled me. I wasn't expecting you back so soon." She stood rigid and bowed her head again.

"It was a too-tedious day and so very ho-hum as always, and I'm nearly exhausted. Come here, Sweetness, and give God's Wife a kiss."

Neferure opened her thin arms in a welcoming gesture and the handmaiden crossed to her, coming face to face. The two young women locked mouths for several long moments, Neferure fondling one of Meket's melon-sized bare breasts. She then sat on the bed, and the handmaiden backed off the dais.

"Be a dear and go fetch some really good Delta to soothe my parched throat. And bring a second goblet for our guest, as well. And, yes, a full pitcher, too."

"He's coming again this evening?"

"As soon as he's tucked in all his delightful Medjays for Re's Underworld crossing."

Captain Nebet rounded the corner of the passageway intersection and came, as he'd expected to, upon the pair of palace guards assigned to the apartment of the God's Wife — except that Princess Neferure required that they stand at the start of the long corridor leading to her doorway rather than right by the entrance itself, as all other Medjays typically did when on "door duty" — which it was called in their barracks at the Residences. The two tall Wawatmen were slouching against the cool plaster of the corridor wall, but came to stiff attention when their officer suddenly appeared. Nebet said something to them in their mutual tongue, straightened the vertically held lance of one guard, then proceeded down the corridor to the double-door panels. Without knocking he opened these and slipped inside.

The antechamber was empty of any occupants, but by the low illumination of its braziers, the tall, leanly muscular native of Wawat noted the discarded linen sheath on the painted-plaster floor, near the now-closed double doors to the bedchamber of the young woman whom he'd been discreetly commanded that afternoon to service this evening. Nebet wore only the short white kilt and close-fitting linen skullcap of the Medjay livery, plus bronze-studded black-leather wristbands indicating his rank, and leather sandals dyed black as well. He unbelted the bronze dagger at his waist and laid weapon and sheath on a table near the doors, stepping out of the sandals at the same time. He had not bathed at the barracks after returning from the west bank, as the God's Wife always seemed to savor his muskiness when he became sweated, as ever, in the course of their vigorous coupling. The "most handsome man in Kemet" — as the Female Horus had once called him to his face — knew he was expected, so did not knock before pulling open the bedchamber door-panels.

The space within was even less illuminated than the antechamber. In its center was a wide bed, on which lounged the fully nude princess, propped up by several feather-filled embroidered bolsters. She was holding a faience goblet to her lips, about to sip its contents. On a small table by the bed was a tray with a silver ewer and another goblet.

Before approaching the bed and its occupant, Nebet scanned the pillared shadows of the chamber and quickly enough made out the dim form of the handmaiden Meket seated on a stool there. The God's Wife always had the servant as an audience of one to her servicings by the Medjay captain; on more than one occasion, she'd summoned the full-breasted young woman to join them in their bed recreation. And Nebet didn't regard this clandestine physical exchange with the God's Wife to be anything more than that for her, plain and simple recreation. He himself expected only a very good fuck.

"Welcome, Captain. Come, have refreshment before we get down to serious business." Neferure indicated the tray and its contents.

Nebet went to the dais and stepped up to stand at the bed's paneled footboard.

"I prefer to work with a clear head," was his reply.

He untied and dropped the kilt.

As always Neferure smiled broadly.

Twelve Floodings Later, Inundation 20
Coregency of Maatkare/Menkheperre
Ipet Isut, the Mansion of Amen-Re, Waset

Dismissing the four-man Medjay escort, to await his return to the Residence, Son of Re Djehutymes passed alone through the first and largest of three successive pylon gateways erected by his grandfather and thereby entered the sacred inner precinct of the Mansion of the Hidden One, Lord Amen-Re. He was responding to a request — although she surely regarded it as a summons — by his Coregent to join her in an inspection tour of the work progressing on the grand Barque Chapel of the god and the surrounding apartments being erected by Daughter of Re Hatshepsut — or, officially at least, by both joint-rulers. The actual construction itself had been completed for some time now, and only carved-and-painted decoration of the many wall surfaces was presently underway — a good portion of that fully finished, as well.

But it seemed that all work had been stopped for the occasion of the royal inspection, as no artisans peopled the scaffoldings still in place. In fact the premises seemed fully deserted, not even a *wab* priest to be spotted. His Majesty walked barefooted on the smooth, cool paving stones, through a roofed narrow columned hall, a second and smaller gateway, another even narrower roofed hall with a single row of columns, and through the smallest pylon of his ancestor, Asar Akheperkare Djehutymes. In the open-to-the-sky, fairly large, porticoed courtyard fronting the Holy of Holies complex, under a portable sun-shade of painted-linen canvas, sat Her Majesty on a throne-chair no doubt brought from the Residence. A similar unoccupied chair faced her and a third seat, between and perpendicular to the others, supported the majordomo of this place, First Prophet of Amen-Re Hapusenub, inarguably the most powerful non-royal individual in all of Kemet. The elderly priest stood when he saw that the awaited Lord of the Two Lands had entered the courtyard.

Djehutymes briskly crossed under the noon-hour sun to the little temporary pavilion. He was casually dressed, as usual for him, not wearing any sort of covering on his closely cropped head, save an inlaid gold fillet sporting the royal rearing-cobra emblem over his brow. His broad chest was bare, as nearly always, and his kilt was pleated but without an apron or sporran. The First Prophet's attire was, well, what all priests wore: a plain ankle-length kilt without a tunic, differentiated in his case by the inlaid-gold pectoral of the priesthood's highest office, which hung around his scrawny neck, centered between his old-man's sagging breasts. Hapusenub's head was completely shaved, as were his eyebrows and all other body hair, as required for service to the god.

What surprised His Majesty, however, was the manner in which the Coregent had had herself arrayed for this presumably informal occasion. Maatkare Hatshepsut was sporting the Double Crown, worn only for highest state-events. And she had on the False Beard, which she almost never donned, even when Djehutymes himself did. Rather than the usual sheath gown, she was attired in the king's pleated knee-length kilt and starched apron with hinged sporran, albeit with the shear-linen tunic that covered her upper torso when she affected royal-male garb. An elaborate bead broad collar, inlaid gold wristlets and gilded-leather sandals completed her regal ensemble. The Crook and Flail scepters were laid across her lap. Djehutymes also noted that her small feet rested side by side on a low Nine Bows stool. She, indeed, and puzzlingly, was decked out in all of her Mistress of the Two Lands, Daughter of Re full glory.

Coming out of the bright sun, Menkheperre Djehutymes addressed the other two.

"Your Majesty. First Prophet."

And Menkheperre took the throne-chair obviously meant for him, Hapusenub sat again.

"So, we did not receive further notification that this was other than an informal walk-through inspection of the decoration work in progress here, as Your Majesty stated when your personally drafted message asked Our Person to join you here today."

"We did deceive Your Majesty somewhat," responded Maatkare. "But *Our* Person desired to have a private audience with the Lord of the Two Lands, and with the First Prophet at the same time, as well."

"We've 'private audiences' all the time, in your apartments or ours, at the Residence, without the extra bother to come here to the

Mansion of the Hidden One." The Son of Re folded his arms across his chest — which he immediately thought might appear a defensive posture to the Coregent, and so grasped his thighs instead.

"We believe this is the appropriate setting for what we plan to speak about with Your Majesty and the First Prophet today." She paused, then continued. "Do you know what is the significance of this particular day, Hawk Beak?"

Wincing internally, as almost always, Menkheperre Djehutymes simply shrugged. "A day like any day, Aunt." If she could address him so informally, he easily enough could do likewise, certainly.

"Not *any* day. This is an anniversary." She looked to the priest. "Since our Coregent is clueless, do you know *what* anniversary, First Prophet Hapu is Well?"

The old cleric seemed to be at a loss. After several moments of reflection, he replied, "No, Your Majesty, I can't think of which one."

"Well, it was exactly twenty floodings ago, *today*, that the Oracle of Hidden One Amen-Re declared us Mistress of the Two Lands, True Soul of Re and the Female Living Horus — when we stepped forward and rescued your Horus Throne, Lasting Manifestation of Re, from pending usurpation by the defunct Taos clan. We would have thought that you might've been counting every single hour of those twenty floodings."

"It's been *that* long? Time's like a diving falcon, is it not? Since we're nearly twenty-four floodings, we must've been a mere toddler when Your Majesty came to our 'rescue'. We really don't have a memory of that. It seems True Soul of Re has *always* been sitting next to us, standing at our side, even making weighty decisions on our behalf!" Son of Re chuckled, tenting fingers on his chest.

"Oh, Hawk Beak! You've been included in High Council deliberations and decisions for very many floodings now! Certainly you are fully adult and of the absolute soundest judgment. We admire your qualities — most, if not *all* — as co-ruler of the Two Lands."

Moving to shift the conversation's now-awkward direction, Djehutymes asked, "Why, Aunt, are you attired so formally just now, like you're greeting the ambassador from Babylon or receiving the legendary Minos of Kheftiu himself? — as if that shadowy figure would ever dain to leave his reportedly strange island-kingdom to visit us here in the Two Lands!"

"Inasmuch as True Soul of Re will be *no more* at the conclusion of this audience, Our Majesty thought it appropriate that she should be in full glory at the end," replied Hatshepsut, picking up the Crook and Flair scepters from her lap and crossing these on her narrow chest in the prescribed manner, all the while smiling at her Coregent.

"You've lost us, Your Majesty," Djehutymes replied, leaning forward, elbows on his knees, "What do you mean that True Soul of Re will be 'no more'?"

"To be very direct about it then, Your Majesty, we have decided to cease *being* True Soul of Re. We're stepping down from the Horus Throne." She thrust the pair of scepters at arms' length towards Menkheperre Djehutymes. "Here, take these from us. We wield them no longer."

Reflexively, he reached out and grasped first the Crook and then the Flail, and Hatshepsut released her grip, bringing empty hands back to her empty lap. Then she reached up and lifted the red-and-white Double Crown, revealing her natural grayed hair coiled on top of her head, held in place with a ribbon of scarlet linen.

"Here, this, too," she said as she held the tall leather headgear out for Djehutymes to receive, as well.

Dismayed and momentarily speechless, he laid the scepters on his own lap and reached for the dual-crown regalia, which Hatshepsut let go of once her Coregent's hands had closed on that symbol of total authority over the Two Lands, North and South, Black and Red, soil and sand.

Immediately she next unfastened the thin leather strap which held the gilded-leather False Beard in place and pulled the latter off her chin. Because Menkheperre's hands were full at the moment, she held this out to the First Prophet, who accepted it, obviously confused by what was transpiring. Next she pulled on the hair ribbon, which In Sitre had carefully arranged so that it would come away with little effort. In moments the thick grayed locks fell to her shoulders and she combed the mass with her fingers.

"There, we're only Noblest Woman Embracing Amen once more. True Soul of Re has ceased to be. Now but one Living Horus is sole ruler of the Two Lands, and that is Lord of the Upper and Lower Black Land Lasting Manifestation of Re, Son of Re Born of Djehuty."

Hatshepsut smiled broadly, first at her former Coregent, then at the First Prophet. She seemed quite pleased with herself.

"But *why*?" asked her still nonplused nephew/stepson.

"Perhaps because we are weary. More honestly though, because we're not *needed* any longer, Your Majesty, even haven't been for some time now. We should've relinquished the shared throne when our great ambition for Beauty of Re — for her to be the next in a continuing line of Female Horuses — was extinguished by her premature flying off to the stars, reckless girl."

"But is this even possible?" Menkheperre Djehutymes immediately asked the old priest. "Surely there's no precedent for a Living Horus voluntarily 'relinquishing' the Double Crown! Just stepping down. Is there?"

"Indeed, the Horus Throne is only emptied when its occupant has flown to the stars — either naturally or by warfare, or, very, very rarely, through regicide," responded Hapusenub, fiddling with the False Beard resting on his boney thighs. "But *I* am not fully expert in what the Archives may contain, not like Brother of Mut was...when he *was*."

"Please, First Prophet, don't sully this special moment by mentioning that name in front of us!" said Hatshepsut tartly. "If a Living Horus going into retirement has no 'precedent', then also nearly without precedent was the situation of there being a Female Living Horus in the first place, at least of one co-ruling alongside a legitimate sovereign for an entire generation, rather than merely safe-holding the throne for just a very few floodings — which, as we understand, has happened only twice before, in any case. If the very fact that there even *was* a True Soul of Re was an anomaly, then her ceasing to be is no more so."

"What are the *rekhyt* of the Black Land, to be told regarding this 'ceasing to be'?" Menkheperre Djehutymes asked. " Or wretched foreign rulers, for that matter? That True Soul of Re has flown to the stars?"

"Lowlies of the Two Lands are indifferent as to *who* occupies the Horus Throne, Your Majesty, as long as there *is* an occupant and that ruler guarantees The River will rise and recede annually, and that the State granaries are full when Hapu is now-and-then less than forthcoming," replied Hatshepsut. "As to barbarian princelings — even the mysterious Minos and the self-important rulers of Naharin and faraway Babylon — they may believe whatever they *will*, even should it be that True Soul of Re has joined the gods among the stars. It's no concern to us, nor should it be to Your Majesty."

"So, what is Noblest Woman planning to do with herself in her 'retirement', since — unless she has talents far greater than we know — she cannot simply, magically *disappear*. Will our now-former Coregent continue living in the Residences, out of sight, if not out of mind?"

"We've already made arrangements in that regard, Lasting Manifestation of Re. Even as soon as tomorrow we shall take ourself off to Wer-Mer. Although we've never visited the Oasis ourself, we're told that the harim residence there — built by Moon Born, Beautiful Companion many floodings ago, as a place for female relatives she didn't choose to endure at court — although presently unoccupied, is reportedly well maintained and even quite pleasant despite, perhaps because of, its remoteness.

"We'll be accompanied by our dear Ancient One, Fish, and others of our present serving staff. And we'll be provisioned there from our personal estates, which we definitely *are* retaining." Hatshepsut rubbed her small, hennaed hands together. "So, you see, there's nothing for Your Majesty to concern himself about regarding our going 'out of sight, if not out of mind'."

Unexpectedly sole Lord of the Two Lands for the first time in twenty floodings, a short while later Menkheperre Djehutymes retraced his steps back through the Mansion of Amen-Re additions of his grandfather, to where his Medjay escort waited. True Soul of Re's discarded Double Crown supported against his hip and her Crook and Flail and False Beard straps gripped in his other hand, he had only a single pressing thought: the present resident at Wer-Mer and his household must be recalled to Mennufer immediately, before Noblest Woman and her entourage arrived at the Ta-She oasis. His order for this would be sent by charioteer that very afternoon.

*   *   *

12

SOME WEEKS LATER
THE PORT CITY OF GUBLA, RESIDENCE OF SENENMUT

Hearing the voice of Minmes calling out cheerfully to one of their neighbors, Senenmut let the scroll he'd been rereading for the dozenth time roll up on itself, and he sat listening as the younger man's footsteps could be heard climbing up the wooden stairs to their second-level apartment. His companion-in-exile had been away most of the morning, shopping for food at the neighborhood bazaar and running errands generally. Thus the young man from Kheftiu hadn't been there when the messenger from Kemet arrived with the papyrus scroll perhaps thirty minutes earlier.

In moments Minmes was opening the wide wood-plank door and entering the not-overly-large chamber, where few-and-far-between guests were received and Senenmut now half-sat, half-sprawled on a wide cedarwood divan loaded with colorfully embroidered pillows of the local style. The shortish handsome slender man with straight shoulder-long raven hair was dressed in the brightly patterned knee-length belted tunic favored by the men of Gubla and he carried two woven-fiber satchels filled with visible produce and various other items gathered during his morning outing. He broke into his pearly perfect grin when he saw Senenmut across the room.

"You're home early, Mut's Brother! Weren't your accounting skills needed inventorying arriving cargo at the wharf today?" Minmes crossed to the older man and he bent to kiss him on the lips.

"I developed an intense headache, so decided to leave work early. The shipment was simply amphorae of Delta wine, so easy enough to tally and tag quickly. The merchant vessel also had a single passenger, who, in fact, sailed here from the Black Land specifically to find me and deliver this message, which he did, and did." He held up the scroll, then offered it to Minmes.

The younger man lowered his satchels to the wooden floor boards and took the small tube of papyrus. He unrolled it and read to himself:

Greetings, Senenmut, son of Hatnefer, from Lord of the Two Lands Men-kheperre, Son of Re Djehutymes. Life! Prosperity! Health! We write to tell you that we have rescinded your exile to Gubla. You are hereby invited by us to return with haste to Kemet, coming up river to Waset, reporting to the Residence, where you will be presented by us with a modest estate on the outskirts of the Southern Iunu. If he is still with you, bring as well your helpmate, the young man of Kheftiu. Your former duties are performed by others now, or else have been eliminated as unnecessary. But there are doubtless still some services you may perform for Our Person by way of your immense experience and yet-uncounted talents. Should you have not learned it as gossip coming out of the Two Lands, your nemesis, our former Coregent, is no more. By that we mean there is no longer a Maatkare. Hatshepsut indeed still lives but rules not, in fact has retired to Wer-Mer. She was told by us that you had gone to the Field of Reeds while there in Gubla, so shall not be advised of your present pardon and recall to Kemet. We are eager to see you again, Senenmut. Life! Prosperity! Health!

Minmes looked up from the scroll, towards the lounging tall man staring at him from the low divan. Senenmut had clasped his hands behind his head, leaning back into the pillows. His white-streaked coppery hair was worn quite long now, secured behind his ears by an embroidered headband, and he sported a wiry squared-off full beard, as was the fashion for mature males at the City in the Cedar Groves; this was fully white, save for bunches of coppery strands. His attire was similar to that of Minmes — a long-sleeved belted woolen tunic of colorful geometric patterns, except ankle-length and trimmed around the bottom hem with sea-green thick fringe.

"This certainly comes as a surprise, doesn't it?" stated and asked Minmes, as he handed the rewound scroll back to Senenmut. "Do you suppose that Lasting Manifestation of Re finally deposed the old bitch?"

"He does say that she has 'retired,' although I do find it hard to believe that of her, to be sure." Senenmut sat upright and placed his elbows on his knees, pulling on his long nose with the arthritic fingers of one hand. "But there's no reason Lasting Manifestation of Re would dissemble about her status now. That's not his nature."

"Where's this Wer-Mer? I've never heard of it." Minmes sat on the divan, pushing pillows aside to make room for himself.

"At the great lake oasis Ta-She, some distance south of Mennufer. I've never been there, actually. It's where Prince Amen at the Head, the secret bastard son of His Majesty and Beauty of Re, has been living since he was just a newborn. He must be at least ten-floodings old by now. I would guess he's not sharing the Wer-Mer harim with his grandmother," Senenmut chuckled. "Born of Djehuty would've brought him back to Mennufer before Noblest Woman took up residence at the oasis, of that I'm certain."

There was a long pause, Senenmut lost in thought. Finally Minmes broke the silence between them, standing again and picking up his satchels.

"What will you do, Mut's Brother?"

Senenmut snapped out of his revery. "About what?"

"Returning to the Two Lands?"

"Do *you* want to go back, Born of Min?" Senenmut leaned into the pillows again.

"I'm rather enjoying our lazy life here at Gubla," Minmes replied. "But I admit to missing the Two Lands, especially fowling in the marshes, hunting by chariot in the desert and traveling on The River, back and forth between the Northern and Southern capitals. I'd be happy to stay here, but will return if that's what you choose to do."

"Our lives wouldn't be the same as before. Mine, certainly, whatever 'services' Lasting Manifestation of Re might think up for me to perform. And could I hold my head high again after the humiliation of banishment, whether or not that was the just punishment for my indiscretions, my reckless abuse of the great power I'd been allowed by the Female Horus?" He laid the back of one hand against his high forehead. "Pondering this has aggravated my headache." He sat upright again, and stood. "I can't make the decision just now. I must give this unexpected pardon and recall home much careful thought."

Listing slightly the tall man walked to their shared bedchamber, to lay down. Minmes was tempted to follow, but instead put his satchels on the floor again, picked up the scroll abandoned on the divan and reread it twice. Gubla or Waset? He'd be content in either place. With Senenmut.

Second Season of Inundation 2
Sole Reign of Menkheperre Djehutymes
The Residence, Waset

Lord of the Two Lands was rearranging a pattern of beads laid out on a table surface in the workroom of his personal apartments of the Residence at Southern Iunu, when his steward, Renna, filled the doorway with his girth and knocked lightly on the jamb, to get his royal master's attention, intently focused just then on jewelry designing. Menkheperre

Djehutymes looked up from where he was seated behind the table.

"Yes? Enter Renna."

"Your Majesty," said the portly servant, bowing his head ever so slightly as he moved into the modest space. "My apology for interrupting this recreational time, but there's a royal messenger at the door to the antechamber, who is requesting — perhaps I should say demanding — to speak to Your Majesty face to face, 'as soon as possible'. He's from the Residence at Mennufer and says the matter is 'most urgent'."

"Which means bad news, no doubt.We should receive him in a more formal situation than right here, Renna. Wait several minutes, then bring the bearer of this 'most urgent' message to our private audience-chamber, where we'll be waiting."

Renna departed and Djehutymes rearranged a few more beads. Then he stood and went directly to his bedchamber, where he put on a gold headband with the rearing cobra and added a shoulder-length wig. He decided against donning a beaded broad collar which he'd made for himself. Minutes later he was in the audience chamber, seated on his throne, awaiting the "bad news."

As soon as they could be brought together, that same evening members of the High Council who were just then present in Waset sat arranged in armchairs before the dais of Lord of the Two Lands Menkheperre's personal audience-chamber, where he was himself enthroned, wearing the blue-leather helmet-crown but without other regalia. Present were newly appointed Vizier of the South Rekhmire, First Prophet of Amen-Re Hapusenub, Lord Chamberlain Meninre, Chief of the Treasury Penemhat, Steward of the Estates of Amen-Re Wennefer and Generalissimo of the Army in the South Neferronpet. Seated crosslegged at a low table behind this assembly was young King's Scribe Tjaneni, ready to record the proceedings.

After goblets of wine had been distributed among the Council members by Residence serving personnel, Menkheperre addressed his advisors without preamble.

"Notables, this afternoon a messenger from the Northern Capital arrived with the most-dire news. It has been learned there just days ago that princeling dynasts of the vile foreign cities of Kadesh and Megiddo have each revoked their long-sworn allegiances to the Living Horus and the Two Lands. They have leagued themselves together and even now are in full revolt, having dragged from their beds and summarily slashed the throats of our legates in each place, and their entire families as well."

Over the resulting murmurings, His Majesty continued. "These wretched rebels of Kadesh and Megiddo are reportedly gathering to them the petty princelings of every foreign city in the Retenu — all which have been loyal to the Black Land, sending annual tribute here since the time of our grandfather, Asar Akheperkare Djehutymes, who brought them every one to their scabby knees in his time. We are told that Kadesh's and Megiddo's call to take up arms against the Horus Throne has gone out as far as Naharin — and the armies of Hurru and Kode and a dozen other lice-infested places already have answered this summons to open rebellion.

"It scarcely needs be said that these brazen provocations are wholly unacceptable to Our Person and to all the people of the Black Land, commoners and high born alike. Immediate and swift response by the Armies of the Two Lands is the sole recourse open to us."

Menkheperre paused to sip his wine and grizzled Generalissimo Neferronpet indicated he wished to speak by showing his just-raised palm.

"Yes, General. Stand, please."

After rising, the stout military man of some years asked, "Will you want the Army of the South to sail to Mennufer, then?"

"We'll need all of the Black Land's manpower to march on the northern barbarians, so, yes, arrange immediately with the admirals here and in Swenet to make all transport vessels available, and begin sailing your troops downstream as quickly as possible. The chariot cavalry, as well. We'll ourself speed to the northern capital on the royal yacht, to rally the Army of the North and begin the marshalling of the vast provisions necessary for the long trek to Retenu."

General Neferronpet sat down.

"Vizier, First Prophet and Steward of Amen-Re, you will remain here in Waset, of course, but our Chamberlain and Treasurer will accompany us north, and also King's Scribe Tjaneni, it goes without saying."

Without further ado, Menkheperre Djehutymes stood, stepped off the dais and, carrying his wine chalice, briskly exited the audience chamber, followed on his heels by Tjaneni. The youthful sole ruler of the Two Lands had clearly risen to the occasion.

FORTY-FIVE FLOODINGS EARLIER, INUNDATION 5
REIGN OF AKHEPERKARE DJEHUTYMES
BANK OF THE EUPHRATES RIVER, RETENU

King's Scribe Senenmut stood watching the engravers as they worked on the tall stela that had been erected on the river bank a few days earlier, having been hastily cut by stone masons from a local rock outcropping. He sensed that someone had approached behind him and turned his head. Standing several cubits off, hands on his hips, as was typical for him, was Lord of the Two Lands Akheperkare Djehutymes.

Senenmut turned fully towards the ruler and bowed his head.

"Your Majesty."

"So your words crafted for us will now be read down through eternity, Brother of Mut." The warrior-king — attired in the bulbous *Khepresh* helmet and a gilded-leather corselet imitating folded falcon wings worn over his simple short tunic — gestured towards the stela.

"If only by literate men venturing all the way here from the Two Lands," replied the tall red-haired young man in a full-sleeved tunic and long overskirt. "That is unless we add a translation at the bottom in the primitive bird-scratch script of this place — of course, who knows how to write it except the barbarians themselves? And how many of them can read, in any case?" joked Senenmut.

"The great gods certainly can read our words in the sacred writing of the Two Lands," replied Akheperkare." It's really for the gods — in particular Lord Hidden One Amen-Re — that we're putting our pronouncement here, stating this wide river marks the physical boundary of our ambition to bring the wretched land of Retenu under the heel of the Black Land and the Living Horus for all time. Let the Mitanni beyond these waters cross over at their own peril!"

With Senenmut walking at his side, the ruler tramped back up the dusty embankment and returned to the temporary tent village of the Armies of Kemet.

If not for "all time," at least for forty-five floodings, Retenu — with its many petty princelings — would remain passively "under the heel of Kemet" and three additional Living Horuses. It would fall to the first Djehutymes's descendent, third of the same name, to come to this very place and restake his grandfather's claim, placing his own stela alongside that of the founder of the House Born of Djehuty.

INUNDATION 3, SOLE REIGN OF MENKHEPERRE DJEHUTYMES
ENCAMPMENT OF THE ARMIES OF KEMET
NORTH OF THE TOWN OF YEHEM, RETENU
FIELD TENT OF THE LORD OF THE TWO LANDS

The several generals of Kemet's massed armies, and lesser-rank infantry and chariotry commanders and officers, had all assembled as a war council in the large field tent of Menkheperre Djehutymes and were seated on campstools arranged in casual rows before the small portable dais slightly elevating the youthful Lord of the Two Lands seated on his folding campaign throne. Being that it was the harvest season of early *Peret* back in Kemet, most of those present — even Djehutymes himself — wore woolen tunics, to lessen the frequent blasts of cold wind which they never experienced at home. King's Scribe Tjaneni — seated cross-legged at his lap-table off to one side of the dais — had even cleverly fashioned for himself fingerless gloves to keep his hands warmer — or less numbed.

The united armies of Northern and Southern Kemet, some 10,000 men strong, now well inside Retenu, had advanced north for twenty crossings of Re, marching inland parallel to the coast, to the foothills town of Yehem, where they were presently encamped. The destination of Megiddo lay in a plain beyond those rugged high foothills. The purpose of this war council was to determine which was the best of three possible routes to reach the rebellious city.

Menkheperre cleared his throat to quiet the whisperings among his war counselors, then spoke.

"Our valiant scouts report they've learned that the vile Prince of Kadesh has come south to take up residency in Megiddo and is there even now, his army camped north of the city walls. He and his cohort, the Prince of Megiddo, have called on all the chiefs of upper Retenu to join them in their rebellion against us, and the scouts of the Black Land have seen these wretches and their rag-tag forces streaming unto the city, as well. Thus, with this present gathering in a single place, it's the perfect time to march forth and crush these gathered vermin with one swift blow."

There were murmurings of agreement and Menkheperre continued.

"These same scouts have discovered that there are three possible ways to advance on Megiddo from here: a long one to the east, leading somewhat indirectly there, via the town of Taanach; another to the west detouring a distance north of the city to the town of Zefti, then requiring a march back south to arrive at Megiddo; and — the most direct route — a central approach via what's called locally the Aruna Pass, as it cuts through the rugged foothills which now separate us from Megiddo.

"The first of these routes will bring us to an encampment of enemy forces east of Taanach. The second likewise would cause the Armies of the Black Land to encounter yet another enemy encampment near Zefti. Only the central route through the narrow pass avoids coming into premature conflict with the foe, in advance of striking at the heart of Megiddo. Our Majesty believes *that* is the route which the armies should take, but we'll entertain other views, certainly."

There was a lengthy pause, then Generalissimo Thuty, commander of the Army of the North stood in the front row of war counselors. He nodded his head towards the seated young ruler, then spoke.

"This middle way, Your Majesty, do I understand correctly reports that the mountain defile is especially narrow?"

"Our Person hasn't seen it, of course," responded Menkheperre, "but the scouts report that, yes, the Aruna Pass is so narrow in most places that chariots will have to pass through single file, infantry no more than four abreast."

"Does that not put the armies at great risk of ambush by bowmen on the heights? I was but a young child myself at the time, but I remember Your Majesty's grandfather, Asar Great Soul of Re, was slain in ambush here in this wretched land, by just such a vile bowman from on high. Or so the story was told." Thuty sat on his stool again.

"Archers on the heights *could* strike in such a fashion, indeed," replied Menkheperre. "However our scouts report that the foothills aren't peopled by even one of the foe, who clearly do not suppose we'd risk advancing on Megiddo by that unlikely route. This is why they have their detachments encamped along the other two approaches, at Taanach and Zefti, to apprehend us *before* we can reach the rebel city from either of those directions. The scouts say there's no such enemy encampment at the exit from the Aruna Pass and a great plain there where our armies may reassemble for the assault."

Generalissimo of the Army of the South Neferronpet rose in his place.

"I'm nervous, Your Majesty, about basing our approach strategy on the eyes of scouts who've already returned here with their reports. Even at this very moment the unseen bowmen of wretched Retenu may be settling into their places of vantage above the narrow pass."

Menkheperre folded has arms across his broad bare chest. "While that would be possible, General, My Majesty already has taken the precaution of dispatching bowmen of the Black Land to those foothills, and they patrol the heights 'at this very moment', ready to slay on the spot the heart of any foe who may dare venture there. Indeed, our armies will be effectively guarded from on high as they pass through to the plain in front of Megiddo."

Neferronpet continued standing.

"Well, General, you have another comment?"

"Yes, Your Majesty. I'm also greatly concerned that this direct middle route will cause the armies to be strung out for far too long at far too great a distance. The first ranks will emerge from the mountain defile while the greater part of our forces will not've even entered it on this side. What if word reaches the enemy at either of their outlying encampments that the Armies of the Black Land are coming onto the Megiddo plain one chariot after one chariot, foot soldier after foot soldier? Wouldn't they rush there and attack us for our advance guard's lack of numbers, with the full force of our rear guard still in formation outside this town of Arunu?"

His point made, Neferronpet sat down.

"My Majesty is told, again by our scouts, whose observations we fully trust," Menkheperre replied, "that Megiddo lies still some distance from the egress of the pass. Even too far off for the vile foe to observe our arrival on the plain from the high towers of his city. We're confident that all the Armies of the Black Land, to the last soldier, will've passed through and reformed well before news of our arrival there reaches those wretched princes of Kadesh and Megiddo.

"So certain are we of this — that the Aruna Pass is the only right approach — My Majesty will be at the very head of the march, showing the way, none having gone before us, and Our Person's chariot will be the first to emerge onto the plain. This is our decision and you may follow us or make your own ways to vile Megiddo by those other roads, as you please, joining us and Lord Amen-Re there in our certain victory."

Lord of the Two Lands Menkheperre, Son of Re Djehutymes rose up from his portable throne. The war council was concluded.

THREE CROSSINGS OF RE LATER
ENCAMPMENT OF THE ARMIES OF KEMET, PLAIN OF MEGIDDO

The passage of the Armies of Kemet through the Aruna Pass did not go entirely without incident. As Menkheperre had been confident, no ambush assault was made on the long file of chariots and infantry as it slowly, carefully wended its way through the narrow mountain defile; but soon after the Lord of the Two Lands in his electrum-plated chariot had emerged into the spreading valley leading to the plain of Megiddo — quickly followed by chariot after chariot, and by reforming ranks and files of foot soldiers — a solitary patrol of a dozen startled Retenu infantrymen were encountered, engaged and easily overwhelmed, arrows from Menkheperre's own bow finding their marks — his first human kills.

Just past midday the swelling force of the Armies of Kemet reached a wide-but-shallow stream called Qina by the locals and the decision was made by Menkheperre to set up full encampment at that spot. This was done without the rebel forces apparently yet aware of the arrival of the Living Horus and the Armies of Kemet. Or if their own scouts had alerted the princes behind the walls of the rebel city to this reality, it was too late in the day to muster the outlying contingents of Retenu hunkered down some distances away at Taanach and Zefti.

Once the royal command-tent was pitched — with a sea of sleeping tents of the foot soldiers and charioteers quickly rising around it — Menkheperre sent out word that preparations should be made to engage the enemy in battle the very next morning. Following a brief war council with generalissimos Neferronpet and Thuty and others of the command staff, the young Lord of the Two Lands — in his blue *Khepresh* with gold bosses and a gilded-leather corselet reflecting the late-afternoon sun — strode informally about the encampment, offering words of encouragement — "Be steadfast! Be vigilant!" — to his troops, whose spirits were recharged, consequently.

Early the following morning, the Barque of Re having just appeared on the eastern horizon, Menkheperre issued orders for the Armies of Kemet to form up and move out in battle formation, fording the ankle-deep Qina and marching measuredly towards Megiddo, the towers of which soon became visible some distance off yet. His Majesty, rode his gleaming chariot at the head of the center contingent of calvary and foot soldiers. Equally wide infantry wings to his left and right were preceded at walking pace by their own ranks of chariotry.

King's Scribe Tjaneni would write in his account of this event:

The Lord of the Two Lands went forth in a chariot of electrum, arrayed in his weapons of war, like Horus the Smiter, like Montu of Waset, like his father Amen-Re, who strengthened his arm. His Majesty led the way at the head of his armies, with a mighty flame of fire wielded as his sword. He went forth, none like him, slaying the barbarians, smiting Retenu, bringing to him their princes as living captives, capturing their chariots wrought of silver and gold still bound to their horses.

In fact, the two detachments which had been lying in wait for the forces of Kemet to approach Megiddo along roads either from Zefti in the north or Taanach to the south, had redeployed overnight, to stand now in wide ranks and deep files before the towered and turreted walls of the city. As the Living Horus and his force of 10,000 came nearer and nearer, the tall gates of Megiddo opened and reenforcements emerged to take positions behind the arrayed Retenu infantry and calvary. Included in their numbers were the oily-bearded princes of Kadesh and Megiddo themselves, bedecked in their bright barbarian finery, standing defiantly tall in their massive wooden chariots heavily embellished with silver and gold.

At a certain distance, the advancing forces of Kemet came to a halt. After a few minutes of silent face-off with the city's defenders, at a signal of drumming, archers moved forward through the files of the Kemet middle contingent fronted by the Living Horus, moved ahead of the long row of chariotry, fell into formation and drew back their long bows, simultaneously letting loose a rain of arrows that fell in torrents on the hapless foe, their round shields raised over their heads. Many slender shafts found their marks and soldiers of Retenu fell left and right. An immediate second barrage of Kemet arrows produced yet more instant casualties.

The barbarian archers moved to the defenders' front rank; but before they could loose their heavy composite bows — at the drop the Living Horus's arm — the center rank of chariots of Kemet began a forward charge, the riders in each rapidly firing arrows as the drivers urged their horse-teams on. At the sight of this thundering onslaught, the Retenu bowmen broke rank and ran back into the files of foot soldiers with shields, some stumbling and falling over the dead and wounded bodies on the ground. As the chariots came on — the sudden flight of the archers having struck additional fear in their hearts — many in the front ranks of Retenu infantry likewise turned to flee towards Megiddo, Kemet's arrows finding their marks in dozens of the exposed backs. Almost instantly there was a general melee among the defenders, a massive rush to get back into the city, the heavy gates of which were being pushed closed slowly. The single rank of Retenu chariotry, waiting in formation behind the infantry, was swamped by the press of fleeing foot soldiers' bodies; and — the tall, cumbersome vehicles not being able to maneuver or even move at all — their occupants began jumping to the ground to join in the mass retreat. This included the princes of Megiddo and Kadesh, as well, who did not succeed in reaching the gates before these finally secured.

Before closing on the mob of fleeing defenders, following the lead of the Living Horus, the chariots of Kemet were reigned to a halt a few dozen cubits from the crush of panicked enemy soldiers. The charioteer bowmen continued firing their missiles into the mass of Retenu bodies, and the dead and wounded began piling up in what amounted to wholesale slaughter. The screaming was deafening, as defenders on the walls of Megiddo began dropping ropes fashioned from clothing down to their desperate comrades, then hauling them up one by one. Included among those rescued in such a manner were the two rebel rulers, the princes of Megiddo and Kadesh.

By the time the Kemet infantry of the middle contingent had marched forward, the quivers of the Living Horus and the other charioteers had been emptied, so it would remain for the foot soldiers to finish off the defenseless foe, using their lances and scimitars. However, as they closed on the abandoned gold-and-silver embellished Retenu chariots and those vehicles' horses in harness, many broke rank to take hold of these. Others began picking up dropped swords, lances and bows. Still other soldiers of Kemet commenced hacking off the right hands of the foe's dead and wounded, slashing the throats of the latter, looting the hundreds of bodies of personal effects, such as body armor, bracelets and rings. In short, discipline was largely abandoned in favor of trophy taking. Those few of the infantry which did close on the remaining defenders, quickly dispatched them, so that none were left alive. Megiddo itself remained unbreached, however.

M enkheperre was dictating to Royal Scribe Tjaneni, when a raspy voice was raised outside the entry hatch to his tent. Lord of the Two Lands recognized this as Generalissimo Neferronpet, addressing the pair of Medjay guards.

"Enter, General," Menkheperre commanded.

The thickset military man — dressed in a gilt-embellished leather corselet worn over a woolen tunic and a tight-fitting leather cap on his shaved head — ducked slightly and entered through the tent hatch. He immediately came to attention, bowing his head.

"Your Majesty. I wouldn't want to interrupt...." He'd noticed young Tjaneni sitting cross-legged at his low lap-table, a scroll of papyrus unrolled, his writing tool in hand.

"No, matter, General. We were just dictating to King's Scribe our extreme displeasure with how the assault on Megiddo went today, when the foot soldiers of the Armies of Kemet — those of the Division of Lord Amen-Re, at least — let personal greed at the sight of war booty cost us the chance to overwhelm the city with the Black Land's sheer might."

"That was most regrettable, Your Majesty, regrettable, indeed, but perhaps also understandable. What I mean is, those particular infantry had never seen actual battle before, so didn't understand the etiquette of collecting the foe's debris. I'm sure that General Horus Victorious never thought to instruct the Army of the North in that."

"Thereby ensuring that we all shall be here, sitting on our hands round about Megiddo, waiting for the vile dynasts within to capitulate finally, after most of their numbers and the city's non-combatants have died of starvation and thirst." Menkheperre had sat on his portable throne. "We understand from one of the few foe captured alive that over 300 Retenu rebel princelings and chieftains are now hunkered down in Megiddo, so that the capture of this one city would've been the capture of 1,000 cities."

Menkheperre looked over to his secretary.

"Did you get that down, Tjaneni? We rather like that. 'It is the capture of 1,000 cities, this capture of Megiddo'." He turned back to Neferronpet. "So what have you come here for, General?"

"A bit of, well, *good* news, Your Majesty."

"Continue."

"On the far side of the city, the soldiers discovered the abandoned encampment of the vile Prince of Kadesh. His attendants and support force had all escaped to within the city by way of a rear gate. All but one, that is. Inside the prince's most gaudy tent — colorfully striped, embellished with what here are called 'fringes' — inside, cowering under the ruler's draped high bed, they found a boy, perhaps ten floodings, who pleaded for mercy in his own gibberish tongue. The soldiers believe he may be the son of the Kadesh rebel. He awaits outside, under guard of course, along with all the furniture and furnishings of the royal tent, which the soldiers have brought here to present to Your Majesty."

Sighing and shaking his closely cropped head, Menkheperre lifted the blue-leather helmet-crown off a low table by his throne. Donning it, he stood, crossed the tent and disappeared through the door hatch. Tjaneni was quickly on his bare feet and following, should the Lord of the Two Lands want a record of whatever would be transpiring. Which he did.

Sixty Crossings of Re Later, the Docks, Mennufer

As sailors of the merchant vessel from Gubla laboriously maneuvered the bulky vessel into dock at Kemet's northern capital, Mennufer, the ship's only two non-crew passengers watched the maritime proceedings from the port-side railing midship. One tall, the other somewhat shorter, the men were similarly attired in the brightly patterned garb of the eastern Great Green coastal cities. The tall one had grayed long red hair, pulled into a tight roll on the nap of his neck; he also sported a mostly white full beard trimmed square. The shorter and younger individual's black hair was worn shoulder length and secured behind his ears with an embossed-leather headband. These seagoers were, of course, Senenmut and Minmes, returning to Kemet from their years of exile at Gubla.

Once the ship was securely docked and its gangplank lowered, the two made their way across to the wharf. While the single modest chest they'd brought back with them from Gubla was being unloaded, they would find passage aboard the first vessel heading upstream that would take on passengers. In his letter of pardon, Lord of the Two Lands Menkheperre had instructed Senenmut to return directly to Waset, where he would be given a "modest estate" on the outskirts of the Southern Capital. The former bureaucrat thought it best, however, to inquire whether the young ruler was at the Residence there, Waset, or if the royal schedule had him just now at Mennufer.

The supervisor-type whom they approached with this query responded with some startling news.

"The Mighty Bull's neither here nor there, foreigner. For some several moons he and the Armies of Kemet have been up north in the land of the barbarians, crushing the vile oily rebels. He's had — so the word came back — the fortress city of Megiddo under siege for a long while now. Even built a high wooden wall, so it's said, around the entire place, which they're calling 'Born of Djehuty is the Surrounder of Retenu'— the wall that is."

If word of Menkheperre's war on Retenu had reached Gubla, the gossip had not gotten as far as Senenmut's ears. His first thought was whether he and Minmes should immediately go on to Waset, or wait at Mennufer for the ruler's eventual return to Kemet.

"Who governs the Two Lands in His Majesty's absence?" Senenmut asked. "Surely not Great Royal Wife Sitiah in capacity of Regent. And Crown-Prince Lasting Manifestation of Re would still be far too young, certainly."

"You seem well informed about matters in the Black Land, for a foreigner, and speak our tongue like a native here," replied the dock foreman, confidently.

"Because we *are* of the Two Lands, friend," was Senenmut's reply, "although have lived abroad for some years now. We no longer have the appropriate clothes, so are attired as we'd dress and groom ourselves where we were, which was Gubla. But, again, I ask, who's in charge with Lord Lasting Manifestation of Re away at war?"

"I can speak only for here in the North, not for Waset. But here day-to-day matters are handled by the Vizier, I suppose, as I've never heard otherwise, or particularly cared. Who governs isn't really my concern. Nor religion for that matter. Business of the gods is in the hands of the First Prophet of Ptah, as far as I know."

"Who is Vizier of the South now?"

The man shrugged.

"And has there been any change regarding the First Prophet of Lord Amen-Re?"

Again, a shrug. "Not much aware of what goes on upriver. None of my business." He turned away to bark orders at a gang of dock workers now intent on unloading the merchant ship from Gubla, the cargo of which included hundreds of planks of cedar.

One of the first things off had been the traveling chest of Senenmut and Minmes, which two dock men had brought up and put down next to where they were standing. The tall man sat on it to think. Minmes squatted beside him and after a few long moments of silence spoke.

"It seems we mis-timed our return, Mut's Brother. At least as far as being welcomed back to Kemet by Lord of the Two Lands himself."

"I wonder how we didn't hear in Gubla of this war in Retenu and the long siege-business? Not that the ruler and greedy merchants of that place are especially attentive other than to matters of the Great Green. What happens beyond the cedar forests and white mountains is far off and not of much concern, to their parochial way of thinking, certainly."

"Are you of the opinion that we should stop here in Mennufer, to wait for Lasting Manifestation of Re's return?"

"No, I'm of a mind to make our way on up river to Waset now, trusting that my old colleague and friend, the First Prophet of the Hidden One Hapu is Well, still lives and holds that post. Perhaps he's fully aware of Lasting Manifestation of Re's intentions to give us a house in Waset, and that such, in fact, is awaiting us even now. Yes, he'd surely be. So, I think Born of Min that we should find ourselves passage to the Southern Iunu without even venturing into Mennufer at this time."

That settled, the two began inquiring after which ships were continuing upstream even that very afternoon. They had their choice of three.

* * *

13

Hatshepsut was not certain she could watch the procedure about to be performed. She sat rigidly in an armchair positioned a few cubits beyond the footboard of the bed now occupied by the prostrate supine form of her lifelong dear friend, Nurse In Sitre. Not fully prostrate, however, as the elderly woman's shoulders and head were propped up by bolsters, her long white hair fanned out on these. A linen sheet was pulled high on her massive bosom, although her fleshy arms rested atop this, reaching along her sides.

Nurse was breathing heavily, but appeared to be no longer conscious, her mouth gaping some, with a rivulet of drool. The drugged wine she'd been given by the young physician summoned to Wer-Mer from Mennufer seemed to have succeeded in its purpose. For some long while now, In had complained constantly of her teeth aching unbearably, making it difficult to chew even soft food. Her gums appeared inflamed and swollen and she frequently spat out small quantities of pussy blood. Recently her left cheek had become clearly swollen, evident despite the natural fullness of her face.

This situation of the terribly agonizing teeth only compounded In's other infirmities. Since her return to Wer-Mer with Hatshepsut from their visit to Waset two inundations before, she had suffered from frequent cramping in her midsection and her legs had been in constant pain, impeding her already shuffling gait due to her considerable obesity. She now needed to lean heavily on one or two of the handmaidens whenever she moved, which was seldom any further than from her armchair to the latrine or to her bed. Occasionally four male servants, sliding poles under her chair, would carry her to join Hatshepsut in the pavilion of the Residence garden — where the two women would chat or play *senet*.

The young physician's examination of In Sitre's mouth determined that her upper left-rear secondary molar was even more abscessed than several others of her teeth. He said the only thing to alleviate the immediate pain and swelling was to extract this particular offending tooth. In's immediate initial reaction was she wouldn't permit that. The physician finally persuaded her, however, that he could do this while she was made to deeply sleep by drinking a potion dissolved in Nurse's favorite Delta vintage. The young man was not only very attractive, but really quite charming as well; and — holding In's plump hand, repeatedly patting it, while he purred his assurances and persuasion — he finally wooed her consent.

Now, with In Sitre apparently oblivious, the physician loomed over her with a small bronze tool in hand, of a sort Hatshepsut had never seen before — inasmuch as she had almost no personal experience with physicians generally and none with tooth extraction specifically. Four handmaidens had been recruited as assistants, positioned to hold In's arms and legs should she attempt to resist the pending violent ministrations to her infected mouth.

The physician clamped the fingers of his free hand onto Nurse's jutting chin and pulled her jaw down so that the open mouth widened. He whispered for the serving girl at In's right arm to grip the chin, and when she did so, he put his fingers into the maw, forcing the mouth as open as possible. The old woman groaned but did not resume consciousness. Immediately he inserted the tool and guided it to the offending molar with his fingers in the mouth. Following some adjustment, making sure he'd closed on the correct place, he suddenly jerked the tool out of Nurse, bringing with it a large bloody tooth. The patient let out a piercing cry, opened her eyes and began struggling against the restraint of the four young women. Immediately blood began gushing, which the physician tried to squelch with a linen cloth inserted into the wide-open mouth — having laid tool and tooth on a small table by the bed.

This cloth quickly turned scarlet as In continued struggling, tossing her head from side to side. Gripping the chin again, the young man pulled the jaw down so that he could extract the soaked fabric and insert another crumpled clean linen square, pushing it with his fingers to the hole where the molar had been. Blood now covered In Sitre's chin and the bedsheet over her heaving bosom; the physician and his assistants had all been splattered, as well. Sickened at this violent spectacle, the Dowager Great Royal Wife twisted in her chair as much as possible, averting her eyes, shielded by her small hand.

The profuse bleeding continued, as cloth after soaked cloth attempted to stop the flow, but without any success. Nurse's struggling quieted and then suddenly ceased. The great bosom stopped heaving. The *ba*-bird of Hatshepsut's companion of some sixty floodings had flown heavenward.

The fatal molar subsequently was recovered and retained by the Dowager Great Royal Wife, placed by her in a wooden jewelry coffer, and would go with her to the grave one day — in the not-so-distant future.

FIVE FLOODINGS EARLIER, INUNDATION 4
SOLE REIGN OF MENKHEPERRE DJEHUTYMES
KEMET COMMAND TENT, THE PLAIN OF MEGIDDO

King's Scribe Tjaneni carefully placed a large rectangle of plain papyrus onto the lowered press-dried plant, washed roots and all, which lay diagonally on another papyrus sheet, itself resting atop a stack of identical sheets. Between all of these were other flattened desiccated botanical specimens that had been personally collected by Lord of the Two Lands Menkheperre during the Armies of Kemet's long stay encamped outside the timber rampart wall enclosing the beleaguered city of Megiddo. Several dozen stacks of papyri sheets and interspersed dried plants were arranged in two orderly rows against an interior wall of the large command tent. Tjaneni next would carefully pack these in specially fashioned wooden chests, for eventual transport — along with numerous still-living specimens in ceramic vessels — back by sea to the Northern Capital at Mennufer. There Menkheperre would continue his careful study of the various unfamiliar flora of Retenu, with which he'd become fascinated over the past months of siege-boredom. His Majesty was at the moment napping in the screened-off rear of the tent that was his private space.

Tjaneni had just placed the final specimens stack on the hard-clay floor, when a voice was raised beyond the tent hatch, seeking admittance from the pair of Medjay guards. The scribe immediately recognized the speaker as Generalissimo Neferronpet, commander of the Army of the South. He crossed to the entrance and pushed aside the hatch flap.

"His Majesty is at his afternoon rest, General," said the shaved-bald young man, dressed in just a simple white kilt because of the sweltering heat. "Perhaps you'd care to return later, when Lord Re has traveled further across the heavens?"

"I've a most-urgent message for His Majesty regarding that vile town under the Black Lands' siege," returned Neferronpet, hands on hips, obviously annoyed by the green bureaucrat's self-importance.

"Come again later, General, in an hour or so, when His Majesty will surely receive you at his convenience."

"Let Our Majesty's general enter, Tjaneni," Menkheperre spoke to the youth's back from across the tent. "Our Person is awake now."

Crossing to his portable campaign throne on its small wooden dais, the Lord of the Two Lands tied the sash of his pleated but-otherwise-plain kilt as he moved. He was barefooted, as always, and wore no adornments, his shaved head without a covering. When Menkheperre had seated himself, the King's Scribe stepped to one side of the hatch; and Neferronpet, ducking his own uncovered, also-shaved head, entered, immediately coming to rigid attention.

"Your Majesty." He lowered his chin.

"At ease, General, and approach. Be seated." The youthful ruler gestured to a folding stool a few cubits in front of the throne dais.

Neferronpet did as instructed. Tjaneni quickly sat cross-legged behind his low dictation desk, pulling a brush from his scribe's palette and unrolling the large leather scroll on which he recorded each day's happenings.

When his secretary was poised to write, Menkheperre spoke. "So, what 'most-urgent message' do you have for us?"

The much older man cleared his throat. "Emissaries have come out of the town to the gate of 'Born of Djehuty is Surrounder of Retenu,' with the message that the vile rebels are now exhausted near to death and wish finally to bow their oily heads in surrender to Your Majesty and the mighty Black Land, offering a great tribute of precious metals and stones and much cattle and grain in return for Your Majesty's kind mercy."

"If they've cattle and grain to give up, we think they're dying from absence of water rather than lack of any food. The wells and cisterns of Megiddo have gone dry, no doubt."

Neferronpet shrugged his rounded bare shoulders. "No doubt."

"This surrender must be done with great formality and Lord Re has traveled too far west now to arrange that for today. Tell the emissaries from Megiddo to return there with instructions that the town's entire population, high and lowly, slaves too, and every refugee within shall present themselves and all their gifts of tribute before our throne at midday tomorrow. The wicked princes of Megiddo and Kadesh shall set their tarnished crowns at our feet and grovel on their faces before us, eating dust and begging to keep heads on their shoulders."

"Only the vile scorpion of this particular place will be so able to eat dust, Your Majesty," the general replied.

"How so is that? The wretched Prince of Kadesh already has succumbed for lack of water?"

"Rather, Your Majesty, the enemy emissaries have relayed that

that cowardly traitor managed to slip out the back gate of this town, under cover of darkness during the absence of Re, that happening immediately following the great victory here of Your Majesty and the mighty Armies of the Black Land. They suppose he's long ago fled north and taken refuge in his own city, and cowers now behind its also towered high walls. His four wives and three of his daughters are still within here, however, and we already possess his young prince and heir, discovered hiding under Kadesh's camp bed immediately after the great battle, Your Majesty will remember."

"To be certain, General." Menkheperre stood. "And the boy should even now be in Mennufer, where he's already beginning to learn to love the Black Land. When the day comes that his wretched father's finally gone for good, we shall send the pale princeling back north here to Retenu, to very Kadesh, to assume governing that place in Our Majesty's behalf, his heart full of gladness for the Two Lands.

"In fact, that shall be our policy for all the future. Tomorrow, when the rulers of 1,000 towns bow and grovel in the dust before us, they shall also hand over their heirs, each and every one, and they, too, shall be sent south to gladly learn love for the ways of the Black Land."

Menkheperre stepped off the dais and walked to his private space.

Generalissimo Neferronpet realized he had been dismissed, so bowed to no one and left.

W riting in his great leather scroll, the Book of Days, young King's Scribe Tjaneni recorded the proceedings of the capitulation and surrender of Megiddo, which would later be transcribed in the annals that Menkheperre Djehutymes caused to be engraved on the walls of the Waset Mansion of the Hidden One, Lord Amen-Re:

"Those Asiatics who were in wretched Megiddo, but not the prince of Kadesh among them, came forth to behold the fame of Djehutymes, who is given life. They spoke, saying, 'Give us a chance to present to Thy Majesty our duties.' And they came, bringing all that belonged to them, to do obeisance to the fame of His Majesty, to crave the very breath of him with their nostrils, because of the greatness of his power. And he treated them with his leniency. But, because that foe of Kadesh was not among them, His Majesty carried off the wives of the vanquished one, and his children as well, and the wives of the 38 other fallen chiefs of Retenu who were there in front of Megiddo, together with their children. These counted for 340 living prisoners. Also taken were the slaves of the place, to the total of 1,796 men and women and their children.

"Among the tribute brought forth that day out of the town were 924 chariots belonging to the wretched armies of Megiddo and Kadesh, including ones wrought with gold and silver belonging to the two princes of those places, who would ride them no more. Added to these were 2,238 horses, comprising 2,041 mares, 191 foals and six stallions. Also there were those vile princes' beautiful suits of bronze armor embellished in gold, and 200 suits of armor belonging to the wretched armies of the foe, to which were added 502 bows and 70 poles of cedar wood wrought with gold, belonging to the tent of the cowardly prince of Kadesh, along with his magnificent household furniture, among it his royal scepter of carob wood fashioned with costly stones, a silver statue in beaten work, perhaps of his god, and an ebony statue of himself, wrought with gold, the head inlaid with lapis.

"And much gold and silver and bronze came forth from the town by the baskets full, being plates and vessels and knives, amounting to 748 deben, to which were added baskets heaped with rings of unfashioned gold, amounting to 966 deben.

"Among these spoils were counted as well 1,929 large cattle and 2,500 small cattle, which had been taken into the town from the country-side, but not butchered for food, proving wretched Megiddo capitulated to His Majesty from thirst not hunger."

Thus was Tjaneni's spare formal account and accounting. The events of the day of Megiddo's surrender were more complicated than simple tallying, however.

When the tall, thick, bronze-fitted cedar gates of Megiddo were pulled open that high noon of the day following the emissaries' appearance at the entry to "Djehutymes is the Surrounder of Retenu," youthful Lord of the Two Lands Menkheperre was already seated outside the timber retaining wall. His campaign throne had been elevated by a specially built, stairs-mounted wood-plank platform, so that all who approached would need to tilt their chins to look up at him, the Living Horus.

The third Djehutymes was arrayed to bedazzle. On his freshly shaven head was the bulbous blue-leather helmet-crown, fronted by an inlaid-gold rearing cobra and embellished all over with sheet-gold bosses that reflected the overhead sun. His gilded-leather corselet was fashioned like spread hawk wings enfolding his broad chest; this too was made even more brilliant by the sun's scorching rays. Embossed-gold bands adorned the wrists and thick biceps of his arms, which were crossed over his chest, hands grasping the Crook and Flail symbols of his authority as ruler of

Kemet and its hegemony. His fresh linen kilt was fronted by the flared gilded-leather sporran apron, and on his feet were ceremonial sandals of sheet gold. Those feet rested on a low stool decorated on its top surface with the prostrate figures of the Nine Bows, Kemet's traditional enemies.

Flanking the platform-elevated Lord of the Two Lands were standing ranks of the officers of the Armies of Kemet, including generalissimos Neferronpet and Hornakht. All were dressed in full battle attire. Seated on the ground to one side of the platform's steps was bare-to-the-waist Tjaneni, his leather scroll spread open on his low dictation desk. Next to him stood the colorfully garbed Asiatic defector who would serve as translator of Menkheperre's words to his humbled foe and whatever might be responded in turn. Many hundreds of Kemet's foot soldiers and charioteers were fanned out in rank and file behind and to both sides of their Living Horus lord, all with their various weaponry in hand. It was an impressive assembly, indeed, bespeaking the might of the Two Lands.

Once the double wings of Megiddo's gate were both flush with the thickness of the entry tower, the vanquished began emerging in mass, the several refugee princes of Retenu in the lead, with the ruler of the town anonymously in their midst. All of these men had dressed in their exotic best finery, for the most part consisting of just brightly patterned or striped knee- or ankle-length kilts or skirts, all with fringes. Most were barefooted, some sported pectorals or other jewelry and each had a gold or silver diadem atop his oily-black long hair. Every last one was full-bearded in various square-cut and pointed fashions. None bore weapons.

Immediately behind these some three-dozen fallen rulers, a sizeable congregation of women and children of both sexes shuffled along the dusty unpaved road. The younger of the latter were naked for the most part, but the older ones and all the women were attired in the same bright colors of their fathers and menfolk, the males in short kilts, the females in fringed ankle-length full-sleeved sheaths and barefooted generally. A great many of the junior women were bare breasted, their jet locks falling free to their shoulders or beyond, while the matrons concealed their hair with white scarves intricately wrapped into turbans. A great many of these in the front ranks wore necklaces and bracelets of gold and semi-precious stones, signaling their high status as wives and concubines of the rulers.

Trailing the elites through the gates were the common townspeople of Megiddo, a motley lot of merchants and craftsmen and their families, also colorfully dressed but not so richly, fringes and jewelry lacking altogether. There were hundreds upon hundreds of these folk; and mixed in with them were the many dozens of armorless, unarmed soldiers who had escaped into the town, plus countless slaves of both sexes, all coming on and on, fanning out to form a wide mass of humanity before Megiddo's walls.

When the vanguard of rulers approached to within a dozen paces of Menkheperre's throne platform, they collectively halted, all looking towards their vanquisher. The translator relayed a command from the Lord of the Two Lands, and the defeated princes dropped to their knees in near unison.

"Tell these worms to fall on their faces in the dust," the translator was ordered by the Living Horus. "To fall flat on their faces and remove their ill-gotten crowns, thrusting these forward towards Our Person at full arms' length, placing these on the ground as offerings to My Majesty and the Black Land."

This was repeated in the language of Retenu and three-dozen princes were soon fully prostrate and without diadems on their heads. The large group of rulers' wives and children had come to a standstill a few paces behind their stretched out husbands and fathers. Menkheperre instructed Generalissimo Thuty to move forward and collect the discarded regalia. This took several minutes, as the officer stepped among the groveled princes, picking up the gold and silver circlets one by one and slipping each over his bare forearm, until that was fully covered from elbow-bend to wrist. Finishing this harvest, he returned to stand at the foot of the platform steps, holding out the diadem-laden limb towards the Lord of the Two Lands. Menkheperre then told the general to pass the surrendered crowns to King's Scribe Tjaneni, which was done, the latter making a jumbled metallic pile on the dusty ground next to his writing desk. In response to his lord's instruction, Thuty resumed his place in the front rank of the officers of Kemet.

After a long pause, still sitting rigidly, his Crook and Flail crossed over his chest, Menkheperre spoke again.

"Tell the wretched fallen prince of this place, this Megiddo, to rise and approach Our Person. To come to the foot of these steps and then to kneel upright facing My Majesty."

The command was repeated by the translator, but no one stood.

Immediately the translator restated the command in the gibberish of Retenu. After several long moments, an individual slowly pushed to his knees near the center of the mass of prostrate figures. His entire front was covered in dust. He stood upright, a portly man in his late middle-age. After a hesitation he moved towards the elevated Lord of the Two Lands, stepping over and around the outstretched forms of his fallen fellows, coming to the stairs as ordered. Looking up at the Living Horus, golden and glittering under the high-noon sun, he quickly bowed his head and sank onto his knees again, hands resting on his heavy thighs.

"You were prince in this place, the dynast of Megiddo, who revolted against your sworn allegiance to the Two Lands, who rallied these other groveling dynast worms of Retenu to your cause, all vanquished in this place by the Mighty Bull, My Majesty?"

The complex question was translated.

His dusty pointed beard still on his grimy fleshy chest, nearly touching the gold pectoral he wore, the kneeling man slowly responded at length, his sing-song voice quavering.

The translator looked up at Menkheperre, smiled, bowed and responded.

"He say father's father of him prince in Megiddo at time other great prince of great Black Land come to here, and he, the ancestor, was who first pledge fealty to that long-ago great prince and send tribute gift to south each year. And his father and him, also. Twelve moons gift of much great, great value, send many, many time.

"Then Kadesh prince, marriage kin to him, persuade — false now he know — that great Black Land long in control by female prince, and distant place female govern weak and tribute gift need send no longer. He greatly regret he seduce to such very falsehood by Kadesh deceiver. He swear more Megiddo's fealty and each year again send many, many gift to you, lord, great, great prince of great Black Land. And he beg to forgive his miserable life and also life these many prince of Retenu here, who fooled by Kedesh, too."

The translator smiled within his oily beard, which he pulled on, bowing again; and there was a long pause, while Menkheperre processed this garbled information. The "long-ago great prince" was clearly his warrior-grandfather, the first Djehutymes, Asar Akheperkare, and the "female prince" was his now-former Coregent, Maatkare. Finally, he spoke again, lowering the Crook and Flail to his lap.

"So, wretched Megiddo, you lay full blame for the failed rebellion of Retenu at the feet of Kadesh." This was translated. "Let wretched Kadesh rise and come forward to also kneel before Our Person, to plead, like Megiddo, for My Majesty's forgiveness." The translator directed this towards the prostrate princes.

None rose, as Menkheperre knew would be the case, the Prince of Kadesh having made good his escape and flight north under the cover of darkness months before. The Prince of Megiddo made a reply, which the translator communicated to the Lord of the Two Lands.

"Him, coward Kadesh, have gone long time. Run away after great, great prince of great Black Land cast down armies of Retenu at this place. Only wives, daughters of Kadesh now here. Them prisoners of great, great prince of great Black Land." The translator gestured towards the large group of richly dressed women and children standing just beyond their still-face-down husbands and fathers.

Menkheperre addressed the translator: "Tell these foolish princes of Retenu to rise and come forward, then to kneel together over there." He gestured off to his left.

After this command had been relayed through the translator, the three dozen rulers began rising, some dusting off their fronts as they walked together to where directed. Soon all were kneeling again, facing towards the Lord of the Two Lands, shoulder to shoulder in an unorganized grouping. Once they were in place, Menkheperre rose from his throne, laying his scepters on the chair's cushioned seat. He stepped off the Nine Bows footstool and out of his gilded sandals. The heads of all present bowed as he measuredly came down off the platform by its stairs, the foreigners taking their cue from the amassed soldiers of Kemet.

Once on the ground, the Lord of the Two Lands turned towards where generalissimos Neferronpet and Thuty were standing and held out his hand, palm up. Thuty stepped forward, was joined by two junior officers, and the three crossed to the Living Horus. Thuty carried a mace, a gilded long handle topped by a diorite sphere the size of a large pomegranate. He passed this ritual weapon to Menkheperre, stepped back two paces and came to rigid attention. The pair of officers moved to where the ruler of Megiddo was kneeling, positioning themselves on each side of him, then pulling the now-quaking prince to his feet. Each gripping a fleshy arm, they pulled him, stumbling as he went, to Menkheperre, then forced him to kneel in the dust again, pushing his head forward. With some difficulty one of the officers undid the knot of long hair resting on the nape of the prince's thick neck, then grabbed a handful of the loosened oily, black-dyed locks, yanking the bearded head upright again, then back so that the chin was elevated. The Lord of the Two Lands raised the mace high above his head, at arm's length.

A collective gasp arose from the countless foreigners present, when they suddenly realized what was about to happen: the braining of the vanquished prince of Megiddo by the victorious Mighty Bull of Kemet, Menkheperre Djehutymes.

But after a long pause, the muscular bare arm of the latter slowly lowered, without a blow being struck. The mace was handed back to Generalissimo Thuty and the officer let go of the hapless prince's hair. The stunned man, who had soiled himself, was pulled to his feet again, turned and led to the cluster of demeaned dynasts of Retenu, where he was pushed to his knees once more, facing towards his would-have-been executioner, who was standing akimbo, the general a pace behind him.

The Lord of the Two Lands addressed the group of kneeling rulers in a loud voice. "Thus My Majesty has given his pathetic life back to the wretch of Megiddo, and so, also, to each of you who blindly rebelled against the Black Land and the Living Horus, for the sake of wretched Kadesh — whose forehead My Majesty *would* have bashed to pulp had the cowardly worm been present this day." Menkheperre addressed the translator. "Tell them Our Person's words, speaker."

The translator did so and His Majesty continued.

"Living Horus has so given back your vile lives, but heavy retribution for your foolish transgressions shall be extracted."

There was a long pause and the translator realized it was his turn again. When he was quickly finished with his Retenu gibberish, Menkheperre resumed.

"In addition to all the riches of this place, which shall be taken back to the Black Land — all of your slaves, men, women, children, as well — so, too, shall each of your wives and every one of your children be transported there by My Majesty, to be slaves or servants as Our Person determines.

"And your sons who are carried off shall be tutored in the tongue and ways of the Two Lands, so they may return to rule in your places one day, possessing great wisdom and with much love for the Black Land and the Living Horus in their hearts, never to rebel like their foolish wretched fathers before them."

This was translated at length.

While the intermediary was speaking, double files began peeling off from both wings of the assembled soldiery of Kemet, trotting around the perimeters of the horde of Megiddo townspeople and entering through the high, wide-open gateway, to commence the formal official looting of the place.

Having finished addressing the still-kneeling dynasts, the Lord of the Two Lands motioned for the translator to follow and he crossed the dusty expanse to where the royal women and offspring of the towns of Retenu were clustered together, over 300 in all. He stopped some paces from the congregation, chin high, hawk-like and impressive in his gilded and golden regal finery.

The translator held back several cubits.

"Speaker, instruct the whore-wives and spawn of Kadesh to make themselves known, to stand here in front of Our Person."

This was relayed; and after some long hesitation — with the command repeated by the translator — four adult women and a trio of teenage girls holding one another's hands collectively took a step forward from the front row. The turbaned matrons wore heavy makeup and excessive, gaudy jewelry, and two were somewhat stout. The gazelle-eyed, pale-skinned slender teenagers, however, were unadorned and rather quite carnally attractive to young Menkheperre, their sheer appeal enhanced by bared breasts in three stages of maturation.

The Lord of the Two Lands would take the eldest daughter of Kadesh, Menhet, to his camp bed that very night; and, back in Kemet, at Mennufer, she would eventually become first his concubine and then his King's Wife, along with her sisters as well, Menwi and Merti, the youngest, one after the other. Two, in fact, would over time bear him five daughters and the third a still-born son.

Two Seasons Later,
Home of Senenmut, Outskirts of Waset

His driver from the royal charioteer-pool reigned King's Scribe Tjaneni's borrowed vehicle to a halt at the gate of Count Senenmut's modest estate. He had ridden there — for the very first time — from the Residence in Waset, where his own simple living quarters were located (so as to be ready at hand when the Lord of the Two Lands summoned his service, and that was more or less daily).

The young man adjusted his new formal shoulder-length layered wig and stepped down from the chariot. He was attired in a short-sleeved linen tunic over which a sheer ankle-length skirt was tied. Except for one leather wristlet, he wore no adornment and his sandals were plain leather. Handsome Tjaneni looked every inch the professional bureaucrat that he was. And there he was, arriving to dine privately with the bureaucrat's bureaucrat, Senenmut, once the most powerful commoner in the whole of Kemet, having begun his long career as a King's Scribe. Tjaneni had been only a young-teenage acolyte in the Waset Mansion of Lord Montu at the height of the count's many achievements in service to the House of Djehutymes, which was also the point at which he had been cast down by the Female Horus, then Coregent with his own master, Lord of the Two Land's Menkheperre Djehutymes. Senenmut had been sent into exile — to the Great Green coastal port of Gubla, Tjaneni remembered — and survived there some years, until, following his Coregent's retirement, the Living Horus had sent the old bureaucrat a letter of pardon (Tjaneni had written this himself), inviting him to return to the Two Lands, specifically there to Waset. This had happened just prior to departure of the Armies of Kemet for the lengthy campaign in Retenu; and Senenmut had, indeed, accepted the royal reversal and was now resident in this present modest villa, a gift by way of compensation from Lord Menkheperre.

Following the return of the victorious Armies of Kemet to the Two Lands, His Majesty had remained at the Northern Residence in Mennufer for several weeks, only arriving in Waset to great fanfare a few crossings of Re before. Thus, Senenmut was still to be summoned for an audience with Menkheperre, and Tjaneni had not yet personally met the former "Lord High and Mighty of This and That" (as His Majesty had referred to him jokingly, at the time of dictating the redressing letter). So the King's Scribe was puzzled, to say the least, why he himself had received an invitation to dine privately with Senenmut at this time. Defanged, so to speak, the old lion surely was quite harmless these days. Obviously Menkheperre thought so.

Tjaneni instructed the driver to wait there in the shadows-darkening deserted residential lane for his return, in an hour, no more than two. He walked to the gateway, but before he could discover how to make his presence known, the painted plank door suddenly opened and he was greeted profusely by the estate butler, a short rotund bald man of indeterminable years. The latter led the King's Scribe through a small formal garden and up steps to a shallow portico and then the front door of the residence, ushering him inside to the smallish, columned audience hall. He was directed to seat himself in one of the several armchairs with seat cushions arranged casually around a low square ebony table, in the center of which was a large bronze bowl with several floating water-lily blossoms. The butler said "the master" would be joining him momentarily, and bustled off, no doubt to inform Senenmut of his guest's arrival.

And it was, indeed, only mere moments before a quite-tall man came into the chamber through the same double-door by which the butler had exited. His short-cropped hair was pure white, and he was attired in a full-sleeved tunic of sheerest linen, worn with an ankle-length overskirt dyed a brilliant scarlet. He wore no adornments and was informally barefooted. With his arms held wide in a gesture of familiarity, he crossed to where Tjaneni was seated, then quickly was standing.

"My dear young man! How good of you to accept our invitation, since we're strangers to you, yet."

He did not embrace Tjaneni, as the scribe thought he might, wondering immediately next at his host's use of the royal-prerogative plural-pronouns, "our, we." Perhaps former "Lord High and Mighty" was not as rehabilitated as His Majesty believed.

"Sit again, please," the sharp-featured man gestured, taking a chair for himself.

As Tjaneni did so, he could not help but notice the other man's pointed long nose and receded chin, the leathery wrinkles and the squared-off, longish white goatee (an affectation out of style at court these days).

Smiling, Senenmut sat back in his armchair, elbows on its arms, his fingers tented on his barreled chest, a gesture surely purposedly meant to echo the well-familiar one of Menkheperre. Tjaneni felt a tinge of uneasiness.

"So," began the old bureaucrat, "our spies have not exaggerated."

After a confusingly long pause, Tjaneni had to ask, "About what, Count?"

Before Senenmut could respond, a third person entered the chamber, again through the only door the King's Scribe had noticed. He was a young-seeming — but probably not so youngish — foreign-looking, somewhat short bronze-skinned male, inarguably handsome in the way some women of Kemet were inarguably beautiful. His shiny black hair, more perfect than any wig, hung straight to his broad shoulders, and he was — startling to Tjaneni — wearing only a loincloth patterned with bright-colored stripes, something decidedly "barbarian." The man's physique was athletic, to say the very least. Like Senenmut he affected no jewelry and was likewise barefooted. He crossed to the seated host, bent down and kissed him unabashedly on the cheek. He then stood and smiled at Tjaneni, who could not help but notice the perfect white teeth.

"Let me introduce my dear companion, Born of Min, who's been my best half since he was just out of boyhood," Senenmut, smiling, gestured up at Minmes beside him.

The man of Kheftiu held out his hand and Tjaneni stood. Minmes stepped forward and the two shook.

"Welcome to our modest home," Minmes offered.

Tjaneni thought he detected just the hint of accent. The two broke their grip and Minmes took the armchair between that of Senenmut and where Tjaneni resumed his previous seat. Almost immediately the butler returned bearing a tray laden with three lily-form faience chalices and a small silver ewer. The conversation did not resume until he had placed these on the table, poured three drinks of the finest Delta vintage and silently departed through the singular side door.

"So, as I was saying, dear man, our spies at the Residence weren't exaggerating when they reported that the young King's Scribe is very *well favored*. You must have the heart of every Residence serving-maiden aflutter." Senenmut paused, smiling over the rim of his chalice. "Even if you're *spoken* for, as you must be, surely."

Tjaneni felt his already-dark complexion growing redder.

"Oh, I haven't taken a wife, yet, if that's what you mean, Count. His Majesty has promised me the pick of the Retenu royal women recently brought back as slaves, whatever — excepting, of course, the three quite lovely daughters of the Prince of Kadesh, which Lasting Manifestation of Re has claimed as his own — but I'm, well, still undecided in that regard, being kept so very busy with His Majesty's business that I scarcely have any time for a personal life, let alone for husbanding a foreigner."

The King's Scribe sipped his wine.

"Well, one's total devotion to the Living Horus can be most rewarding, as I certainly know," Senenmut replied, "having served five of them, beginning like you as King's Scribe for Asar Holy Soul of Re, Amen is Pleased, when I was even younger than you, before I'd seen seventeen floodings."

"And your own family, Count Brother of Mut, you managed to find the time to wed a wife and then father children?"

"The family of my husbanding sits right there beside you." Senenmut gestured towards Minmes. "Born of Min is in many ways the one true child I've created and, all in all, my helpmate in every possible way a *wife* might be." He smiled at the black-haired handsome man and pursed his thin lips in the pantomime of a kiss. Minmes returned the smile and sipped from his chalice.

Senenmut looked back to an uneasy Tjaneni. "Surely Lasting Manifestation of Re, knowing of your coming here this evening, advised you of my 'nature' and that of Born of Min."

"I didn't inform His Majesty of your invitation, since I don't bother him with my private affairs." Tjaneni sipped again. "Consequently he knows nothing of my acceptance nor presence here now. He's never spoken of you to me, Count, except regarding your...well, banishment by his former Coregent, and that only at the time he dictated to me the letter inviting you back to the Black Land."

"So that was *your* hand. Very crisp and readable penmanship."

"If I may be so blunt, sir, at that time he did refer to you, I believe it was, as 'Lord High and Mighty of This and That,' laughing when he said it."

"Yes, that was what the princess and God's Wife, Beauty of Re, would blurt out when she was angry with me, which was often while she was going towards womanhood. She was in many ways the other one of my children — at least when I was still her tutor. She was less of a success than Minmes."

Senenmut sharply clapped his hands and the butler immediately appeared.

"Have the food brought now, Saroy."

The servant departed.

Senenmut turned back to Tjaneni and changed subjects abruptly. "You know Prince Amen at the Head, I presume."

Tjaneni nodded. "His Majesty's first son, but not the Crown-Prince. Only by sight. I've never spoken to the youth, who has trouble forming sentences, I understand, a stammerer. He came to stay at the Residence here in the Southern Capital when the Dowager Great Royal Wife Noblest Woman retired to Wer-Mer at Ta-She Oasis, where the prince'd been living since immediately after his birth, as I heard it."

"A stammerer? Like his grandfather then," mused Senenmut. "I didn't now that."

"His grandfather?"

"Yes, the second Born of Djehuty, Lasting Manifestations of Re's father, he also stammered all his life. Asar Great Form of Re was father of God's Wife Beauty of Re, His Majesty's half-sister and Prince Amen at the Head's mother, who died in childbirth, along with the princes' twin sister, who was never given a name that I heard of. Very confusing, the family relationships of the House Born of Djehuty."

"Mut's Brother had a hand in all of that," said Minmes, speaking for only the second time, "in the begetting of Prince Amen at the Head, that is."

"You're such a *gossip*, Born of Min!" Senenmut laughed. "But I can see from his expression that our young King's Scribe here is understandably curious about these people from before his time as the third Born of Djehuty's intimate, or at least confidante." There was a pause. "Well, would you like to know all the sordid details of the 'stammerer's' rather unorthodox conception?"

At that moment the door panels off to the chamber's far side opened again and Butler Saroy entered, then held one panel wide so that a trio of male servants could pass through, carrying trays with food for the meal. The three youths from Wawat were well above the norm in foreign facial and physical attractiveness, the latter quite evident inasmuch as they were attired in only the skimpiest of bright scarlet loincloths and their jet skin had been lightly oiled to a subtle sheen. Their heads were shaved and shiny and they were all barefooted. When the third server was through the doorway, Saroy led them to the center of the chamber, and the foodstuffs they carried were placed on the large ebony table. The Wawatans all emitted a faint aroma, which Tjaneni thought was probably the result of "bathing" in the fumes of smoldering frankincense — something of a sacrilege.

The meal placed before the three diners consisted chiefly of spit-roasted young ducks stuffed with pickled onions and dates; dom-palm nuts that had been thinly sliced, soaked in wine and pan-roasted; and honeyed bread-cakes dusted with sesame seeds. Chalices were brim-filled with the Delta vintage. Indeed, thought Tjaneni, Senenmut and his Kheftian "wife" set as sumptuous a table as His Majesty at the Residence.

Although the conversation resumed, off to one side the lithe Wawatan trio performed graceful juggling and acrobatic feats, as the evening's entertainment — to the accompaniment of an elderly male harpist led into the chamber by Saroy, so probably blind.

"Well then," Senenmut returned to where he'd been interrupted, "do you want the details of Prince Amen at the Head's conception, and why he's not Crown-Prince?"

"I'm certain that you're going to tell me, whether I should hear them, the details, or not, so continue." Tjaneni tore a leg from the small duck carcass on his plate, then bit off some of the crispy flesh.

Senenmut began, "As you must know, in the tradition of the houses of Tao and Djehuty, when young Lasting Manifestation of Re reached sexual maturity, he should have been married to his older half-sister, Beauty of Re, and gotten about the business of making himself a Horus-in-the-Nest." Senenmut paused to chew and swallow some roasted dom-nut slices. "She, however, despised him and had ever since their childhood. Besides which her mother, the Coregent, had other plans for Beauty of Re, intending that the girl should remain unmarried, so that she could eventually succeed True Soul of Re as the next Female Living Horus — which wouldn't have been conceivable if she was Lasting Manifestation of Re's Great Royal Wife and mother of his brood, producing his Heir or not.

"It was widely known in the Residences that the young God's Wife had lost her virginity soon after commencing to bleed, and that she went on to receive *any* erect Min that presented itself: charioteers and stable grooms, the captain of the Medjay royal guards, her mother's King's Scribe and, the gods forbid, none other than her pet dwarf! She even tried her very best to seduce *me*, her tutor of all people! It was my turning her advances aside — falsely claiming impotence — that initiated her subsequent great distain for me. Beauty of Re expected to *always* get her way.

"As you're well aware, His Majesty is not, how shall I say it, especially favored by Min —"

"I'm his *scribe*, not his body servant. I take dictation, but I don't *bathe* him!" Tjaneni interrupted emphatically.

Smiling thinly, Senenmut waved the objection aside and continued. "In any case, *I'd* been instructing young Born of Djehuty in the purpose and function of his modest Min since he reached puberty, which I'd done with his father, as well. He had no experience laying with females, and was fully intimidated by his sharp-tongued half-sister, so likely wouldn't have been able to adequately perform his husbandly chores, even had Beauty of Re pointedly wanted to wed and bed him against her mother's wishes."

Senenmut chewed some duck, sipped wine and went on.

"Because the young God's Wife took her sacerdotal duties way too seriously — ritually stroking the erect Min of Lord Amen-Re's effigy being one of them — she began to insist that the Hidden One himself regularly visited her bed and laid with her as would a mortal male. She was quite adamant about that — most likely inspired to such fantasy foolishness by the fiction her mother had created to account for True Soul of Re's self-proclaimed semi-divinity: that she herself was conceived when Lord Amen-Re, in the guise of her father, had played husband to her mother.

"So an idea came to me. Young Hawk Beak — that is, Born of Djehuty — could lie with his sister if she thought it was Amen-Min who had entered her. And if he wasn't able to perform, as he feared, then she'd never dare complain about the god's inadequacy — although I didn't present that part of the ruse to His Majesty, not wishing to discourage him before he'd even made the effort."

Interrupting himself, Senenmut refilled his chalice and that of Minmes. Tjaneni gestured that his drink was still fine.

"To shorten the tale, I managed to arrange for an hallucination-inducing herb to be slipped into the God's Wife's wine ewer on the appointed evening. Meanwhile, I personally converted His Majesty into the god. With him stripped naked, I painted his head and face with a washable blue pigment. The very act of doing this excited him, and his — well, as said, modest — Min became fully rigid in anticipation of the forthcoming event. With gilded feathers banded to His Majesty's head, and resin gum being chewed by him, we managed to slip into the God's Wife's Residence apartment without being discovered.

"Everything went as I'd hoped. Beauty of Re received Amen-Min/ Born of Djehuty with jutting tongue, tight embrace and widespread moist thighs. His Majesty performed faultlessly, achieving his first orgasm with a female, perhaps rather too quickly, but to his own satisfaction. I'd achieved a revenge of sorts on my sharp-tongue former pupil, and Lasting Manifestation of Re had proven his manhood to himself."

A bite of sweet cake and a swallow of wine.

"But the unanticipated unfortunately had happened. In a few short months it became apparent that Beauty of Re was with child. She genuinely — or insanely — believed it was the seed of Lord Hidden One growing in her, of course. Her mother confided to me that she feared it was that of the Wawatan captain of the Medjay guards or, far worse, of the disgusting dwarf, Khawi. There was nothing to be done, after all, but let the God's Wife reach her full term and deliver. She grew and grew and finally the time came.

"I wasn't present at the coming forth, naturally, but learned later from Noblest Woman's companion, Royal Nurse Fish, Daughter of Re, that it had been a total disaster. Beauty of Re labored on the birthing blocks for hours, not able to release her fetus, being that it was feet-first. In desperation for the lives of both mother and child, the attending physician sliced open the God's Wife's belly to extract the infant. To the great surprise of all present — which did not include either Noblest Woman or Nurse Fish — not one but two came forth, doubles, one living, a boy, the other dead, a girl. Beauty of Re, of course, very soon died. The infants, without breath and breathing, had been taken away by the time Noblest Woman and Fish returned to the birthing chamber, from which they'd earlier fled in frustration. Her Majesty was led to believe that she'd lost both her only daughter and an unliving granddaughter. She never demanded to see the tiny corpse, perhaps privately fearing it would be either black-skinned or stunted of limb. I thought it best not to pry her motive.

"Without Noblest Woman's awareness, the boy infant was delivered to his young father; and Lasting Manifestation of Re had his son — whom he named (since *he* was in the correct birthing position) Amen at the Head, sent, as you know — to be raised in secret at the oasis harim residence of Wer-Mer, a full-day's journey south of the Northern Capital. Over the floodings, as the opportunities of royal hunting expeditions to the oasis permitted, His Majesty would visit the growing prince, whom he took to his heart, despite the boy's obvious speech problem. Amen at the Head was a bastard, of course — as the third Born of Djehuty himself had been — so couldn't be declared the Heir, unless, matter of factly, a Great Royal Wife ultimately failed to produce a dynastically legitimate Horus-in-the-Nest. This didn't happen, obviously, being that Her Highness Sitiah finally delivered a son who has indeed lived, Crown-Prince Lasting Manifestation of Re."

Senenmut sipped more wine.

"You've a mind for great detail, Count. My personal strength is in distilling rather than embellishing. I limit my observations to the obvious rather than the particular. His Majesty seems to prefer that approach."

Tjaneni popped a piece of sesame cake into his mouth, chewed and sipped wine to wash it down. After a pause he continued. "I confess to being somewhat confused as to your reasons for inviting me here, other than to gossip."

"Well, beautiful young man, besides the rather, well, obvious one of hoping to seduce you into our bed this evening, Born of Min's and mine — and that would seem to be a vain goal — I was hoping to enlist your support in my endeavor to return to some significant degree of influence with Lasting Manifestation of Re. You, I'm informed, as no one else, have the ear of the Lord of the Two Lands; and the merest suggestion from you in my behalf would be most effective, I've certainly no doubt."

"In the first regard, Count, you flatter me greatly. But thank you very much, no, I've never any felt inclination to lie with men — if only very little more to enter a woman. My needs in the matter of Min are all but non-existent, perhaps regrettably, although perhaps not. I don't choose to treat this subject further with you, but I will say that Born of Min" he gestured towards him, "is obviously most fortunate to have been, to be your 'best half', as you put it earlier. And your selection of him for that very special role demonstrates your exquisite good taste, to say the least." Tjaneni shrugged. "If I had any carnal needs whatsoever, he'd satisfy them most fully!"

Minmes grinned and bowed his head. Tjaneni continued:

"Now, as to the matter of my serving as your agent with His Majesty, you indeed over-estimate my personal influence with the Lord of the Two Lands, Count Brother of Mut. I function as his cipher only. He's never once sought my personal counsel, has never confided to me his intentions or plans. Inarguably, I spend more time in His Majesty's presence than any other single person, but I'm neither his 'confidante' nor 'intimate'. Nonetheless, as it's possible, I'll put forth your case. I can't promise results from doing so."

"I couldn't really hope for anything more, realistically." Senenmut stood.

With that, King's Scribe Tjaneni took his leave of "His Lord High and Mighty." Their paths would cross again, repeatedly, however, to neither man's real regret.

TWO SEASONS LATER, INUNDATION 5
SOLE REIGN OF MENKHEPERRE DJEHUTYMES
HARIM OF THE RESIDENCE, MENNUFER

His staff of office in hand, King's Steward Renna preceded His Majesty as they walked to the harim wing of the Mennufer Residence.

Tjaneni, secretary of the Lord of the Two Lands, trailed a few paces behind, carrying his scribal gear, as always, should Menkheperre Djehutymes want anything recorded — as he often did.

The young ruler was paying the initial visit to a his newly born
first daughter. Her mother was Menhet, eldest of the three princesses of
Kadesh brought to Kemet by His Majesty, as hostages following the campaign in Retenu that had climaxed with the capitulation of the town of
Megiddo — where the teenage girls, their mother and other wives of the
prince of Kadesh had taken refuge during the three-month siege of the
town. By the calculations of Kemet, Menhet was seventeen floodings old.
Menkheperre was ten floodings her senior. He had a Great Royal Wife,
Sitiah — who now lived full-time at the Residence in the Southern capi-
tal, Waset — and by her one living young son, his Namesake and Heir,
Crown-Prince Menkheperre. Menhet and her younger sisters, Menwi and
Merti, were His Majesty's first concubines, and so were occupants of the
Mennufer harim. Also resident there were the girls' mother and three step-
mothers, all hostages.

A pre-teen full brother, heir to the prince of Kadesh and captured
at Megiddo, was now in Kemet as well, but at Waset, living in confinement with other young heir-princes of Retenu, likewise taken prisoners at
Megiddo. It was Menkheperre's plan that the youths learn the language
and customs of the Two Lands, so that they'd feel predisposed towards
Kemet, when eventually they'd be sent home to succeed their fathers on
the various petty thrones of Retenu.

Renna, His Majesty and Tjaneni rounded the corner of the final
hallway to the harim and beheld Chamberlain Nay, the very obese eunuch
in charge of the place, waiting for them in front of the harim's wide-open
doorway. As soon as the Lord of the Two Lands and his small entourage
came into view, Nay bowed as much as his sagging vast belly allowed.

"Greetings, Chamberlain," intoned approaching Steward Renna,
to the bent-forward bald man in an ankle-length linen skirt. "His Majesty
Lasting Manifestation of Re has come to meet his new daughter," Renna
stated the obvious. He was only a little less fat than the chamberlain, and
not a eunuch.

"Our humble establishment is greatly honored by the Living Horus's presence," lisped Nay, still looking at the painted gypsum-plaster
floor.

"Lead us to the new princess," ordered Menkheperre. He was
dressed simply as usual in private, wearing only a short linen kilt without
adornments. His close-cropped head was uncovered, so no cobra graced
his brow; and he typically was barefooted. Tjaneni was identically attired,

except for the leather wristband he always wore on his writing arm.

Nay uprighted his bulk and waddled into the harim's central chamber. This was the same place where Menkheperre himself, as a small child, had sometimes lived with his mother, the late Dowager Royal Wife Iset — this prior to his father's unexpected death when the prince was but three floodings old. The space had a two-column deep colonnade running along three sides, off of which opened doors to individual apartments for the harim's residents, usually secondary royal wives and the Lord of the Two Lands' concubines and their children (boys just until their Horus Sidelock was cut). Presently the harim's only inhabitants were the seven royal females of Kadesh. At the moment there was no evidence of the occupation of any of these persons, however, as everyone, including servants, apparently had retreated to the individual quarters, in anticipation of the arrival of the Living Horus; all the apartment doors were closed. What the Reteni women did to occupy themselves was not apparent, as nothing personal had been left on the chamber's sparse furniture or the floor painted in imitation of garden ponds populated with fish, flora and waterfowl. Not even the omnipresent cats were to be seen.

Chamberlain Nay waddled through the center of the long space, with Steward Renna, His Majesty and King's Scribe Tjaneni in his wake. Passing under the colonnade opposite the harim's main entry, the four men came up to the closed wooden panels of an apartment's door. Menkheperre knew what awaited on the other side: the suite he had shared with his mother more than twenty-five floodings before, when the court was resident at the Northern Capital. The eunuch knocked, then pushed the panels inward without waiting a reply and entered. King's Steward Renna stepped to one side, so that the Lord of the Two Lands and his secretary could follow behind the Chamberlain. He then closed the doors, to wait where he was: his duty had been to lead His Majesty to this appointment; he was not expected to be present at the audience with the new mother and infant.

Menkheperre had supposed that young Menhet would still be recuperating in her bed, as the delivery had been only three days earlier. Rather, she was now sitting in a cushioned armchair, bare to the waist and nursing the tiny pink infant cradled in her arms. The pale teenager's raven long hair was held behind her ears by a simple gold fillet and she wore no eye makeup or jewelry.

Seated in armchairs to either side of Menhet were her mother, three stepmothers and two younger sisters. The older women had abandoned the brightly patterned attire of Retenu in favor of all-black garments, including their wrapped turbans, perhaps in protest of their hostage status; but the girls now sported the plain-linen sleeveless sheath dresses favored by the females of Kemet, although these had been retailored so that their small breasts were fully revealed, in the manner of the Reteni. Unadorned hair hung loose to their shoulders, kohl lined their large eyes and each wore a simple beaded collar of the current Kemet fashion, plus narrow wristlets of braided gold wire. So close were Menwi and Merti in age and appearance, they might have been mistaken for twins. Each sister had gone to Menkheperre's bed on several occasions, qualifying both as his concubines. Eventually proving fertile, they would be made King's Wives, like their elder sibling recently had been.

At the sudden arrival of the Lord of the Two Lands, all of the women save Menhet rose to their feet, heads bowed.

"His Majesty, Son of Re, the Living Horus, Mighty Bull, Lasting Manifestation of Re, Born of Djehuty," intoned the eunuch loudly — and unnecessarily.

"Thank you, Chamberlain," said Menkheperre. "You may take your leave now."

"But I must chaperone the ladies," he protested, nearly pouting.

His Majesty pointed to the closed doors. "Go exchange Residence gossip with the King's Steward. We won't be long. And our wife and mothers-in-law and sisters-in-law will be perfectly safe with Our Person and our King's Scribe."

His mound of bare shoulders slumping, Nay waddled off, closing the double-door behind himself.

"So, greetings, your highnesses. Please, be seated again."

Although the Retenni royal women had been taking daily instruction in the spoken language of Kemet, their comprehension was less than might be desired after several months. So Menkheperre gestured with both hands for them to sit. They did and he stepped to in front of Menhet, indicating he wished her to hand him his tiny naked daughter.

The King's Wife pulled her nipple from the infant's mouth, shifted position and held the little body out to His Majesty, facing towards him. As soon as Menkheperre had gripped the infant's sides, she began to scream and kick. Menhet released her hold and father and daughter were then face to face. The Living Horus pursed his lips and kissed the bump of nose. She reached out and gripped his "Hawk Beak" with her tiny fingers. Menkheperre laughed and held her out at arm's length.

"Yes, My Majesty shall name her 'Beautiful Bee,' after the step-aunt I never knew."

He passed the still-squalling infant back to her mother. The Lord of the Two Lands could have no way of knowing, of course, that the toddler Neferubity also would die from the bite of a cobra.

*   *   *

14

The royal flotilla of eight small barques in single file approached the Pleasure Island in the middle of The River, a short distance up stream from the Southern Capital at Waset. Each vessel was rowed by six nearly nude muscular men of Wawat, their ebony bodies oiled for the occasion and thus glossy in the late-morning sun. The occasion was a picnic outing from the Residence and passengers on the river craft were: Great Royal Wife Sitiah; Nurse of the God Ipu, Sitiah's mother; teenage Crown-Prince Menkheperre; his elder brother, Prince Amenemhat, and that young man's recent bride, Lady Isety; her mother, Adoratrix Huy, and teenage sister, Merytre Hatshepsut; plus a number of the women's handmaidens and the Crown-Prince's two hunting hounds.

An advance group of Residence servants and a pair of Medjay guards had arrived at the island earlier that morning, to drive off any sons of Sobek which might be sunning on the embankments and to make preparations for the royal picnickers — freshening up the small permanent pavilion there by entwining flower garlands on the brightly painted slender wood columns, arranging pillows and bolsters for lounging, setting up amphorae of Delta vintage, positioning small low rush-work tables and stools to dine from and situating baskets of food for ready access when it came time for the royals and their in-laws to take refreshment. Two lute players and a piper were prepared to entertain, as well.

Lord of the Two Lands Menkheperre, Son of Re Djehutymes was not present that fateful day, being far off campaigning in Retenu, as had been his annual habit for the previous six floodings. More correctly the current campaign was a naval one, His Majesty and the marines of Kemet assaulting the Retenu coastal cities of the Great Green Sea (including Gubla), forcing submissions and laying up provisions for future inland forays.

Princes Menkheperre and Amenemhat, Lady Isety and the lanky

dogs rode in the lead barque. The closely cropped heads of the two youths were uncovered and they wore only simple linen kilts and reed sandals; each had a sheathed dagger belted at his waist. The new bride, in a white sleeveless sheath, had eschewed a wig, her long raven hair adorned with a thin wreath of blue cornflowers; she wore only a single bracelet of braided gold wire and was barefooted. The hounds, sporting gilded embossed-leather collars, stood shoulder to shoulder in the barque prow, like double figureheads. They began barking in unison as the vessel approached the island embankment, already occupied by numerous skiffs used earlier by the Residence servants and Medjay guards. The youthful Crown-Prince twisted on his padded-plank seat to address his half-brother.

Pointing, he asked, "What's that disturbance over there, Amen at the Head?"

Some distance off, further upstream and many cubits from the island, the bluish-green waters of The River seemed to be roiling. This apparently was what had set the dogs barking.

"Sub...merged ri..ver ho...hors...ses, prob...bly," the young man stammered his reply, as usual. "Se...ev...eral, from the lo...o..ks of it. A herd."

"Will it be safe to go ashore, with the beasts out there?" Lady Isety innocently asked.

Amenemhat thought so. He would soon enough be proven very wrong.

T he gala picnic was well under way, when Menkheperre's hounds resumed their barking, bounded off the pavilion and raced towards the tall stand of papyrus that formed a backdrop at one side of the large man-made clearing, in the center of which was the barely elevated wooden structure now housing the sizeable party of diners and their servers. The Crown-Prince's shouted commands for the pair to "come back" went unheeded, of course, and the dogs disappeared into the dense greenery, their barking even more agitated. Menkheperre rose and stepped down to the grassy ground, to go impulsively in pursuit of his pets. The two Medjay guards were immediately at his heels. The three of them were just a few cubits from the wall of papyrus, when one of the hounds yelped loudly, then was silent. His mate continued her panicked barking, yelped as well and was also silent. Medjays and prince halted in their tracks, however, when a loud, netherworldly bellowing began a short ways off within the stand of thick water foliage.

In only moments a gigantic green-black river-horse bull burst through the papyrus, pink maw — with its wrist-thick bloody ivory pegs

— stretched wide open. Before either stunned Medjay could raise his spear, or the Crown-Prince could draw his dagger, the bellowing beast was upon them, trampling the hapless youth underfoot and tossing the Wawat men, one after the other, aside, into the air, so that, their weapons flying, they crashed to the ground unconscious.

Immediately, there was mass pandemonium among the picnickers — the women all on their feet, scattering furnishings, wine goblets and food, and screaming hysterically, Prince Amenemhat drawing his useless dagger. When the huge-headed monster closed its great mouth on the broken body of the already-dead Menkheperre, raising this into the air and shaking it furiously, bellowing all the while, Great Royal Wife Sitiah mindlessly was off the pavilion and dashing across the lawn to aid her hapless, helpless son. Instantly Amenemhat was running after her, but not soon enough. As the screeching small woman in a heavy wig went up to the behemoth shaking the bloodied Crown-Prince like a rag doll, the beast tossed its victim forward so that the mangled body literally slammed the frail Sitiah to the ground with great force, killing her on the spot.

The raging river-horse ignored Amenemhat — who was now kneeling beside the equally dead Heir and Great Royal Wife — turning its attention to one of the sprawled fallen Medjay, closing its bloody jaws on the prone black body. The prince seized the opportunity and grabbed up the spear of the other unconscious guard. Rushing from the animal's blind side, he ran the weapon with all the force he could muster through the thick hide and nearly a cubit into the body, just behind the tree-trunk of front leg. Amenemhat lunged backwards and fell onto his rump, as the monster dropped the Medjay's lifeless corpse and rose, roaring in great pain, on its rear haunches, stubby front legs thrashing the air. The prince quickly scrambled backwards on all fours, regained his footing, stood and ran without consideration towards the pavilion filled with fear-frozen wailing women. Spear shaft protruding from its side, the fately wounded bull charged after Amenemhat.

But by the time the fleeing prince had almost reached his destination, some three-dozen black marines had burst into the clearing — having heard the hysterical commotion and bellowing from where they were hunkered some ways off by their beached ferry-crafts, awaiting the royal party's return trip across The River. Several carried spears, which were launched at the lumbering beast. Four or five of them embedded in its wide snout, the animal suddenly halted, crumpled and rolled onto the bulbous side without the Medjay's spear shaft. Not realizing that his pursuer had dropped in its tracks, Amenemhat leapt onto the pavilion and into the waiting wide-open arms of Lady Isety. He was quickly surrounded by the other grief-stricken women.

It would be many crossings of Re before word reached campaigning Lord of the Two Lands Menkheperre that he was, in one fell sweep, without both a chief spouse and the Heir. When he finally returned to Kemet, he partially corrected that situation by naming his first and only surviving son, Neferure's bastard Amenemhat, Horus-in-the-Nest. The following flooding he took as Great Royal Wife his stammering new heir's sister-in-law, teenaged Merytre Hatshepsut. After another three floodings, in Inundation 36 of Menkheperre's reign, she gave birth to a son, who was named Amenhotep. The infant immediately replaced his elder half-brother as designated successor to the Horus Throne. Amenemhat was then given the title of Overseer of the Cattle of Amen-Re, an important and lucrative administrative post he'd hold well into the reign of his much-younger sibling.

EARLY IN INUNDATION 33, REIGN OF MENKHEPERRE DJEHUTYMES
THE RESIDENCE, MENNUFER

His Majesty was dictating to King's Scribe Tjaneni, when the Northern Residence's recently named Chamberlain, the eunuch Nay, appeared at the doorway of the ruler's bed chamber. The third Djehutymes looked up and saw the obese bureaucrat, fingers interlocked on his bare belly.

"Yes, Chamberlain?" The Living Horus acknowledged the other's quite large presence.

Tjaneni twisted around from his seated position at the low writing table.

"Excuse me, Your Majesty." Nay nodded his shaven head. "But a messenger has just arrived from the retirement residence at Wer-Mer, with word that her highness Dowager Great Royal Wife Noblest Woman is gravely ill. Servants there seem to feel that her days are numbered to a very few. A physician is in constant attendance."

Menkheperre rose from his armchair. Bereft of adornment, barefooted and attired in only a short wraparound coarse-linen kilt, he might've been taken for a thickset common farmer of Kemet, rather than as mighty Lord of the Two Lands and persistent scourge of the hapless princelings of Retenu.

"This news was to be expected, sooner or later. Our former Co-regent has outlasted most of her generation. The few floodings since Nurse Fish's passing have been very empty for her at Wer-Mer, we've been told. She's been left with only her many memories." He sat again. "Thank you, Chamberlain. You may go."

"But, Your Majesty," the eunuch protested, bowing his head once more, "the messenger awaits for word whether the residence at the Oasis should prepare for the Lord of the Two Lands' visit there, to offer his farewell to True Soul of Re...ah, that is...to Noblest Woman, of course."

Menkheperre looked to Tjaneni, who nodded in the affirmative.

"Yes, yes, well, of course. Tell the messenger that the Wer-Mer serving staff should expect Our Person and Crown-Prince Amen at the Head to arrive in, what?, say three crossings of Lord Re. We shall stay there overnight, departing for here the next dawn."

As the fat bureaucrat turned to go, Menkheperre asked rhetorically at his wide back, "May we presume, Chamberlain, that the former Mistress of the Two Lands is still alert enough and will know that Our Person and her grandson have come for a final audience?"

Nay turned back. "I'd suppose so, Your Majesty, but will ask the Wer-Mer messenger for confirmation." He waddled off.

LATE AFTERNOON, THREE CROSSINGS OF RE LATER
THE RETIREMENT RESIDENCE, WER-MER

Dowager Great Royal Wife Hatshepsut dreams: She enters through a wide stone gateway into an immense high-walled sunny garden of songbird- and monkey-filled acacia and dom-palm groves, interspersed by free-form papyrus ponds abloom with the largest blue and white water lilies she has ever seen. These are populated by plentiful, colorful fish and swimming and wading waterfowl of every describable sort, butterflies and dragon-flies darting about in aerial swarms. The lawns are uniformly lush dark green and clipped as short as the hair on a hunting hound. Wandering freely is a menagerie of seemingly tame gazelles and assorted horned small antelopes, antlered deer, even clusters of young ostriches.

She quickly is aware that besides all the fauna, humans are standing and sitting in numerous conversation groups throughout the garden. Like herself the men and women are dressed in linen finery and formal wigs, wearing jewelry appropriate to their sex. Naked children of various ages are engaged here and there in childhood games of ball tossing, tag and spinning, some young boys wrestling and riding piggyback. Faint piping and string music can be heard, although no musicians are evident.

It is all very idyllic.

She approaches one of the standing groups of adults, all of whom hold chalices of gold or silver, or else the finest faience. Walking up to them, she immediately realizes that she knows every single one of the half-dozen individuals — who halt their conversing and look her way, all smiling.

"Welcome, daughter," greets one of the women, a rearing inlaid-gold cobra fronting her tripartite long wig. "We've been expecting you."

This is Great Royal Wife and Regent Ahmes, her mother, as young-seeming as she'd been when she was married to her cousin, Generalissimo Djehutymes. Standing beside Ahmes, sporting an old-fashioned Hathor-wig is Mutnofret, her father's first wife, whom she'd never known — because she'd died — but recognizes now, nonetheless. And beside the latter is none other than that beloved father, Lord of the Two Lands Akheperkare Djehutymes. The close-filling cap-wig he wears makes his nose seem larger than she remembers. He, too, has a golden cobra on his brow and exhibits the muscular, if thickset, physique of a man in no more than his late twenties. The slight paunch is gone.

"Our warm greetings, too, daughter. It's seems like only yesterday that we bade you farewell, when we departed for our final, ill-fated campaign in Retenu."

Next to her father is her half-brother, Amenmes, Crown-Prince when he disappeared while River-swimming in Wawat. He's still a stocky teenager, a young copy of her father, and only offers her a nod, raising his faience chalice to sip from it.

And beside him are two other youths, whom she never knew but recognizes as her father's elder sons by Mutnofret, thus her half-brothers, Wadjmes and Remes. They likewise are shyly silent.

Before anything more is said, a small, very pretty naked girl in a sidelock comes running up to beside Ahmes, gripping the woman's free hand, grinning widely. This is Neferubity, her little sister, looking exactly as she had that afternoon of the fatal family outing by The River, when their father was still a generalissimo.

"Sister!" the child exclaims, "You are so grownup!"

"And you are so *not*, Beautiful Bee." This is the first thing she has uttered since entering the garden.

"Come," the girl took her hand, "Let's go see Great-auntie."

Without resisting — or taking her leave — she allows herself to be led away from the family group and across the lawn towards persons seated a ways off. For the first time she realizes that she, too, is carrying a chalice, a solid-gold one in her case, which is half-full of red wine.

Those they approach occupy gilded armchairs arranged in a conversational circle. When she and Neferubity are closer, she immediately recognizes each individual, although she has only known one of them personally. This is the petite female of uncertain age wearing a massive tripartite wig fronted by a rearing cobra, who is the indomitable Great Royal Wife, Regent and God's Wife of Amen-Re, Ahmes Nefertari, her great-aunt; she is addressing the others. Seated to one side of her is a small-boned, slender man in a short-curled wig with cobra on his brow: The Liberator, Nebphetyre Ahmes, Ahmes Nefertari's brother-husband. And next to him are their mother and father: stately Great Royal Wife and Regent Ahhotep and her brother-husband, Ruler of Waset Seqenenre Tao, who had begun the Wars of Liberation. Beside him is their petite mother, Great Royal Wife Tetisheri, matriarch of the House of Tao; her wig might appropriately be described as "old fashioned." And, finally, occupying the chair between his great-grandmother and mother is Lord of the Two Lands Djeserkare Amenhotep, attired in an elaborate shoulder-length wig of tiered braids fronted by a golden cobra; he holds a rolled handkerchief in one hand. All six possess gold chalices from which they sip at random intervals.

As she and her sister go up to the group, little Neferubity pips, "Great-auntie, see who's just arrived!" All look their way.

"Well, our dear, it's high time, is it not?" Ahmes Nefertari states and asks. She raises her chalice in a greeting gesture. "How are things in the Two Lands?"

She is standing outside the circle of ancestors, Neferubity still clinging to one hand, the chalice in her other.

"From what we know, your highness, the Two Lands continues at annual war with the wretched Reteni," she replies. "His Majesty Lasting Manifestation of Re has become addicted to conquest and tribute, it seems. And he continues adding to the Mansion of Lord Hidden One, Amen-Re, we understand — finishing constructions we began jointly, initiating his own projects. His Majesty hasn't regularly communicated with us following our retirement."

"And for how many floodings has that been?" bird-like Great Royal Wife Tetisheri asks, then sips from her chalice. "That is, your 'retirement'?"

"Eleven now, if we remember correctly."

"So, exactly why was it that you saw fit, as a female, to personally assume the Double Crown in the first place, great-grandniece?" It was The Liberator speaking.

"To secure the throne of our nephew, Lasting Manifestation of Re, who was a young child, just five floodings old. We believed it was about to be seized from him by your passed-over middle offspring, Son of Amen, and his conniving son, Prince Tao. That would not've been possible, or certainly less likely, with duo Horuses, one adult, co-ruling. Which correctly proved to have been the case."

"And you co-ruled for how many floodings?" The Liberator continues.

"Twenty," she replies.

"Was that not about ten longer than really necessary?" Djeserkare Amenhotep interjects, sniffing at his handkerchief.

She shrugs. "Certainly Lasting Manifestation of Re was fully capable of sole rule even before he reached his majority, Your Majesty, but our arrangement, the sharing of responsibilities for the Two Lands, had become a matter of mutual convenience. We and our nephew were quite compatible, or so it always seemed to Our Person. By the time Lasting Manifestation of Re was in his teens, matters of state were decided jointly. It was then a coregency of fully equals."

Ahhotep — longtime Regent for her own minor son, The Liberator — speaks up. "We understand from your daughter, Beauty of Re, that you were of a mind to establish a permanent institution of co-ruling male and female Living Horuses. Is that correct? If so, an explanation, please."

"Indeed, that unique concept was considered, Your Highness, but it never materialized."

"Only because Beauty of Re came here unexpectedly, isn't that right?" Ahhotep continues.

"Our daughter was key to the concept. Without her it wasn't possible, so abandoned." She suddenly feels the need to sip her wine, and does so. It is the best vintage, even the very best she has ever tasted.

Ruler of Waset Seqenenre Tao speaks for the first time. He's had to twist in his golden armchair to see her. "If your coregency was going so well, why is it that you decided to doff your Double Crown? To our admittedly limited knowledge, no Living Horus has ever voluntarily relinquished the throne of the Two Lands. We certainly never would have, had it been ours to occupy."

"The simple answer, Revered Ancestor, is that True Soul of Re grew bored," she answers simply. "Even *weary* with day-to-day governing. We broke precedent by becoming True Soul of Re, but certainly no more so by ceasing to be that entity. Beauty of Re was gone and Lasting Manifestation of Re no longer required Our Person at the rudder, so to speak. Thus, it was, well, farewell."

She releases her sister's hand, quickly bows her head, abruptly turns and walks away from her seated grand jury of ancestors. As she crosses the verdant lawn, she passes standing groups of persons she doesn't know, but who, nonetheless, acknowledge her passing with nods of apparent recognition.

A spotted young gazelle approaches fearlessly, even boldly, so she stops, pats its smooth head several times and moves on. For a few moments, a group of naked small children link hands and gambol in a circle around her, while she stands and sips the really excellent wine. When they break and dash off, squealing and laughing, she continues her stroll, very soon spotting a conversation group standing at the edge of a large water-lily pond, several of whom she knows for certain.

Two men have their backs to her, but next to one is unquestionably her brother-husband, Lord of the Two Lands Akheperenre Djehuty-mes, less paunchy and fleshy-faced than she remembers him, his baldness covered by a short wig with the frontal cobra in gold. Beside him, in her typical immense wig of layered braids, is King's Mother Iset, "Harim Mouse," scarcely taller than a prepubescent girl. And next to her — and only a very little taller — is none other than God's Wife of Amen Neferure. Lithe as ever, she wears a close-fitting wig of tight curls with modius and holds a small linen-wrapped bundle in her slender bare arms.

These are not persons that she's anxious to encounter just now, if ever, but before she can turn away and move off, she's spotted by her half-brother, who calls out.

"So, Sister, you've finally arrived. Come, come, join us." He broadly gestures for her to approach.

At which moment the two whose backs have been to her turn in unison. To her surprise they are her father-and-son old nemeses, Prince-Count Siamen and Prince Tao. She can't help but notice — to her greater surprise — that her father's uncle is no longer lame, his withered leg now quite normal in length and natural looking, under his knee-length linen kilt. He also seems far younger than she ever knew him. And his son, her once-only lover, seems scarcely more than a man in his early twenties, attractive physically in every way that her brother-husband never was — or is not even now. Both men smile, not exactly benignly.

She could just move off, but goes up to the small group instead.

"Greetings, Dowager King's Great Wife," Siamen speaks first. "It's been too long, but we knew you'd be arriving here eventually."

"Need we say that you're looking exceptionally fit, Son of Amen. Certainly all would have been quite different, had that always been the case, we suspect."

"Still using the ruler's plural, then?" It is Tao's question.

"*We* are surprised to find *you* here, Cousin. Kheftiu was not to your liking?" she asks coldly.

"Oh, Kheftiu suited me quite nicely, indeed," Tao replies." I married the Minos's sister and sired him a nephew, who himself is even now the current Minos, my late brother-in-law having no surviving sons of his own. I may have never been a ruler myself, but am the proud father of one, to be sure. And, indeed, I was quite surprised to find myself in this place, when I first arrived. Frankly, being father of the Minos, I rather expected to go to the Realm of the Mother Goddess."

"And exactly what place *is* this?" she asks — although she believes she knows.

"The Blessed Gardens of Asar and Iset, of course, Mother," replies Neferure. "Really quite lovely, if also really, really quite *boring*, as you'll discover, soon enough."

"What are you holding, Daughter?" She moves past Siamen and Tao and goes up to the petite young woman.

"Your granddaughter." The girl holds out the bundle. "Would you like to hold her?"

She takes it and pulls up the flap of linen covering the tiny red face. The infant is sleeping, it seems.

"Does she have a name?"

"None that I ever gave her. None is necessary here. She's simply 'Little One'."

"You do know, Beauty of Re, that she has a brother?"

"So I've been told. He's grown now, apparently."

"We only finally met when Amen at the Head — *his* name — was sixteen floodings. His existence had been kept a secret from us by his father, our former Coregent, your half-brother." She sips her wine. "He reminded us very much of his grandfather when young," she looks contemptuously at Akheperenre, "even to the way he speaks." It suddenly dawns on her that her brother-husband had not stammered, when he addressed her, called her to join them.

"So then, our daughter's son will succeed Lasting Manifestation of Re on the Horus Throne?" asks Akheperenre rhetorically.

"Not so, Brother. Your bastard son finally took a Great Royal Wife, and — after several attempts — she produced him a *legitimate* heir, whom he named after himself, Lasting Manifestation of Re. Amen at the Head is like Count Son of Amen, a passed-over prince."

She hands the still-sleeping infant back to her daughter.

"Seemingly you don't know, Sister, that Crown-Prince Lasting Manifestation of Re and his mother are both here in the Gardens of Asar and Iset, arriving together some short while ago," Akheperenre informs, smugly. "Which means — unless the third Born of Djehuty has yet another son waiting behind a bush you're not aware of — our mutual grandson, Amen at the Head, is currently Horus-in-the-Nest, or so it must be presumed."

"But a temporary expedient, certainly, as Lasting Manifestation of

Re will surely have himself a new Great Royal Wife and seed her with more sons of his body," she responds, then suddenly turns — without taking her leave — and walks away across the lawn, past clusters of chatting strangers and groups of playing children, and through the menagerie of free-roaming creatures.

It's not too long before she spots someone a ways off who causes her heart to surge. There, in animated conversation with two others she knows well, is her dearest lifelong friend, Royal Nurse In Sitre. Her male companions are King's Scribe Senimen and First Prophet of Amen-Re Hapusenub. In is as she knew her when she was herself a child: imposingly tall, a bit thick-waisted and certainly full-bosomed; and she, as always, sports an elaborate wig and plentiful jewelry, with perhaps a bit too much kohl and rouge. The shaved-bald priest is no longer stooped and paunched, and seems in his middle age. Senimen is as youthfully handsome-featured and leanly muscular as she remembers him to have been when they were, well, very intimate for a considerable while.

The two women embrace unabashedly. Then In Sitre holds her at arm's length, looking her up and down, smiling approvingly.

The nurse speaks first. "I was waiting, Mistress. I knew it'd probably not be a very long wait."

"It was indeed lonely those long months at Wer-Mer without you, Daughter of Re. You'd always been seldom further than the next room, since we were aware of anything, nursing at those great udders of yours," she laughs, loosening her grip on In's thick forearms. She turns to Hapusenub.

"So, Hapu is Well, your retirement was somewhat brief, it seems."

"Not even one flooding, Your Highness. I fully expected to go to the Field of Reeds, rather than to the Blessed Gardens of Asar and Iset, however. I believed this particular place was reserved strictly for the royal ancestors and descendents. But when I arrived here, there are the likes of Daughter of Re and Brother of Amen, as well." The priest indicates his conversation companions.

"Yes, even Brother of Mut made it, too." A well-familiar voice speaks behind her and she quickly turns.

There stands Senenmut, and at his side, the beautiful Kheftiu youth, whose name she can't recall at the moment. She's quite stunned to see "Lord High and Mighty of This and That" again. She'd presumed, with certainty, that his black heart was gobbled up at its weighing by The Swallower. He is as she remembers him when he first entered the service of her father, as King's Scribe and royal tutor: taller than most men, broad-shouldered, his face still dominated by the long pointed nose, but un-creased yet and without the wattles that came later. He wears a cap-wig of tight curls, his hallmark head-covering. His companion appears to be no more than a young teenager.

"We are most displeased by your presence, Great Steward. We'd supposed — mistakenly, it now seems — that Lord Asar had sent you, once and for all, to an eternal exile, that the god had let Devourer Amam wholly consume your wicked soul."

"Oh, it definitely wasn't to her liking and she spat it right out!" Senenmut laughs. "So, having no other option, Lord Asar graciously as-signed me here. Born of Min, grieved by my absence, chose to join me very soon after. And Asar was..." As he speaks his raspy voice grows in-creasingly fainter.

She opens her mouth to respond, but finds herself suddenly speechless. Immediately the airy, bright Blessed Gardens of Asar and Iset dim to black nothingness. And Hatshepsut ceases dreaming.

Crown-Prince Amenemhat leaned forward in his armchair. The frail old woman supine on the bed, sunken into several soft pillows, her thin grayed hair fanned out, framing her delicately wrinkled oval face, appeared to be returning to consciousness — at least her eyes had begun to blink very rapidly.

"S...she s...s...eems t...to be wak...ing, Your M...Majesty," he loudly whispered towards the Lord of the Two Lands, who dozed in the armchair beside him, chin resting on his collar bones.

Menkheperre jerked up his head and looked at his son, then to the woman. In moments she was staring, eyes wide, towards the high ceiling. He rose and moved to the side of the bed, so that she might see him, if she still had vision.

"Welcome back, Noblest Woman," Menkheperre addressed her, arms folded under his broad bare chest.

Her head moved just enough to make eye contact.

"It was quite lovely there, Hawk Beak."

"Where is that, Your Highness?"

"Where we've just been. In the Blesssed Gardens of...ah, Asar and Iset. We didn't suppose we'd...be returning here just now, or ever again."

"You were dreaming, no doubt." Menkheperre motioned for Am-enemhat to move the armchair he'd occupied to alongside the bed. "There's no such place."

The young man did so, then returned to his own seat.

"Is that...Amen at the Head?" Hatshepsut asked faintly.

"I a...am here, Gr...Grandmo...ther," the Crown-Prince responded. He stood again, so that she could see him.

"Are there...others?"

"No, Your Highness. Just Our Person and your grandson."

"Who is now...Horus-in-the-Nest, is he not?"

"That's true. But how did you know?" Menkheperre had sat down again.

"I was told...in the Gardens of Asar...and Iset. Rather, I was told that...Great Royal Wife Sitiah and...her son, Lasting Manifestation of Re, were...both there, rather newly... arrived. Thus, it follows that...Amen at the Head is...now fully Heir, as appropriate." She spoke barely above a whisper.

"There was a terrible accident at Waset, while we were away, campaigning against the coastal towns of Retenu." Menkheperre had tented fingers on his chest.

"A river horse attacked a picnicking party from the Residence and our beloved wife and son fell victims to its mad rampage. Amen at the Head and his recent bride were there at the time, but luckily they escaped injury."

"So you have...taken a wife already, Grandson?" Hatshepsut looked towards the still-standing youth.

"In...deed, Your High...ness," he replied. "Her na...name is Iset...ty, and sh...she's now wi...th ch...child. You sh...shall b...b...be a gr...great... gr...grand...moth...er."

"Not unless...she goes on the blocks this...very hour, we're afraid. But your mother...will be pleased to learn...when we return...that she'll soon... have a grandchild." She smiled. "Then again, perhaps not ...after-all...Beauty of Re being, well, who...she is."

After a lengthy pause, she continued towards Crown-Prince Amenemhat. "She asked...after you, your mother did. We held...your womb-sister, who will...forever be a new-born infant...apparently. She has no name... except 'Little One'...which seems a shame."

Amenemhat supposed that his grandmother was speaking from delirium.

Hatshepsut turned her head enough to see her former Coregent.

"So, Hawk Beak...you've bothered to travel...all the way here to Wer-Mer...to see with your own eyes...that we've, indeed...flown to the stars." It was a statement rather than a question.

"Word came to us in Mennufer that your departure was imminent, Aunt. We've a long history together, you and Our Person. It was no bother to come to speak with you, face to face, one last time."

He reached out placed his calloused brown fingers atop the skeletal, large-veined hand resting on the bedsheet at Hatshepsut's hip. He couldn't remember having physically touched her before, at least not since his childhood, during the assassination attempt. Hatshepsut was very cool, if not actually cold.

"We've never thanked you for saving our throne for us, Noblest Woman, for sparing the Two Lands the strife and turmoil an usurpation by the defunct Taos would've brought. All in all, in hindsight, the joint reign of you and Our Majesty was very successful, we think, if lasting somewhat longer than was really necessary — and even if we didn't agree with a few of your independent actions.

The old woman had closed her eyes, mouth a hard line. "Such as?"

"Your sudden, wilful exiling of Brother of Mut comes immediately to mind."

"He... overleapt himself. Far more than deserved it, finally." She sighed. "You reversed us on...that one, in any case. Calling him back. Into the sphere of...influence once more." She paused again, then continued. "We were amazed to encounter him. In the Gardens of Asar and Iset."

She chuckled to herself. "Said Amam had...spit out his heart. Too bitter." Another pause. "Brother of Mut's pretty whore boy...he's there with him. In the Gardens."

"Born of Min let his blood flow, very soon after Brother of Mut's *ba* flew off. We laid them side by side in the simple rock-cut Mansion for Eternity the Great Steward had hewn, following their return from Gubla."

"His third."

"Third what?"

"Mansion...for Eternity. After the grand one we...caused destroyed. And that greatly offensive...other one we ordered...filled in." She paused. Sighed. Continued, "Ours was never...fully completed, we suppose."

Menkheperre uncovered her hand, tenting fingers on his chest again.

"*Your* own Mansion for Eternity? As much as could be accomplished, we were told. The First Prophet reported the quality of stone in the resting chamber wouldn't permit the full veneering that was originally planned. It should be comfortable enough, nonetheless, or so we were assured."

"So you...*will* put us...there." Her voice was barely a whisper.

"Unless, you'd prefer the Mansion for Eternity you caused to be made when you were our father's Great Royal Wife."

There was no response. After a few long moments, Menkheperre leaned towards her, reached out and took the cool frail hand at her side. The reed-narrow lips were parted, eyes covered by papyrus-thin blue lids. Noblest Woman's *ba* had just flown. She was returning to her Blessed Gardens of Asar and Iset.

TWO SEASONS LATER, INUNDATION 33, REIGN OF MENKHEPERRE DJEHUTYMES EAST BANK OF THE EUPHRATES RIVER

S oldiers were nearly finished taking down the scaffolding used by artisans to engrave His Majesty's declaration on the tall slab of local stone, which Lord of the Two Lands Menkheperre had caused to be erected as a notice to the recently defeated-and-fled present ruler of the kingdom of Naharin. It was a warning that Najehmne and future wretched rulers there would face the swift wrath of His Majesty should the army of Naharin ever dare cross over the close-by wide, slow-flowing river that delineated the boundary between that vast place and Retenu to the immediate west, the latter now being fully and firmly in the possession of Kemet and the Lord of the Two Lands, as well as His Majesty's successors on the Horus Throne for all time — or so Menkheperre optimistically hoped.

Attired in his bulbous helmet-crown of blue leather and a gilded-leather corselet fashioned as opened hawk wings embracing his stocky torso, the third Djehutymes to rule Kemet in succession stood akimbo in a wide stance, clenched fists on kilted hips. He was supervising the scaffolding dismantlement. To each side of him and behind, as well, were the pair of generals and numerous lesser commanders of the victorious forces from the Two Lands that had routed the superior numbers of the army of Naharin — and subsequently reaped a great quantity of booty on the battlefield. The latter — plus harvested grain and many living prisoners, as well as the wounded and slain of Kemet — already was taken across the river by a score of barges, which'd been specially constructed on the distant shore and employed to transport thousands of Kemet's soldiers and chariotry for the invasion and then the subsequent return to Retenu.

Menkheperre looked to his left, past Generalissimo Neferronpet to Chief of Chariotry Amenemheb. "General Amen in Jubilation, go alert the boatmen that we'll be departing for the banks of Retenu shortly."

The tall, broad-shouldered officer came to attention, raised one forearm across his corseleted chest in a salute, turned on his heels and strode off down the knoll to where several small barques were pulled out of the lazy waters of the green-brown river, their numerous rowers hunkered about on dry land.

Addressing no one in particular, perhaps just musing out loud, the Lord of the Two Lands said, "We suppose our present effort here," he gestured towards the stela, now almost free of all scaffolding, "is more for show than serving any real practical purpose, inasmuch as the wretches of this place won't be able to read our exhortation against their trespassing into territories under the protection of the Two Lands."

"By this monument Your Majesty has declared, to the Hidden One and the other blessed gods, Your Person's determination to safeguard the far boundaries of the Two Lands." It was Thuty, generalissimo of the Army of the North, speaking on Menkheperre's right. "But, the Living Horus is correct. The Black Land's forces no doubt shall have to return to this remote place from time to time, so that the Nahari keep toeing the line."

In fact, Menkheperre Djehutymes never again gazed on the Euphrates, though he'd continue campaigning throughout Retenu — suppressing revolts of the local princelings and collecting vast quantities of tribute — each fall for the following eleven floodings, until Inundation 42 of his reign. The kingdom of Naharin, however, would still loom large in the foreign affairs of Kemet for the next three generations of Lords of the Two Lands.

FOURTEEN CROSSINGS OF RE LATER
PLAIN OF NUKHASHSHE, ENVIRONS OF THE TOWN OF NIYA, RETENU

Menkheperre was dictating to King's Scribe Tjaneni, when someone beyond the tent hatch was requesting to be announced. His Majesty thought he recognized the voice as that of General Amenemheb, chief of all chariotry.

"Enter, Amen in jubilation," Menkheperre responded.

He was bareheaded and wearing only a short kilt, relaxed on the campaign throne, with Tjaneni a short ways off, seated cross-legged at his low scribal table, covered by the partially unrolled leather Book of Days in which he had been writing.

The young chariotry officer ducked his uncovered head and stepped through the opening, standing immediately upright, at attention.

"At ease," instructed Menkheperre. "Is there news?"

"Yes, Your Majesty. Scouts have returned to camp to report that a large herd of great leathery beasts with serpents for noses has been spotted at pasture along the banks of a wide stream not more than an hour's ride from here. Most are very tall adults with long tusks seemingly of ivory, very much larger than those of river horses. I thought Your Majesty might want to go see these strange creatures for yourself."

Menkheperre stood. "We've heard of the existence of such monsters, General, but have never beheld such. Perhaps an infant one might be captured for Our Majesty's menagerie at Mennufer!"

He started towards the living quarters of the command tent, then turned back to the officer. "Go, Amen in Jubilation, organize a hunting party of, say, twenty charioteers and as many bowmen from the officer corps. Plus as at least a dozen spear men from the infantry. And bring nets and rope, in case we may take a captive. Our Person will be ready to depart in a few minutes."

He pushed a linen hanging aside and disappeared within the Lord of the Two Lands' private space. Tjaneni allowed the Books of Days to close, rose and followed, to assist the Living Horus in attiring himself for the "monster" hunt.

The company of chariots was arrayed in a single line at the top of a low rise still some distance from the grazing herd of perhaps three-dozen elephants, most adults but also a few young calves just visible within the forest of log-like tall legs. Several others of the adults were partially submerged in the shallow stream. Though some ways off from the hunting party's vantage, trumpeting of the beasts wallowing in the water was clearly audible. The men of Kemet had never heard such a bellowing noise, even coming from river horses, the largest creatures of their experience.

Menkheperre Djehutymes stood barefooted alongside his driver, attired in his blue helmet-crown, a simple corselet of leather scales and a wraparound kilt, with a sheathed dagger on one hip, suspended from a leather belt. His only other weapon was a longbow of the Asiatic composite type. His companions that afternoon numbered both generalissimos Thuty and Neferronpet, Chief of Chariotry Amenemheb and several other senior and junior officers. All were likewise armed with hunting bows and wore daggers; some, including Amenemheb, had brought along scimitars, as well, these strapped over their shoulders. In a chariot at one end of the group was unarmed Tjaneni, driving himself, who had come along as His Majesty's omnipresent observer. Interspersed within the row of chariots were some dozen kilt-clad infantrymen with bronze-tipped spears, many with bows and quivers slung across their bare backs. Four porters, waiting a few paces behind the vehicles, were loaded down with coils of thick rope and bundles of netting. They were sweating profusely, clearly exhausted by their long trek on foot from the encamped Army of Kemet.

The Lord of the Two Lands turned towards and addressed Amenemheb, whose chariot was next to his own.

"Do you have any idea, General, how to approach the beasts? Before they see or smell us and either stampede or else charge?"

"I've certainly no experience with hunting such fantastic brutes, Your Majesty," Amenemheb replied, "but would suppose that at least the largest males would take the offensive rather than run off. The females and few little ones might wade or swim across the stream, in which case it would be impossible to pursue them, except on foot, and that probably not very successfully."

"May I suggest, Your Majesty," Thuty offered, "that the spear men approach first. If these creatures are anything like river horses, their vision is likely quite limited. Men on foot might not be noticed, especially if they crouch and move slowly. There seem to be numerous small boulders nearer the stream, so they might be mistaken for those. When they get within lethal throwing-range, they could simultaneously hurl their weapons at a just few of the smaller beasts, which are likely females."

What the generalissimo did not say was that, should the assaulted herd charge rather than run, the infantrymen, even though officers, were expendable. The boulders were not large enough to offer them real protection from rampaging males.

"In any case," Menkheperre observed, "it won't be possible to finally get very near by chariot, due to the boulders. Perhaps we should all dismount here and, likewise crouching, follow the advance infantry at a reasonable distance, so that it'll be possible to instantly employ our bows once their spears are exhausted."

No one thought it prudent to challenge the Living Horus, even if any present had wiser tactics to suggest — which none did, in fact. So His Majesty and his officers dismounted their vehicles, as did the drivers — the latter to hold the horses' reigns. Tjaneni remained aboard his chariot, not being one of the hunters. The dozen elite spear men were given their instructions by Generalissimo Thuty, and they began their cautious advance on the near-distant elephant herd. When they had gone several dozen cubits, the Lord of the Two Lands gave the command for his other officers to follow. The milling and bathing animals remained seemingly indifferent to the slowly approaching, roughly parallel two lines of humans.

The elephants' vision was indeed poor, but not their sense of smell. When the infantrymen were some 100 cubits from the first of the scattered small boulders, one of the largest bulls ceased grazing at the outer perimeter of the herd and raised his massive trunk high, flexing pink nostrils to check the air for a faint alien odor he had just sensed. Almost immediately he slowly moved away from the other elephants, directly towards of the first line of humans. The crouching spear men all halted in their tracks, low to the ground as possible. Menkheperre and his officers likewise halted and stayed crouched. Two smaller bulls, their trunks raised menacingly, also broke away from the mass of grazers and followed at a measured lope after the principal herd guardian.

When the first bull was only three-dozen or so cubits from the unmoving spear men, he halted, raised his especially long trunk high again and, after several moments, let forth with a loud bellow. The other bulls were immediately flanking him on his bulging sides, their massive heads and snorting trunks swaying. Whether they could now actually see the humans was impossible to know. More or less shoulder to shoulder, they presented an inviting target to only the two or three spear men on the far ends of their forward line.

No order was given, but one of those outlying hunters suddenly stood fully erect, brought his spear into the throwing position and hurled it with practiced force, so that it sank a couple of hand spans into the leathery broad side of the male elephant nearest him. The huge animal seemed to stagger into the lead bull, then recovered his footing and reared, thrashing the air with his columnar forelegs, tusks and trunk high, and bellowing in pain.

The other spear men immediately likewise stood and in near unison cast their weapons towards the three roaring behemoths. Several of these merely bounced off the broad foreheads, while others found shallow marks in the waving trunks and heaving chests. Two additional spears penetrated the side of the first bull to be wounded, bringing him crashing to the knees of his forelegs. The other outer bull was likewise wounded by two spears to his side, and reared before falling sideways, driving the shafts deep into his body. The middle, principle bull, two spears dangling from his bleeding, thrashing trunk, charged towards the puny humans directly in front of him. All the spear men had turned and were running back towards where the Lord of the Two Lands and the chariotry officers were now fully standing and drawing their bows.

The assault on the herd guardians caused immediate panic among the many cows and half-dozen calves, which, as predicted by General Amenemheb, began stampeding into the shallow, suddenly churning stream. Several other younger bulls, however, came rushing towards the melee, bellowing, tusks waving menacingly. Three halted their charge, to examine with trunks the two fallen and dying or already dead guardians.

The others thundered on towards the strung-out line of bowmen.

A score of arrows flew towards the oncoming lead behemoth, most finding marks in the huge moving target, but not bringing him down. The fleeing spear men passed through the line of officers, stopped in their tracks and turned back towards the oncoming elephants — those who were carrying them, pulling their bows over their heads and frantically fitting these with arrows from their quivers.

Before the Lord of the Two Lands — or any of the chariotry officers, for that matter — could get off a second shot, the wounded lead bull was but several cubits away. Although the spears had fallen from his blood-oozing trunk, his bloodied high shoulders and barreled sides dangling a dozen arrows, the great beast only suddenly stopped his charge when he came up to within less than a half-dozen cubits from Menkheperre in his blue *Khepresh* — who stood his ground in a wide stance, his long bow fully drawn back, arrow in place. Roaring, spraying the Living Horus with blood from his waving trunk, the bull reared, his thick forelegs treading the air. Menkheperre loosed his arrow, which sank deep into the broad exposed chest of the animal. The ground actually shook when the forelegs came crashing down, narrowly missing the now-defenseless ruler, who nonetheless was pulling his long dagger from its sheath. But that was no more than in hand, when the blood-slick thick trunk struck a heavy sideways blow to Menkheperre's shoulder, sending him flying and crashing supine to the ground, his helmet thrown off.

Just as the elephant was about to club again the downed Lord of the Two Lands with his raised trunk, Amenemheb rushed up to straddle Menkheperre, his scimitar lifted with both hands above his head. He struck before the crazed bull could, the sideways sweeping curved bronze blade of his weapon severing the upraised proboscis cleanly in half.

The sliced-off long, thick member actually struck Amenemheb across his chest, covering the charioteer general-officer with viscous crimson and knocking him to the ground. The stunned bull, the stump of amputated snout gushing red, staggered a few steps backwards, sank to his four knees, then toppled onto his arrow-filled side, dead. Lord of the Two Lands Menkheperre, Son of Re Djehutymes regained consciousness quickly enough and proved, on his physician's later examination, to have suffered only a badly bruised, dislocated shoulder. He later rewarded Amenemheb's bravery handsomely, with much gold and — as the captain recorded — "three changes of clothing."

The other berserk young bulls were soon enough dispatched by retrieved spears and barrages of arrows, so that the elephant tally that afternoon was nine slain males or eighteen large tusks. General Amen-emheb, in his tomb biography, would later greatly exaggerate that total to 120 slaughtered beasts. A singular female calf was apprehended, floundering in the stream where she had been summarily abandoned by her panicked and fleeing mother. With some difficulty she was roped and ultimately manipulated ashore, then forced to walk the considerable distance to the Kemet encampment. Taken by oxen cart to the coast of the Great Green — along with the Eighth Campaign's considerable other booty and tribute — she died of starvation on the sea voyage back to the Two Lands, mashed greens and donkey milk not particularly to her liking.

* * *

15

L ord of the Two Lands Menkheperre, Son of Re Djehutymes quickly strode into the audience chamber of his private apartments in the Residence at Waset, followed by Great Royal Wife Merytre Hatshepsut, scurrying to keep up with His Majesty's pace. She gripped by his hand six-floodings-old Crown-Prince Amenhotep, who pulled back in silent protest, slowing her pursuit. The third Djehutymes had taken off the stiffened-felt White Crown he'd been wearing for that day's ceremonies and carried this regalia under one arm. He crossed the expanse of the spacious columned room and stepped onto the painted dais at its far side opposite the entry, seating himself on the gilded throne positioned in the low platform's center.

His Majesty unceremoniously placed the tall crown on the floor beside the throne, and it unceremoniously fell onto its side, which he ignored, tenting his fingers on this tunic-covered, broad-collar-draped chest and glaring intently at his still-youthful wife and their son, who had stopped in front of the dais and stood side by side facing him. More or less side by side, as the prince had moved as far away from his mother as her tight grip and their arm lengths made possible. Well above average height for his age, young Amenhotep's head would have come to the Great Royal Wife's shoulder, had they been truly at one another's side.

Menkheperre, his chief spouse and their sole offspring had just returned from across The River, where His Majesty had been participating in the week-long ceremonies of the Beautiful Feast of the Valley, Merytre Hatshepsut and the Crown-Prince being among the many spectators from the court and priesthoods of the Hidden One and the Great Mother — Amen-Re and his spouse, Mut. It was on the return trip to the east bank via the royal barque that the Great Royal Wife had demanded — and loudly enough so that all on board could hear — an immediate audience with the Lord of the Two Lands.

After several long moments of strained silence, Menkheperre Djehutymes spoke.

"Now, wife, what is so important that you need Our Person's private attention at this busy time?"

"To wage my complaint, yet again, Born of Djehuty, against your foreign bitches!" the slender, plain-featured woman — in tripartite wig and inlaid-gold Vulture Cap-Crown with modius and tall pair of ostrich feathers — replied shrilly.

"Our *wives*," Menkheperre corrected. "And mothers of our several daughters."

"Who you clearly favor over myself in every way, in the harim and beyond, even in public, as today."

"You were right at Our Person's side at the appropriate moments in the processional and other parts of the ritual, as avatar of the Great Mother, which is the Great Royal Wife's and God's Wife of Amen's *role*, we needn't remind you, Beloved of Re." He smiled indulgingly. "Menwi, Merti and Menhet never participate in the ceremonies, are onlookers only."

"But they're all too obvious, even so, wearing as they do those ornate golden headdresses you designed for them, unlike anything ever seen before. You've never gifted *me* with jewelry from your own hand." She yanked on Crown-Prince Amenhotep's hand, so as to pull him closer. He wouldn't budge.

"Your public regalia is governed by tradition, Noblest Woman Beloved of Re," His Majesty lectured his somewhat-younger spouse. "The only headgear you may appear in on formal occasions is the Vulture Cap with its modius, disk and feathers, as Great Royal Wife, and the simple gold fillet worn when you're functioning as God's Wife. The three headpieces we caused fashioned for our Reteni wives were so that they may appear at public functions attired in an appropriate manner — reminiscent of their foreign origin, but which is also acceptable by standards of the Black Land. And, surely you haven't forgotten, Our Majesty *has* given you gifts of jewelry we've designed, bracelets and bead collars."

Amenhotep suddenly jerked his hand free from his mother's grip.

"She's jealous you fuck the foreigners but not her, is all," Horus-in-the-Nest blurted, his thin arms now folded on his narrow bare chest.

Without saying anything, Merytre Hatshepsut stepped to her son and slapped him forcefully with her small palm, alongside the shaved head above his ear, opposite where the braided thin Horus Sidelock hung to his shoulder.

"Wife!" Son of Re Djehutymes barked, standing. "You will *not* strike the Heir, mother of him, or not."

"She does *all the time!*" the boy asserted, rubbing above his ear, where he was smarting.

Merytre Hatshepsut turned back to the Lord of the Two Lands, glowering. "Your son is a foul-mouth brat and deserves every smack I *do* give him, husband. He terrorizes the harim, terrorizing always the bastard girls of those foreign bitches! He even exposes his not-so-little Min to them, so they'll scream. It's disgusting."

"Do *not!*" The boy pouted, arms folded once more. His facial features, even at his young age, favored those blunt ones of his common-born mother, rather than most beaky-nosed royal males of the House of Djehutymes.

Menkheperre sat again. "Amen is Pleased, come up here. Bring that over and sit by Our Person." He indicated a gilded stool, with openwork between the four legs representing the entwined symbolic flora of Upper and Lower Kemet.

The Crown-Prince did as told, then stuck out his tongue at his mother — a gesture that the Lord of the Two Lands failed to notice.

"Perhaps, dear Noblest Woman Beloved of Re, it's time to move Horus-in-the-Nest out of the Royal Wives' quarters, to an apartment of his own in the Residences. We had our personal spaces when about his age, we remember, even younger, actually."

"He requires constant supervision, Born of Djehuty," the Great Royal Wife responded, "with double Medjays posted at every door, to keep him from wildly running about, making trouble, as he always does."

"Amen is Pleased is now of an age to begin his formal tutoring, to learn to read and write the script of the Black Land. Also to learn the craft of the hunt and warfare. Yes, Our Majesty will commence the grooming of Horus-in-the-Nest for his future role as our successor to the Double Crown. Once the Beautiful Feast is finished in two crossings of Re, appointment of a proper tutor will be a first priority."

Young Amenhotep had picked the toppled White Crown off the floor beside his stool and lowered this onto his head. Even with the Horus Sidelock, it was far too large and covered his ears and eyes, the protective golden cobra resting on his pug nose. He giggled.

Menkheperre reached over and, by its knobbed finial, lifted the tall regalia of Upper Kemet off the young Heir.

"It would seem you've some growing to do, Amen is Pleased, before you'll be ready for our throne." The Lord of the Two Lands replaced the White Crown on his own shaved head. It fit him perfectly, of course, serpent centered above the brow.

Merytre Hatshepsut's private audience was concluded. Defeated and depressed, she returned to the harim alone, her estrangement from her difficult son now having begun in totality. Which had not at all been her intention when she ineptly confronted her seemingly indifferent, disinterested god-incarnate husband, regarding the three foreign rivals for his conjugal affections

ONE FLOODING LATER, INUNDATION 43
REIGN OF MENKHEPERRE DJEHUTYMES
THE RESIDENCE, MENNUFER

The six-man Medjay escort of the Lord of the Two Lands burst through the ajar double doors of the Residence harim without knocking, followed immediately by barefooted Menkheperre Djehutymes himself, the King's Scribe Tjaneni in his wake and, waddling several paces behind, Chamberlain of the Mennufer Residence Nay. His Majesty and Tjaneni had been taking the evening meal together in the King's Apartments, when a frantic messenger from the harim had interrupted to report to that "something terrible" was happening at that very moment in the Royal Wives' quarters. Menkheperre and his scribe departed immediately for the far side of the Residence and, coming upon the obese Chamberlain on the way, had brought Nay along with them — to encounter whatever was awaiting where the Lord of the Two Lands' four spouses and several young children resided.

As he and his guard-contingent and tagalongs abruptly entered the spacious high-ceilinged, columned women's quarters of the Northern Residence, Kemet's ruler and the other intruders into this always-off-limits place confronted mass pandemonium. The large central space — shared by all of the residents of the harim as a common recreational room — was populated by numerous crouched or sprawled prone wailing serving women, royal nurses and several girls ranging in age from a toddler to a teenager. In the midst of this distraught assembly stood the immensely fat superintendent of the harim, the eunuch Hray, perspiring and wringing his hands. Stepping over and around the obviously mourning females, Menkheperre went up to Hray, who immediately bowed as much as his great paunch permitted, fleshy arms held straight, pointing towards the colorful painted-plaster floor.

"What's going on here, eunuch?" Menkheperre demanded. He'd been joined at his elbow by Tjaneni. The Medjays and Chamberlain Nay remained just within the open doorway, however.

Still bowed, Hray replied in his high-nasal voice, "Great tragedy Your Majesty, Lord of the Two Lands, Son of Re. All of the wives are already gone or going."

"Gone, going where?" The bawling toddler, his fourth daughter by Menhet, had come running to him and wrapped her short arms around Menkheperre's knee. He lifted her into his arms and she buried her wet face against his neck.

"I think he means they're dead or dying, Your Majesty," Tjaneni offered.

Indeed, the Reteni sisters, their mother and the other three hostage wives of the Prince of Kadesh were not among the wailing women, and looking about now Menkheperre could see that the doors of their private chambers all stood open and were dimly lighted within. Handing the child to Tjaneni, he crossed through the prostrate women to the personal space he knew was Menhet's. He stopped at the doorway and peered in.

On the bed in the center of the smallish chamber, supine, lay his favorite of the Reteni wives, the mother of his first daughter, Neferubity, who had perished from a cobra's bite. Menhet's head was sunk into the embroidered pillows the foreign women all preferred, eschewing the headrest used by the people of Kemet. Her jet long hair was fanned out, her open eyes stared unseeing at the high ceiling and her mouth gaped wide as if in a silent scream. Her bare full breasts and pregnant belly were awash with what appeared to Menkheperre to be drying vomit and blood. Seated rigidly in an armchair by the head of the bed was one of the wives of Kadesh, wearing the black garment and peculiar turban the elder foreign women had stubbornly affected during their long years of captivity in Kemet. Her heavy eye makeup was smeared from dried tears, and she was focused on vacant air, so did not seem to notice the Lord of the Two Lands at the open door.

Menkheperre didn't enter the chamber, instead going to the next open doorway. Within, the sleeping space of Menwi was empty, save for decorated storage chests against the walls, two wooden armchairs and the bed on a low dais in the room's center. The latter supported a form covered by a plain linen sheet with a patch of dark scarlet at one end. The Lord of the Two Lands already knew what he would find, but entered nonetheless and crossed to the bed and its hidden burden. He pulled the sheet back and stared at his Reteni wife, Menwi. She, too, lay supine against a mound of pillows, damp hair fanned by her cheeks, though her kohl-rimmed eyes and rouged lips were closed; dried bloody vomit also covered her chin and naked front, however. With the sheet recovering the *ba*-less husk of Menwi, Menkheperre backed out of the chamber and went next door to the apartment of Merti, youngest of the daughters of Kadesh whom he had taken to bed and made his Royal Wife some years before.

Compared to the two previous spaces, this room was virtually crowded. Merti lay on her bed in its center, but appeared to be still living, though her eyes were closed. Arranged in armchairs at both sides of the bed and at its foot end were Menkheperre's mother-in-law and the two other captive wives of Kadesh, all in their usual black attire and peculiar turbans. Also present was Merti's personal serving woman and bending over his patient, wiping at her drooling slack mouth with a small towel was the Residence physician, Petweri, who stood erect when he sensed the entrance of the Lord of the Two Lands. Both he and the serving woman bowed towards the ruler from their waists. The Kadeshi women sat rigidly erect without acknowledging their captor's presence.

"What has happened, physician?" Menkheperre went to the foot of the bed, standing next to Merti's seated mother.

"Your wives've been poisoned, in my opinion, Your Majesty," replied Petweri, looking at the ruler. "They all became violently ill shortly after finishing the evening meal. Two have died and she," he indicated Merti, "certainly will, as well. Although her reaction to whatever caused this hasn't been as extreme as those of her sisters."

Menkheperre looked down at his mother-in-law, who still had not looked at him.

"Didn't you and the other wives of Kadesh eat and drink the same meal, Lady Nahti?" he asked her.

Her gaze still focused on her stricken, unconscious daughter, she replied in a hoarse loud whisper, " We eat not with them, us daughters. They with Greatest Wife in space of hers."

Menkheperre addressed the physician again. "Is Noblest Woman Beloved of Re stricken, as well?"

"I wasn't told so. I was summoned by the eunuch only after the first wife began vomiting food and blood. Her *ba* flew before I could make my way here. If the Great Royal Wife is also sick, the Chamberlain surely would've said so."

Menkheperre turned and quickly left the chamber, going into the central hall with all the still-wailing serving women. Chamberlain Hray, perhaps in shock, had not moved. Tjaneni had taken a chair and gathered the nude royal daughters around him, the toddler on his lap. He was talking quietly to them and they'd ceased their crying, the younger girls all sucking on their thumbs. The Lord of the Two Lands went to the closed double doors of the apartment he'd shared as a small boy with his late mother, King's Mother Iset. He raised his hand to knuckle one panel, but changed his mind and pushed on both panels to open them. They wouldn't budge, apparently bolted from within.

"Two guards, come here!" he called across the wide hall to the group of Medjays still standing with Chamberlain Nay at the open entrance to the harim.

A pair of the Wawat mercenaries, spears in hand, immediately crossed through the mourners to where the Lord of the Two Lands stood.

"Shoulder it open," was the royal command.

The guards simultaneously pushed their shoulders against the panels. The ebony bolt securing them snapped immediately and the pair of doors swung inwards. The Medjays stepped aside, so that Menkheperre could enter. The well-furnished space was dimly lighted by two floor braziers and a portable table lamp. The latter served to illuminate the *senet* board game being played at that moment by Merytre Hatshepsut and her handmaiden, both seated on gilded stools at a low table with the game between them. The Great Royal Wife looked up, feigning surprise.

"Why, Born of Djehuty, husband, you seldom are so very *anxious* to visit me!"

"You're not ill, obviously."

"Not that I know of, husband."

"Did our other wives dine with you here this evening?"

"I do believe they did, Born of Djehuty. Yes, I remember now that they did, did they not, Tesit?" she addressed the other woman who vigorously nodded in the affirmative. "Such tedious bores, really, they can barely make simplest conversation in their poor command of the speech of our Black Land."

"Did they become ill while here?"

"They're *ill*? Oh my! I hope it wasn't something *I* served them." The Great Royal Wife was making a move on the game board.

"If you're attempting to be amusing, Beloved of Re, you're failing miserably. Certainly you can't have *not* heard the commotion in the common chamber." Menkheperre angrily gestured in that direction. "Menhet and Menwi are both very *dead*, as well as Menhet's and Our Person's unborn child; and Merti will likely also be gone soon. The physician believes they all were poisoned by whatever they'd just eaten or drunk. And their last meal was served them by you."

"On his *opinion* are you accusing your Great Royal Wife, the God's Wife of Amen, the mother of your Heir of committing such a heinous deed as *murder*, my lord? I know truly *nothing* of poisons and poisoning." Merytre Hatshepsut ran fingers through the short-cropped dark hair on the crown of her head. She then made another *senet* move.

"Your dissembling and absolute lack of remorse betrays you, 'mother of the Heir'. We've decided that you're to be confined solely to this apartment — until Our Majesty determines what further to do with you. You may not enjoy your private garden, however. Guards'll be posted beyond those doors to ensure that," Menkheperre pointed to the double ones open to the outside, "and at these," indicating the entrance to the Great Royal Wife's apartment. "Your personal needs'll be provided for, as always, of course."

The Lord of the Two Lands rapidly strode from his defiant spouse's presence. If anything the wailing of the harim serving-women had increased in volume, although the fully calmed royal daughters were still clustered adoringly about Tjaneni. Hray was in conversation with Petweri. When Menkheperre came up to them, the physician looked at him, nodded and shook his head in the negative.

"Royal Wife Merti's *ba* has now flown, Your Majesty. She went more peacefully than her sisters, who were in great agony to the end."

"See to it that they're taken to the preservers as soon as possible," he ordered both the fat eunuch and rail-thin Petweri. "We shall send word to Vizier of the South Rekhmire, instructing him to seek out for our wives an already available suitable Mansion for Eternity at Waset, where they'll be laid together in seventy crossings of Lord Re."

Menkheperre Djehutymes broadly gestured for Tjaneni to follow after him; then, before departing the harim, he spoke briefly with Chamberlain Nay and the Medjay captain, instructing them to affect the Great Royal Wife's just-ordered confinement. Shed of the royal daughters with some difficulty, Tjaneni came alongside his lord, and the two of them departed the harim premises, Menkheperre of course in the lead.

Back in the King's Apartments, the Lord of the Two Lands and his secretary resumed the meal that had been interrupted — with warm food and fresh drink provided. In their ensuing conversation, Tjaneni once again made the case that he was far too busy with His Majesty's many tasks to undertake the tutelage of the young Crown-Prince, as well. Menkheperre finally accepted Tjaneni's previous proposal that the probably challenging task be assigned to a talented young scribe presently employed in the Mansion of Amen-Re by the name of Min, who was highly recommended by the newly named First Prophet of the Hidden One, Menkheperresenub. Min, himself only some twenty floodings old, was a bachelor and thus free to move into the Crown-Prince's Residence quarters and devote full time to teaching the high-strung boy his script and numbers, as well as etiquette, protocol and all else that a future Lord of the Two Lands needed to master. In the case of young Amenhotep, it would prove to be a challenging task, indeed.

THIRTEEN FLOODINGS EARLIER, INUNDATION 30
REIGN OF MENKHEPERRE DJEHUTYMES
HARIM GARDEN, THE RESIDENCE, MENNUFER

Word had reached the Residence the day before that Lord of the Two Lands Menkheperre, Son of Re Djehutymes was two day's sailing away from Mennufer, returning to the northern capital following conclusion of the Festival of the Opet upstream at Waset, Kemet's other administrative center and home to the Hidden One, Lord Amen-Re. His Majesty, Great Royal Wife Sitiah, Crown-Prince Menkheperre and Prince Amenemhat — as well as those several members of the court who traveled between the two capitals, as occasions such as the festival required — had been up south for nearly a month; and consequently life in the harim of the Northern Residence had been even more humdrum than usual. The Great Royal Wife's chatty presence would be welcome again, in fact.

Lord of the Two Lands' Royal Wives, sisters Menhet, Menwi and Merti — and the young women's mother, Nahti, as well as their three Reteni stepmothers — were lunching together, as was their habit, in the colorfully painted pavilion of the large walled garden, accessed from each Royal Wife's private apartment. In addition to the seven women, half-a-dozen small girls played in the nude on the clipped lawn of the lushly landscaped space. They were the three Royal Wives' various daughters, fathered by Menkheperre Djehutymes. Merti, in fact, was in the last weeks of still another pregnancy. The youngest girl, Menwi's, had yet to take her first steps; and the eldest, Neferubity, Menhet's first child, was only six floodings old.

Refills of wine were being poured by two harim serving-girls, when a bald, very fat eunuch named Hray, Chamberlain of the place — Nahti called him "jailer" in her native tongue — came through the doors to Menhet's apartment, crossed the loggia and stepped ponderously down into the bright sunlight. He followed his huge bare belly across the lawn, long linen skirt flapping, and came up to the pavilion. Conversation in the language of Retenu ceased and he addressed Nahti.

"Lady of Kadesh" — what Hray always called her — "your son's at the doors of the harim and requests to see you and his sisters."

Although the former chief wife of the Prince of Kadesh well enough understood what the Chamberlain had said — having been forced to learn at least a little of the gibberish of Kemet — her eldest daughter translated Hray's remark.

"Let the turncoat come to us," she replied to Menhet in Reteni.

Although Nahti did not criticize her daughters for taking on the fashions of Kemet and learning the local speech, she held it against her teenage son that he'd done likewise, even becoming fluent in the aliens' language; in her mind this wasn't appropriate for the future Prince of Kadesh, which Menkheperre had vowed he'd send her son home to be, once word of her husband's death reached Kemet.

Hray waddled off and conversation resumed. In a few minutes, a pale-skinned, quite slender youth of fourteen floodings, by the reckoning in Kemet, emerged through Menhet's doorway, crossed the shaded loggia and stepped down into the sunny garden. Moments later he was bowing formally to the "Lady of Kadesh," his three older sisters and the other wives of his father. Meru — here in the Two Lands he was called Meketre — was, by the standards of Retenu, a very handsome young man, his thick black brows meeting over his narrow nose, his lips sensuous, his jaw and dimpled chin having a bluish tint, suggesting that he already was shaving daily. His well-shaped head also was shaven, except for the black braided sidelock that was required of the youths of Kemet until they came of age, which Meru would in two floodings of The River. He wore only a wrap-around plain-linen kilt and plaited-reed sandals. Except for his complexion, he could have easily enough passed as a son of Kemet rather than of Retenu.

"So, Meru the Traitor, what is your pleasure today," Nahti haughtily addressed her son in their mutual language.

"I've come, our mother, to ask a large favor of you and of my beloved sisters."

There was a long pause, Menwi sipping her wine, Merti suppressing a laugh.

"Well, speak up, traitor to Kadesh. What sort of 'large favor' could you want of us four helpless prisoners?" Nahti prompted.

"There is a...." Before Meru could continue, the child Princess Neferubity came running up beside him.

"See what I find!" she squealed. In her chubby hand the small girl clasped at one end what appeared to be a short, thin length of brown cord. Giggling, she instantly laid this on top of her shaved head; and, before anyone could move, it coiled, reared up and flared a colorful hood just beneath a blunt head the width of a child's fingernail. A forked tongue flicked.

"Cobra!" Meru blurted and reached out to sweep the tiny serpent off his young niece. Quick as he was, it struck his hand nonetheless, then was flung onto the lawn a few cubits away.

Neferubity ran to where the cobra had begun moving away and attempted to snatch it up again. It reared once more and struck her small hand, as well.

In short minutes both the would-have-been future ruler of Kadesh and the Lord of the Two Land's first female offspring were in their painful death throes. Nahti and her daughters would never know what favor son and brother Meru was seeking.

FIFTEEN FLOODINGS LATER, INUNDATION 45
REIGN OF MENKHEPERRE DJEHUTYMES
MANSION OF THE HIDDEN ONE, LORD AMEN-RE, WASET

First Prophet of Amen-Re Menkheperresenub rubbed his oily palms together, then ran them over his freshly shaven pate. He had just returned to his modest apartment in the priests' quarters adjacent to the Mansion of the Hidden One, after having ritually bathed in the Sacred Lake of the god's precinct, as was his required daily routine. Not only was his head shaved, but his entire body, eyebrows and pubes included. While his beard required daily attention, the razor skimmed the rest of him but once a week, or so. The act of shaving was performed by a young acolyte, who was also Menkheperresenub's regular bed mate those nights the high-priest did not spend at home with his wife and children, at his comfortable estate on the far outskirts of Waset.

The First Prophet wiped his hands with a small towel and then tied on his loincloth and secured his wraparound ankle-length linen skirt. Stepping into the plain reedwork sandals all priests wore, he finally lowered the woven-gold cord over his head from which hung the simple solid-gold pectoral that was his mark of office as the most senior of the Amen-Re priesthood. Menkheperresenub was now properly attired for the series of ritual ceremonies he would lead that day. And it was a special day involving consecration of the finally completed first pylon-gate on the processional way leading from the Mansion of the Hidden One to the Mansion of Mother Mut, his divine spouse, some distance to the south. This gateway had been initiated and mostly constructed by the late ruler Asar Maatkare Hatshepsut. When she unexpectedly retired as the Female Living Horus some twenty floodings before, work on the structure had come to an abrupt halt, however, inasmuch as her Coregent and successor as sole-ruler, Menkheperre Djehutymes, had been preoccupied a part of each of those flood-years with campaigning in far-off Retenu, subduing the wretched barbarians there and collecting rich booty and tribute for eventual deposit in the Hidden One's treasury.

When the Living Horus was back in Kemet, his building activities at Ipet Isut had been focused on expanding and completely remodeling the core part of the god's mansion, including additional obelisks and a brand-new granite Holy of Holies, to replace the quartzite one he had raised together with his co-ruler, Maatkare (now dismantled, the blocks in storage beyond the priests' quarters). And Menkheperre also had raised a unique structure just to the east of the main mansion, a huge Festival Hall dedicated to Amen-Re, in which the Lord of the Two Lands had celebrated his *Heb-Seds*, commencing in his thirtieth inundation on the Horus Throne, and that festive jubilee renewed each third inundation thereafter. Indeed, like his grandfather, Asar Akheperkare, the third Son of Re Djehutymes proved to be a major contributor to the Mansion of the Hidden One and its walled precinct.

Having crossed an open area between the priests' quarters and the god's mansion, the First Prophet was entering now a modest side portal used by only the priesthood and acolytes. As planned he would rendezvous with Lord of the Two Lands Menkheperre in front of the Holy of Holies, so that His Majesty might be given a preview of the finished new gateway, in advance of that early afternoon's official dedication ceremonies, with the Hidden One himself in attendance. After making his way through a series of dimly illuminated connecting passages, the chief priest finally emerged into the open-air portico court fronting the god's inner abode. To his surprise, there in the bright sunlight already stood the middle-aged ruler, in full Double Crown regalia, along with his nine-floodings-old son, Horus-in-the-Nest Amenhotep, Vizier of the South Rehkmire, the omnipresent King's Scribe Tjaneni and several members of the King's Council of high governmental officials.

Bowing his head, arms thrust at a downwards angle in front of himself, First Prophet Menkheperresenub went up to the group. Tjaneni said something inaudible to the Lord of the Two Lands, who turned to face the approaching cleric.

"Greetings, Lasting Manifestation of Re is Healthy!" His Majesty spoke when the First Prophet was still several cubits away. "It seems Our Person is early for the advance look at the new gateway."

"My embarrassed apology for being *late*, Mighty Bull! It is my role to *receive* the Lord of the Two Lands when he visits the Mansion of the Hidden One, not be received by *him*." The high-priest's glossy head was still bowed, his arms stiffly at his sides, fingers pointing to the ground.

"No matter, First Prophet." Menkheperre smiled at the top of the bald pate. "Crown-Prince Amen is Pleased was anxious, as always, to be on his way here, so our company arrived from the Residence sooner than you were expecting is all. Next time we shall be more respectful of Mansion protocol. Now lead us to Our Majesty's latest achievement."

And they moved, Menkheperresenub at the fore, across the courtyard towards a large side-portal opening onto the paved avenue leading in a straight line to the distant Mansion of Mother Mut.

S haded by a portable canopy, Lord of the Two Lands Menkheperre, Son of Re Djehutymes sat enthroned atop a stairs-mounted high dais centered directly on the processional way a short distance beyond the new pylon gate — the latter's wedge-shaped paired tall towers decorated with brightly painted huge reliefs that depicted a victorious, superhuman Living Horus smitting the collective heads of wretched Asiatics on the northern tower and, in a mirror image, the collective heads of even-more wretched savages of Wawat on the southern one. Youthful Crown-Prince Amenhotep was seated beside His Majesty on a gilt-appointed armchair. Notables of the Two Lands, dressed in their finest court attire, stood in ranks and files on both sides of the dais, facing in the same direction as His Majesty and the Heir.

First Prophet Menkheperresenub officiating, ritual dedication of the gateway had taken place with fullest pomp and circumstance; and the Hidden One's gilded barque — bearing his solid-gold image, housed in a red-linen-draped gilded shrine — was once again resting on its pedestal in the Holy of Holies, carried there aloft on the shoulders of a contingent of sixteen bare-chested junior servants of the god. An interlude entertainment of drumming soldiers and gyrating male-and-female temple dancers was just concluded, the performers bounding and marching off; and now the second half of the afternoon's ceremonies could begin. This was the formal presentation of gifts and tribute by delegations of foreign peoples, standing amassed some ways off, looking towards the Lord of the Two Lands and the colorful — if intentionally menacing — pylon backdrop. Once again Menkheperresenub officiated, in conjunction with Vizier of the South Rekhmire. The rail-thin vizier, in his billowing long skirt reaching from his armpits to nearly the ground, presented each delegation to the First Prophet, who in turn announced their identity to His Majesty and the Heir.

First of the waiting groups to approach the enthroned Lord of the Two Lands was the delegation from Kheftiu, that distant exotic island-nation in the Great Green Sea. Son of Re Djehutymes smiled to himself as he thought of the handsome native of the place who had been the male intimate of "Lord High and Mighty of This and That," long-late Great Steward of Amen-Re, Senenmut. And he was also remembering that he was himself a cousin to some degree of the present ruler, as far as he knew, of

Kheftiu, the Minos — as all of the island's kings were styled, one after the other — the half-Kheftian son of a prince of the Two Lands, Tao, grandson of The Liberator, who had been exiled to the Great Green when Menkheperre was very young and coregent of Asar Maatkare.

The two dozen or so representatives of Kheftiu that day were all olive-brown youngish, uniformly handsome, clean-shaven men with long, thickly curled and coiled, oiled jet hair, their muscular-lean torsos bare to tapered waists above colorfully patterned and fringed layered kilts, some wearing laced leggings reaching to their knees. They carried as their gift-offerings to the Lord of the Two Lands — never having been subjected to Kemet's will — various large, elaborately fashioned gold-and-silver vessels (rhyta and craters and ewers in their alien tongue), presented individually on large solid-gold trays, or else carried atop their coifed heads. A few men of the delegation bore long strands of large beads of raw amber and semi-precious stones, others carried pillow-shaped ingots of copper on their shoulders and still others elevated long, slender, sea-motif-decorated ceramic amphorae filled with their island nation's much-desired finest vintage. These gifts were, one after the other, deposited on rush-work matting covering the sandy ground on each side of the processional way, in front of Menkheperre's reviewing dais.

When the Kheftis had dispersed and filed to the rear of the grouped foreign delegations, the second contingent to move in front of the waist-high platform elevating the present and future rulers of Kemet was composed of three-score and more representatives of the various tribes of Wretched Wawat, the vast River-flanking region spreading far south of the First Cataract, but nonetheless within the hegemony of the Two Lands. These black-skinned men and women (and even a few small children) — savagely, if skimpily, attired in animal-hide garments with opulent feathers tucked into their wiry hair, ears and nostrils pierced with rings of gold or ivory, arms and ankles loaded with more ivory and solid-gold adornments — carried or led a wide variety of bona fide tribute. This included numerous logs of ebony, a dozen huge tusks of bull elephants, piles of animal hides and wooden trays heaped with quantities of unsmelted gold. And on leashes they led hunting hounds, two cheetahs, several monkeys and an immense tame male baboon, as well as several particolored cattle with long horns.

But what immediately captured the attention of both the Living Horus and Horus-in-the-Nest was a young giraffe, much like the one which had been brought back from Punt when Menkheperre was a boy-ruler sharing his throne with the Female Horus, Maatkare. This second spotted "antelope" with the incredibly long neck would find a new home (along with the other exotic beasts brought by the Wawatans) in the royal menagerie of the Residence there in Waset. It would survive but two floodings of The River, however.

The southern tribute was piled and stacked behind the gifts of Kheftiu, the animals handed off to gamekeepers from the royal menagerie; and the black primitives all returned to stand behind the island dwellers. Next to process to in front of the Lord of the Two Lands and his young Heir was the delegation from legendary Punt, also bearing gifts rather than tribute, as their coastal homeland far to the south was not under the political control of Kemet. These fine-featured slender brown-skinned men in colorful kilts, with braided hair and pointed beards, carried wooden trays, some heaped with beads of incense, others with piled strands of semi-precious stones. Several men held aloft large bunches of ostrich feathers or carried baskets filled with the huge eggs of the ostrich. A dozen men even bore, suspended from poles carried on their shoulders, six small gum trees in baskets, intended for replanting. And there were still more animals for the royal menagerie — ibexes and gazelles on leashes — plus several leashed hunting hounds. When these gifts had been laid out or handed over, the delegation from Punt retreated as a group to the rear of the other gathered foreigners.

The final and largest delegation to be presented to His Majesty by the Vizier and First Prophet, to stand before the royal viewing-dais that afternoon, definitely presented tribute, inasmuch as Menkheperre Djehutymes had repeatedly brought the vast and varied land of Retenu under the heel of Kemet during the seventeen floodings spent campaigning in the north.

As the Asiatic tribute bearers began approaching, the Son of Re was wondering whether his Reteni mother-in-law, Nahti, and the other three hostage Wives of Kadesh had made it home some two floodings earlier, sent north with a military escort by him soon after the simultaneous poisoning-murders of her three daughters, Royal Wives of Menkheperre's and mothers themselves of several daughters by him. He'd not really expected that the haughty old woman would send word to Mennufer of their safe arrival back at the fortified town of Kadesh.

The tribute offerings of Retenu were the most varied presented to the Lord of the Two Lands that afternoon, as were the pale-skinned, large-nosed Reteni bearers themselves, in their close-fitting embroidered robes and wide-ranging hair and beard styles. In addition to large, finely worked vessels of both silver and gold, even electrum, there were numerous amphorae of the finest Asiatic vintages; logs of aromatic cedar-wood; ingots of copper; trays heaped with large rings of cast smelted gold; baskets of unworked turquoise and carnelian; four gilded chariots (fashioned in the lightweight Kemet style rather than the bulkier one preferred by the Reteni themselves) and eight thoroughbred horses to pull them; scores of composite bows and many embossed-leather quivers of arrows; and a dozen or more elephant tusks. But of greatest interest to the third Djehutymes and his prepubescent son were the muzzled young brown bear lumbering on a leash and, best of all, a shuffling baby elephant, like the one captured in Retenu on the Eighth Campaign, which however had died of starvation en route back to Kemet.

When most of the Retenu tribute had been deposited with the other foreign offerings, one of the Asiatics approached Menkheperresenub and, speaking passably in the tongue of Kemet, requested permission to approach the royal dais, to deliver directly to the Living Horus a verbal message from the Great Wife of Kadesh, Nahti, mother of the late Royal Wives, Menhet, Menwi and Merti. Instructing the fully bearded young man to stay where he was, the First Prophet himself went up to the foot of the short stairs centered at the front of the dais.

Menkheperresenub bowed his shaven head, waiting for His Majesty's acknowledgement. He fingered the pectoral on his chest.

"Speak, First Prophet," the Lord of the Two Lands commanded.

"Mighty Bull, one of these wretched Asiatics here would deliver directly to Your Person a verbal message from the Great Wife of Kadesh," Menkheperresenub relayed.

"Send him forward," the ruler replied.

The priest returned to where the man of Kadesh was standing and told him he could approach the Lord of the Two Lands. The youth — dressed in a colorfully patterned long-sleeved, ankle-reaching garment, its front open to the waist exposing his lean hirsuteness, his oiled jet hair tied in a large knot on the nap of his neck — made his way between the piled offerings and went up to the steps accessing the royal dais. He did not kowtow or even bow, merely nodding his head once, then stepping out of his pointed sandals, to stand barefooted before addressing Menkheperre Djehutymes, his bearded chin held high.

"Mighty Kemet Prince, I say now message memorized from Great Princess Nahti, Kadesh ruler for her not good health husband, Great Prince Haniglah. Great Princess send 'greetings to assaulter of slaved daughters, who die in huge pain from hand of Wife of Kemet.' She say 'Kadesh Great Prince not for live much long, but is no new ruler to follow, since Kemet Prince capture Great Prince Haniglah just son, take here so too he die from Kemet wicked serpent.' Great Princess Nahti much sad, always much, much anger to Kemet Prince. But, she from her sad anger send gift for him, which give I now."

Before anyone realized exactly what was happening, the messenger reached inside the open front of his robe and drew a long bronze dagger from its concealed sheath. Simultaneously, he bounded the few dais steps and threw himself at seated Menkheperre with such force that the throne toppled backwards, carrying its startled occupant and his assailant crashing to the platform's floor. Because His Majesty was holding his Crook and Flail scepters crossed over his chest, he had been able to push these forward at the moment of the frontal impact, thus just barely deflecting the assassin's downwards thrusting stab at his exposed torso.

A contingent of a dozen Waset Residence guards — armed with their signature spears — had been standing in formation a dozen cubits from the back of the dais, and the whole lot of them were instantly closing that distance and leaping onto the waist-high platform. But before the first Medjay plunged his weapon into the back of the thrashing emissary of Kadesh, young Crown-Prince Amenhotep had pulled a small dagger out of the sheath he wore suspended from his kilt belt and thrust the slender gold blade between the ribs of his father's would-be assassin. Although the foreigner was quickly dispatched by half-a-dozen spear points, Amenhotep would long brag that his was the fatal first blow.

Thoroughly shaken by this second attempt on his life, of course, Menkheperre Djehutymes suffered only minor bruises and scratches, as well as a protracted headache from his Double Crown having forcefully banged against the dais. Certainly King's Scribe Tjaneni never recorded this event in his Book of Days. And neither First Prophet of Amen-Re Menkheperresenub nor Vizier of the South Rekhmire would make any mention of it in their elaborate tomb depictions of the great presentation of foreign tribute and gifts to the Lord of the Two Lands, at which they had officiated.

TWO MONTHS EARLIER, PALACE OF THE PRINCE, KADESH IN RETENU

Lieutenant Weshptu could only wonder why he had been summoned that morning from the army barracks to go to the palace of his native city, the mighty Kadesh. All he was told by the messenger was that Her Highness Great Princess Nahti desired to speak with him in her private apartment there. She was the *de facto* ruler of the city, inasmuch as her husband, Great Prince Haniglah, was purportedly very much enfeebled in his old age, in fact was mostly unaware of what went on around him. Thus, he had not been seen publically in a great while, prompting persistent gossip on the streets of Kadesh that he had already died. This was made the more urgent because it was known by all of the city's residents that the much-beloved Haniglah had no designated successor. His heir, young Prince Meru, had died while being held hostage in far off Kemet, and it was likely that the adult sons of Haniglah's deceased brother would contend for the throne of Kadesh, once their uncle was truly in his grave. This might prove bloody. It therefore seemed probable, as the rumors would have it, that the elderly Great Princess Nahti would hold on to power, as her husband's regent, for as long as possible.

Lieutenant Weshptu had never met the Princess, of course, never even been in her presence, except at a considerable distance. Thus, he was understandably nervous at the imminent prospect of confronting her face to face. She was not in the spacious, well-appointed chamber he had been taken to by a palace guard, after arriving at the entrance portal and identifying himself. Although there were several chairs and a cushioned divan in the space, he didn't think it was appropriate to seat himself, while he waited — for the royal lady to appear, presumably. So he assumed a stance of relaxed attention a few feet beyond the doorway he had entered.

It was several minutes before his waiting was over. Princess Nahti, unaccompanied, came through an arched open doorway on the opposite side of the chamber from where the young soldier stood. Wearing heavy makeup, bejewelled and dressed in a richly patterned, fringed woolen gown with long sleeves and reaching to the floor — her hair hidden in a cylindrical turban, equally colorful — the stout elderly woman crossed silently to one of the chairs, seated herself and gestured for Weshptu to sit upon the divan facing her a couple of paces away. Once he was seated, it was long moments before the Princess addressed him.

"We would guess that you were but a boy when the mighty Kadesh was attacked and besieged by and finally succumbed to the raptor Hawk God of Kemet and his blood-thirsty, rampaging armies."

"Indeed, Your Highness, not a 'boy', but into my teens, if just," Weshptu replied. "I do remember very well the long months we all were prisoners within the city walls, the rationing of food down to stale, moldy bread crumbs, when the cisterns went bone dry — and that there was no recourse, finally, but to surrender, lest every man, woman, child and slave died of thirst and starvation."

"So you also remember, surely, that the Royal Wives and several daughters of the Prince, and the young heir, too, were all carried off to the fly-infested land where the red-skinned inhabitants grovel before animal-headed gods, and every manner of beast and bird, as well." Nahti affected a shudder of disgust.

"There was much lamentation when you were led away in bindings, Your Highness. There was also much joy when yourself and the other Great Wives returned. Word had reached the city some years before that teenaged Prince Meru died in captivity. There was much lamenting then, too, Great Prince Hangilah even renting his royal garments in public to show his terrible grief."

"Our daughters, mine and the Prince's, all died in Kemet, viciously, painfully poisoned by the vulture-headed, cow-horned wife of the wicked Hawk God — gone mad because he preferred to lay always with them rather than her wither-teated, repulsive self — impregnating our daughters again and again. The so-called 'Great Wife' had managed, after several miscarriages and still-born deliveries, to produce only a single foul-tempered male-child. Beautiful Menhet, Menwi and Merti — all 'Royal Wives', too — gave birth, on the other hand, to many fair-skinned girls, which greatly pleased the Hawk God — so much so that he gifted the princesses of Kadesh over and over with jewelry and golden headwear — which he claimed to have designed himself, though small likelihood of that!"

The elderly Great Princess paused in her bitter litany, as if she was expecting some sort of response from the lieutenant. After an awkward pause, Weshptu replied, "I'm at a loss, Your Highness, as to why you're telling me this very personal information."

"Because, brave young warrior of Kadesh, you have been specially selected by the priests of the Great God Ehsehru to be the instrument of our — Great Prince Haniglah's and our own — revenge on the wicked Hawk God of fetid Kemet, and thereby on all the abominable people of that place, as well. It is you who personally shall render justice for Meru, Mehet, Menwi and Merti!"

Lieutenant Weshptu continued listening in stunned disbelief, as Great Princess Nahti told him in much detail of the large tribute-bearing delegation from all of Retenu departing in a few days for the interior of Kemet, which he would nominally lead. She then coached him in the speech that he would deliver to the Hawk God in the spoken gibberish of the place, just before plunging a dagger — Prince Haniglah's own — into the bird-headed man-god's wicked heart. Weshptu would be instantly slain, himself, almost surely, but would be rewarded beyond measure in the next life by Ehsehru, or so the god's priests were confident.

The distressed lieutenant lay awake on his barracks cot that evening, wishing he had never learned some of the difficult spoken tongue of Kemet, from the handsome young soldier of that place who had been minimally wounded and captured at the Battle of Kadesh, then held prisoner in the city, eventually becoming young Weshptu's secret lover during the Hawk God's months-long siege.

RE ASCENDING

TWO FLOODINGS LATER, YEAR 47
REIGN OF MENKHEPERRE DJEHUTYMES
THE RESIDENCE, WASET

Eleven-floodings-old Crown-Prince Amenhotep and his "milk brother," Qenamen, were wrestling again. As usual the boys' roughhousing had wrecked havoc to the sitting chamber of the prince's apartment in the Waset Residence. Chairs and a table were overturned, the latter even split through its middle when the bare young bodies fell across it in their good-natured grappling. Although one flooding younger than Qenamen, Amenhotep was half-a-head taller and clearly the stronger of the prepubescent youths. He now held his foster-brother in a head lock and the two of them were spinning in a circle, as Qenamen struggled to pull loose.

The infant Amenhotep had been nursed by Qenamen's mother, Amenemopet, inasmuch as his own mother, Great Royal Wife Merytre Hatshepsut could not lactate. As Royal Wet-Nurse, Amenemopet and her infant son had moved into the Residence harim at Mennufer, living there among all the foreign women of His Majesty — and the several daughters fathered by Lord of the Two Lands Menkheperre, Son of Re Djehutymes. When high-strung Crown-Prince Amenhotep was extracted from the harim by his father at age six floodings — and given his own apartment in both the Northern and Southern Residences — Qenamen had accompanied him as his "chamber-mate"; and, since the two boy's were long-before weaned, Amenemopet retired as Royal Wet-Nurse and returned to being a Lady of the House for her husband, an officer in the Army of Kemet stationed at Mennufer. Taught together by the same patient tutor, one Min, the youths became virtually inseparable and full confederates in boyish crimes.

A major one of those was committed when the two decided to practice their growing archery skills on the grounds of the Royal Menagerie at Waset, an animal compound created by Amenhotep's father when he was himself a boy early in his coregency with Asar Maatkare Hatshepsut. By Inundation 45 of Menkheperre's reign, the menagerie had been extended several times and was quite literally a sprawling walled park adjacent to the Residence, with small herds of free-roaming gazelles and ibexes, scores of unhampered monkeys and some dozen baboons, flocks of wing-clipped ducks and geese and ibises, plus numerous caged animals of a more dangerous sort: hyenas, jackals, cheetahs, two lions and even a bear. There were a dozen or more large ponds throughout the park, stocked with every sort of fish imaginable — one of these, fenced all around, even home to several smallish, hissing crocodiles. All in all, the

Royal Menagerie was the dream hunting-ground for a pair of daredevil boy-archers.

And wildly laughing Crown-Prince Amenhotep and cohort Qenamen nearly emptied their quivers, bringing down (if not always slaying) some two score of the menagerie inhabitants — including several gazelles, three ibexes, six monkeys, a baboon, more than a dozen fowl and ibises, even a caged hyena, two penned crocodiles and one large fish — before they were discovered red-handed at their thoughtless deed by grounds keepers and brought to a sudden halt by summoned Royal Tutor Min. Floodings later, reminiscing with his life-long companion, Lord of the Two Lands Akheperure, Son of Re Amenhotep thought he and Qenamen might have completely decimated the animal park had not Min arrived on the scene when he did. The prissy tutor could be such a total spoilsport.

As that afternoon, when Min entered the Crown-Prince's in-shambles apartment and found the two boys, naked but for loincloths, clenched in physical combat, Qenamen trying without success to free himself from Amenhotep's headlock.

The King's Tutor, shortish, slightly built and in his late twenties, dashed up to the boys and yanked Amenhotep's head back by the prince's Horus Sidelock.

"Amen is Pleased, let him go, right now!"

"You let go, Prick!" the Heir yelled back, calling the tutor by the two boys' nickname for him, "Or I'll have your *prick!*"

Min yanked a second time, harder. "Let go, *now!*"

Which Amenhotep did so suddenly that Qenamen fell to his bare knees. The Crown-Prince pulled his sidelock free from Min's grip and spun around, his fist drawn back, as if he meant to strike the adult no taller than himself. His eyes flashed real anger. Own hands clenched at this kilted thighs, Min tilted his chin, as if challenging his charge to land a blow.

But young Amenhotep lowered his arm and began laughing loudly, bent forward, hands on his knees. He raised up and was eye-to-eye with Min.

"One of these days, believe me I will, Prick. I *will.*"

And he would, two floodings later, during the harvest season, at the Residence in Mennufer. King's Tutor Min abruptly awoke in the middle of the night, not remembering what he'd been dreaming. His tiny sleeping chamber, his sole private space, was immediately adjacent to the much larger one with two beds, shared by Crown-Prince Amenhotep and Qenamen, son of Amenemopet, since they were young boys six- and seven-floodings-old. Now both in their very early teens, the youths had discovered the pleasurable release derived from stroking themselves under the bedsheets nocturnally. Each knew what the other was doing at the time, but was never inclined to take their intense boyhood camaraderie to a mutual sexual intimacy.

Min, on the other hand, often was the unnoticed voyeur in the deep shadows of the narrow colonnade separating his chamber from that of the youths. Never, however, would he've dared risk the trust of the Lord of the Two Lands — let alone his rather privileged Residence employment — to actually make an inappropriate advancement towards either of his charges. Besides, in his gut he knew that neither young teen, particularly the Crown-Prince, would be in any way receptive, were he to have ventured even the subtlest seduction.

Once wide awake that particular night, Min lay on his low bed, neck supported by a headrest, and listened in the still blackness for any low moans in the connecting space. Detecting nothing of the sort, he guessed both youths were indeed sleeping. But to satisfy his nagging curiosity, he finally arose, naked, and crossed in the dark the short distance to the open single door of his room. From the colonnade he peered into the sleeping chamber only very dimly illuminated by cloudy moonlight leaking through the high clerestory windows in the opposite wall. The two beds, spaced a couple of cubits apart in the center of the space, were both empty, although mussed sheets on each indicated they'd been occupied earlier.

Min backtracked, tied on a loincloth and wrapped a short kilt around his narrow hips, stepped into his sandals and, for good measure, donned his one wig, adjusting it as he entered the neighboring sleeping space once more. Crossing to the closed double doors and pulling these abruptly open, he encountered the standing-but-slouched, snoring form of the tall Medjay assigned bed-chamber door duty that evening. The ebony mercenary jerked to attention, then grinned when he recognized the tutor. Understanding immediately what the much shorter man of Kemet was about, the Medjay nodded and pointed across the wide sitting chamber in the direction of the hallway doors. Outside these Min's sudden presence awoke two additional guards, who, likewise grinning, both pointed down the corridor, indicating the truant youths had departed in that direction.

At various brazier-illuminated corridor intersections of the Residence, posted guards continued revealing the route of the teens. Suddenly it dawned on Min that their destination was the kitchens. He remembered Amenhotep and Qenamen, heads together, rather audibly assessing the somewhat obvious physical attributes of one of the women servers at a small banquet His Majesty Menkheperre had hosted the previous evening for the four Prophets of Ptah and the Vizier of the North. Clearly the two had somehow arranged a rendezvous with the buxom youngish woman, likely a slave of Asiatic origins, if Min remembered correctly. The Residence kitchens — midway through the twelve hours Re's barque was transversing the Underworld — would be the perfect place for an undisturbed liaison of the sort the pair apparently had in mind.

When Min reached the open doorway to the first of the several food-preparation spaces, a distinct moaning punctuated by grunts brought him up short. He cautiously looked into the room illuminated by several small oil lamps. There were half-a-dozen domed ovens in a row lining the far wall, and against the low curve of one of these, his rapidly thrusting naked buttocks towards the tutor, a standing-but-hunched-forward Crown-Prince Amenhotep was coupling dog-fashion with someone, no doubt the female slave. The moans were hers, the grunts his. Half-a-dozen cubits to one side, fully naked and stroking his erection, stood Qenamen, clearly waiting his turn.

That was coming sooner rather than later, as Horus-in-the-Nest raised suddenly upright on his toes, shuddered and climaxed with loud, protracted growling. He quickly pulled free and stood to one side, so that his "milk-brother" could take the vacated position behind obviously female broad buttocks.

Rather than watching Qenamen commence loosing his virginity, young Amenhotep picked up a discarded kilt from the floor, shook this twice and wrapped the linen rectangle around his hips. As he was re-tying the waist strings, the Crown-Prince happened to look to where Min was standing at the door.

A broad smile halved his plain features. Without speaking the youth walked barefooted across the hard-packed dirt floor, to stand less than two cubits from the tutor. After a long pause, still smiling, he said, voice husky, "Some things *you* can't teach us, Prick."

With that Amenhotep delivered the slug to Min's jaw that he'd once promised, sending the tutor stumbling backwards, to fall flat on his buttocks. The two of them, royal pupil and commoner teacher, never spoke of the incident. It was many floodings later — when he was mayor of This in the Delta and Akheperure Amenhotep occupied the Horus Throne — that Min, laughing about it, told the story at a bachelor dinner party.

*　　*　　*

16

The gilded Barque of Amen-Re had reached the paved avenue extending away from the foot of the long, wide ramp of Djeser Akhet, "Sacred Horizon," the recently completed barque-chapel Lord of the Two Lands Menkheperre, Son of Re Djehutymes had raised next door to Djeser Djeseru — "Holiest of Holy Places," the unfinished grand memorial mansion of his former Coregent, the long-deceased Asar Maatkare Hatshepsut. Although much more modest in scale, this new focus of the Beautiful Feast of the Valley festival was a perfect compliment to its neighbors (the renewed ancient structure to its south being the joint funerary monument and tomb of a long-ago ruler of Kemet). Like them it was raised on two tiers of porticoed terraces and built of gleaming white limestone quarried far to the north and transported to the Southern Capital on barges.

With it serving as such for many floodings, Menkheperre finally decided that the incomplete nature of Maatkare's Djeser Djeseru made it unsatisfactory as the ultimate destination of Lord Hidden One, as the god undertook his annual rounds of several sacred west-bank sites during the Beautiful Feast. These included the memorial mansions of his father and grandfather; as well as his own such monument, still under construction; and, most importantly, the smallish chapel he and his Coregent had jointly erected many floodings before on the Mound of Creation (one of the holiest places in all of Kemet).

Rather than Menkheperre leading the Sacred Barque with its portable shrine that housed the Hidden One on his journey (as had been his role throughout the rest of the Beautiful Feast processional), during the recessional First Prophet Menkheperresenub and the three other prophets were his escorts for the return trip to Ipet Isut, Amen-Re's sprawling abode across The River. Wearing the blue-leather helmet-crown (its many gold bosses glittering in the afternoon sun), His Majesty strode alone several paces behind the slow-moving barque swaying ever so slightly on the bare shoulders of sixteen shaven-headed acolytes. Following him in rank and file walked several barefooted female musicians, who had shaken sistrums during the offering and lustrating rituals performed for the god within Djeser Akhet, and who continued doing so, providing a march cadence.

Beyond the ramp, lining both sides of the avenue, stood several-dozen members of Menkheperre's court and the city government of Waset. These formally attired individuals — all male — had not been permitted into the sacred space of Djeser Akhet proper, so had waited during the ceremonies within the smallish chapel, in order to join the recessional. Among those in attendance that day were Vizier of the South Rekhmire; Mayor of Waset Amenmessu; Crown-Prince Amenhotep (plus, of course the latter's figuratively joined-at-the-hips companion, the youth Qenamen); and — chiefly because he resided in Waset — Menkheperre's eldest son, Prince-Count Amenhemhat. When His Majesty and the musicians had filed past, the group would fall in behind, although no effort would be made by them to proceed in any way approaching an orderly military fashion. That would be for the sizeable contingent of Medjay royal guards, who flanked the avenue a cubit apart for some distance, and who would bring up the rear.

Both the god's barque and Lord of the Two Lands Menkheperre had moved down the paved way to just past the waiting royals, officials and courtiers, when a sound as deafening as a lightening bolt striking rent the air above the very high tan cliffs that formed a dramatic backdrop to the side-by-side sacred structures. The vanguard of priests, the barque bearers, ruler and the musicians all came nearly simultaneously to a halt, the former and latter turning to look back towards Djeser Akhet. The gazes of all present — save those who carried the god on their shoulders — were drawn up the rugged cliff face to the summit source of the thunderous cracking.

"What is happening?" asked Vizier Rekhmire of Mayor Amenmessu at his side.

"Look, t...the cl..cliff is f...fall...ing *away!*" Prince-Count Amenemhat stammered at the top of his voice, pointing towards the rim of the massive rock formation.

This did seem to be shifting downwards, if barely perceptibly. Then, almost immediately, with another ear-shattering explosion of breaking stone, a huge section of the rim did indeed pitch forward into a free fall, plummeting downwards, crashing with tremendous force, half a moment later, onto the collapsing flat roof of Djeser Akhet and sending up a high spray of gray dust in its wake.

Instantly more and more huge vertical slabs of limestone separated from a wide section of the cliff rim, peeled off and dropped or slid with acceleration down the rock face. These too crashed onto the chapel.

Someone among the onlookers shouted "avalanche!" and everyone, the Lord of the Two Lands included, began running away from the continuing rock fall. Everyone that is but the acolytes; they first had to shift the Sacred Barque off their shoulders in unison, setting it on the ground, then picking up the carrying poles at arms' length and moving off as quickly as their heavy burden allowed, being engulfed before they had gone far in a gigantic rolling cloud of smarting dust particles.

At a safe distance away, but still not out of range of the settling dust cloud, Menkheperre and his Heir and courtiers, the Amen-Re high priesthood and musicians, and the Medjay guard stood looking back in dumbfounded disbelief for several long minutes, as rock still continued to fall, piece by increasingly smaller piece, until the avalanche was exhausted and collapsed Djeser Akhet had totally disappeared under a massive mound of raw-limestone debris.

Against his will, but having no other option, Lord of the Two Lands Menkheperre, Son of Re Djehutymes would complete the decoration of neighboring Djeser Djeseru, returning it to its longtime Beautiful Feast of the Valley function. He thus converted the structure into his own monument, conveniently erasing the original authorship of Maatkare Hatshepsut in the process.

None of the clustered ant-like figures far below could possibly have seen the activity at the cliff top, even if any of them was looking skyward — and all eyes were certainly directed towards the new chapel, wherein the ruler was even now interacting with the god. The dozen or so men, naked to their loincloths, had already worked up a sheen of sweat, as they strained at the six stout wooden tent-poles deeply wedged into a wide fissure running several cubits along the ridge. Their objective that afternoon was, quite simply, to force the uppermost part of the upper cliff face to separate off and fall the great distance to the chapel directly below, crushing the building and everyone inside at the moment, which purposely included the ruler and the god himself.

This was not a course of nefarious action that these simple laborers had collectively devised on their own. Rather, they'd secretly been individually recruited — with an irresistible enticement of several *deben* of gold each — by an unnamed individual acting on behalf of "one close to the Horus Throne," who desired that particular seat to be vacated so that a new ruler could claim it as his own. One Lord of the Two Lands or another, it didn't really matter to these always-hungry men. Most of them had never laid up-close eyes on the present living-god, an old man who had begun his rule of Kemet when their own hoary (or deceased) fathers were very young, or else not even born.

A cohort in the murderous plot, situated on the rim of the ridge running alongside and high above the abandoned monument of a Female Living Horus — who only a few of the men recalled hearing stories of as small boys — had signaled with a waving white cloth when the god's golden boat, preceded by the ruler, ascended the long ramp of the chapel and disappeared inside. None of the men knew how long whatever happened there would take, so they immediately commenced their wedging and pulling on the pole-levers.

After a time it seemed that the fissure was, indeed, finally widening — the rock emitting a faint groaning, grinding sound — when almost simultaneously two of the poles snapped under the pressure being applied, sending the laborers manning them falling abruptly onto their rumps. Regaining their feet, each of the four took a new place on one of the remaining levers. A third splintered and its team recovered and repositioned themselves along the last three poles. It seemed very possible that they had underestimated what it would take to force the section of separated rock far enough forward so that it would break off and fall. In any case they were so concentrated on their effort that none of them noticed the signal flag indicating that the god had begun recessing from the chapel, the golden boat now descending the long ramp, his bald priests in the lead and the targeted ruler following close behind.

All dozen men fell backwards onto one another at the same time, at the moment a ear-shattering cracking signaled their great effort was at last realized. The narrow fissure had widened to a gulf and all of a sudden a mass of the cliff ridge dropped out of their view. New cracks began opening under their tangles of naked flesh, but all dozen sweat-soaked, dust-streaked men managed to separate themselves and scramble backwards on the wide trail which ran along the top of the cliffs. More and more of the ridge broke away and fell amid a great roaring. None of the twelve waited to see the exact consequence of their labor. They would only learn later that, although the chapel had been utterly destroyed, the ruler had survived unscathed. Their promised *deben* never materialized, of course.

E arly that same evening, Menkheperre Djehutymes sat enthroned in his private audience chamber of the Residence, his two sons and the

High Council occupying chairs arranged informally in front of the low dais. The First Prophet of Amen-Re Menkheperresenub and Vizier of the South Rekhmire were in the assembly, as well. Omnipresent King's Scribe Tjaneni sat cross-legged at his low writing table, off to one side of his master, poised to record the proceedings.

Attired in one of his stripped starched-linen *Nemes* headcoverings, Menkheperre cleared his throat, indicating he wanted the whispering to cease so that he could speak. All were immediately silent, full attention directed towards the Living Horus.

"It would seem that this day's unprecedented great catastrophe was neither a fateful accident nor a wilful random act of Set, Lord of Chaos. Mayor Amenmessu has just earlier reported to Our Person that his investigators sent to the cliff top found parts of broken tent poles there, which appear to have been employed to wedge the already splintered rock on the heights to such a degree that a great portion collapsed, subsequently creating the violent avalanche that totally buried our Sacred Horizon chapel — which act was witnessed by most of you here."

He cast a sideways glance towards Tjaneni, then continued. "It is believed by the god's priesthood that all officiants today had exited the building before the first section of sheared cliff face crushed its roof, and that, by the grace of Lord Amen-Re, no lives were subsequently lost to the many falling rock slabs and boulders.

"Since this gross disaster was wholly manufactured, it is only too clear that the timing of its perpetration was in no way pure happenchance, occurring as it did precisely when Lord Hidden One and My Majesty were together at the chapel for the Feast of the Valley celebrations. Thus, it can only be concluded that both the god's new structure raised by us and Our Person were dual targets for mutual destruction!"

There was murmuring among the counselors.

"Our Majesty wonders who the perpetrators of this vile deed might be. We don't doubt that those who actually levered the rock were other than desperate men in the temporary servitude of another or others. Our Majesty welcomes any ideas regarding the identity or identities of whomever masterminded today's attempt on Our Person's life."

Vizier Rekhmire rose after a few moments of hesitation.

"Mighty Bull, none here this evening — excepting yourself, of course — are old enough to remember the time when the House Born of Djehuty was under silent assault by survivors of the defunct House of Tao, who sought to overturn Maat and return the Horus Throne to the old order."

"That, at least, was the conviction of Asar Maatkare Hatshepsut, and her rationale for declaring herself a Female Living Horus and Mistress of the Two Lands, thereby buffering Our Majesty's inherited claim to the Double Crown, even though we were just five floodings old at the time," replied Menkheperre. "As a consequence, Prince Tao, the senior of his house, was sent into exile in the Great Green. His son, Prince Amen is Pleased, was allowed to retire to the Tao country estate in the Delta, where it is our knowledge that he still lives a quiet life, surrounded by a large family in his old age. And he is even older than Our Majesty, by ten floodings or more, if we remember correctly."

Rekhmire continued, asking, "Is it not possible, Mighty Bull, that the Taos — and by them I particularly mean a younger member of that family, a son or grandson of this Prince Amen is Pleased — may have rekindled an imagined claim to the Horus Throne, and so desire that Lord of the Two Lands Lasting Manifestation of Re be sent to the stars well before his time?"

"That would be worth considering as a faint possibility, Vizier, except for the fact that Our Majesty has a newly adult Heir in the person of Horus-in-the-Nest Amen is Pleased. And the security of a reserve son, as well, in Prince-Count Amen at the Head."

Menkheperre gestured to the half-brothers seated side by side in the midst of the assembly. Amenhotep had only recently reached sixteen floodings and shaved off his Horus Sidelock. Amenemhat was a well-mature twenty-four floodings older. Even in spite of their great differences in age, the two bore no physical resemblance to one another — nor to their mutual father, for that matter. Amenhotep facially favored his mother, the exiled Merytre Hatshepsut; Amenemhat looked like his grandfather — Asar Akheperenre Djehutymes — probably would have, had he lived to reach forty floodings.

"What's more," Menkheperre continued, "who is to say there may not be even more princes to come, inasmuch as Our Majesty once again has a new Royal Wife and she is, even now, with our child?"

This was a reference to Nebtu, a commoner whom Menkheperre had married two floodings previously, despite the fact, at only eighteen, she was young enough to have been his granddaughter.

"No, Vizier, the Taos harbor no secret desires to return to power, of that Our Person is confident."

"Your Majesty is doubtlessly correct. The House Born of Djehuty is, indeed, safe from usurpation, especially with the Heir having reached his majority."

Rehkmire twisted to smile lopsidedly at the Crown-Prince and then resumed his seat.

First Prophet Menkheperresenub spoke without standing.

"Could this have been a vile foreign plot, Your Majesty? Might the wretched Witch of Kadesh still seek her personal revenge against Kemet for the deaths here of her son and three daughters many floodings ago?"

"It is unknown whether our erstwhile mother-in-law even still lives," Menkheperre replied. "With her nephew now Prince of Kadesh, it is most unlikely she wields any power in her advanced old age, or could have mounted a complex scheme to murder Our Majesty in the distant Black Land, in any case."

There were no further responses from the counselors.

"So, is that all you have to offer in this matter, two not-probable theories? A villain or villains wait to be revealed, Notables of the Black Land."

Menkheperre stood and there was a scraping of chairs as the several counselors did likewise.

"Our Majesty suggests all of you deeply ponder other possibilities. Speak to us in private of your ideas, if that would be preferable to this present open forum."

He stepped off the dais, then a thought came to him.

"First Prophet, completion of the decoration at the Holiest of Holy Places shall commence immediately. Come and see us tomorrow, for Our Majesty's ideas in that regard."

The Lord of the Two Lands exited the doorway to the rest of his apartments. Tjaneni rolled up his scroll, rose and followed. The others quickly dispersed without further conversation. Prince-Count Amenemhat hung back. Rather than be the last to depart the audience chamber, however, he left through the same doorway as his father.

M enkheperre had pulled off the *Nemes* and tossed it onto a table as he came into his bedchamber. He now sat in a gilt-enhanced ebony armchair and held up his goblet for Tjaneni to fill from a small ewer. Prince-Count Amenemhat sat across from him, a low table between them. He, too, held a goblet, which the King's Scribe also filled nearly to its brim with the finest Delta vintage.

"So, Prince, may we rightly presume that you have a theory about today's incident that you wish to share with Our Person privately?"

"I hes...it..ate to d...do so, fa...ther. Be...cause I have no ac...tual p...proof of any...thing I'm a...about to sug...gest." He sipped his wine.

"Would you excuse us, Tjaneni? Our son would be more comfortable without extra ears present."

The King's Scribe merely nodded and departed.

"So, on with it." His Majesty also imbibed.

"Wh...who w...would have be...ne...fited m...most if Your Ma...jesty had b...been kill...ed this af...after....noon?"

"Benefited? Well, we suppose it would have been Our Majesty's Heir. Yes, of course, obviously Amen is Pleased would now be the Living Horus, not just Horus-in-the-Nest." He sipped again. "Are you suggesting, then, Amen at the Head that your young half-brother managed to mastermind a plot to have Our Person's *ba* winging it to the stars ahead of schedule? So that he could don the Double Crown and ascend the Horus Throne sooner rather than later?"

"I ha...have h...heard him, w...with m...my own ears, s...s...speak con...con...temp...tu...iously of Your Maj...esty. He g...g... great...ly re...sents t...that you ex...exiled his mo...mother and ha...ave not let h...h... him v...visit her a...all these f...flood...ings."

"He never liked his mother. They fought constantly when he was a young boy."

Amenemhat shrugged. "He h...has said to me th..that his f...f...irst act as Lord of t...the Two L...Lands will to b...bring her b...b...back from Swe...net, and to re...store her as G...God's Wi...Wife."

"Amen is Pleased is a risk-taking young hothead, to be sure," his father responded. "Sometimes reckless even. He thinks with his mouth, more often than not. His passions are martial rather than mental. Certainly his horsemanship cannot be equalled by those twice his age. Our Person was never the archer that the Crown-Prince has become, piercing copper ingots with arrows shot from a speeding chariot."

Menkheperre chuckled. "Few men can even draw his bow, we are told. Our Majesty will never be embarrassed by even trying!"

Although father and stammering son continued conversing over wine awhile longer, His Majesty remained unconvinced, finally, that he should be concerned about the ambitions of his Heir.

M enkheperre looked up from his work table, where he sat planning the stringing of a bead collar. Crown-Prince Amenhotep had entered the smallish chamber that the Lord of the Two Lands used for his various sedentary pastimes. Answering his father's summons, he had come directly from the stables, so was without a wig and wearing only a soiled short kilt and leather sandals. His leanly muscular torso was also smudged in places. Neatness was not one of the youth's priorities. Son of Re Djehutymes smiled at the offspring who was, at just sixteen flooding, half-a-head taller than himself. The Heir spoke first.

"So, father, what is important enough that you sent the lackey Tjaneni looking for me? Interrupting my grooming work."

"We are glad that our long-time loyal King's Scribe is not present to have heard that. His feelings would have been bruised." Menkheperre gestured towards the armless chair across the table from himself. "Take a seat, Amen is Pleased. We have something to tell you, which you certainly will want to hear."

The youth pulled the chair back and sat heavily, slouched, arms folded across his chest, bare legs splayed. He frowned, mouth in a hard line. He was expecting a reprimand.

After a long pause, the Lord of the Two Lands continued.

"The tragic event of yesterday has given Our Person cause for considerable reflection. As you well know, Lasting Manifestation of Re, Born of Djehuty has occupied the Horus Throne for fifty floodings now, albeit twenty of those shared with our late Coregent, the Female Living Horus, True Soul of Re. To Our Majesty's knowledge, very few have ruled the Black Land for as long, far fewer still for any *longer*. While we are yet vigorous of body and sound of heart, and we fully expect to see many more floodings of The River before joining Lord Re on his heavenly barque, it is perhaps advisable to once again take a Coregent — one of our *choosing* this time — who can share the day-to-day heavy burden of governing the Two Lands alongside Our Person."

"So, you are going to make me Co-Lord of the Two Lands," Amenhotep stated rather than asked, a broad smile brightening his blunt features, as he unfolded his arms and sat upright, placing calloused palms on his knees.

"There are some few at court here — and at Mennufer — who might think that naming you co-ruler would be ill advised, Amen is Pleased, some who do not presently regard you as yet temperamentally suited to govern the Black Land, even in a shared capacity with Our Majesty. Who believe your demonstrated judgment is flawed. Who believe your youth causes you to jump to rash conclusions and then to stubbornly refuse to admit it when events subsequently prove you wrong."

Amenhotep bristled. "Who are these 'some'?" he demanded.

Menkheperre chose to ignore the pointed question and continued, "It has even been suggested to Our Person that it was the Crown-Prince himself who orchestrated yesterday's disaster, in order to speed his ascension to the Horus Throne. We rejected that possibility, of course."

Amenhotep met his father's stern gaze, then looked quickly away.

"It was the Vizier of the South, was it not? he stated and asked. "That scrawny rodent has always disliked me." He nearly said, "And Qenamen, too," but thought it best to not share his present victimhood.

"You do not deny the charge, then?"

The Crown-Prince bristled again. "Of course I *deny* it! What opportunity would I have to 'orchestrate' such a vile deed? I'm virtually a prisoner of the Residence."

"Who escapes his 'prison' on occasion, to go carousing during Lord Re's transit of the Netherworld, in the drinking establishments of Waset and Mennufer, in the rough company of royal-stable grooms. Our Majesty's eyes and ears are everywhere." Son of Re Djehutymes smiled, sat back in his armchair and tented fingers on his barreled bare chest.

"If you know this and disapprove, Father, why haven't you said so before?"

"Should Our Person forbid it, you'd only go out of your way to defy us. That is your regrettable nature, Amen is Pleased. Losing the Heir in a common drunken brawl is a risk Our Majesty has decided to take. Should something happen to you on one of your 'escapes', there is always Amen at the Head — waiting in the antechamber, so to speak. He already has two maturing, healthy sons of his own, so the House Born of Djehuty would be guaranteed continuance with him as Lord of the Two Lands."

"You prefer the Stammerer over me, isn't that so? I'm only Horus-in-the-Nest because he's your bastard by your unmarried half-sister — who was a whore, or so I've been told — and I'm the *legitimate* son by your Great Royal Wife."

"Who, *shamed*, lives in confinement at Swenet, because of her unforgivable deed a decade of floodings ago!" Menkheperre himself bristled. "Our Majesty is recently told that you've wanted to visit her for some long while, but that *we*'ve forbidden it. That is a falsehood, as you well know, Amen is Pleased — that you've been prevented from seeing Noblest Woman, Beloved of Re — inasmuch as you've never made your desire in that regard known to us."

"Had I requested it, you would've denied me." Amenhotep ran a rough palm over his burry head.

"Perhaps. Certainly so when you still wore the Horus Lock. Now that you are in your majority, probably not. In any case, once you are Co-Lord of the Two Lands, you may do as you chose in that regard."

"Including recalling her to court, restoring her as God's Wife of Amen," the Crown-Prince stated rather than asked.

"Not that — at least not until Our Person has flown to the stars."

"That, *then*, shall be my first act as sole ruler, when the day comes, one day." He folded his arms across his chest again. "So, when I'm wearing the Double Crown, I'll want my own Residence. Here and in

Mennufer, as well."

"Not that either. When Asar True Soul of Re shared Our Majesty's throne, we joint-rulers occupied the same Residences, both here in the South and down North, too. That shall be the case again.

"It is our plan that you shall spend the greater share of your time at Mennufer — hunting and fowling are better there — and Our Person will be most often here at Waset, where we can more conveniently oversee our building projects and check progress on our Mansion for Eternity.

"You will, of course, come south for the Festival of the Opet and the Beautiful Feast of the Valley. And Our Majesty will sail downstream for the annual celebrations of Lord Ptah at Mennufer and Lord Re at Iunu. The Double Lords of the Two Lands will be under one another's feet, so to speak, only multiple crossings of Re out of a flooding."

"Thus, in effect, I shall be the Lord of the Lower Black Land, and you the Lord of the Upper Black Land." Again, a statement rather than a question.

"In practice, yes, but it shall never be stated as such." Menkheperre put his elbows on his knees and leaned forward. "Now to another matter, Amen is Pleased, that of finding you a Great Royal Wife — so that you can get to work making your own *legitimate* Horus-in-the-Nest. Which should be easy enough for you, husbanding, inasmuch as you already have several 'bastards' of your own, fathered on kitchen help and other common 'whores' — or so it's been reliably reported to Our Person."

The Crown-Prince smiled broadly, but thought it best to bite his tongue on the matter of whores and bastards, clearly sore subjects for his father.

"So, do you have someone in mind, for the role of my Great Royal Wife?" he asked instead. "The only suitable females close to my own age *I* know of are your pale daughters by the Reteni women, and none of those bitches have any appeal for me, quite honestly. And I'm certain the feeling is mutual for them."

"There is someone who has been highly recommended to Our Majesty. The first prophet of Lord Min in his mansion at Ipu — one Yey — has a daughter thirteen floodings old, whose name, if we remember correctly, is Tiaa. She is said to be quite more attractive than average; and the family of Yey is an old noble one, going back to before The Liberator, to even before the time of the hated Foreign Princes. The girl has several married sisters, we are told, all of whom have produced male offspring, so she's almost certainly fertile."

Crown-Prince Amenhotep merely shrugged his broad shoulders.

"It seems I haven't a say in the matter."

A Great Royal Wife was merely an expediency. In any case, he didn't expect to cease laying with his several "whores" anytime soon — although it would doubtless be necessary to put a halt to the carousing when Co-Lord of the Two Lands. He'd simply invite his drinking cohorts to whichever Residence, instead.

Three Weeks Later
The Country Estate of Yey at Ipu

It had been decided by Menkheperre that a marriage would be concluded between Crown-Prince Amenhotep and young Mistress Tiaa, maiden daughter of First Prophet of Min Yey, prior to the youth's coronation as Co-Lord of the Two Lands Akheperure, Son of Re Amenhotep — in order that his new spouse could be crowned Great Royal Wife and installed as God's Wife of Amen at the same time. Thus, it was necessary for him to finally meet his bride-to-be, and he had sailed from Waset half-a-day north to the provencial town of Ipu for that purpose. Amenhotep was accompanied, of course, by his inseparable companion, Qenamen.

With an armed escort of Medjay on foot, the two young men, each driving his individual chariot, arrived at the entry gate of the walled country estate of Yey. This lay on the outskirts of the sleepy town of Ipu, long the cult center of the ithyphallic fertility deity Min. The docking of the royal yacht at the modest wharf there shortly before and been noted by a posted servant of Yey's, who then hurried to the estate, to alert the cleric to the imminent arrival of the Crown-Prince. Thus Amenhotep and Qenamen were very much expected, and the estate chamberlain had hobbled through the gate to welcome them even before they handed off the reins to a couple of Medjay and dismounted their vehicles.

The quite elderly servant bowed from his thick waist, arms extended towards the dusty ground. "Greetings, Your Highness. The First Prophet is greatly honored by your visit and awaits within with his family. I will lead you to them, when you choose."

"Yes, yes, let's be on our way!" Amenhotep gestured impatiently.

The chamberlain turned to proceed to the wooden gateway; and the Crown-Prince immediately mimicked the old man's lurching gait, which set Qenamen laughing. The chamberlain stopped and turned back to see what was so funny.

"Go. Go! We're impatient to meet our waiting bride!" Amenhotep shooed the servant. He had begun to practice the prerogative of the royal first-person plural.

The Crown-Prince and his companion were dressed almost identically, in short, tiered wigs then in style at court, and lightweight tunics, each wrapped around by a knee-length pleated kilt. Bead broad collars draped their chests and leather sandals shod their feet. As always, Amenhotep additionally wore an embossed-leather archer's guard on one wrist. Although the Crown-Prince had tucked his own into the waistband of his kilt, Qenamen still sported red-leather driving gloves.

The two youths plodded along a few paces behind the slow-moving chamberlain, tall Amenhotep affecting the old man's hobble a couple of times, shorter Qenamen suppressing laughter. The gravel path leading to the sprawling whitewashed house took them through a well-tended garden with aged tamarisk trees shading flower beds in bloom, and clumps of plumed grasses waving in the gentle breeze. They were greeted at the paneled double doors of the house by a bald florid fat man, who identified himself as the butler of Yey and explained that the "master" and Lady of the House, plus several of their younger children were waiting for their guests in the audience chamber of the estate.

This proved to be high-ceilinged and spacious, with four tall wooden columns painted bright red, the papyri-form capitals multi-hued. Several doorways opened off the walls, except for the one opposite where Amenhotep and Qenamen entered. Centered on it, in front of a colorful large painted scene of Yey and his family fowling in a marsh, sat the First Prophet himself, in an inlaid armchair; to one side of him, seated on an armless chair was a mature woman, doubtless the Mistress of the House; and arrayed on stools placed back from their parents' seats were two small boys and three older girls, one of them presumably the expectant bride-to-be, Tiaa.

After his presentation of the Crown-Prince and his "friend," the butler backed out of the chamber, his head bowed.

Yey — a large-nosed man of middle age, wearing a layered long wig of the sort no longer considered fashionable in Kemet's two capitals — rose in the presence of Horus-in-the-Nest, soon to be crowned the Co-Living Horus, but sooner still to become the provencial cleric's son-in-law.

Bowing just slightly, Yey addressed both the quite tall and shorter, otherwise somewhat identical, youths — clueless as to which of them was Crown-Prince Amenhotep, never having seen the Heir before.

"Greetings, Your Highness. My family and I are greatly honored by your royal presence in our humble home today."

"And we are pleased to be here, First Prophet of Lord Min," responded Amenhotep, revealing himself. He had crossed his wrists on his solid buttocks, wide shoulders squared, broad chest thrust forward.

"May I introduce my family, Your Highness?" A rhetorical question, Yey continued without a reply from the Crown-Prince, indicating, "Here is my dear wife, Lady of the House Thuit." She bowed her head, lappets of the heavy, old-fashioned wig swinging forward. "And these are my youngest sons, Yetu and Yuya." The naked small boys stood in unison and bowed from the waist. "And, yes, my three youngest daughters, Tesu, Iba and — of course — the lovely Tiaa."

Amenhotep had already figured out that the clearly oldest of Yey's girls present was his intended bride. And he was, perhaps surprisingly, not disappointed. Almost not. The youth was decidedly attracted to full-breasted females; and fresh-faced, yes, even quite pretty Tiaa might have been a teenaged boy, in that regard, from what he could tell. But then, again, she was only thirteen-floodings-old, so — hopefully — might still fully "blossom," as was said.

The Crown-Prince and Qenamen, too, made awkward back-and-forth conversation with Yey, wife Thuit and their brood (not that the latter had much to offer) for several minutes, before Amenhotep abruptly terminated the introductory audience by saying, "We shall see you all, very soon, in Waset, for the ceremonies. The Vizier of the South will arrange the details for you. We now must be on our way." He bowed his head ever so slightly towards his prospective Great Wife.

Without further ado, Horus-in-the-Nest and his companion turned on their sandaled heels and were quickly gone. Once they were a family alone again, Yeh could not resist asking his demure daughter, still seated, head bowed, with hands clasped on her lap, "Well, soon-to-be King's Great Royal Wife Tiaa, what do you think of your future husband?"

After a pause, she looked up and demurely replied, "I like the shorter cute one better."

The Next Day, on The River, near Swenet

Having a royal yacht at his disposal, Crown-Prince Amenhotep decided to bypass the Southern Capital and ordered his rowers to push on to the frontier quarry settlement of Swenet, where his mother, Merytre Hatshepsut, had been under royal confinement for ten floodings, in a nearby villa previously used as a vacation retreat by second-tier members of the House of Tao.

The Heir was six-floodings-old when he last saw the woman who was generally believed to have collectively poisoned — though never formally accused of doing so — the three Reteni Royal Wives of her still-husband, Menkheperre Djehutymes. Quite honestly, Amenhotep had only the vaguest recollection of what the former Great Royal Wife even looked like. He did vividly remember that she had screamed at him a great deal, and had violently struck him on several occasions, including once in front of the Lord of the Two Lands — fortunately in private. To say the least, the youth was conflicted that he even had a lingering desire to reconnect with this long-gone female so far removed in every way from his present situation, especially his imminent elevation to co-ruler of Kemet. He could not quite admit it was not out of any lingering, suppressed affection for Merytre Hatshepsut, but simply to spite his father.

When the royal yacht finally came — near to the slipping of Lord Re's golden barque beyond the western horizon — within view of Swenet, a whitewashed sprawling town on the east bank of The River, Crown-Prince Amenhotep's thoughts were not on the pending unannounced reunion with his estranged mother, but rather on how he planned to share his father's crowns and what portion of ultimate power he would claim as specifically his own. He certainly did not intend his kingship to be purely symbolic until aging Menkheperre finally got around to booking passage on the sun's barque. Amenhotep had already determined to have himself crowned in one of the open-air courts of the ancient Mansion of Re at Iunu rather than at the traditional coronation venue of Ipet Isut, the Hidden One's mansion at Waset. And he would take the throne name of Great Manifestation of Re. At the moment, he did, indeed, feel "great."

After docking at Swenet, Amenhotep and Qenamen disguised themselves as common sailors and ventured into the frontier town for a night of heavy imbibing and intense gambling in several drinking establishments of the rough-and-tumble place, ending up at a brothel, where the Crown-Prince sampled three and Qenamen two of the less-unattractive employees there.

T he next morning Merytre Hatshepsut relaxed in one of the tree-shaded gardens of her villa-prison, seated in a small, colorfully painted pavilion, playing *senet* with the eldest of her daughters, Sitmin. Yes, her *daughter*, of three by her lover of nearly ten floodings. The prepubescent's skin was the color of Kemet's flood soil, which was not at all surprising, given that her father was a pureblood man of Wawat — ostensibly one of the former Great Wife's "jailers," named Pemitu. He was presently upriver at the Second Cataract's Fortress of Buhen, on "business" of some sort. As always Merytre Hatshepsut was totally disinterested in what exactly that might be.

She made her move on the game board and waited for Sitmin's counter. Both barefooted mother and daughter were attired in strapped plain-linen sheaths, their heads uncovered, hair cropped short, the girl without a Sidelock of Youth. Merytre Hatshepsut looked up as her butler approached along the garden path. He seemed in a hurry, unusual for his advanced age and immense girth.

As the ebony-hued servant came up to the pavilion, before he could address her, his mistress noticed — as well as her unadmitted diminishing vision allowed — that he was being followed at some dozen paces by two other men whom Merytre Hatshepsut didn't recognize, even as they moved closer.

"Highness," the butler bowed his head.

"Do we have visitors, Bete?" she asked before he could continue, putting down the game piece poised to trump Sitmin's likely move.

"Yes, My Lady. They were insistent on seeing you immediately, but would not identify themselves. By their attire, they would seem to be officials from down river, if a little youthful." By the time he'd finished speaking, the two were standing a few cubits behind him.

"You are dismissed, old man," instructed the taller, broader-shouldered of the pair.

Bete moved his bulk to one side, nodded, and waddled off, back down the path leading to the villa.

Both youths — they were certainly only teenagers, Merytre Hatshepsut assessed — were wearing knee-length, pleated kilts belted at narrow waists with embossed leather; they also wore leather sandals and sported tiered short wigs probably in style now at Mennufer and Waset. The shorter visitor was quite good looking, she thought; the more muscular, tall one's unrefined features reminded her of someone, but she couldn't quite decide who — maybe her own long-dead father.

"Dismiss your slave-girl, mistress," the latter youth ordered flatly.

"My *daughter*, young lord, and she shall stay put, is my wish."

"Daughter?" Amenhotep asked incredulously, then quickly laughed. "So we have a black half-sister! Which doesn't surprise us, actually."

"Half-sister? Just who *are* you, calling my Daughter of Min your own blood?" Merytre Hatshepsut sat rigidly back in her armchair, blinking.

"We didn't suppose you would recognize us," Amenhotep responded, fists on his hips. "We're your all-grown-up son, Amen is Pleased, our mother, Noblest Woman, Beloved of Re." He just barely nodded at her. "And this is our milk-brother, Strong is Amen, who you may remember as a Child of the Nursery," gesturing to his companion, who also nodded, but more pronouncedly.

"Well, grown *up* to be sure. Yes, tall, really quite tall. I never supposed I'd lay eyes on you again, Amen is Pleased. Are you still a wilful, ill-tempered brat?"

Qenamen snorted a laugh. The Crown-Prince roughly elbowed his friend, but good-naturedly.

"We do have our moments, certainly," Amenhotep chuckled.

"Why are you using the ruler's personal plural? Has Born of Djehuty flown off and you are now the Living Horus? I don't see a cobra on your brow."

"Not quite yet, our mother. Lasting Manifestation of Re still lives and governs, but has elevated us to be Co-Lord of the Two Lands. When The River's flood recedes in some three-dozen transits of Lord Re, we shall don the Double Crown and reign from Mennufer as Great Manifestation of Re, Amen is Pleased, Ruler of Iunu. Before that we are taking a Great Royal Wife, a commoner girl whom we've only just met yesterday. And our plurals are practice for being My Majesty."

Merytre Hatshepsut would have offered her unexpected guests seats, but there were only two chairs on the pavilion.

"I would invite you both to sit, but there's a lack of furniture out here, obviously."

"That's all right," said Amenhotep, suddenly squatting and assuming a cross-legged position on the clipped lawn, a couple of cubits or so from the platform. Qenamen followed his example. "We can't stay very much longer, in any case. Lasting Manifestation of Re expected us back in Waset yesterday. We wouldn't want His Majesty to send out a search party."

"So, your father is well, I trust, if certainly getting a little snaggle-toothed by now?"

"He does cough a good deal and has shortness of breath of late, but still appears quite fit for a man of his many floodings. All his seasons of campaigning in vile Retenu toughened him for his old age." Amenhotep leaned back on his straightened muscular arms. "He's recently taken a quite young wife, but not made her Great Royal Wife. If she gives him a child yet, he'll likely do that, we would think."

Young Sitmin had become bored with the adult conversation, so stood, crossed around the low table with the *senet* board and whispered into her mother's ear. Merytre Hatshepsut nodded assent, and the girl hopped off the pavilion, hiked her sheath and ran away up the path leading to the villa.

"She's going to play with her little sisters," her mother offered. She gestured for her son to take the vacated chair, but he shook his head negatively.

"Oh, so there're more little half-sibling black ones." It was a statement by the Crown-Prince rather than a question. "You were raped how many times, our mother?"

"Not 'raped' even once. All three daughters are from the same father. His name is Pemitu, and he's been my lover for nearly a decade of floodings now. Quite frankly, he's much more accomplished with his Min than your father ever was." She wigged the middle finger of one hand and the little finger of the other.

"We've heard that men of Wawat have really immense ones. Mins, that is. May we meet him, this Pemitu?" Amenhotep sat upright again, resting his elbows on his thighs.

"He's upriver at Buhen, on business."

"What sort of 'business'?" Qenamen suddenly spoke for the first time.

Merytre Hatshepsut looked at him and shrugged. "I've never asked. Some sort of trading, I imagine. Flesh of the gods, possibly." She moved to change the subject. "Are all the little Reteni bitches still alive?"

"Our other *white-skinned* half-sisters? All but one, the youngest, who succumbed to a long fever — three floodings ago, wasn't it?" he directed at Qenamen, who nodded in agreement. After a pause, Amenhotep, folding his hands on his stretched kilt, asked, "We would like to know the truth from your own mouth, our mother. Did you poison the three Daughters of Kadesh, as father believed then, and still does?"

"Would you believe *me*, Amen is Pleased, if I professed my innocence?" she responded, laughing, after a long hesitation.

"The Great Royal Wife, our mother, was very angry always, as we remember. She greatly resented that Lasting Manifestation of Re, Born of Djehuty regularly fucked the Reteni bitches, but herself only rarely. We never questioned that you wished your foreigner rivals dead, and so probably arranged for them to travel to the West well ahead of their time, or wherever it is the *bas* of wretched Asiatics go — if they even have a *ba*. Perhaps you didn't add poison to their meals with your own hand, Noblest Woman, Beloved of Re, but almost certainly managed it done, has always been our own belief."

"And so you won't have to change that, your belief, Amen is Pleased. It was *my* plan, but the deed of the handmaiden, Tesit, who slipped a tasteless potion into their wine, actually. In her guilt, she swallowed the same stuff herself, two floodings after our arrival here in exile." Merytre Hatshepsut suddenly swept the gaming pieces off the *senet* board. They clattered to the pavilion's painted floor. "I suppose Amam gobbled her soul at the Judgment, as it surely will my own, one day."

After some further conversation on a lighter note, Co-Lord of the Two Lands-to-be Amenhotep and his lifelong companion, Qenamen, took their leave of Merytre Hatshepsut, returning to the royal yacht and sailing north to Waset that early afternoon. She would never be visited by her son again, although living on in exile at Swenet for another seventeen floodings, totally blind well before the end. Because of her admitted guilt, Amenhotep, once he was ruling alone, decided against restoring his mother to her former role as God's Wife of Amen; Great Royal Wife Tiaa already held the position, in any case. The unfinished Mansion for Eternity which Menkheperre Djehutymes had long before been hewing for her in the Great Place would be given to the Mayor of Waset and his family by Akheperure Amenhotep-Heqaiunu. He never knew his mother's actual final resting-place, and only learned of her death some while after the fact of it. He brought grown-up Sitmin and his two other part-Wawatan halfsisters to live at the Residence in Mennufer at that same time. Son of Re Amenhotep never met his stepfather, who had predeceased his mother.

Merytre Hatshepsut's and Pemitu's youngest daughter would one day become a concubine of Amenhotep's son and successor, and mother of another Child of the Nursery.

*　*　*

17

Her naked legs wrapped around his narrow hips, ankles crossed above his buttocks, she dug her fingernails into his damp bare shoulders, arching her back against the rapid thrusting at her crotch. He would achieve his release soon — or so she could only hope — and push away, breaking the grip of her legs, roll off her onto his back, spent, his cleaved broad chest heaving. And that finally happened, moments later. She drew up her knees and lay listening to his gasping breathing quiet. Her arms rested flat on the twisted bedsheet, along her sides, one pressing against his extended hard arm, her small fists clenched. Very often his erection did not subside and, after resting awhile, he would remount and begin all over again.

His Majesty, seventeen-floodings-old Co-Lord of the Two Lands Akheperure, Son of Re Amenhotep, Ruler of Iunu, was determined to get his three-floodings-younger Great Royal Wife Tiaa seeded with his first child (well, first legitimate one, at least), hopefully also his own Horus-in-the-Nest. To that end he'd taken her to his bed every single night since their marriage some two seasons before, and often during the daytime, too — even when her bleeding was happening. To no avail, so far. At least there'd been no subsiding of her flow and not even the slightest swelling of her belly, yet.

The youthful Horus was not a great lover — if that concept involved romantic foreplay prior to and following coupling. Her mother, Lady of the House Thuit, had instructed Tiaa to expect prolonged gentle caressing and kissing as part of the marriage act — at least that was Thuit's personal experience throughout her many years of connubial exchange with Tiaa's father, First Prophet of Min and Father of the God Yey. His Majesty Amenhotep had clearly never been schooled in the finer points of lovemaking, however.

His sexual approach to his young wife bordered on the violent, which involved his stripping away her garments, often by tearing these in his haste. He had never really kissed her, rather forcibly thrusting his hard tongue into her mouth repeatedly, until tiring of it. Amenhotep would bite her ear lobes, sometimes so they bled; he also would suck her only-budding small breasts, as if a giant ravenous infant, even pinching the tender nipples until she whimpered. He often roughly grabbed her long hair in both fists while mounting her, whether from behind — with her standing upright or on her hands and knees — or lying face-to-face on his bed, him on top always. Frequently, His Majesty seemed to be intoxicated, at least Tiaa could smell sour wine on his breath, taste it on his violent tongue. He would have been drinking prior to her arrival at his Residence bedchamber, plus there were always the two or three chalices drained prior to his eventual physical onslaught.

Thankfully there might not be a second round of coupling this particular evening. A few minutes after his breathing had subsided to normal, His Majesty Amenhotep rose up, swung his long legs off the bed and sat at its edge, elbows on his knees, his hunched bare broad back to her. After a few moments, he stood and walked naked across the brazier-illuminated chamber to a low table between two gilded armchairs and poured himself a faience chalice of Delta vintage from the ewer positioned in its center. He immediately gulped this down and poured himself a refill. When he turned back to her, she was relieved to see that his Min was utterly exhausted, shrunk back to its still-impressive flaccid state. He again drank deeply from the lily-form vessel, then carried it back to the bed and sat there once more, so that he was looking down at her.

"Well, little Great Wife, do you suppose it took this time? Did our seed fall on fertile soil? Will your belly be filled with Our Person's Horus-in-the-Nest soon, do you think?" He gently — for him — rested his free warm calloused palm on her concave bare abdomen.

"We can only hope, Amen is Pleased." She forced a smile. He'd instructed her on their wedding night to always call him by his birth name when in private. "We shall know if I don't bleed again on schedule. In twelve crossings of Re. Or so my mother has told me."

"And Lady Thuit should well know, having been successfully sown eight times with the Father of the God's seed, isn't it?"

"Ten, actually, as two went West soon after dropping. Her first and second, both boys. Lady Tausret and Lord Bes didn't look favorably on them, or so my mother has said."

"And your three older sisters all have several brats each, right?" Amenhotep swallowed more wine. It was a rhetorical question.

"One, the eldest, has two boys. The other two both have three girls. 'Breeding stock', my father calls them. I should certainly follow their example, he thinks. But you very well know all this, Amen is Pleased. We've discussed it again and again."

"Repetition makes for reassurance, our little Tiaa," Amenhotep responded, his open rough palm moving to her freshly shaven pubic mound, finding the moisture there, kneading, squeezing. He inserted his longest finger. She moaned, more from raw tenderness than any pleasure.

While they were talking, Tiaa had raised herself on her elbows, so could see now that her husband was becoming engorged again. After several more long moments of his fingering, Son of Re Amenhotep placed his empty wine chalice on the painted-plaster floor and remounted and re-entered the pubescent Great Royal Wife, for his second "sowing" that evening.

She didn't realize that there was an invited secret audience for the royal coupling this particular time (as there often was): masturbating Qenamen admired his "milk brother's" performance from behind a pillar of the King's Bedchamber. The fact that he knew his dearest friend was watching served as a stimulus for the Co-Living Horus.

It would be three more floodings before Tiaa became pregnant, finally — not from lack of husbandry on the part of the young Lord of the Two Lands, however. A Horus-in-the-Nest would not be conceived and born alive until Inundation 10 of his sole reign.

Two Seasons Earlier, Inundation 51
Reign of Menkheperre Djehutymes
The Mansion of Re, Iunu

Unlike the typical residence of a deity, the generations-old Mansion of Re in the ancient Eastern Delta town of Iunu did not have a Holy of Holies as such, housing a cult image of the god kept there in a golden boat-shrine. Rather, the divine essence of Kemet's sun god was thought to reside in the *Ben Ben* "sun stone," a massive, covered-all-over-in-sheet-gold, squat pyramidion elevated by a tall, masonry-built rectangular base situated on a stairs-mounted stone platform in the middle of the rearmost and largest of three adjoining open-to-the-sky rectangular courts separated by soaring pylon-gates. There were, however, any number of colossal quartzite and red-granite standing and seated statues of the hawk-headed deity — a large gilded sun-disk crowning each one — situated around the columned perimeters of the two outer open-air courts. It was in the middle one of these that the coronation of Co-Lord of the Two Lands Akheperure, Co-Son of Re Amenhotep was underway.

Placed between the Re colossi were a half-dozen temporary smallish open pavilion-shrines, each veneered in gold foil; they housed seated human-sized gilded-wood images of Kemet's principle pantheon: Amen, Ptah, Asar, Hathor, Iset and, of course, Re himself. In the middle of the court there was also a somewhat-larger, more-elevated painted-and-gilded pavilion, reached by two parallel flights of stairs, on which a pair of gilded cube-thrones were centered side by side. The right or southern-most of these was presently occupied by Co-Lord of the Two Lands Menkheperre, Co-Son of Re Djehutymes, just beginning the fifty-first flooding of his reign over Kemet. Barefooted, he was attired without adornment in a simple red-linen kilt and sported the molded-felt White Crown of Upper Kemet. Crook and Flail scepters of the ruler of the Two Lands rested on his lap.

The second throne was presently empty.

This was because its former occupant, youthful Akheperure Am-enhotep, was making the rounds, in turn, of the deity shrines. Likewise barefooted, unadorned and kilted identically to his father, wearing a fully gilded version of the bulbous *Khepresh* and carrying another set of the Crook and Flail, he would mount three steps and enter each structure. Within he would be greeted by the First Prophet of the particular god or goddess, then kneel in front of the deity's image, the scepters crossed on his bare chest. The First Prophet would position himself directly behind Akheperure Amenhotep and, after uttering the appropriate litany, would carefully lift the golden helmet-crown off the young man's clean-shaven head, elevating it at arm's length. After more ritual pronouncements — vocalizing on behalf of the god or goddess he served — the cleric would lower the crown onto Akheperure's head again. The latter would then stand upright, bow ever so slightly towards the deity image, turn and dis-mount the pavilion-shrine by its steps, turn to his left and move at a meas-ured pace to the next structure glistening in the high-noon sun.

When he had been de-crowned and re-crowned six times, now fully the co-ruler, Akheperure Amenhotep moved on a diagonal course to the center of the courtyard, to stand a few paces in front of the throne-pavilion. He was joined there by the six First Prophets in a single rank behind him. The clerics then formed two parallel files of three each, mov-ing around the new co-ruler and going up to the high throne platform. The file of Amen, Asar and Aset climbed the southernmost stairway, that of Re, Ptah and Hathor simultaneously mounted the other, northern one. Once on the platform, they all moved behind the pair of occupied and empty thrones and reformed a single standing line in front of the several persons seated at the rear of the structure. These individuals included:

young bride Great Royal Wife Tiaa, in her vulture cap-crown, modius and double tall plumes; recent Royal Wife Nebtu; viziers of the North and South; just-appointed King's Chamberlain Qenamen; mayors of the duo capitals, Mennufer and Waset; as well as King's Scribe Tjaneni and more than a score of notables of the Two Lands, generalissimos of the Northern and Southern Armies of Kemet, and admirals of The River and Great Green fleets.

When the first prophets were in place, Menkheperre Djehutymes stood up, scepters now crossed on his chest. All those seated stood, as well. He moved to the front of the platform. This was the cue for the Second Prophet of Re and two acolytes to enter the courtyard through its pylon gate, and measuredly approach the solitary Akheperure Amenhotep from behind. Each acolyte bore on outstretched, paralleled forearms a cushioned tray. One of these was empty and the other supported the upright basket-work Red Crown of Lower Kemet. Uttering something inaudible to those on the high platform, the Re cleric lifted the golden *Khepresh* off the tall young co-ruler's head and placed it upright on the empty tray. He then raised the Red Crown at arms' length and lowered this onto the Co-Living Horus's shaven pate. The three then exited the court-yard, moving backwards in practiced unison.

Akheperure Amenhotep now slowly strode to the throne platform and climbed the northern stairway, turning to stand facing the courtyard, side by side with his Co-regent, half-a-head taller. Father and son each counted silently to ten, then began moving down their respective stair-ways one step at a time. When they reached the courtyard pavement, they began walking in unison towards the pylon gateway. Before they got to the portal, the assembly on the throne platform had begun dismounting it by the paired stairs, the files of high-priests first, followed by the two Royal Wives, the Viziers, the rest of the courtiers and the military men.

The Co-regents slowly passed into the first court of the Mansion of Re, where two gilded cube-thrones fixed with long carrying poles wait-ed, side by side, oriented towards the first court portal, the high gilded ce-dar gates of which were closed. Two parallel lines of bearers faced towards the thrones, a few cubits from their long sides. These sixteen were young men of Kemet rather than of Wawat, all the exact same height and trim physique, barefooted and attired in short white kilts, each sporting a small white ostrich feather in his cap-wig.

Menkheperre and Akheperure seated themselves on the backless thrones, scepters still crossed on their chests; the lines of bearers ap-proached, assumed their assigned positions and simultaneously lifted the two rulers, first to arms' length and then to bare shoulders. By this time the coronation audience had begun to file into the first court. Coming from the court portico, a contingent of tall Wawatan drummers, colorfully attired in native garb, took their place a few cubits in front of the two elevated thrones. The six First Prophets moved past the rulers and drummers and reassembled in front of the latter.

As host of the coronation, the First Prophet of Re raised one arm over his head, then dropped it. Immediately the drumming cadence began and the procession moved measuredly towards the first pylon. Half-a-dozen porters waiting there began pulling the high, glistening double door-panels inward, slowly revealing the amassed townspeople of Iunu beyond, waiting to greet the two Living Horuses. Cheering began when both door panels were pushed against the gateway thicknesses and the closest persons lining the processional way could see the elevated Co-rulers approaching from within the sun-god's dwelling.

The royal processional continued to a nearby resthouse specially constructed for the coronation event. There Menkheperre and Akheperure changed from their ritual attire into daily kilts and wigs and personal adornments. Great Royal Wife Tiaa likewise doffed her Vulture-Cap and feathered modius. They then mounted chariots and, side by side, began the lengthy land trip back to the Mennufer Residence, leading at a walking gait the chariots of the courtiers and military, and the carrying litters of the Royal Wives pair — cheered all the way by curious farmers in their fields and inhabitants of the villages through which the royal progress passed. That evening aged father and youthful son co-hosted a banquet to celebrate the commencement of a new era for the Two Lands. No one imagined then that it would last for less than two floodings.

THREE SEASONS LATER, INUNDATION 1
COREGENCY OF MENKHEPERRE/AKHEPERURE
TIME OF THE BEAUTIFUL FEAST OF THE VALLEY, THE RESIDENCE, WASET

Seated Akheperure Amenhotep-Heqaiunu poured himself another helping of wine from the Asiatic-crafted silver ewer he'd lifted off the low table separating him from his also-seated father. He tilted his head and drained the chalice, refilled it and returned the ewer to its matching small tray. He then held the gold drinking vessel in both hands, at chest level, elbows on his chair arms.

"We don't see why you are so resistant to our proposal, Your Majesty. You've already had her images, names and many texts erased from the Holiest of Holy Places, now that you are finishing and otherwise remodeling it as venue again for the Beautiful Feast rituals."

Menkheperre Djehutymes wasn't imbibing. "That is merely expediency, Amen is Pleased, to give the place a consistency of decoration. Only depictions of her as True Soul of Re have been replaced with those of our justified father and grandfather, or else by offering tables and fetish stands. Our Person left the narratives of her imagined divine birth and the expedition to the land of Punt intact, and the sun-needles account, too, since the lower colonnades are not visited during the Feast celebrations."

"The Punt adventure and sun-needles at least were real events," Amenhotep countered. "The birth business was just justification for Noblest Woman co-opting your throne by declaring herself the daughter of Lord Amen-Re's own body." He sipped his wine.

"We think she sincerely believed that, or at least convinced herself of it."

"She was no more the god's blue flesh-and-blood than was Amen at the Head!" the younger ruler laughed. His elder half-brother had told him the bizarre story of his own deceitful beginning. Amenhotep had never known his father's first Coregent, of course.

Menkheperre chuckled at the distant memory. "It's certain that Brother of Mut didn't have a hand in Noblest Woman's conception." His present Coregent only knew the late High Steward of the Estates of Amen-Re by his controversial reputation.

"Whether she believed her own preposterous fiction or not, Your Majesty, the fact is Noblest Woman wilfully violated *Maat* when she declared herself a *female* Living Horus." Amenhotep sipped more wine. "That very concept is simply contradictory. Horus is a *male* deity and the *Lord* of the Two Lands is his visible manifestation...or in our cases, his double manifestation. Plurality isn't alien to *Maat*, father, but a male god transformed willy nilly into a goddess certainly is."

"You needn't lecture Our Person on theology, Amen is Pleased."

"If her offense to *Maat* is so obvious to someone as unschooled in 'theology' as ourself, then...."

Menkheperre raised a palm to cut his son short. "Noblest Woman's motives were never theological but merely pragmatical, Your Majesty. You know very well that Our Majesty was but five floodings old when...." The older man suddenly lapsed into a fit of violent coughing — a frequent occurrence of late.

Akheperure waited until this eruption subsided, handing his father his half-full chalice — which Menkheperre drained.

The two rulers' conversation continued in the same vein awhile longer, concluding with the aging Conqueror of Retenu agreeing to give "serious thought" to his young Coregent's nagging insistence that all physical evidence of Maatkare Hatshepsut's twenty floodings of impostoring as a Female Living Horus be obliterated from Kemet's record. And more importantly, that her unfitting kingly burial be removed from the Mansion for Eternity she'd had made for herself in the Great Place; and that the reburial she'd caused there of Menkheperre's grandfather, the Asar Akheperkare Djehutymes, be returned to his original Great Place Mansion for Eternity, as well.

A DOZEN CROSSINGS OF RE LATER
STORAGE YARD AT THE MANSION OF AMEN-RE, WASET

After taking their plain lunch of bean mash and bread — washed down with a shared jug of beer — stonecutters Webmut and Tefmin resumed their tedious chore in the shadow of the surrounding wall of Ipet Isut, the vast domain of the Hidden One, Lord Amen-Re. Their assignment — given them directly by the Fourth Prophet of the god — was to chisel out the many relief images and name-rings of the long-gone former Mistress of the Two Lands, Maatkare, from the surfaces of the massive stack of dismantled red-and-yellow-painted stone blocks that once had constituted the god's Holy of Holies. This structure had been taken down floodings before, to make room for a new, even larger Holy of Holies barque shrine commissioned by the elder one of the current Co-Lords of the Two Lands — who had begun ruling Kemet long before either callow mason was born.

The scores of large red-stone blocks quarried at Swenet had been piled up more-or-less neatly in a far corner of the divine precinct, somewhat beyond the clustered dwellings of the Amen-Re priests and acolytes and the storehouses of the god's vast treasury. Nearby were the dismantled white-stone blocks from an even-earlier Ipet Isut structure, taken down on the order of Maatkare when she had remodeled the innermost part of the divine mansion. The surfaces of these blocks still bore the jigsawed pigmented scenes of an ancient Lord of the Two Lands — whose image Webmut and Tefmin didn't recognize; nor could they read his name-rings, since both men were illiterate, of course.

For that matter, they were only able to tell which name-rings, and consequently the accompanying figures, they were to hack out of the assigned shrine blocks by referring to an ink sketch of the Maatkare Hatshepsut throne and personal names on a white-stone chip given them by the Fourth Prophet. Although she'd been female, the priest had instructed the masons that the ruler's accompanying figures would be those of a male. Webmut and Tefmin vaguely remembered stories from their childhoods that Maatkare had pretended to be a man during her long reign.

The shrine blocks were stacked three high in a roughly rectangular grouping some forty by sixty cubits, the back side of which was nearly against the precinct's surrounding wall. Cornice sections and roof and flooring slabs were piled off to one side, without any sense of order. No thought had been given by the dismantlers of the Maatkare/Menkheperre monument to position the loose wall blocks so that the relief-decorated surfaces were all facing out; many of these displayed just their unsmoothed, undecorated backsides.

In any case, only those tiers of blocks forming the three accessible sides of outer perimeter of the grouping were actually visible to the two stone masons. Although of varying sizes, the blocks were all too heavy to be lifted or maneuvered by only a couple of men, even had the indifferent pair been motivated to access every single decorated or inscribed surface. Thus just those images and names of Maatkare that were readily seen and easily reached would be attacked that and subsequent days by Webmut and Tefmin.

Consequently, because the shrine blocks were later reused as partial filler in a huge new pylon gateway erected to front Ipet Isut by Menkheperre Djehutymes's great-grandson — then were rediscovered some 3,300 floodings in the future by men dismantling that later monument — the stone masons' efforts to erase the memory of Mistress of the Two Lands Maatkare Hatshepsut were found to have been haphazard at best.

SEVERAL CROSSINGS OF RE LATER
MANSION FOR ETERNITY OF ASAR MAATKARE HATSHEPSUT
THE GREAT PLACE, WEST OF WASET

The work gang of some ten sweat-glistening naked laborers (removed loincloths tied over their noses and mouths) and four equally damp mortuary priests (hems of their long kilts pressed to their faces) squatted in tandem along the dusty short tunnel opening off a steep flight of a roughly hewn stairs leading from the funerary-furnishings-filled antechamber of the Mansion for Eternity of Asar Maatkare Hatshepsut. A variety of gear rested on the uneven passage floor around their feet. By dim flickering torchlight, two other naked laborers were taking down the stacked smallish stones which were blocking the doorway of the late Mistress of the Two Lands' resting chamber — which she had shared for many floodings with her father, Asar Akheperkare Djehutymes.

When the last blocking stones had been removed and stacked again to one side of the roughly squarish opening, the chief mortuary priest in the Great Place — named Amenkhau — ignited a torch from one of the many resin-saturated ones brought along by the laborers. Ducking his head, the sputtering new light thrust out at arm's length, he entered the pitch-black space. Amenkhau was followed in turn by the three other now-also-light-bearing priests.

The quartet carefully made their way to the far end of the rectangular rough chamber, the low ceiling of which was supported by a row of three rock-cut squarish pillars. Separated by the third pillar, but parallel to one another, were two, nearly identical massive red-stone flat-lidded sarcophagi. Centered at the foot end of the leftmost of these was a much smaller square, lidded box of the same material. A similarly sized painted-wood chest was in the same position by the other sarcophagus. The black openings of storage side-rooms were visible in the end- and one sidewall of the large chamber. The surfaces of the space seemingly had proven too irregular to plaster for decoration, so a wall veneer of smoothed white-stone blocks had been started, then apparently abandoned early in the process. The priests just could make out on these the faint red-and-black ink sketches of linear figures and glyphs from the relatively new *What is in the Underworld* funerary text.

After the priests' inspection of the situation, Amenkhau loudly called to the laborers waiting in the passageway, "Light the rest of the torches and come in here!"

One by one the nude men with heads swathed in loincloths entered the space, which became gradually more illuminated with each additional torch. At the instruction of the chief priest, eight of the sweaty laborers propped their firebrands against the walls and positioned themselves around the head end of the left-most of the great red-stone sarcophagi. Two of the men had brought along lengthy bronze crowbars, the chisel-shaped ends of which they inserted into the narrow join of the lid and basin. The weight of two men pressing down each bar raised the lid, just enough so that wooden wedges could be shoved into the resulting opened space. When the lid had thus been elevated all around, freeing it from the inset lip of the basin, the eight men began working in unison to move the heavy slab onto the basin's long top-edge nearest the rock-cut pillar.

As soon as a wide-enough space had been exposed, Amenkhau ordered, "Stop! Let me look inside."

He went up to the sarcophagus and held his torch so that the interior was dimly illuminated. Within the depths was a faint metallic glow from the gilded serene coffin-face of the occupant. The inlaid cobra on the brow of the *Nemes* head-covering and the base of a False Beard jutting from the chin told him this was indeed the coffin of a ruler of the Two Lands. But which one? The priest backed away from the box and scanned its long side with his torch, until the flickering light revealed the name-oval he was looking for: "Maatkare."

"This is her," Amenkhau announced to his fellow priests. "Continue," he ordered the laborers, who stepped up to the sarcophagus again.

And the shoving in cadenced unison resumed, until the heavy lid-slab teetered on the basin rim, then fell of its own weight with a loud thud to the chamber floor, resting angled against the sarcophagus's long side.

"All right, take it out," was the priest's next command.

Two of the naked men hoisted themselves and climbed over the rim into the basin and onto its contents, one at the head — squatting so that his genitals dangled over the coffin's face — and the other hunkered on the foot end. simultaneously, they each worked a thick length of sailor's rope under the two extremities of the gilded-and-inlaid human-shaped container. Once the ropes were in place, the pair climbed out of the stone box and were joined by the other six, two on each protruding length of ship-line. At Amenkhau's count, "One-two-three," the ropes where pulled, hand over hand, until the glimmering coffin rose into full view. With some difficulty two long wood planks were inserted under it, across the basin's void, so that the elevated container finally rested on them.

Pushing from the far side moved the coffin to the rim nearest the pillar. Next the laborers were able to manhandle it to the chamber floor. With a copper chisel, Amenkhau wedged loose the lid and two of the laborers lifted it off. Nested inside, as he fully expected, was a second, similarly gilded and inlaid coffin, the head-piece of this one being fashioned with a stylized blue-and-gold stripped wig, but the brow also adorned with a protective cobra and a False Beard protruding from the chin of the golden face. Leaning over the exposed inner coffin, Amenkhau reached down and pulled on the inlaid gilded-bronze serpent, working it until the protective image finally came free of the wig brow. Then he yanked forcibly on the False Beard, which was pulled out of the chin-notch with surprising ease.

One of the other mortuary priests stepped up, holding open a large leather bag, and the cobra-and-beard royal insignia were dropped inside. Next Amenkhau pulled from sheet-gold hands the gilded Crook and Flail scepters, which also went into the bag. Extracting a small mallet and bronze chisel out of a pouch hung from his kilt belt, the priest carefully chiseled two name-ovals of Maatkare from the gilded text band running down the coffin's front. These foil pieces were likewise added to the bag, its contents to be presented later to First Prophet of Amen-Re Menkheperresenub, as proof of an accomplished mission.

"Take this one out of the other," the lead priest now ordered. "It will be a lighter burden for the long haul back up to the surface."

While the laborers struggled to extract one coffin from the other, Amenkhau turned his attention to the much smaller rectangular red-stone box located by the sarcophagus' foot end. At the cleric's instruction, one of the head-swathed nude men single-handedly shoved off the lid, which fell to the floor, splitting across its middle. Inside the box, separated by a pair of intersecting wood partitions were four large veined-white-stone vases, each with a stopper fashioned as a small human head wearing the *Nemes* and sporting a small cobra on its brow. Although the laborer was clueless, the mortuary priest knew that each vessel contained a small bundle of one of Maatkare's preserved internal organs. Using his little mallet, Amenkhau proceeded to carefully smash the four miniature serpents into smithereens. After the laborer had lifted out the heavy vases, one at a time, the Maatkare name-ovals on their sides were likewise quickly but neatly chipped away. The priest left all Hatshepsut name-ovals intact, however.

By now the still-closed inner coffin rested at an angle across the rim of the outer coffin's basin. So by the flickering firebrands, Amenkhau proceeded to cut out the throne name wherever it appeared in texts on the coffin's gilded sides and foot end. These pieces of foil also were deposited in the leather "proof" bag.

On further orders from the chief cleric, two long carrying poles were produced from the resting chamber's entry-passage and the inner coffin was lashed to these by the ropes used to lift the nested coffins from the sarcophagus. The eight laborers who had done the latter, recovered their torches (some of which had sputtered out and were relighted) and now positioned themselves along the poles; at a command from Amenkhau, they raised the altered coffin and moved back towards the door opening onto the passageway. Two of the necropolis priests, also bearing firebrands, led the little procession.

"Go on ahead," Amenkhau called after them. "We'll follow on your heels."

When the priests and coffin-bearers had disappeared through the doorway, and the resting chamber was considerably darker, Amenkhau addressed the one remaining cleric and the four additional laborers.

"We shall return tomorrow to deal with the burial of Asar Akheperkare." He gestured towards the still-sealed other red-stone sarcophagus. His orders from the First Prophet of Amen-Re had been to remove the coffin of the long-dead Lord of the Two Lands and return it (along with the ruler's organ vases) to Asar Akheperkare's original Mansion for Eternity on the far side of the Great Place.

So he directed the four laborers to each pick up one of the white-stone vessels he had only just mutilated and to then follow the other light-bearing necropolis priest single-file out of the resting chamber and on up the long way out of this unbearably suffocating Underworld hole. He would follow with his own firebrand (which had gone out and so was rekindled from the other priest's now-sputtering torch).

This rear-guard contingent had reached the furniture-and funerary-goods-filled antechamber of the joint Maatkare/Akheperkare Mansion for Eternity, and was moving through the narrow aisle down the middle of the clutter, when the firebrand of the cleric in the lead did finally flicker and go out. Cursing, Amenkhau pushed his way past the four naked laborers with their arms full, to go relight the extinguished torch. Doing so, he shoved aside the man just ahead of him in line, who, startled, dropped his burden to the antechamber floor. The white-stone vase shattered into large pieces, the little human-head lid flying off. Apparently unaware of the accident, Amenkhau elbowed his way to the front of the line and rekindled the other cleric's torch. The laborer, meanwhile, crouched in the near blackness and gathered up the stopper and fragments of the vase, cutting fingers on the sharp edges. He didn't notice, or else ignored it as of no importance, the small linen-wrapped dark bundle that had been laying amid the vase debris. By the time Amenkhau had made his way back to his earlier last-in-line position, the laborer held the large fragments clutched to his bare chest. He turned slightly away as Amenkhau moved by, so that the chief in the Great Place would not see yet what had happened. As the little group began moving again, the cleric stepped on a lump in the dark and kicked it aside with his bare foot.

When somewhile later Amenkhau's heavy-breathing, perspiration-drenched little procession finally re-emerged through the roughly hewn entrance to the Mansion for Eternity, back into the bright light of Re's orb moving towards the western rims of the Great Place, the other necropolis priests and the coffin bearers were waiting, hunkered around their golden burden resting on the gravel-strewn inclined ground. The chief of the Great Place walked to the edge of the slope and looked down on the scene many cubits away.

A large hole gaped at the base of a ledge of rock outcropping. Heaped close by were the white-stone splinters and small boulders that other workmen of his necropolis team had only just finished removing from the entrance stairwell to the Mansion for Eternity of the long-gone Royal Nurse Asar In Sitre, who, it had been explained to Amenkhau, was the lifelong companion of the defunct Female Horus, Maatkare. Since they had been so close in this life, First Prophet of Amen-Re Menkheperresenub had reasoned that the latter — now officially demoted to status of Great Royal Wife Hatshepsut — should share her friend's Mansion for Eternity, once she'd been evicted from the regal one she'd had hewn for herself.

A young necropolis priest, whom Amenkhau had assigned the job of overseeing the reopening of the In Sitre burial place, spotted the senior cleric, so stood where he'd been squatting in the shade of the cliff with the naked workmen and waved at him.

"The stairwell is fully cleared and the door blocking completely taken down, sire," he shouted.

Amenkhau merely waved his acknowledgement, then turned attention back to his own crew. The bearers of the white-stone organ vases had placed these on the ground and, having unwound their perspiration-damp loincloths from their shaved heads, were using these to attempt to towel themselves dry. All but one of the laborers, that is, who — head still swathed and body glossy with sweat — squatted with his back to the chief cleric. When Amenkhau walked up and looked over the quivering man's shoulder, he saw that he was clutching to his bare chest what appeared to be broken large pieces of the vase he'd been carrying, the human-head stopper held in one grimy hand.

"What's this?" the priest demanded. When the man didn't respond, Amenkhau struck him forcefully on his wet shoulder with the back of his hand. "You've broken the vase," the priest loudly stated the obvious.

"It slipped from my arms — when you shoves past me after fire went out," the man cowered.

"Put the pieces down," Amenkhau ordered. When this had been done, he asked angrily, "Where is the bundle it held?"

The laborer only shrugged. The necropolis chief struck him again, this time with an open palm alongside his loincloth-swathed head.

With a torch-bearing Amenkhau in the lead, the eight coffin-bearers with their burden and three laborers carrying organ vases, plus another priest with a firebrand following, all made their way along the low-ceilinged, narrow, irregularly hewn tunnel leading to Asar In Sitre's resting chamber, passing a small black opening in the right wall along the way.

Amenkhau ordered the others to wait, then stepped down nearly a cubit into the smallish space. His firebrand revealed it was all but filled with grave furnishings, the nurse's oversized gilded coffin resting directly on the floor up against the wall opposite the opening from the entry passage. Inasmuch as there was only a rather small clear area in the middle of the chamber, the necropolis chief ordered the eight men carrying the coffin, to lower that and come on into the space, to move furniture and restack chests and boxes, so as to make enough room for the royal nurse's unexpected guest.

When the coffin of Great Royal Wife Hatshepsut was positioned alongside and parallel with the somewhat larger one of In Sitre, her three remaining organ-vases were lined up beside it, placed on the resting chamber's uneven floor. Amenkhau had been instructed by First Prophet Menkheperresenub to leave all of the personal possessions of Hatshepsut in her original Mansion for Eternity, so the necropolis chief supposed that the former "non-ruler" would now have to be satisfied forever after with the grave goods she'd herself no doubt sent to the Afterlife with Nurse In.

Their work there finally finished, Amenkhau and his crew exited the resting chamber, retraced their steps back up the entry passageway and climbed the awkward irregular cuttings that served as the crude stairwell. He ordered the entry to be walled up again, and the stairwell to be refilled with the rock debris removed earlier. He, of course, didn't standby watching this done. However, when he returned to the Great Place the next day — to recover and re-inter Asar Akheperkare — he would check to see that the joint Mansion for Eternity of Asars In Sitre/Hatshepsut had been properly hidden from sight and thus forgotten for all time.

313 FLOODINGS LATER, INUNDATION 14
REIGN OF NEFERKARE SETEPENRE RAMESES
THE GREAT PLACE, WEST OF WASET

Foreman Pedjetnuf went to see what apparently had been discovered by one of his rock-masons. The man, who had called his superior over, was on his bare knees and running fingers along one side edge of the wide cutting being leveled and hewn as the grand approach to the future Mansion for Eternity of Prince Montuhirkhopshef.

"What have you found, Khonsu is Well?" Pedjetnuf squatted beside the other man.

"It seems someone's been here 'fore us, chief. See, 'neath the small boulders we removed, where bedrock ends there and there, and 'tween them clear mason's cuttings, that's rock-chip fill. Perhaps an older Mansion for Eternity, do ya think?"

"Let's see, shall we? His Majesty Beautiful Soul of Re wouldn't want to have squatters on the very doorstep of his precious prince."

With his firebrand held at arm's length ahead of him — and the mason Khonsusenub close on his heels — Foreman Pedjetnuf moved down the rough, narrow, low passage. An unblocked doorway appeared on their right. The foreman in the Great Place thrust the torch into the opening and a small, irregular chamber — partially filled with large ceramic jars and amphorae and pitch-covered cases of preserved fowl and beef legs — was illuminated: clearly this was the storeroom of a Mansion of Eternity, but a rather humble one, it would seem.

The two pushed on, and immediately a larger, squarish opening or unblocked doorway could be seen through the gloom. When they reached the end of the passage, Pedjetnuf stuck his torch into the darkness, suddenly illuminating a smallish, low-ceilinged chamber filled with piled-up furniture and stacks of chests and boxes, which cast exaggerated shadows on the irregular walls of the space a cubit lower than the floor of the passageway. Directly opposite where the foreman and mason stood, shoulders touching, were two gilded coffins resting side by side, parallel to one another, directly on the floor. The one closest to the chamber wall was somewhat longer and higher than the other.

"Looks we got us a still-occupied Mansion for Eternity, chief," observed Khonsusenub. "And not no poor one neither, from looks a all the gold." He pointed towards the coffins.

Holding his firebrand high, so that the flames licked the rough ceiling, the foreman stepped down into a small empty space beneath the door opening. A very narrow aisle had been left between the piled and stacked grave furnishings, so that the two coffins were accessible. Pedjetnuf began to make his way towards the glitter of gold.

"Careful," he cautioned the mason, who had also stepped into the chamber.

In moments both men stood looking down at the pair of coffins.

"Looks like somebody's got at this one," said Khonsusenub, pointing at the oval holes in the gilding and where a false beard and protective cobra had been pulled away.

"There's still a name-oval there," Pedjetnuf pointed. He lowered the torch, bent closer to the coffin and read, "It says 'Noblest Woman Embracing Amen'." As chief in the Great Place, the foreman was passingly literate.

"Never heard a her, m'self." replied Khonsusenub. "But if she's a 'woman', how come there woulda been a beard there under the chin? And musta been somebody high 'n mighty, too, since that hole's where a royal snake once was."

"Seems I remember from scribal school that there was once a female who disguised herself as Lord of the Two Lands. When she died, though, her name was erased from royal records. Maybe that's what we've got here." He pointed at the empty ovals in the line of inscription running down the front of the gilded coffin. "Maybe this is her."

Work was brought to an abrupt halt on Prince Montuhirkhopshef's Mansion of Eternity. The boy had died after a prolonged illness, only a few short months before his father himself flew off to the stars; and he was interred in a makeshift spot cut into the floor of what was intended only as the long entry-passage in the tomb's original design.

The nearby humble Mansion for Eternity discovered some three floodings earlier by Foreman Pedjetnuf and the mason Khonsusenub was consequently filled in and quickly forgotten. Using the handy space as a storage and resting spot, the workmen hewing and the artists decorating the Montuhirkhopshef monument systematically — if secretly — thoroughly looted the tomb's double burial over time, carrying away all of the grave furnishings, with a few things of no real value being simply smashed to pieces. The two coffins were opened, of course, and the elderly-female mummies therein stripped of their wrappings in a rewarding search for jewelry and other gold. The coffins themselves were adzed of their gilding, most of one and the lid of the other subsequently hacked up for firewood — to keep off the chill of *Peret*. Emptied of their useless contents, the three white-stone organ vases were carried off for recycling.

Just prior to the sealing and reburying of the tomb, however, Foreman Pedjetnuf had entered the emptied space one final time. As his sign of respect for one of the Two Lands' ancient — if apparently discredited — rulers, he lifted from the floor the denuded corpse of the elderly female whom he had found occupying the coffin belonging to "Noblest Woman Embracing Amen." Because that container had been destroyed for the most part, Pedjetnuf laid the nearly weightless rigid remains in the surviving, if mostly denuded, basin of the large second coffin. He left that container's original aged occupant on the chamber floor, however. After thousands of floodings, it would be found still lying there by a young explorer from a faraway place.

SOME 105 FLOODINGS LATER
REIGN OF AKHEPERRE PSIBKHANIWT (PSUSENNES)
THE GREAT PLACE, WEST OF WASET

Chief Priest in the Great Place Djemutefankh and his dismantling party were surprised to find that the large antechamber of the Mansion for Eternity listed in the records as once jointly belonging to Asars Akheperkare Djehutymes and his daughter, Great Royal Wife Hatshepsut, was still filled with funerary furnishings and to all appearances undisturbed.

The resting chamber beyond — down a rough steep stairway and a short declining passage — proved to be a different matter, however. There they found two huge red-stone sarcophagi, both with their lids thrown off and standing empty. On the floor by one was an intact large human-form gilded-and-inlaid coffin, its lid resting upside down on the chamber floor. When, on Djemutefankh's order, two of the Great Place workers turned the latter over, it was discovered to have royal insignia — brow cobra, False Beard and crossed scepters — and a text band down the front containing the name-rings of "Mistress of the Two Lands Maatkare," "Daughter of Re Hatshepsut Embracing Amen." Similar identifications were noted within the texts covering the sides of the coffin basin. One of the sarcophagi also bore identical name-rings, as did a rectangular smaller red-stone box, empty, but with four equally sized compartments created by wooden partitions. The box's lid, broken in half, lay on the floor beside it.

Djemutefankh's inspection of the second sarcophagus revealed the name-ovals of "Lord of the Two Lands Akheperkare and "Son of Re Djehutymes." There was no sign of a coffin for him, however; nor any chest for his organ vessels. Other than the empty coffin, there didn't seem to be anything to salvage in the resting chamber. The chief priest ordered the basin and lid to be taken to the surface; they were a rich find, indeed, and would yield significant bullion for the First Prophet of Amen-Re Pinudjem's treasury, when stripped of their gilding and sheet-gold face-piece and hands.

On second thought, Djemutefankh commanded two of his workers to carry away the red-stone halves of the broken box lid; he had something personal in mind for their recycling.

It took the workforce of dismantlers many long trips to empty the antechamber of its clutter of rich grave goods. Much of the furniture — armchairs, straight chairs and beds especially — was either gilded all over or else generously embellished with gilding or even sheet gold. Many of the chests contained quantities of fine linen, very old to be sure, but well preserved and fully usable, nonetheless. A number of ritual vessels of solid gold and solid silver were a welcomed discovery; and even a quantity of inlaid-gold jewelry bearing the names of the royal owners was recovered. Additionally there was a dismantled chariot with Maatkare Hatshepsut's names and titles; this was veneered in sheet gold that would be melted down to a quantity of bullion for the First Prophet's treasury.

When most of the major pieces had been carried out, one of Djemutefankh's men brought him a small bundle wrapped in brown-linen bandaging. It had been found by him on the chamber floor, under the chariot. The chief priest immediately recognized it as a preserved organ, doubtless belonging to one of the Mansion of Eternity's missing occupants. There had been no organ vases in the resting chamber. Perhaps this particular bundle had somehow gotten separated from its vase, when those organ containers were carried off with the royal remains.

Looking about he spotted a smallish wooden, lidded coffer detailed with ivory still sitting on the antechamber floor. He picked this up and saw it was incised with the throne and personal names of Maatkare Hatshepsut. The bundle was really too large for the empty little box — probably some sort of jewelry container originally — but Chief Priest of the Great Place Djemutefankh forced it in nonetheless, even though the hinged lid wouldn't close consequently.

The cleric's thought was that this single preserved organ very probably was all that still existed of the legendary Female Horus. He thus developed a mental plan to anoint the bundle with unguent and to include the coffer containing it in the eventual caching of recovered royal corpses that were even then being assembled, restored if damaged and rewrapped in fresh bandagings. A token survival was better than none, he figured.

418 FLOODINGS EARLIER, YEAR 1
COREGENCY OF MENKHEPERRE/AKHEPERURE
THE RESIDENCE, WASET

Vizier of the South Rekhmire and First Prophet of Amen-Re Menkheperresenub stood together outside the Residence apartment of His Majesty Menkheperre, waiting to be admitted. The rail-thin chief bureaucrat wrinkled his long nose: the musk of the Medjay armed guards stationed on either side of the doorway's double cedar-wood panels was quite pronounced — and clearly annoying to him. The high-priest didn't seem to notice the distinctive odor, however, or at least seemed focused on rereading the scroll he held in front of him. After long moments, the doors were pulled inwards and His Majesty's recently named Chamberlain, Roy, stood in the opening.

"Lasting Manifestation of Re will see you, notables." The relatively young man bowed ever so slightly, then stepped aside, gesturing for the two to enter.

After the bureaucrat and priest walked side by side into the columned antechamber of the King's Apartment, Roy closed the doors and quickly moved around the pair, in order to lead them to the closed single-panel door to Menkheperre's bedchamber in the far wall. As they came up to that, harsh coughing could be heard from within. Roy waited until it subsided and ceased before knocking. A few moments passed and then a woman's voice commanded, "Enter." Roy opened the door and led the others in.

Seated — or more accurately, slouched — in a gilded armchair, Lord of the Two Lands Menkheperre held a faience goblet from which he had been drinking. Beside him, hand atop His Majesty's bare forearm resting on the chair arm, his own hand clutching a crumpled square of linen, was the Living Horus's recent bride, Royal Wife Nebtu. She was very much her husband's junior, enough so to have been his granddaughter, in fact. Her fresh features were rather commonplace — not so surprising, since she was of peasant stock, in fact hailed from Ipu, the same town as her new son-in-law's recent bride, although they'd not known one another there. Nebtu was attired informally and her glossy-black natural hair hung well past her shoulders.

Menkheperre had not summoned either his chief administrator or the First Prophet of the Hidden One to the Residence in perhaps three-dozen crossings of Re. Both men were silently stunned to see how much the Mighty Bull's appearance had altered, in even so short a time. The third Djehutymes's head was freshly shaven, shiny even, which added to the new gauntness of his face: the eyes seeming sunken into dark holes; the cheekbones chiseled ridges, skin tight; the prominent nose more beak-like than ever. And he'd lost body weight, as well. Small-boned, the Co-Son of Re had nonetheless always had a muscular physique bordering on stocky. Now his clavicles protruded and his breastbone was evident. And the slight paunch he'd developed in recent years was no longer apparent, even with him seated.

Chamberlain Roy bowed towards the royal couple and backed out of the bedchamber, closely the door behind himself. Menkheperre was the first to speak, his voice somewhat hoarse.

"Take a seat Vizier and First Prophet," he said, gesturing with the hand holding the goblet towards a pair of armchairs positioned opposite himself and Nebtu, on the other side of a large, low table, in the middle of which was a wide bronze bowl with floating water lilies. When they'd seated themselves, he asked, rhetorically, "So you have a report for Our Majesty?"

Rekhmire looked at Menkheperresenub beside him. The priest held out the rolled papyrus scroll he'd been reading earlier. Royal Wife Nebtu stood and took it from him, handing it to her husband, then resuming her seat.

"This is the official accounting, Your Majesty, as dictated by myself to the chief scribe in the Mansion of Lord Amen-Re. The Vizier of the South has also read it through and concurs with its completeness and accuracy." Menkheperresenub looked to the bureaucrat, who nodded his agreement.

"We shall read it at Our Person's leisure, but give us a verbal summary," the Lord of the Two lands commanded hoarsely, taking the roll from his wife and laying it on the table.

"Perhaps starting with the acts I was responsible for," replied the priest.

Menkheperre merely nodded assent and sipped from his goblet.

"Well," the First Prophet continued, "Firstly, the remodeling of the Holiest of Holy Places has been completed, the previously undecorated columns of the porticoes all now having images of Your Majesty and Lord Amen-Re. The new reliefs of the Third Terrace reflect Your Majesty celebrating the Beautiful Feast of the Valley festival. The many niches there now have depictions of Your Majesty's father and grandfather, Asars Akheperenre and Akheperkare. All of *her* images have been erased altogether, or else replaced by ones of those Lords of the Two Lands, and also by offering tables and fetish stands. Her names have likewise been carefully chiseled away throughout. Statues of her and the many lion-images with her features lining the processional way have been broken up and the pieces dumped into the quarry there, then buried as well. The great Asar statues fronting the portico of the Third Terrace, as well as the two colossal ones on the First Terrace, have been left intact, but her names erased from the inscriptions on them.

"Also on the West of Waset, the chapel commemorating the burial place of the Divine Eight, which Your Majesty raised in conjunction with her, has now been thoroughly altered to reflect your presence alone — along with that of Asars Akheperenre and Akheperkare, of course.

"At the Mansion of Lord Amen-Re itself, the apartments she raised around the Holy of Holies, at least the ones with her images, have been walled up — those same images and her names erased even so. The lower portions of her needles of the sun have been walled in, to the height of the roof of the forecourt where they stand. No effort was made to put up scaffolding so as to erase her images or names on the upper shafts of the needles, as these can only be seen from a distance, outside the Mansion, and therefore are not readable, in any case. Lastly, masons have even chiseled off her images and names from the dismantled blocks of the Holy of Holies chapel which Your Majesty caused to be taken down many floodings ago, and are now in storage at the far rear of the Mansion."

The First Prophet paused, then looked to Rekhmire.

"Why don't you continue, Vizier, as my throat has gone dry?"

"How rude of us to not offer refreshment," stated Royal Wife Nebtu. She loudly clapped her hands, and a male servant appeared from out nowhere. "Wine for our guests, and hurry."

He turned and disappeared the way he had come.

After a few moments, the shaven-headed thin bureaucrat picked up the narration in his somewhat shrill voice.

"Although it was not my responsibility, Your Majesty, I have been shown the proof of it by the First Prophet, that the Mansion for Eternity of Noblest Woman was entered by agents of the Great Place and her burial removed to the nearby Mansion for Eternity of the royal nurse, Asar Fish, Daughter of Re."

"What proof is that?" Menkheperre spoke for the first time since the accounting began.

"As instructed he should, the agent in charge of the transfer removed the royal serpent from the coffin brow and the beard from the chin and the royal scepters, as well. He brought these back to Waset, and also the gold-foil name ovals of 'True Soul of Re' he cut out of the coffin's inscriptions. He presented all these to the first prophet, who has shown them to me," Rekhmire explained.

"You still have these 'proofs', Lasting Manifestation of Re is Well?" His Majesty asked.

"Indeed, Mighty Bull."

"My Majesty should like to possess them for ourself," Menkheperre replied, and then suddenly began coughing again. When he'd recovered and sipped more wine, the Living Horus continued, "And what of our grandfather's reinterment?"

Rekhmire looked at Menkheperresenub, who did not make eye contract with him. So the Vizier answered the question.

"The transfer of Asar Akheperkare back to his original Mansion of Eternity was accomplished successfully, Your Majesty. He was placed in his two coffins within the red-stone sarcophagus already there. And his organ vases in their gilt-wooden chest were returned, too. Additionally, his grave furnishings and food offerings were renewed, as Your Majesty had instructed be done."

The male servant returned as the Vizier was concluding, and wine was presented to him and the First Prophet. Menkheperresenub accepted a refill. Nebtu was not drinking.

Next the bureaucrat launched into a rather tedious account of how the names of Maatkare Hatshepsut had been deleted from all documents in the House of Records at both Waset and Mennufer, so that everything therein now indicated that her acts alone or else jointly with him had been strictly Menkheperre Djehutymes's doing only. Any references to her as the Great Royal Wife of Akheperenre had been left intact, however.

Rekhmire droned on until interrupted by another fit of royal coughing. When the Lord of the Two Lands, Son of Re had recovered, he dismissed the Vizier and First Prophet. He'd heard enough. Fact made fiction was now fact again.

*   *   *

18

Menkheperre Djehutymes dreams: On hands and knees and stretching as far as possible over the water, he finally touches the floating small leather ball with the dead papyrus stalk he has pulled from the clump at one end of the garden pond. User, his pet hunting-hound pup paces excitedly by his side for the throw-thing to be retrieved. It'd been tossed with too much force and the gangly young canine had failed to catch it, so that it bounced off User's muzzle and into the pond. As he is maneuvering the half-submerged red sphere through the water-lily leaves and towards the water's edge, he hears a woman's loud shriek coming from inside his mother's and his apartment. He pays it no heed, as Itbet, the young woman who nurses him, often screams in excitement when she beats her mistress at the board game they are always playing.

He has just plucked the wet sphere from the water, when suddenly he is grabbed from behind by two large hands gripping him under his bare arms. He drops the ball — which bounces back into the water — as he is lifted off the grassy ground. This abrupt action so startles him, he lets out a boyish scream of his own. User yaps with glee, anticipating a new game.

He is turned around by his assailant, so that they are quite literally face to face. It is his big sister's tutor, the very tall man with the pointed long nose, whose name he can't remember just then. He continues screaming and begins pounding the man's wide chest with both small fists. And he kicks bare feet against the adult's hard thighs.

"We're going back inside, Prince," the tutor says matter of factly in his raspy high voice.

And so, moments later, he is carried — still kicking and pounding his fists, but bawling now — into the large chamber that serves as the living quarters for Horus-in-the-Nest and his mother, Royal Wife Iset. In addition to the latter and the wet-nurse, there are several other people in the space: many of the black-skinned men who guard the doors with spears and two persons he recognizes — his aunt,

Noblest Woman, and the boss of this place where he's always lived, the very fat Ruru.

The aunt grips his mother's shoulders from behind and keeps her from coming to him when she cries out, "Give me my son!"

He is being held tightly to the tutor's chest and being shushed by him, his bawling reduced now to sobs, the kicking having stopped. The aunt is telling his mother that he is now ruler of the Black Land and so will be taken away from her. She says more adult-talk things he doesn't understand, then tells the tutor to "bring the infant" and turns to leave the chamber. As the tall man — name remembered now: Brother of Mut — begins to follow, his mother imploringly reaches out her small hand, which triggers more screaming by him. He closes his tear-wet eyes as tight as possible.

The dreaming continues: When he opens them again, he is being held in the arms of a very different man, a skinny old one with a bald head, ugly with fat nose, big yellow teeth and such sour breath. He places his small palms against the man's bony chest and pushes back at arms' length — not so much to get a better view of him but because of the foul smell from his mouth. After the old man says "Greetings," a shiny large object with a dangling chain is held up. He reaches for it, grabbing the chain, but the old man attempts to pull it out of his grip, saying "Not yet." When he won't let go, someone is whispering in his ear, "Let him have it for now, Your Majesty. He'll give it back." It is his tutor, Brother of Amen, whom he likes a lot. So he releases the chain.

The old man carries him over to a rather large face made of shiny yellow stuff, which is higher even than his own head and that of the one who holds him. The eyes of the face are large and scary, and the nose is too, large, very large, that is. The big lips seem about to smile, though.

The old man says, "When I hand this back, Your Majesty will put it up to the statue's mouth, like this." He demonstrates what he wants him to do. "Understand?"

He nods that he does, and points at the statue face, saying loudly, "Nose!"

"Yes, a big one," replies the old man, holding up the shiny object and chain again. "Now touch this to the mouth."

He suddenly snatches the object away from the old man and — squealing "Nose!" — throws it as hard as he can directly at the face. It strikes the nose on its tip, then clatters to the floor.

Someone shouts from off behind him, "Hawk Beak, behave!" It is his aunt, grumpy old Noblest Woman.

The dreaming continues: The rhythmic drumming has suddenly stopped. Only moments before both he and Aunt Noblest Woman have noticed some commotion a ways ahead of them on the processional route to the Mansion of Lady Mut, now looming only a short distance off. It appears that the Sacred Ram of Amen-Re has fallen to the ground and its priestly handlers are gathered around it. The two of them have halted in their tracks, consequently.

Simultaneously, he and Noblest Woman turn completely around, to look back at the no-longer-moving elevated golden barque-shrine of Lord Hidden One, only some three-dozen cubits behind them.

"What's happening, Aunt? he asks. "Has the drumming stopped because something's wrong?" She is standing rigidly and does not respond. "What are we supposed to do now?" he asks.

Suddenly his nose itches and he reflexively tries to rub it with the back of his hand holding the walking staff that is part of his regalia that day. In doing so he lets go of the golden rod, and it falls clanking to the stone pavement. Impulsively he squats down to retrieve the staff and at the same moment feels a sharp blow to the back of his *Khepresh* helmet-crown. Already off balance, the force of this sends him pitching forward, his bare knees striking the processional avenue with painful force.

"Hawk Beak!" Noblest Woman cries out, bending sideways towards him.

He has turned his head to look up at her, and so sees the arrow graze the top of her left shoulder, shattering when it smacks into the paving stones four cubits or so away. By the time his coregent has also sunk to her knees, her superficial wound is bleeding profusely. Attempting to assist her in sitting, he is also bloodied. In no time at all, the struck-down Lord and Mistress of the Two Lands are surrounded by a forest of black legs belonging to their Medjay bodyguards.

Menkheperre's eyes blink open. His scribe, Tjaneni, is standing across the chamber, his back to the bed. He is whispering with the King's Physician and King's Son Prince-Count Amenemhat. Menkheperre succumbs to sleep again.

The dreaming continues: They have decided to forego the total blue body-paint, he and Brother of Mut, as impractical, and they've opted instead to merely paint his face, shaven head, neck and shoulders bright blue. In her drugged state, and dim brazier light of her chamber, that is all that Beauty of Re is likely to see, in any case. The sheet-gold headband with the twin gilded ostrich feathers stuck into it behind his ears will fully convey who he is supposed to be. And the idea of him chewing on a lump of myrrh, so that he would have the breath of the god, is a stroke of genius on Brother of Mut's part.

The Chief Steward has, as always, managed all of the details. Beauty of Re's wine has been drugged by him and the Medjays guarding her apartment door dismissed for the event — rather, given official orders by the Medjay captain of the Residence to abandon their post until dawn. It is certain that the young God's Wife shared her evening wine with her handmaiden, and so the girl will also be drugged, with any luck completely passed out.

He now stands stark naked outside the double doors to his half-sister's sleeping space, Brother of Mut kneeling in front of him. As so often before, the mouth of the older man is impaled on the pretending Amen-Min's now-rigid member. After several more deep-throating strokes, he pulls off, rests his kilted buttocks on his heels and looks up at his co-conspirator.

"That should do it, Your Majesty." The Chief Steward smiles and winks. "Now go in and pay your 'wife' a visit like none other she's ever imagined having from the Divine One." Brother of Mut stands, a whole head taller than the tumid nude teenager in face paint, gold band and artificial feathers.

So, he quietly pulls open the door panels and slips into the darkened bed-chamber, closing them behind himself. In the center of the space, raised on a low dais, is the God's Wife's bed, with her on it, dimly illuminated by a nearby low-burning brazier. As supposed the handmaiden seems sound asleep on her cot well back in the room's colonnade. Removing the small myrrh lump from his mouth and tossing this into the dark, he approaches the apparently sleeping figure on the bed.

Bed sheet tangled about her feet, fully nude Beauty of Re sprawls on her back, headrest supporting her neck, her slender legs invitingly spread wide, as if in anticipation of what is to transpire. He stands for several long moments at the bed's foot end, stroking his Min to keep it rigid. He can't help but notice that her pubes are shaved, as is required for her cultic role, which makes her cleft all the more exposed — and inviting. Then he comes alongside the bed and carefully climbs onto it, lowering his naked flesh against that of his half-sister, guiding his Min into her moist warmth. She does not stir until he begins his thrusting, exactly as instructed by Brother of Mut. She groans pleasurably and her kohl-rimmed eyes slowly open only some three hand-spans from his own. He has never been this close to her face before. She looks nothing like her mother, the Coregent: her features are less sharp, her nose definitely smaller, her lips far fuller.

At first Beauty of Re seems disoriented, then seemingly realizes that she is, in fact, not dreaming any longer. She reaches behind her neck and pushes the headrest off the bed. Lying flat now, her cool small hands grip his narrow, hard buttocks, long fingernails pressing into his heated flesh; and the God's Wife begins pushing upwards with her lower body, forcing his thrusts even deeper.

Neither Hand of the God nor make-believe fertility deity speak. And it is over far sooner than he had thought it might be, his release coming in several quick spasms of pleasure. He might linger within her gripping warmth, but his arms have begun to grow numb from supporting his own torso; so he pushes away and raises to his knees, extracting his still-turgid Min as he does so. Swinging off the bed, he stands upright, turns and, with a quick look over his shoulder, leaves the chamber, going to where Brother of Min is waiting to hand him his kilt and escort him back to the King's Apartment. In some 270 crossings of Re, he will be a father.

A fit of coughing brings Menkheperre to waking consciousness again. Tjaneni and the physician administer wine, while Amenemhat stands silently at the foot of the bed; the hacking and spewing subside.

He is soon dreaming once more: The stationary grazing herd of monsters probably numbers hundreds of the bizarre hairless gray creatures, most standing at least five or six cubits high on long legs like dom-palm trunks, with massive serpent-like snouts between very lengthy, thick tusks of what appears to be ivory, like that of river horses, except very far larger. A few infant beasts can be seen within the dense forest of legs.

As the advance guard of a dozen elite spearmen approach the herd in low-crouching positions — bows in hand, he and the officers following similarly on foot at a distance of several dozen cubits — one of the larger of the behemoths, probably a male, suddenly moves away from the herd in the direction of the now-halted spearmen. It is joined almost immediately by two others, their long snouts raised high; all three begin an unearthly bellowing. Without any command being given — at least none that he hears — one of the spearmen at the far end of the line of the advance guard stands and hurls his bronze-tipped spear with such force that it deeply penetrates the leathery barreled side of the beast nearest him.

The huge creature staggers, then recovers its balance and even rears on its log-like rear legs, thrashing the air and bellowing. Immediately the other spearmen stand erect and hurl their weapons. Most find their marks, though three or four merely bounce off the wide foreheads. The legs of the first beast wounded crumple and it crashes to the ground, dead. The other outer one also rears and then falls over sideways, driving shafts penetrating its side deep into the swollen body. Although wounded by two spears dangling from its snout, the still-standing central creature now charges the line of upright spearmen.

At once he and the chariotry officers, and the archers behind them, are also fully upright and drawing their bows. Two score of arrows fly in whirring unison towards the oncoming beast, some bouncing off its bony forehead, the others penetrating bulged leathery sides, forelegs and bloody snout (from which the dangling spears have fallen away). But it charges on, only stopping when it is but a few cubits in front of him, now standing ground in a wide stance, a second arrow ready to let fly. As it rears, massive forelegs thrashing the air, hot blood from the beast's wounded snout sprays his face and corseleted torso. He looses the arrow, which finds its mark deep in the exposed wide chest. The raised legs hit the ground with a loud thud, just missing him, and he is now drawing his dagger, a puny defense against such a violent huge creature. Even before that blade is fully in hand, however, the blood-gushing snake-snout — far thicker than any man's arm — swings sideways and strikes him a blow on the shoulder, so that he goes flying several cubits through the air, crashing to the ground with such force that his *Khepresh* flies off. Which is all he remembers.

Dreaming still: When he opens his eyes, he wears full formal regalia and is enthroned on a high dais under a painted-wood canopy, with his young Crown-Prince seated in a child-sized armchair at his side. Under the midday sun, arrayed in row upon row before the dais are gift-offerings of great quantity and variety; and beyond these, in many ranks, are colorfully attired delegations of tribute bearers from the wretched land of Wawat to the south of Kemet, from exotic far-away Punt and from the distant island of Kheftiu in the Great Green, as well as the large and diverse delegation from the large vile land of Retenu to Kemet's north. First Prophet of Amen-Re Menkheperresenub stands at the foot of the stairs leading up to the dais, his shaven head bowed. Realizing that the priest wishes to address him, he commands:
"Speak up, First Prophet."

In a loud voice the cleric explains that leader of the Retenu delegation wishes to approach His Majesty and present a personal message from the Great Wife of Kadesh. This would be Princess Nahti, formerly his mother-in-law — her three daughters, his hostage wives, having been foully murdered in the Residence harim at Mennufer only some two floodings before. Nahti and her sister-wives had subsequently been sent home to Kadesh.

He replies that the delegate should come forward. The First Prophet returns to where the youth is standing in the aisle bisecting the piled tribute, many cubits in front of the dais. When the priest gives the command, the fully bearded, colorfully robed young man of Retenu comes to the foot of the stairs and, without bowing as is convention for foreigners, steps out of his sandals and begins addressing the Living Horus in a very garbled attempt at the language of Kemet — which His Majesty understands only very little of.

Then, suddenly, the speaker is bounding up the stairs two at a time, pulling off his fake bushy beard and so revealing himself to be none other than Princess Nahti herself — at the same time drawing a large dagger from out of the front of her robe. Once on the dais, she literally throws herself at him, thrashing downwards with the bronze blade. He raises the Crook and Flail scepters crossed on his chest, warding off the blow; but the impact of Nahti's stout body causes the throne to topple over backwards with both its occupant and his assailant; and the Lord of the Two Lands' Double Crown smacks the wooden floor with such force that all goes black.

Dreaming still: He opens his eyes and finds himself standing within the shadowed thickness of a high, wide, deep stone gateway, but one without any inscriptions that he can see in the dimness. Nor is there a gate or any door to bar his way. So, barefooted, he walks on through and into the open and suddenly very bright daylight, the cloudless sky overhead a brilliant blue-faience hue. It appears that he is in an immense lush park of closely clipped lawns and paved pathways wending this way and that through dom-palm, acacia and tamarisk groves, which are interspersed with free-form wide ponds filled with thick papyrus stands and remarkably large water lilies in bloom. There are also varied sorts of colorful blossoms in many neat flowerbeds. Butterflies hover and dart among the blooms.

In addition to all this flora, the place is populated with fauna of the sort he has collected for his personal menageries at the northern and southern Residences: clusters of horned small antelopes and gazelles, young ostriches, free-roaming chattering monkeys and baboons grooming one another; there is also a great variety of birds, such as ibises, cranes and storks wading in the ponds and any number of brilliantly plumed songbirds flit about in the trees or else swoop about on wing.

Strolling along the path he has chosen, the beasts and birds pay him no heed, although an occasional gazelle or antelope will raise its head from grazing and stare unblinking as he passes by. He has gone some distance into this arcadia, when up ahead he spots what appears to be a sizeable garden pavilion, although not one like even he's ever seen before, since it quite glows in the sunlight and seems to be gilded in its entirely. As he draws nearer, he determines that it is being occupied by several persons, half a dozen or so, both men and women, seated in fully gilded armchairs casually arranged in a circle at the pavilion's center. None seem to notice his approach, as they are engaged in conversation with one another. That is, until he is a couple of dozen cubits off, when one of the bewigged women facing his way spots him and raises a slender arm in waved greeting.

"Born of Djehuty!" she calls out. "We thought you'd be arriving soon." The speaker is none other than his Great Royal Wife, Sitiah, whom he's not seen in a very long while. She seems to have not aged, however.

All seated on the golden pavilion look his way, those with their backs to him twisting in their chairs — and he recognizes everyone of them. Next to Sitiah is their teenage son, his namesake and his one-time heir, Crown-Prince Menkheperre — looking much as he supposes he also must have at the same age. To the youth's left, side by side, sit the Kadesh sisters, his Royal Wives, exotic Menhet, Merwi and Merti. Next to the latter, fully turned now in her gilded armchair, is none other than his own mother, Royal Wife Iset, petite and childlike as always in her oversized, old-fashioned wig and over-kohled eyes. And looking back at him as well, smiling crookedly, is someone he scarcely remembers but now immediately knows as the man who gave him life so very long ago, Lord of the Two Lands and the Son of Re, Akheperenre Djehutymes — an inlaid-gold cobra at the front of his out-of-style cap-wig testifying to that status.

Sitiah stands and holds out her arms as if to embrace him.

"Come, come, Born of Djehuty! You must be very much thirsting after your journey here. Join us in the cool shade for some soothing refreshment and give us the news we all so long for."

As he steps up onto the pavilion — even its floor appears gilded — he can see that everyone there holds a gold liliform goblet, and a golden table in their midst supports another, unused goblet and a gold-inlaid silver ewer. There also is one unoccupied armchair — wholly gilded, of course — between Sitiah's and where his father is seated. After lightly embracing his Great Royal Wife, he takes his place there, seating himself as she is indicating he should.

His mother leans forward and pours wine from the ewer into the goblet on the table, then says, "Please, Born of Djehuty, refresh yourself."

He lifts the goblet and sips the very best vintage he can remember ever tasting.

"You must have enjoyed the Horus Throne, our son, as you occupied it for so long." It is the other Djehutymes speaking.

"Fifty-two floodings," he replies, "although twenty of those sharing it with your wife, our father. On our own only a little more than enough to have qualified for a Renewal Festival."

"And how many of those did you finally celebrate, Lasting Manifestation of Re?" Royal Wife Iset asks.

"Eight, we believe, Mother." He counts on his fingers. "Yes, it was eight all totaled. One every three floodings after the first at Inundation 30."

"He raised an amazing venue for that, in the precinct of the Mansion of the Hidden One, I remember." It was Crown-Prince Menkheperre speaking. He sips from his goblet, as if remembering to be seen and not heard.

"Born of Djehuty made very many amazing buildings, even in my time," adds Great Royal Wife Sitiah. "Like the new Barque Shrine for the Holy of Holies at Lord Amen-Re's mansion," she continues, "replacing the one built by *her*, glorifying herself and her false reign."

"We completed much that she'd left unfinished," he inserts, "including that; but then decided the Hidden One deserved better, so did such for him."

Suddenly Royal Wife Menhet speaks up. "Does our mother live still, do you know, Born of Djehuty?" Her accent seems less pronounced than he remembers.

"We really doubt it, wife, as she would be very ancient by now, wouldn't she?" he replies, then continues, looking at the princesses of Kadesh, "You three probably don't know it, but Princess Nahti sent an agent to publicly slay us, at an annual presentation of tribute from all the places bowing to the Black Land and Our Majesty. He failed, obviously. We later sent our own agent to pay her in kind. He never returned to the Black Land, so may have failed his mission. We never heard that she'd been slain, however."

"Who governs Kadesh today?" asks Royal Wife Merwi, as she pours more wine for herself. Her accent is also not as thick as he remembers.

"A prince named Kelijti, as we recall. He's peaceful."

"Youngest son of our father's youngest brother," comments Royal Wife Merti. "So a cousin we really never knew before leaving our city." She, too, has only very little accent. "Our brother, Meru, he would've been prince of Kadesh, if not for the serpent accident, which our mother she blamed on you, my husband."

He shrugs, looking directly at Menhet. "Our little daughter died in the same accident, as if we would have caused that. And Our Person was on campaign, at the time, as we recall."

"All of your other daughters by us, they lived, are living now?" asks Menhet.

"Two succumbed to fever, but the others still reside in the harim of the Mennufer Residence, the last we knew. We spend all our time at Waset these latter days." He pauses, then smiles. "Or did."

"None have married, then?" It is Merwi speaking.

"We would've that our Horus-in-the-Nest had chosen one of the princesses for his chief spouse," he responds, "but Amen is Pleased protested that none were to his liking. So, he selected instead a commoner bride, who became Great Royal Wife."

"You speak in the past tense, son," inserts Akheperenre. "Horuses-in-the-Nest do not have Great Royal Wives, just wives." His father sips his wine.

"Ah, yes, but we made Amen is Pleased fully Horus, nearly two floodings ago."

"As your Coregent?" Royal Wife Iset asks incredulously, then adds, "I thought you'd had your fill of sharing your throne?"

"We thought it prudent to offer him his own throne before he pushed us off of ours, Mother." He puts his goblet on the table, rests his elbows on the chair arms and tents fingers on his bare chest. "Great Manifestation of Re — the throne name he took — is something of a hothead, like his mother." He turns to the princesses of Kadesh again, "Whom we banished to Swenet, for your sakes, although she still draws breath, as far as we know. Knew," he corrects himself. "It was our Coregent-son who insisted on eliminating all evidence of the reign of our former Coregent-aunt from the official record. Now there never was a True Soul of Re, only a Great Royal Wife Noblest Woman Embracing Amen."

Akheperenre chuckles. "She'll be most displeased, angry even, when she learns of that, you can be certain. You've then not seen her yet, here that is?"

"We've only but arrived, Father, so no. And just where *is it* that we all are, now?"

"The Gardens of Asar and Aset, of course," his mother replies.

"So there really *is* such a place. When Noblest Woman came awake for a few moments before her *ba* flew, she spoke of having been there; but we thought she was delirious and only imagining it, as the sacred texts have nothing to say about such gardens in the West. So it seems she was right, and Our Person was not."

Prince-Count Amenemhat sat up and leaned forward. He had been dozing in an armchair positioned beside the bed of his father, Menkheperre Djehutymes. Opposite, on the other side of the bed, also seated, was Royal Wife Nebtu, who likewise had been dozing. She, too, sat up.

"Wh...at d...did you s...say, Your M...Majesty?" the prince asked of the prone man, whose eyes were still closed, bare thin arms resting at his side, atop the bedsheet.

"That she was...right and we were...not" he replied, then opened his eyes, which seemed sunken into his skull.

"About what, dearest Born of Djehuty?" asked Nebtu. "And who is 'she'?"

He slowly turned his head on the cushions supporting his neck, to look towards his questioner with eyes that seemed unseeing. King's Scribe Tjaneni, who had been across the bedchamber in a whispered conversation with the King's Physician, came up to the foot of the bed.

"Noblest Woman said...just...before her *ba* flew...that she'd been to the Gardens of Asar and Aset, and we didn't...believe her then, since we'd...never heard of such...a place." Menkheperre's voice was little more than a hoarse whisper. He turned his head to look at Prince-Count Amenemhat. "But we've just... been there ourself and it...is very real."

"What is there?" asked Nebtu, taking her husband's cold hand in her warm one.

He turned back to her, but with his eyes closed, as if attempting to revisualize what he'd just been seeing.

"A beautiful...very...large, lush garden with...all sorts of gentle...beasts and birds. In it...a golden pavilion, where...sitting together...were some whose *bas* had... flown long ago." He paused, then resumed. "Our mother and father...our wives and...our son...who'd been Horus-...in-the-...Nest."

"Your Majesty spoke with them?" It was Tjaneni who asked.

There was no response. Menkheperre's eyes were still closed. Then, "Yes, a...conversation with...many questions...from them." Another pause. "It seems...the only news...they have is...from those who...just arrive."

"Was Noblest Woman there, Your Majesty?" Tjaneni again.

Another pause.

"Apparently. Our father, Great Form...of Re, implied as...much. Said... she'd be...angered to learn...that we erased...all record of True Soul of Re's....reign."

"As she...s...s...should be," remarked Amenemhat. "Y...our M...M... Majesty should ne...ver have b...b...been sway...ed to do th...that by our h...alf-b...brother, is my per...sonal op...op...inion."

Menkheperre parted his thin lips as if to reply, but no sound came forth.

"Born of Djehuty?" Nebtu squeezed her husband's hand, then looked towards the physician.

The bald old man moved to the head of the bed, then bent to put his ear next to the Lord of the Two Lands' gaping mouth. After a few moments, he laid his bony hand on Menkheperre's barreled bare chest. After another pause, he stood upright again.

"The *ba* of the Mighty Bull, smiter of vile Retenu, has flown to ride the Barque of Re," the King's Physician announced solemnly.

Or at least returned to the "Gardens of Asar and Aset," thought Tjaneni, wiping at his eyes.

FIVE CROSSINGS OF RE LATER
A DESERT CANYON OUTSIDE THE NORTHERN CAPITAL, MENNUFER

Lord of the Two Lands Akheperure, Son of Re Amenhotep and Ruler of Iunu — Heqaiunu — squatted behind a large boulder, only his shaven bare head not concealed by it. Others of his party were likewise crouched behind their own boulders, or else were far enough back down the slope to not be visible to the pride of half-a-dozen adult lions and two cubs intent on a feast of antelope in the shallow canyon below the hunters' elevated vantage point. It would be their last meal. The desert breeze was blowing so that the tawny felines were unaware of the close-by humans' presence.

It was customary for Lords of the Two Lands — or at least those so inclined — to pursue fleeing lions, one at a time, from a moving chariot; but eighteen-floodings-old Living Horus Akheperure preferred a more dangerous sport. With his hunting party of young notables from court, he would set up a temporary desert encampment and then send out scouts, at least one of whom eventually would discover a lion pride and return to report its location to His Majesty. In their chariots Akheperure and his cohorts would travel close to where the group of great felines had been last spotted by the scout. Abandoning their chariots to drivers and groomsmen, His Majesty and the others would begin to scour the rugged landscape on foot, seeking the pride at its rest — or, as this particular day, at its feeding activity. Then, they would burst from hiding and confront the unsuspecting ferocious beasts, slaying them at close quarters — by arrow and spear — to the very last one; almost never did any manage to escape.

Akheperure looked over to where his "milk brother" Qenamen crouched behind his boulder. Like his friend from childhood, the just-older youth was bare-headed and attired in only a simple short kilt and leather sandals, a sheathed dagger attached to his narrow belt. He gripped a short bronze-tipped spear. Unlike the Co-Lord of the Two Lands, archery was not Qenamen's forté. His throwing arm was fairly accurate, however.

"Psst. Brother," Akheperure whispered loudly, to get Qenamen's attention.

When the other youth looked towards him, he continued, "On count of three, we shall all stand and go around these stones into the open. The beasts will see us then and perhaps the single male will charge. He is Our Person's today. Understand?"

Qenamen nodded that he did. The eight other crouching young hunters nodded affirmatively, as well. Following the ruler's example, they all notched arrows to their strung Asiatic-style composite bows.

"So, then," Akheperure responded in full voice. "One. Two. Three."

All ten raised up simultaneously. The others waited for the Co-Living Horus to move from behind his hiding place, then followed suit.

One of the feeding lionesses raised her head when she sensed the sudden presence of the humans, then stood and roared a warning. The other adult felines likewise were quickly on all fours and facing towards the graveled hillside down which the young hunters were approaching the pride. Oblivious, both cubs continued tugging on a still-attached haunch. Shaking his thick mane, the large male advanced a few steps and hissed loudly, then roared even more ferociously than the lioness had.

The humans were now some sixty cubits off and still moving towards the alerted pride, the steep slope's deep, loose gravel making their footing a little uncertain, however. Qenamen actually stepped out of one sandal, slipped and lost his balance, then quickly recovered. A few cubits from the floor of the canyon, His Majesty halted and raised his free arm, signalling the others to do likewise. The lions were now only forty or so cubits away, the adults grouped in a ragged line and the cubs — having abandoned their haunch — standing a ways back, on the far side of the carcass. The male and two of the lionesses roared simultaneously.

As a challenge to the male, Akheperure raised both of his muscular arms rigidly over his head — bow and notched arrow, too — and mimicked the roar at the top of his voice. Before he could lower the weapon, however, the maned beast began bounding towards him. It was less than two-dozen cubits off by the time His Majesty had the bow drawn back to its full extent. Not able to sight properly, he let his arrow fly at the charging huge feline only when it was actually leaping through the air at him. The slender shaft found its mark deep in the shaggy chest, and the animal was already dead when its full weight slammed into Akheperure, knocking him backwards onto the slope.

The lionesses now charged, as well. And a rain of arrows brought down all but one of the beasts. She came on, abruptly halted and was about to pounce on the prone — and unconscious — Lord of the Two Lands, when Qenamen's thrust spear penetrated two hand spans into her neck, killing her instantly.

S lung on poles which the groomsmen had brought along for that purpose, the slain adult lions were carried back to His Majesty's temporary desert encampment. They were even now being skinned on the spot and the fresh pelts would be delivered to a Mennufer tannery, to be made into rugs for the Residence there. The two cubs — only a few months old — had been captured and secured with ropes, to be taken to the northern capital's Royal Menagerie. A couple of the young hunters had been bitten in the process of overcoming the cubs, but not seriously so.

Lord of the Two Lands Akheperure, however, sat on a folding camp-stool in front of his tent, submitting to his cuts and scratches being cleansed by Qenamen using a cloth dampened with water from a canteen. He had suffered more damage from the sharp gravel he'd been violently slammed backwards onto than from the heavy blow of the dead lion itself — although his ears were still ringing and his head ached worse than following a long night of heavy reveling. He had not yet been informed that his closest companion since their harim-nursery days together had almost certainly saved his life — by dispatching the about-to-spring lioness. When later told this, he would reward Qenamen with the position of King's Great Chamberlain of both the Mennufer and Waset Residences. A formality, really.

His Majesty was being helped on by him with a clean tunic, when, in a flurry of dust, a chariot came rapidly into the encampment and was reined to a halt. The driver and his passenger wore the royal livery — green headbands and waist sashes. The latter man jumped to the ground and strode barefooted through the startled hunting party and attendants, parting to make way for his quick advance. He came directly up to within a few cubits of the Living Horus and bowed deeply, his head down.

"Speak your piece, messenger," Akheperure directed, adjusting the tunic and wincing at the slight foreward movement of his own head.

The man straightened to a rigid stance, pushing his bare shoulders back. "News has arrived from the Waset Residence, Your Majesty."

"And?"

"And it is sad news for the Black Land, unfortunately." He paused, staring into the space above Akheperure's uncovered shaven head. Then he cleared his throat and continued his rehearsed speech. "The Mighty Bull, Co-Lord of the Two Lands, Lasting Manifestation of Re, Co-Son of Re, Born of Djehuty has flown up to the stars!"

"Our father has died?" His Majesty rubbed a calloused palm over his shaven pate, realizing that he was not wearing the royal cobra. "How did this happen? Naturally? Or otherwise?"

"During His Majesty's sleep or, more accurately, while in a deep silence. The messenger from Waset reported that, before the royal *ba* finally flew, the still-Living Horus had been slipping in and out of awareness during many crossings of Lord Re."

Akheperure looked towards Qenamen. "His vigor had been declining for some long while. The thinness. The coughing. He was very *old*, after all. Not many still draw breath who were alive when our father became Lord of the Two Lands."

He looked back to the messenger still at attention. "Return to the Residence and convey to the bad-tidings bearer from Waset that Our Person will be sailing up south as soon as is feasible — not that there is any real need now for rushing, certainly. We are confident that our officious half-brother, Amen at the Head, is already overseeing arrangements for Lasting Manifestation of Re's grand funeral." With a wave of his hand, he abruptly dismissed the messenger.

Akheperure stood up, wincing again. He looked again to Qenamen.

"Fetch our wig and browband with the Lady of Wadjet." He pointed to his tent. "Now that we are sole Lord of the Two Lands, Our Person must fully look the part when we ride into Mennufer."

SIXTY-FIVE CROSSINGS OF RE LATER, INUNDATION 1
SOLE REIGN OF AKHEPERURE AMENHOTEP-HEQAIUNU
MEMORIAL MANSION OF OSIRIS MENKHEPERRE DJEHUTYMES, WEST OF WASET

Qenamen held wide the door-flap so that His Majesty Akheperure could pass out of the midday sun into the Great Pavilion of Anpu, which had been erected temporarily in the forecourt of his late father/Coregent's memorial mansion, Henket Ankh, on the west bank of Waset. The air inside was heavy with incense, masking earlier odors. For some sixty-five crossings of Re, the mortuary priests had labored there to prepare the body of the great conqueror for his eternal existence among the stars. As soon as he had "flown," on the orders of Prince-Count Amenemhat, this great tent had been taken out of storage and hastily installed. Then the frail husk that had been Menkheperre Djehutymes — face and head freshly shaven by Tjaneni —had been brought there with much pomp from the Waset Residence, ferried over The River on the royal barque and borne across the flood plain high on the shoulders of his Medjay bodyguards, to begin the lengthy process of "beautification."

Following certain surgical procedures — which Lord of the Two Lands Akheperure hadn't chosen to have described to him — Asar Menkheperre Djehutymes had been laid prone, arms folded over his chest, on several blocks of white stone and was then quite literally buried under great quantities of drying salts. Over the course of fifty-five crossings of Re, these had been changed several times. Once thoroughly liberated of all moisture, the desiccated royal cadaver had been rubbed all over with aromatic oils and the wrapping of the limbs, torso and head with long strips of the finest linen begun.

Although the living Menkheperre had worn jewelry on only the most-formal of occasions, he might chose to adorn himself more ornately in the Afterlife among the gods, so numerous bracelets and rings were placed on his withered arms and each gold-sheathed finger; and sheet-gold sandals protected his feet (which had gone unshod more often than not in life), the toes also individually encased with gold stalls. An inlaid-gold sporran apron, ritual bull tail and girdle-belt, and several broad collars and pectorals were appropriately positioned within the wrappings, as were scores of magical amulets, including an obligatory heart scarab of solid gold, as well as an inlaid-gold cobra insignia which had been worn with His Late Majesty's wigs. A dagger he had always carried was positioned in its sheath along one hip. And a set of the Crook and Flail scepters were crossed over the waist.

Once the elaborate adorning and wrapping had been completed, the entire bundle was enclosed in a shroud of sheer linen dyed red and the whole bound by two longitudinal and three transverse inlaid-gold bands. Two hands of burnished gold, holding a second set of crossed Crook and Flail scepters, were sewn onto the breast; and over the head was placed a sheet-gold mask with Asar Menkheperre's idealized serene features, the royal serpent on the brow of the *Nemes*, a False Beard pendant from the chin. Thus, His Late Majesty was laid out on a high gilded-and-inlaid funerary bed, its frame fashioned as two side-by-side spotted Hathor cows with sun disks between their long horns.

And this is what Lord of the Two Lands Akheperure, Son of Re Amenhotep Heqaiunu beheld at its center when he walked into the dimly lighted, smoky Great Pavilion of Anpu, the cow-bier supporting his cocooned late father and Coregent, a tall, low-burning brazier at each corner. Besides the shaven-headed mortuary priests — one wearing a polychrome-and-gilt wooden mask with the jackal features of Lord Anpu — several other persons were visible in the tent's shadows. Among them was First Prophet of Amen-Re Menkheperresenub, that god's other three prophets, Vizier of the South Rekhmire, Vizier of the North Penab, Prince-Count Amenemhat and King's Scribe Tjaneni — the latter accompanied by his teenaged son, Amennahkt, whom His Majesty had recently appointed as his own King's Scribe. Additionally, there were the generals of the Armies of Northern and Southern Kemet, admirals of the fleets of The River and the Great Green, and all the members of the High Councils of the North and South. Akheperure's Great Royal Wife, Tiaa, Dowager Royal Wife Nebtu and the royal daughters by Asar Menkheperre's foreign wives were not present; but all would be attending the Opening of the Mouth and the Going into the Mansion of Eternity rites in five more crossings of Re.

King's Great Chamberlain Qenamen let the door flap drop behind him and followed His Majesty to the middle of the space. Without acknowledging those present, Akheperure slowly walked completely around the bier. When he came to the foot end again, he stopped and bowed his blue-leather *Khepresh*-crowned head for several long moments.When he raised his wide chin again, he asked of no one in particular:

"Where are the coffins? Our Majesty would view these, as well."

Prince-Count Amenemhat answered in his usual stammer, gesturing, "They are r...resting b...by the pavil...ion rear w...w...all, Your M...ajesty. Cover...ed with sh..hrouds as pro...tection from d...ust."

"Show them to us, Brother Amen at the Head."

His Majesty's half-sibling gestured again and moved towards two large side-by-side forms draped with dark-red linen and so barely visible in the weak light. Akheperure walked back around the bier and come up alongside the shorter man. Without any formality Amenemhat gripped and simultaneously pulled the shrouds from the two gilded-wood human-shaped coffins, one somewhat larger than the other. Each rested on a low lion-bier. The incised feather-patterned lid of both bore an idealized likeness of Asar Menkheperre Djehutymes wearing a False Beard and the *Nemes* fronted by a rearing cobra — very much like the sheet-gold mask, except far larger in scale. Hands grasped crossed Crook and Flail scepters on both lids.

"When will our father be placed in these?"

"He w...will be t...transport...ed to the G...Great Place in the s...small...er, in...ner one. The l...l..arger will be ta...ken there t...t...tomor..row and p...put empty in...to the Man...sion for E...Eternity and its g...great r...red-stone chest w...w...waiting there. F...Following the Go...ing In s...service, the cof...fin with As...ar Menkhep-er...re will b...be lower...ed into the f...f...first one and its l...lid will be p...put in p...place, and the l...l...lid of the g...great ch...est pos...sitioned."

Akheperure looked directly at the man more than twice his age and laid a hand on his bare shoulder, smiling.

"Our Majesty very much appreciates his big brother's steady efforts over-seeing all of these many detailed arrangements. It would've taxed our own patience. Not in the lifetime of Our Person has there been the occasion to send a Lord of the Two Lands off to sail the barque of Lord Re. We are satisfied that it shall now be done for Asar Menkheperre Djehutymes in a fashion fully suitable to his very long time on the Horus Throne and many lasting accomplishments for the Black Land."

With that Akheperure's rough palm slid off Amenemhat's shoulder and he abruptly turned and strode rapidly from the Great Pavilion of Anpu, saying to Qenamen as he passed him,

"Come, Great Chamberlain Amen is Strong, you and Our Person have some serious hunting to do!"

FIVE CROSSINGS OF RE LATER, THE GREAT PLACE, WEST OF WASET

The funerary banquet for Asar Menkheperre had only just begun, when some-thing totally unexpected happened. The banqueters within the three adjoining temporary pavilions set up in the narrow wadi included Lord of the Two Lands Akheperure; his Great Royal Wife, Tiaa; young Dowager Royal Wife Nebtu; five daughters of Asar Menkheperre by his long-dead Retenu wives, all now teenagers; Prince-Count Amenemhat, his wife, Princess Isety, and their twelve-floodings-old son, Prince Amenmesse, whom Akheperure had only that very morning named Horus-in-the-Nest, until such time as His Majesty fathered a son of his own.

Also present were the viziers Rekhmire and Penab and their wives; First Prophet of Amen-Re Menkheperresenub and the three other prophets of the god;

King's Great Chamberlain Qenamen; young King's Scribe Amennakht and his father, former King's Scribe Tjaneni; plus a score more notables of the court of Asar Menkheperre Djehutymes and their wives; representatives of the military; and the chief priests of Lady Mut and lords Khonsu and Montu; as well as the Mayor of Waset, one Sennefer, and his wife. The males of this assembly were seated on folding stools (His Majesty on a portable throne, of course), the females lounging on large cushions, all arranged informally around small tables loaded with platters of roasted fowl and grilled dom-nuts, fresh green onions and other raw vegetables and fruits. Moving among the diners, ready to refill goblets from silver ewers were a number of serving women from the Waset Residence.

The murmurs of polite conversation suddenly halted and all heads turned to look in the same direction, towards the sound of loud crackings and shouts coming from the massive wooden staircase which had been rigged on scaffolding so that the two coffins of Asar Menkheperre Djehutymes (the smaller one containing him) and all of the cultic paraphernalia, necessary furnishings and food and wine provisions for his Mansion of Eternity could be taken there, its entrance being very high on the cliff face, hidden in a deep natural crevice near the top. The long single staircase without any railings was peopled in single file by well over three-dozen male servants from the Residence — carrying up, individually or in teams of two, chests and furniture pieces and the parts of His Late Majesty's dismantled chariots — and it was clearly sagging in its center and buckling dramatically to one side, causing the men on it to lose their balances and footings and even to put down what they were transporting, so as to keep to keep from being flung off.

Before the funeral assembly had all risen to their collective feet, the sagging complex scaffolding supporting the stairs did begin to fully collapse, the uprights and bracing poles at the structure's midpoint splintering and snapping, so that several of the desperately shouting porters and their burdens were indeed suddenly dropping amid the detached wood-plank steps and scaffolding debris, falling many cubits to the wadi rock floor below. Those men on the topmost reaches of the disintegrating stairs began scrambling further upwards as quickly as they could, most having abandoned whatever they were carrying. Those on the lower steps turned in their tracks to retreat in a mad dash towards the bottom, likewise putting down or dropping chests and chairs and chariot wheels.

As a cloud of dust began to rise from the large tangle of fallen men, grave goods and broken wood, the contingent of armed Residence Medjays — which had been waiting with the chariot groomsmen and carrying-chair porters further down the wadi — rushed by the pavilions, to offer whatever assistance they could to the injured. Lord of the Two Lands Akheperure stepped off the central pavilion where he'd been seated and slowly approached the chaotic scene. Close behind him was Prince-Count Amenemhat and Great Chamberlain Qenamen.

Looking at the broken bodies being pulled free of the heap of dead and dying, His Majesty could only shake his *Khepresh*-crowned head and say to the others now flanking him, "Thank Amen's blue balls that the coffin with our father made it safely inside before this tragedy happened. What an inauspicious start for our sole reign!"

SIXTY-FIVE CROSSINGS OF RE LATER
HIGH COUNCIL CHAMBER, THE RESIDENCE, MENNUFER

L ord of the Two Lands Akheperure, Son of Re Amenhotep, Ruler of Iunu sat enthroned on a low dais with the hastily summoned members of his High Council arrayed before him, the notables seated in armless chairs positioned in a wide semicircle. King's Scribe Amennakht was positioned off to one side of the dais, crosslegged at his father's well-used low writing table, a papyrus scroll open on it, from which he was reading aloud to the others.

"After the usual formal salutations to the Living Horus, life, prosperity, health, the Black Land's deputy at Gubla writes: *'It has only this very day come to my ears, direct from the tongues of traders journeying with their merchandise out of wretched Retenu to this portal to the Great Green, that the devious princes of that place are even now in full-scale revolt against the Two Lands, having taken hostage the deputies of the Mighty Bull in the foul cities of Megiddo and Kadesh. Rumor has it, these same traders further report, that those deputies of the Black Land even may have been executed, their wives and children slain, too.*

'Again, these bearers of bad tidings have told my own ears this day that the reason for the present uprising against the Two Lands is because word reached those wicked princes of wretched Retenu that Lord of the Two Lands Lasting Manifestation of Re, Son of Re Born of Djehuty, the constant smiter of Retenu, has gone to sail the heavens on the Barque of Lord Re. Thus those pointy-beards of foul Megiddo and Kadesh have declared that their allegiances to the Two Lands are no longer in force and burdensome annual tribute shall cease flowing south to the coffers of the Black Land, as well. They have posted envoys to other towns of Retenu, enlisting their own wicked princes to join in ousting the several garrisons of soldiers of the Two Lands there. Rumor is that they each also have sent letters encouraging the prince of wretched Naharin to ally with their cause.

'And further, and these are the words of the traders, not my own, oh Living Horus...' King's Scribe Amennakht raised his chin enough to see His Majesty was frowning, since he already knew what was coming. *'...that the rebels are confident of the success of their revolt because they are told the Black Land is ruled now by a "castrated calf" rather than a "mighty bull" and that —'*

"Enough!" Akheperure Amenhotep Hequaiunu literally shouted. He slammed calloused palms against his throne arms and stood bolt upright. "Our Person shall show these foolish cursed wretches of Retenu that we are indeed a bull with horns even longer and sharper than Our Majesty's

341

late father's!"

He crossed the High Council chamber, kicking off his sandals as he went, then pushed the door panels wide open and exited. Qenamen quickly bent and collected these, then followed in his barefooted friend's wake.

Continued in Book Two

Re Dazzling

CHARACTERS
In Alphabetical Order

Akheperenre Djehutymes (II) "Great Form of Re" "Born of Djehuty." Youngest son of Generalissimo/Lord of the Two Lands **Akheperkare Djehutymes** (I) and his deceased wife Mutnefret; Crown-Prince to his father, then, at an early age, himself **Lord of the Two Lands** Akheperenre Djehutymes (II); reluctant husband to his half-sister, **Hatshepsut**, and father of their only non-stillborn child, **Princess Neferure**; father by Harim **Lady Iset** of **Prince Djehutymes** (III), his successor. Insecure, withdrawn, reticent, gluttonous as a child, with a consequent weight problem; stammers; fatally bisexual.

Akheperkare Djehutymes (I) "Great Soul of Re" "Born of Djehuty." Son of Prince Ahmes Sipari and non-royal **Lady Senisonbe**, so grandson of **Seqenenre Tao** II and nephew of The Liberator; selected as successor to **Lord of the Two Lands Djeserkare Amenhotep** (I) by his aunt, Dowager **Great Royal Wife Ahmes Nefertari**; father of four sons (the younger two Amenmes and **Djehutymes** [II]) by his non-royal first wife, Mutnefret, and of two daughters (one **Hatshepsut**) by his royal second wife, **Ahmes**; resumes the empire building of **Lord of the Two Lands Nebpehtyre Ahmes**; slain by a bowman sniper while on campaign in Western Asia; default founder of the **House of Djehutymes**.

Ahmes "Moon Born." Cousin to and **Great Royal Wife** of Lord of the Two Lands Akheperkare Djehutymes (I); mother of his two daughters, eldest **Hatshepsut** and **Neferubity**, who tragically dies young; regent to her juvenile stepson, **Lord of the Two Lands Akheperenre Djehutymes** (II).

Ahmes, Prince Four-floodings-old son of **Prince Amenhotep**, so a scion of the **House of Tao**.

Ahmes Nefertari "Moon Born" "Beautiful Companion." King's Daughter, King's Sister and **Great Royal Wife** of The Liberator, **Lord of the Two Lands Nebpehtyre Ahmes**; first **God's Wife of Amen** and mother of Lord of the Two Lands **Djeserkare Amenhotep** (I) and his elder brother, **Prince-Count Siamen**; as Dowager **Great Royal Wife**, ultimate powerbroker of the **House of Tao**; she is neither a tolerant nor an endearing individual.

Ahmes Son of Ebana Marine admiral, grizzled veteran of the Wars of Liberation; still in the service of **Lord of the Two Lands Akheperkare Djehutymes** (I).

Ahmesti Fourteen-year-old half-Kheftian son of **Taotios**, nephew of the Minos; himself ultimately the Minos; cousin of **Menkheperre Djehtymes** (III).

Amenemhat, Prince-Count "Amen at the Head." Teenaged bastard eldest son of **Menkheperre Djehutymes** (III) by **Princess Neferure** and grandson of **Hatshepsut**, initially unknown to her; awkward, he stammers. Later briefly Crown-Prince, succeeding half-brother **Menkheperre** in that role, until he is himself succeeded by half-brother **Amenhotep**, son of **Great Royal Wife Merytre Hatshepsut** (see below); married to **Lady Isety** and father of **Prince Amenmes**, first Horus-in-the Nest to **Akheperure Amenhotep** (II); holds title Great Steward of the Cattle of Amen-Re.

Amenemheb General and Chief of Chariotry during **Menkheperre**'s sole reign. Accompanies him on the Eighth Campaign to **Retenu** and performs a service for his sovereign, for which he is richly rewarded.

Amenemope, Count Vizier of the South of **Kemet** at the outset of the reign of **Menkheperre Djehutymes** (III).

Amenhotep, Crown-Prince Son of **Menkheperre Djehutymes** (III) by Great Royal Wife **Merytre Hatshepsut**; coregent with his father for two floodings and succeeds to the Horus Throne as **Akheperure Amenhotep** (II) **Hequaiunu** ("Great Manifestation of Re, Amen is Pleased, Ruler of Iunu").

Amenhotep, Prince "Amen is Pleased." Son of **Prince Tao**, grandson of **Prince-Count Siamen** and great-grandson of The Liberator, **Nebpehtyre Ahmes**; scion of the **House of Tao**; husband of commoner wife **Lady Bastet**.

Amenkhau Chief in the **Great Place** given the assignment to remove the body of **Hatshepsut** from her kingly tomb, obliterate her identity as **Maatkare** on the coffin and canopic jars, and re-inter her in the nearby Tomb of **In Sitre**.

Amenmes, Prince "Born of Amen." Eldest surviving son of **Lord of the Two Lands Akheperkare Djehutymes** (I) and heir-apparent; dies tragically by crocodile(s) in Wawat, inadvertently thereby elevating his younger brother, **Prince Djehutymes** (II), to the role of crown-prince and successor of their father.

Amenmes, Prince "Born of Amen." Young son of **Prince-Count Amenemhat** and **Lady Isety**; named **Horus-in-the-Nest** by childless **Akheperure Amenhotep** (II).

Amennakht "Amen is Victorious." Son of King's Scribe **Tjaneni** and himself King's Scribe to **Akheperure Amenhotep** (II).

Amenneferu, Count Vizier of the North of **Kemet** at the outset of the reign of **Menkheperre Djehutymes** (III).

Amenuserhat, Count Vizier of the North of **Kemet** during the coregency of Maatkare/Menkheperre.

Amenwashu, Count Vizier of the South of **Kemet** during the reign of **Akheperenre Djehutymes** (II).

Archer Discharged soldier of **Kemet** with a mission to restore the order of **Maat**; becomes a snack for **the sons of Sobek**.

Bastet, Lady Commoner wife of **House of Tao** prince **Amenhotep** and mother of his two sons.

Besenmut Generalissimo of the army of **Kemet** during the reign of **Akheperenre Djehutymes** (II) and into the Maatkare/Menkheperre coregency; leads a policing campaign to **Wawat** during the joint-reign.

Bek A charioteer and personal driver of teenaged **Lord of the Two Lands Akheperenre Djehutymes** (II); also secret male lover of the latter.

Bete Aged and grossly overweight Wawatan butler of **Merytre Hatshepsut** at her villa-prison in **Swenet**.

Djemutefankh Chief-Priest in the **Great Place**, who leads a workforce to dismantle the joint-tomb of **Hatshepsut** and her father, **Akheperkare**, and rescues one of the preserved viscera of the Female **Living Horus**.

Djeserkare Amenhotep (I) "Holy Soul of Re" "Amen is Pleased." **Lord of the Two Lands**; youngest surviving son of The Liberator **Nebpehtyre Ahmes** and **Great Royal Wife Ahmes Nefertari**, the latter choosing him as successor to his father, bypassing his elder brother, **Prince Siamen**; in poor health (tuberculosis?); homosexual and childless; his last male lover being teenaged King's Scribe **Senenmut**.

Emissary from Kemet Carries a pardon from the **Lord of the Two Lands Menkheperre**.

Ety Wife of **Pererhu**, chief of **Punt**; excessively obese.

Fourth Prophet of Amen (unnamed).

Handsome Young Physician from **Mennufer**, sent to **Wer-Mer** to attended to Nurse **In Sitre**'s dental problems.

Hapusenub "Hapu is Well." **First Prophet** (high-priest) of **Amen-Re** and thus one of the most-powerful figures at the royal courts of the first two Djehuty-meses, **Hatshepsut** and, finally, the third Djehutymes, during whose reign he retires at the advanced age of eighty-three floodings.

Hatshepsut "Noblest Woman." Eldest daughter of **Lord of the Two Lands Akheperkare Djehutymes** (I) and **Great Royal Wife Ahmes**; half-sister of and **Great Royal Wife** to **Akheperenre Djehutymes** (II); Regent for her stepson-ne-phew, **Menkheperre Djehutymes** (III), then Coregent with him as the Female Horus **Maatkare** ("True Soul of Re"); and, finally, Dowager **Great Royal Wife** in retirement. Mother of **Princess Neferure**. Tomboy as a girl; petitely pretty, with an iron will; adores her father, despises her half-brother husband; dominating mother and wholly efficient ruler. Has a secret lover during her first years as **Mistress of the Two Lands**.

Hray Chamberlain of the harim of the **Residence** at **Mennufer** during the latter part of the reign of **Menkheperre Djehutymes** (III); a eunuch.

Huy Adoratrix of **Amen-Re** and mother of daughters **Isety** and **Merytre Hat-shepsut**, thus mother-in-law of both **Prince Amenemhat** and his father, **Men-kheperre Djehutymes** (III).

Ineni Chief Royal Architect, in service under kings Amenhotep (I) and Djehu-tymeses I and II; designer of the "hidden" tomb of **Akheperkare Djehutymes** (I).

In Sitre "Fish" "Daughter of Re." Royal Nurse to Princess **Hatshepsut**, then her constant companion through to the very end. Tall, very heavyset, exceedingly buxom and blindly vain; affectionately called "Ancient One" by Hatshepsut.

Intef, Count Lord Chamberlain at the court of **Menkheperre Djehutymes** (III).

Ipu Nurse of the God (**Amen-Re**) and mother of **Great Royal Wife Sitiah**, thus mother-in-law of **Menkheperre Djehutymes** (III) and grandmother of Crown-Prince **Menkheperre**; niece of Royal Nurse **In Sitre**.

Irterau, Count Chief Treasurer during reign of **Akheperenre Djehutymes** (II).

Iset, Lady Concubine of **Lord of the Two Lands Akheperenre Djeutymes** (II) and King's Mother of his only son, **Menkheperre Djehutymes** (III); thin, di-minutive in stature and totally deferring in manner; dubbed "Harim Mouse" by rival **Hatshepsut**.

Isety, Lady Daughter of the Adoratrix **Huy** and wife of Prince **Amenemhat**; sis-ter of **Merytre Hatshepsut** and thus sister-in-law of **Menkheperre Djehutymes** (III); mother of future Horus-in-the-Nest **Amenmes**.

RE ASCENDING

Itbet Wet nurse to young Crown-Prince **Djehutymes** (III) at the time of his unexpected elevation to the **Horus Throne**.

Khaemehet, Count Chief Treasurer at the outset of the coregency of Maatkare/Menkheperre.

Khawi A male dwarf, attendant and "First Companion" of **Akheperenre Djehutymes** (II), then "pet" of **Princess Neferure**.

Maid-Servant to **Dowager Great Royal Wife Hatshepsut**.

Meket Young handmaiden to **God's Wife Neferure**, grandniece of Royal Nurse **In Sitre**; audience of one to Neferure's sexual liaisons.

Menhet, Menwi and **Merti** Sisters and teenage daughters of the Prince of Kadesh, taken hostage at the surrender of **Megiddo** and sent to **Kemet** to be the concubines of **Menkheperre Djehutymes** (III), subsequently bearing his children and made **King's Wives** in turn; all reside at the **Residence** harim in **Mennufer**; their mother is **Princess Nahti**.

Menkheperre Djehutymes (III) "Lasting Manifestation of Re" "Born of Djehuty." Bastard only son of **Lord of the Two Lands Akheperenre Djehutymes** (II); infant crown-prince to his father, then himself suddenly **Lord of the Two Lands** at the tender age of three; nicknamed "Hawk Beak" by his stepmother-aunt, **Hatshepsut**, who briefly governs on his behalf as Regent, before ascending the throne and ruling as his co-king for twenty floodings; once ruler in his own right, resumes the empire building advanced by his grandfather, **Akheperkare Djehutymes** (I).

Menkheperre, Prince "Lasting Manifestation of Re." Third son of **Menkheperre Djehutymes** (III) and **Great Royal Wife Sitiah**, and first Crown-Prince to his father; enthralled by naked dancing girls; dies tragically.

Menkheperresenub "Lasting Manifestation of Re is Well." **First Prophet** of Amen-Re, successor to **Hapusenub**; previously First Prophet of **Ptah**.

Mentu Marine captain, banished by order of **Maatkare Hatshepsut** to the Fortress of **Buhen**, where he serves as second-in-command and is responsible for the garrison's provisions and the local population living in proximity to the fort.

Meru Son and heir of the Prince of Kadesh and **Princess Nahti**, captured at the siege of **Meggido** by **Menkheperre Djehutymes** (III) and taken hostage to **Kemet**, to be inculturated in the customs of the **Two Lands**; brother of Royal Wives **Menhet, Menwi** and **Merti**, and uncle to Menhet's daughter, **Princess Ne-**

ferubity; known in Kemet as Meketre.

Merymaat, Count Vizier of the South of **Kemet** during the latter part of the coregency of Maatkare/Menkheperre.

Merytre Hatshepsut "Beloved of Re" "Noblest Woman." Daughter of Adoratrix **Huy** and **Great Royal Wife** of **Menkheperre Djehutymes** (III); mother of his heir, **Akheperure Amenhotep** (II); exiled to **Swenet** for her role in the poisoning deaths of the three **Royal Wives** from **Kadesh**.

Messenger from the **Residence** at **Mennufer**, with news of the unexpected death of **Lord of the Two Lands Akheperenre Djehutymes** (II).

Minatis Sister of the **Kheftiu** ruler, the Minos; wife of **Taotios** and mother of **Ahmesti**.

Minmaat Tutor of **Prince Djehutymes** (II).

Minmes "Born of Min." Aide-de-camp and body-servant of Chief Steward of the Estates of Amen-Re **Senenmut**, his bed mate as well; son of a Kheftian merchant resident in **Kemet**.

Minnakhte, Count Chief Chamberlain of the Royal **Residence** at **Waset**, during the reign of **Akheperenre Djehutymes** (II).

Nahti, Princess Wife of the Prince of Kadesh, held hostage in **Kemet** by **Menkheperre Djehutymes** (III), to whom she is mother-in-law when he marries all three of her daughters, also hostages; resides in the **Residence** harim at **Mennufer**.

Nay Chamberlain of the harim of the **Residence** at the Northern Capital, **Mennufer**; a very fat, self-important eunuch; later chamberlain of the entire Northern Residence.

Nebet Captain of the **Medjay** palace guard and secret lover of teenage **God's Wife of Amen Neferure**; tall, muscular, black-skinned native of **Wawat**, whom **Mistress of the Two Lands Maatkare Hatshepsut** regards as possibly the most handsome man in **Kemet**.

Nebpehtyre Ahmes "Re Lord of Strength" "Moon Born," dubbed "The Liberator" for having driven out the Hyksos (foreign rulers of the North of **Kemet**) and reuniting the **Two Lands** under his rule; second son of **Seqenenre Tao** (II); husband to his wilful sister, **Ahmes Nefertari**, and father of several children by her, including two surviving sons, **Prince-Count Siamen** and **Lord of the Two Lands Djeserkare Amenhotep** (I).

Nebtu Late in his life **Royal Wife** of **Menkheperre Djehutymes** (III); a commoner young enough to be his granddaughter.

Neferronpet Generalissimo of **Kemet**'s Army of the South; accompanies **Menkheperre Djehutymes** (III) on several campaigns to **Retenu**.

Neferubity "Beautiful Bee." Youngest daughter of **Generalissimo Djehutymes** (I) and his second wife, Princess **Ahmes**; sister of **Hatshepsut**; tragically dies very young.

Neferubity "Beautiful Bee." Daughter of **Menkheperre Djehutymes** (III) and King's Wife **Menhet**; dies young, in the same tragic manner as her father's aunt of the same name.

Neferure "Beauty of Re." King's Daughter, born to **Akheperenre Djehutymes** (II) and **Great Royal Wife Hatshepsut**; **God's Wife of Amen** following her mother's assuming the co-kingship. Tomboy like her mother; detests her younger half-brother; teenage nymphomaniac; mother of bastard twins (one **Prince Amenemhat**), dying in childbirth.

Nepu Butler of the Taos at their Delta country estate.

Neshi, Count Chancellor of **Kemet** during the first part of the Maatkare/Menkheperre coregency; successfully leads the trading expedition to **Punt** and is awarded the Fly of Honor.

Pairi Fourth Prophet of **Amen-Re** during the coregency of Maatkare/Menkheperre.

Paneb **First Prophet** of **Ptah** during the coregency of Maakare/Menkheperre.

Pedjetnuf and **Khonsusenub** Foreman in the **Great Place** and a stone mason, respectively, who discover the Tomb of **In Sitre** and enter it, to find the reinterment of **Hatshepsut**.

Pemitu Native of **Wawat**; first "jailer" and then lover of **Merytre Hatshepsut** during her exile at **Swenet**; father of their three daughters.

Penab, Count Vizier of the North of **Kemet** during the brief coregency of **Menkheperre Djehutymes** (III) and **Akheperure Amenhotep** (II).

Penemhat, Count Chief of the Treasury in the first part of **Menkheperre Djehutymes**'s sole reign.

Pererhu Chieftan of **Punt**.

Petweri Physician of the **Mennufer Residence** in the latter part of the reign of **Menkheperre Djehutymes III**).

Prince of Megiddo Leads rebellion against **Kemet** along with the Prince of **Kadesh** and other petty rulers of **Retenu**; taken prisoner at the surrender of his city, but **Menkheperre Djehutymes** (III) spares his life.

Qenamen "Amen is Strong." "Milk-brother" of Crown-Prince **Amenhotep** (II) and his confederate in "boyish crimes"; later Great Chamberlain at the court of **Lord of the Two Lands Akheperure, Son of Re Amenhotep** (II).

Rekhmire, Count Vizier of the South of **Kemet** in the reigns of **Menkheperre Djehutymes** (III) and **Akheperure Amenhotep** (II); short, rail-thin, with an irritating personality.

Renna King's Steward for **Menkheperre Djehutymes** (III); middle-aged, portly, officious.

Roy Chamberlain for **Menkheperre Djehutymes** (III) at the **Waset Residence**, at the end of his reign.

Ruru Chamberlain of the harem of the Royal **Residence** at **Waset**; a eunuch.

Saroy Butler and estate manager for **Senenmut**, following the latter's return from exile in **Gubla**.

Senenmut, Count "Brother of Mut." King's Scribe successively to **Lords of the Two Lands Djeserkare Amenhotep** (I) and **Akheperkare Djehutymes** (I); royal tutor to **Princess Neferure**; Great Steward of the Estates of **Amen-Re** during the Maatkare/Menkheperre coregency; taller than most men, with red hair and a pointed long nose; behind-the-scenes manipulator; unabashedly homosexual.

Senimen Youthful tutor of the juvenile **Lord of the Two Lands Menkheperre Djehutymes** (III). Also King's Scribe to **Maatkare Hatshepsut**, with a special relationship to her and, ultimately, **God's Wife Neferure** as well.

Senisonbe, Princess King's Mother of **Ahkheperkare Djehutymes** (I); widow of Prince Ahmes Sipari, eldest son of **Seqenenre Tao** (II) and brother of The Liberator, **Lord of the Two Lands Nebpehtyre Ahmes**, and **Great Royal Wife Ahmes Nefertari**.

Sequenenre Tao (II) Prince of **Waset**, father of The Liberator, **Nebpehtyre Ahmes**.

Siamen, Prince-Count An elder son of **Lord of the Two Lands Nebpehtyre**

Ahmes and **Great Royal Wife Ahmes Nefertari**; bypassed in the line of succession by his younger brother **Prince Amenhotep** (I), due to his lameness; married to **Lady Teyit**; father of a single son, **Prince Tao**; eventually titular head of the **House of Tao**.

Sitiah First **Great Royal Wife** of **Menkheperre Djehutymes** (III) and mother of his initial Heir, Crown-Prince **Menkheperre**; a commoner, the daughter of Nurse of the God **Ipu** and grand-niece of Royal Nurse **In Sitre**.

Sitmin Half-Wawatan eldest daughter of former **Great Royal Wife Merytre Hatshepsut** and so the half-sister of **Akheperure Amenhotep** (II); her father is **Pemitu**.

Steward of the **Waset** estate of **Senenmut**.

Suitnub Butler and personal body-servant to **Lord of the Two Lands Djeserkare Amenhotep** (I); a eunuch.

Tao, Prince Son of Prince-Count **Siamen**, grandson of The Liberator, **Nebpehtyre Ahmes**; married and father of Prince **Amenhotep**; hope of the **House of Tao**, physically attractive (at least to **Hatshepsut**) and ambitious regarding the continuance of his line; exiled to **Kheftiu**; changes his name to **Taotios** and marries the sister of the Minos, ruler of Kheftiu; father of a half-Kheftian son, **Ahmesti**, who becomes the Minos.

Tesit Handmaiden to **Great Royal Wife Merytre Hatshepsut**; accompanies her in exile to **Swenet**; commits suicide.

Tesu and **Iba** Youngest daughters of **Yey** and **Thuit** and sisters of **Tiaa, Yeta** and **Yuya**.

Tetisheri Commoner consort of **Sequenenre Tao** (II) and mother of **Nebpehtyre Ahmes** and **Ahmes Nefertari**; regarded as ancestress of the **House of Tao**.

Teyit Non-royal Mistress of the House; wife of **Prince-Count Siamen** and mother of their son, **Prince Tao**.

Three Men of Wawat Servers and entertainers at **Senenmut**'s dinner for **Tjaneni**.

Thuit, Lady Mistress of the House, wife of **Yey**, mother of **Great Royal Wife Tiaa**.

Thuty Generalissimo of **Kemet**'s Army of the North; accompanies **Menkheperre Djehutymes** (III) on several campaigns to **Retenu**.

Tiaa Fourth daughter of **Yey** and **Thuit**, and **Great Royal Wife** of **Akheperure Amenhotep** (II).

Tjaneni Young King's Scribe for **Menkheperre Djehutymes (III)**; accompanies him on the campaigns to **Retenu** and keeps the ruler's **Book of Days**, which will be the basis for the Annals of Djehutymes (III) engraved on the walls of **Ipet Isut**, the **Waset** mansion of the **Hidden One, Amen-Re**; an acolyte and then *wab* priest in the Mansion of Montu at **Waset**, prior to being selected as **Lord of the Two Lands'** personal secretary; father of **Amennahkt**, King's Scribe to **Akheperure Amenhotep** (II).

Tje A female servant of **Great Royal Wife Hatshepsut**.

Translator at the surrender of **Megiddo**, who conveys **Menkheperre Djehutymes's** sentiments to the vanquished princes of **Retenu**.

Unnefer Commandant of the Fortress of **Buhen** at the Second Cataract.

Webmut and **Tefmin** Illiterate stone masons given the assignment of removing the images and names of **Maatkare Hatshepsut** from the dismantled blocks of the **Ipet Isut Holy of Holies** barque-shrine built by her and coregent **Menkheperre Djehutymes** (III), then dismantled by him to make room for a new, larger shrine of his sole authorship.

Wennefer, Count Steward of the Estates of **Amen-Re**; successor to **Senenmut** in that role.

Weshptu Young lieutenant in the Army of **Kadesh**, selected for a fatal mission to **Kemet** because of his ability to speak (barely) the tongue of the **Black Land**.

Yeta and **Yuya** Young sons of **Yey** and **Thuit**.

Yey First Prophet of **Min** in the god's mansion at **Ipu**; husband of **Lady Thuit** and the father of two sons and six daughters, the fourth one, **Tiaa** selected to be **Great Royal Wife** to **Lord of the Two Lands Akheperure, Son of Re Amenhotep** (II). Thus Yey is given the honorary title "Father of the God."

GLOSSARY

Akhet The four-month spring season in ancient Egypt, during which the inundation of **The River** (Nile) occurred.

Amam The Devourer; a composite creature, part crocodile, hippopotamus and lion, which eats the hearts of those individuals who tip the scale balanced with the Feather of **Maat** at the Last Judgment.

Amen-Re Chief god of the Egyptian pantheon; epithet is the **Hidden One**. Merged with Ithyphallic god **Min**, as **Amen-Min**.

ankh The glyph representing life, cross-shaped with a loop at the top; ritual emblem carried by deities and the **Lord of the Two Lands**.

Anpu The canine-headed god of mummification, renamed Anubis by the Hellenes, which is how he is known today.

Answerers Mummiform figurines placed in a tomb to magically perform Afterlife chores as might be required of the deceased; called ushabtis or shabtis by Egyptologists.

Apep Giant serpent which attempts to impede the passage of the **Barque of Re** as it passes through the Underworld.

Asar The god of the Afterlife and ruler of the Underworld; renamed Osiris by the Hellenes, which is how he is known today. A deceased person was referred to as Asar (and their name: e.g. Aser Djeserkare Amenthotep).

Aset Goddess and sister/wife of **Asar**; renamed Isis by the Hellenes, which is how she is known today. The mother of the god **Horus**.

Asiatic composite bow Introduced into **Kemet** by the Rulers of Foreign Lands (Hyksos); made of bonded strips of wood, giving it greater strength and firepower than the simple bow.

Atum Egyptian god, who created the universe by masturbating.

ba The Egyptian equivalent of the soul; represented as a human-headed bird.

Barque of Amen-Re Large-scale model boat bearing a shrine housing the cult figure of the god; borne by priests in religious processions; otherwise housed in the **Holy of Holies** of the **Mansion of Amen-Re, Ipet Isut**.

Barque of Re Vessel on which the sun-god **Re** traverses the daytime heavens and nighttime Underworld.

Beautiful Feast of the Valley Annual celebration on the **West of Waset**, when the **Barque of Amen-Re** visits sacred places on **The River's** west bank, and the people of **Waset** honor their deceased ancestors.

Ben Ben A monumental gilded truncated-obelisk-like stone sacred to the sun god, Re, in his mansion at **Iunu** (modern Heliopolis).

Bes Dwarf demigod with lionesque features, associated with childbirth.

Black Land Name of ancient Egypt, written as **Kemet**; refers to the black soil deposited by the annual inundation of **The River** (Nile).

Blood of the Line Male members of the ruling family of **Kemet** eligible for inheriting the throne.

Book of Days A record kept by the King's Scribe; Tjaneni writes his on a leather scroll, which became the basis for **Menkheperre Djehutymes**'s Annals inscribed at **Ipet Isut** (Karnak).

Buhen Fortress at the Belly of Stones (Second Cataract of the Nile).

clerestory Windows in Egyptian temples and palaces, parallel vertical slots placed near the ceiling.

Crook and Flail The paired scepters of the **Lord of the Two Lands**, usually held crossed over the ruler's chest.

Crossings of Lord Re The barque of the sun god, **Re**, sailing from horizon to horizon during the twelve hours of daytime, then passing through the twelve hours of night in the Underworld.

Daughter of the King's Body A princess.

deben A measure of weight equal to 93.3 grams.

Divine Hand of the God Sacerdotal title; see **God's Wife of Amen**.

Djehuty The god of the moon and of writing, renamed Thoth by the Hellenes, as he is known today.

Djeser Akhet "Sacred Horizon"; the name of **Menkheperre Djenhutymes**'s **Beautiful Feast of the Valley** chapel destroyed by an avalanche shortly after its completion.

Djeser Djeseru "Holiest of Holy Places"; the name of **Maatkare Hatshepsut**'s memorial monument on the **West of Waset**; completed and appropriated by **Menkheperre Djenhutymes** (III).

Double Horuses Coregents sharing the throne; occurring infrequently; the king was called the **Living Horus**, as the human embodiment of **Horus**, the male god of kingship.

Father of Inundations Epithet of **Hapu** (Hapi), god of **The River** (Nile).

Field of Reeds The ancient Egyptian equivalent of Heaven, where the Afterlife was spent.

First Prophet Title of the chief priest of a deity cult; there were a total of four prophets for every cult, each with a different ritual or administrative specialization.

flesh of the gods Gold.

flooding The annual inundation of **The River**, by which time is reckoned.

Fly Whisk Scepter of the **Great Royal Wife**.

God's Wife of Amen-Re Sacerdotal title created for **Ahmes Nefertari** and usually held by subsequent **Great Royal Wives**, but by **Princess Neferure**, as well; also the **Divine Hand of the God**.

Great Bay of Merstseger Modern-day Deir el Bahari, site of **Hatshepsut**'s mortuary monument.

Great Green The Mediterranean Sea.

Great Pavilion of Anpu The mummification tent where the deceased **Lord of the Two Lands** was prepared for Eternity over a period of seventy days.

Great Place, The royal necropolis on the **West of Waset**. Initiated by **Akheperkare Djehutymes** (I), first **Lord of the Two Lands** to locate his hidden tomb there.

Great Royal Wife Principal spouse of the **Lord of the Two Lands**, usually mother of the Heir; sometimes referred to as King's Great Wife.

Gubla The name of Byblos, the Mediterranean port city, in New Kingdom times; place of Senenmut's exile..

Guft A southern port on **The River** (Nile), where the returning Expedition to **Punt** sailed from to **Waset**.

Hathor Mirror Toiletries object, the handle of which is the image of the cow-eared goddess of love.

Heb Sed Renewal festival celebrated by the **Lord of the Two Lands** after thirty years of rule, and at irregular intervals thereafter.

Heket Frog-headed goddess of childbirth.

Hidden One Epithet of the god **Amen-Re**.

Holy of Holies Shrine structure housing the **Sacred Barque** (and cult statue) of a god or goddess.

Horus Hawk-headed god of kingship, son of **Asar** and **Aset**.

Horus-in-the-Flesh The ruler of the **Two Lands** as the human embodiment of the god **Horus**.

Horus-in-the-Nest The Heir to the throne of **Kemet**.

Horus Sidelock The braid of hair worn by Egyptian children of both sexes, whose heads were otherwise shaved bald; also called Horus Lock and Sidelock of Youth; shorn when puberty was reached.

Horus Throne The throne of **Kemet**, the **Two Lands**.

House Born of Djehuty The ruling royal family of the Eighteenth Dynasty, initiated by **Akheperkare Djehutymes** (I).

House of Beautification The facility for preservation of the body (mummification).

House of Tao The royal family ruling **Kemet** during the latter part of what today is termed the Seventeenth Dynasty; responsible for the Wars of Liberation which ousted the Rulers of Foreign Lands (Hyksos).

Inundation The annual flooding of **The River** (Nile); a reckoning of one-year's time.

Ipet Isut the Mansion of **Amen-Re** (modern-day Karnak).

Ipu Town downstream from **Waset**; cult center of the ithyphallic god **Min**, whose **First Prophet** is **Yeh**, father of **Great Royal Wife Tiaa**.

Iunu The Mansion of **Re**, the sun god; location of modern-day Heliopolis.

Kadesh City in **Retenu**, home of the three foreign wives of **Lord of the Two Lands Menkheperre Djehutymes** (III).

Kemet The name of Egypt in dynastic times, translated as the **Black Land**, in contrast to Deshret, the Red Land (desert).

Khat Cloth head-covering worn by the **Lord of the Two Lands**, sometimes called a "wig bag" by Egyptologists.

Kheftiu Island nation in the **Great Green** which is ruled by the Minos; inhabitants are Khefti; modern-day Crete.

kheker Design repetitive motif generally similar to the *fleur-de-leis,* used as a border at the top of tomb walls.

Khepresh A bulbous crown-helmet made of blue-dyed stiffened leather and often decorated with gilded bosses.

Kherp Scepter with a wedge-shaped terminus.

King's Wives Secondary spouses of the **Lord of the Two Lands**.

Lady of Buto The cobra goddess **Wadjet**.

Lord of the Two Lands One of the five titles of the ruler of **Kemet**.

lector priest Responsible for recitation of the liturgy during cultic rituals.

Living Horus The ruler of **Kemet**, as the human embodiment of **Horus,** god of kingship.

Maat Goddess responsible for order in the universe, thus also the abstract concept of truth and justice.

Mansion for Eternity The tomb.

Mansion of Millions of Years Funerary monument of the **Lord of the Two Lands**, where his mortuary cult was maintained.

Medjays Mercenary black-African soldiers from **Wawat** who, during the Eighteenth Dynasty, are employed as royal bodyguards and as the police forces of **Mennufer** and **Waset**.

Megiddo City in **Retenu**, the ruling prince of which revolts against **Lord of the Two Lands Menkheperre Djehutymes** (III).

Mennufer Northern capital of **Kemet**, renamed Memphis by the Hellenes; modern Arabic name is Mit Rahina.

Min God of fertility, depicted mummiform with an enormous erection; merged with **Amen** as **Amen-Min**.

Mistress of the Two Lands Maatkare Hatshepsut's title while Coregent with **Lord of the Two Lands** Menkheperre Djehutymes.

Mitanni People of the area of modern-day Syria known anciently as **Naharin**.

Mound of Creation Site on the **West of Waset** (modern Medinet Habu) where **Maatkare** and **Menkheperre** build a chapel to **Amen-Re** in his creator-god capacity.

Mut Mother goddess, consort of **Amen-Re**; mansion nearby **Ipet Isut**.

Naharin Area of modern-day northern Syria peopled by the **Mitanni**.

Nemes Linen head-covering worn by the **Lord of the Two Lands**, with lappets and usually striped.

Nine Bows The traditional enemies of **Kemet**.

nomen The personal name of the **Lord of the Two Lands**, written in a *shenu* (cartouche).

Opening of the Mouth Ritual to revivify a mummy or give life to a statue.

Opet Festival Annual two-week celebration at **Waset**, during which **Amen-Re**, his consort **Mut**, and son, Khonsu, traveled in procession to the **Southern Harim** (Luxor Temple).

Peret The four-month fall/winter season in **Kemet**.

pesesh-kef Flint ritual knife used at the **Opening of the Mouth** ritual.

prenomen The throne name of the **Lord of the Two Lands**, written in a *shenu* (cartouche).

Ptah Creator god, chief diety of **Mennufer**, his cult center.

Punt A location on the east coast of Africa (modern Somalia?), to which **Maatkare Hatshepsut** sends a sea-borne expedition to acquire valuable goods with which to reward **Amen-Re**.

Re The sun god. Merged with Amen as **Amen-Re**.

Red Crown of Northern **Kemet**; probably originally fashioned of basketry.

rekhyt The common people of **Kemet**, symbolically represented by a lapwing (bird).

Residence, Northern and Southern Palaces of the **Lord of the Two Lands** in **Mennufer** and **Waset**.

Retenu Name during the New Kingdom of the coastal area of Western Asia sometimes referred to by historians as Syria-Palestine; composed of numerous city-states ruled by hereditary princes. Inhabitants called **Reteni**.

River, The The Nile, personified by the hermaphroditic deity Hapu.

Sawu Port on the Red Sea.

senet A board game for two players.

Shemu The four-month summer season in **Kemet**.

shenu Oval containing the **prenomen** and **nomen** of **Lords of the Two Lands** and **Great Royal Wives** (cartouche).

sistrum Rattle played by temple women during cultic ceremonies.

Son of His Body Prince fathered by **Lord of the Two Lands**.

Son of Re Title of **Lord of the Two Lands**, preceding his **nomen** (personal name).

Sobek A crocodile-headed god.

sons of Sobek Crocodiles.

Southern Harim Focus of the **Opet Festival** (Luxor Temple).

Southern Iunu Another name for **Waset**.

sporran Inlaid-gold, hinged apron worn by **Lord of the Two Lands**.

Swenet Town at the First Cataract on the border of southern **Kemet** and **Wawat**; site of granite and quartzite quarries; today known as Aswan.

Ta-She Oasis today called the Fayum.

Twelve Gates In the Underworld, through which the **Barque of Re** passes at night.

Two Lands Northern and Southern **Kemet**, as well as the **Black Land** (flood plain) and the Red Land (desert).

Vulture Cap-Crown Headdress of the **Great Royal Wife**, often surmounted by a modius and a pair of tall feathers.

***wab* priest** Lower-level member of the priesthood.

Wadjet, Lady of Cobra goddess who is protectress of the **Lord of the Two Lands**.

Waset The southern capital of **Kemet**, renamed Thebes by the Hellenes and now modern-day Luxor; cult center of the god **Amen-Re**; also known as the **Southern Iunu**.

Wawat Northern part of Kush (modern-day Sudan) bordering on **Kemet**; populated by black Africans.

Wawish Language of **Wawat**.

Wer-Mer Royal residence at **Ta-She** (oasis), where **Hatshepsut** retires to.

West of Waset West side of **The River** at **Waset**, location of the **Mound of Creation**, **Djeser Djeseru**, **Djeser Akhet** and the **Great Place.**

What Is in the Underworld Funerary text originating in the early Eighteenth Dynasty (*Amduat*).

White Crown of Southern **Kemet**; probably fashioned from felt; looks like a bowling pin.

Yellow Land Wawat, modern-day Sudan.

8948841R0

Made in the USA
Lexington, KY
15 March 2011